THE CAPTIVE BORN

Book One In The Captive Series

LK MAGILL

First Hale Press

The Captive Born/ LK Magill – 2nd ed.

Ebook ISBN 978-1-7336155-1-8

Paperback ISBN 978-1-7336155-0-1

Hardcover ISBN 978-1-950928-03-3

DEDICATION

To God, without whom I would not have been able to write a single word.

ACKNOWLEDGMENTS

To my early readers: Ali, Jenna, Krystal, and Sara. Your advice, support and enthusiasm were invaluable to this process. I truly appreciate the time that you took to read and discuss with me.

To my mother, Jan. For the unending support, emotional and financial. For all of the phone calls, pep talks, tears shed, encouragement and unconditional love. I thank you. I thank you. I thank you.

To my father, Wally and step-mom Kathy, thank you for always being there for me.

To my children, Jack and Molly, I love you so much.

CHAPTER 1

PRESSING SLENDER FINGERS AGAINST THE THICK GLASS SHE leaned forward onto the tips of her three-inch heels, watching as the people walked by. Her feet ached, demanding relief, but she was forbidden from removing the torturous shoes in public. This was day three at the business trade show and still no interest.

Professional men and women in their fitted suits of navy, gray and black moved past steadily. The occasional flash came from a daring red shoe or a striped tie that dangled around an accepting neck.

Tap, tap.

Startled, she straightened to the disapproving stare of the sales manager, Ronald. One chunky knuckle had rapped on the glass to remind her... but she didn't need reminding. She knew.

"No leaning on the glass, Val," he said, and moved off.

Slowly rounding the corner of the clear box, he retreated to his seat behind her in the trade show booth. The flimsy metal of the folding chair creaked unhappily as he settled in.

He was free to sit because he was exactly that… free. She was not. Being a Domestic Level 2 Captive, her life was not her own. Never had been.

A group of men in their early twenties stopped to linger in front of the display next to her. The collection of young women inside smiled and laughed. These were hourly D2s, dressed and trained accordingly.

Short skirts, tight tops, high heels and outgoing personalities. All of them had passed the aptitude tests for such a vocation and enjoyed the bustle of activity and attention. The agency that owned them rewarded their efforts with luxury items, special food and favors. In a world where you could purchase nothing for yourself these perks were everything.

Coolly, she watched from her solitary chamber, the climate controls set at seventy-two degrees. She kept her face passive with a mild pleasant expression perfected by years of training. Her neighbors flirted shamelessly, pressing themselves against the glass as the men joked and gestured in turn. Ronald's thick frame could be seen stepping into view. It was time for negotiations to begin.

Smoothing at hair and adjusting their clothes, each girl that was requested stepped away from the others. There was a blonde with beautiful curls and then a brunette whose dark skin matched her eyes. The Cambric Agency kept a variety of women to attract a wide customer base. Business was booming.

Bending at the knee slightly, Val leaned all of her weight onto her left foot, trying to provide momentary relief to the right. She knew many of these women, had grown up with them, lived with them and trained with them. But there were none close enough to call a friend. Only one girl had ever been that, and now Bee was long gone.

"What about this one?" A dark-haired man spoke.

"She isn't hourly. Permanent placement only," Ronald answered.

This caught Val's attention, she was the only permanent D2 on display. Blinking back into focus she watched as if at a distance. Her mind had been drifting elsewhere at the thought of Bee, a coping mechanism.

The well-meaning portly Ronald shook his shiny bald head, causing the overhead lights to glint off its dome surface. Tugging at his expensive suit, the other man frowned. He did not appear accustomed to hearing the word *no*.

As the two discussed whether an exception could be made, Val's gaze drifted idly out over the crowd. She didn't look at the free people, not really. But years of training had her sweeping the space anyway. It was better to appear open and interested.

Stopping short in her survey, Val's pulse quickened reflexively. A pair of arctic-blue eyes evaluated her. They belonged to a man, one who kept both hands stuffed casually in the hip pockets of his gray slacks.

Attractive, even without a smile, he held her gaze. His short waves of chestnut hair were styled, but messily so, as if in just running his hands through it once, he had done enough. She got the feeling he was searching for something, the way his eyes shifted across her face.

All at once, an unfamiliar heat rose to her cheeks.

She wanted to look down, wanted to reach for her face, press her palms against the blush spreading there. But she didn't. Those gestures weren't allowed. It was only the years of steady discipline that helped her to keep her outward composure. This fluttering of nerves... it was new. New and unwelcome.

Purposefully, she shoved back at her own unusual reaction and tilted her chin up just a touch. It didn't matter what this man was looking for, he wouldn't ever lay a finger on her. There was a quiet sort of comfort in that fact, and so she clung to it, which was rare.

She may be a D2 captive, but she would not be sold to any of these men. They weren't the target market for which she had been trained and priced. They were all too young and not nearly wealthy enough.

Left foot cramping now, Val shifted once more, transferring the bulk of her weight to the right.

"I'm sorry but I can't make exceptions on this one." Ronald was firm.

The dark-haired man shrugged before muttering, "She can't even stand up straight anyway."

Quickly, Val evened her weight out between both feet. Would Ronald report her for appearing tired in public? It was a minor transgression but in combination with her leaning on the glass... one could miss a meal over it.

Swallowing nervously, Val let her hands flutter up and smooth over the soft pink chiffon of her dress. The layers of scalloped material felt like slippery soft clouds moving under her palms. Purposefully she checked her expression, and brought the lines of her face back to their former serene composure. *Don't look at him. Don't let him know you've made a mistake.*

Afraid to turn her head now, she listened to the man complete his transaction. The easy banter of her fellow D2s could be heard moving off with him through the flow of people.

Holding her breath, Val waited for Ronald to confront her but after thirty-seconds he failed to show. No warning?

No punishment? It was turning out to be an unusual day indeed.

And in the end, maybe it was that exact lack of enforcement that started something within her. Looking back, she could never be sure. But a sudden impulse had her scouting the press of faces, searching for the man with icy-blue eyes. He was no longer there, however. Like free people were want to do, he had moved on.

For a moment, she wondered about him, and then at her own unusual reaction. Agency rhetoric sounded in her head. *Unwarranted emotion of any kind is intolerable. There is no happy, no sad, no anger, no jealousy. There is only acceptance, fear, and respect.*

Breathing in, she worked to reconstruct her mind accordingly.

"Break time for you Val." Ronald came to stand still in front of her, but he was distracted.

Absently, he pulled his cell phone from his back pocket and glanced down at it briefly. Making no move to type on it, he wedged the phone back into his pants before walking around to the rear of the box. Val waited until he entered a code and the back door clicked open before turning around.

Pausing at the threshold, she offered him her right forearm to scan. He huffed a breath, apparently having forgotten this part of the procedure. Grumbling, he fished again for his phone and waved it over her arm until a sharp beep registered her as exiting the display.

The Agency kept record of all of its captives using an electronic code system. Each individual had a tracking device inserted into their forearm. They did the insertion procedure early on because Val had no recollection of it, only the incessant beep that accompanied her every significant movement.

Stepping down from the clear box, she walked obediently to the enclosed break area located in the rear of the large booth. It was long and narrow, with no windows and only one thin door. Some might find that claustrophobic, but being kept in a box was all Val knew.

Sitting demurely on a padded bench, she slipped the stiletto heels off with a moan and listened to the click of Ronald locking her inside alone.

Per procedure, she changed out of the expensive dress, hanging it neatly on the clothing rack, and into a set of charcoal colored sweats. There was a small refrigerator in the far corner where she was relieved to find bottled water. Gulping at it greedily, Val held the door open and scanned the remaining contents for signs of lunch.

On the top rack, just behind another container, she located a Styrofoam box marked *Val*. With a sigh, she sat back on the bench and devoured the small chicken salad with its meager diet dressing.

When they were kids growing up, The Agency had fed them better. The portions were larger and occasionally they were even offered second helpings. Things changed sometime after they completed middle school, though. That's when Bee started complaining that the calorie police had taken over.

Closing her eyes, Val leaned her head back against the wall and let herself think of her oldest friend, her possible sister. Everyone had said they looked so much alike with their same dark brown hair and unusual green eyes.

The Agency had never confirmed they were family, though. Technically there were no such relations for a captive. But between sharing a room and almost every memory, the two of them might as well have been. From Val's earliest recollection, she had shared her life with Bee.

Of course, that was before the incident. Before things had unraveled so quickly and in such an awful way.

Squeezing her eyes shut, Val worked to wipe her mind clear while the other D2s were rotated in and out for lunch and bathroom breaks. She wasn't sure why Ronald left her off display for so long, but the rest for her feet was much welcome.

Several hours passed that way, with Val blinking at the blank wall and the others making little to no conversation. If it had been Bee in here, Val thought ruefully, the boredom would have gotten the better of her. She would have paced and picked and looked for mischief.

But Bee wasn't here and never would be. No, it was only Val. And for whatever reason it had always been so much easier for her to just breathe and drift.

She did it even now, letting her eyes blur and her mind wander. As children, when Bee had raged against locked doors and withheld food, Val had been the one to shush her. *Let's not make too much noise. You don't want them to come back.* Wrapping her arms loosely around Bee's shaking shoulders, Val would simply sit as the tears flowed down her friend's frustrated cheeks.

Why don't you ever fuss? Bee had questioned. But Val didn't know the answer and so had remained silent.

Looking back, Val wished she had something better to say. But foolishly the idea of not seeing Bee again hadn't yet occurred to her. Now all she was left with were those final moments. The ones filled with screaming.

"Val, you've got a clothing change coming," Ronald said, as he let Alicia inside.

Huffing a breath, the redhead blew a lock of hair out of her face, but said nothing. The woman's arms were full of dress bags and a makeup kit, the tools of her particular trade. Specializing in fashion, Alicia was a C1, or Corporate Captive, also owned by Cambric Agency. Her job was to make D2s presentable for sale.

Standing to make room, Val watched her hang the collection of thin black totes on a nearby metal rack.

"We have a full-length satin gown for you tonight." Alicia gestured to the longest of the bags now neatly arranged in the tight quarters. "It's green, of course, to bring out your eyes."

Val bobbed her head in agreement, as if she had any say in the matter. That color was one they used on her often. That, and blue.

Alicia pulled out a portable mirror and propped it up in front of the bench seat. This wasn't the first time she had worked on Val. She did hair and makeup for a lot of the D2s at Cambric, some more often than others. Their proximity, though, had not made them friends.

In fact, Alicia mostly kept quiet as she worked her transformation magic. Her manner was always reserved, meticulous and benign. And it was that way now as she gestured for Val to sit. This process would take over an hour.

There was a time when things for a captive weren't quite so orderly. Long before Val was born, the slave industry had been a brutal one. Back then the practice was based mainly off of race, with free people being sold into captivity without control. The country became so divided that a civil war nearly broke out.

But that was before all of the government oversight. It was before the institution of captive law that made things equal, made things acceptable.

The Captive Trade Reorganization Act mandated the slave trade be a frozen industry. Each race and gender had to be represented equally from among the general population.

During the great reorganization, a sifting occurred. Certain types of slaves were released while already free people were conscripted to replace them. Fathers sold daughters, mothers sold sons, brothers sold sisters. Families were made wealthy on the backs of their most vulnerable members.

Records of just where each captive came from were then systematically destroyed. From that point on, the industry was legal only if the person was born into it and could only be sustained through deliberate breeding. Though Val didn't know her mother or father, she was the product of many generations of nearly inescapable captivity.

"The formal dinner is tonight," Alicia offered, pressing her lips together occasionally as she applied touch-up foundation. "A lot of executives will be here, this could be it for you."

"Yes," Val replied, for lack of anything else to say.

Cambric Agency had prepared her for this final outcome, had spent every moment of her entire life preparing for it. Because Cambric's owner didn't see the company as just another agency selling sex. Oh no, that wasn't nearly lucrative enough. Like any other multi-million dollar business, they hunted down profit like a dog with a bone.

And in the end, it's that devotion to money that made them the best. Constant market research. Sales techniques. Superior product. Exceptional service. The Agency kept up with current trends, styles, demands. In this way, they lent a new spin to an old trade. You get what you pay for. And at Cambric, you get the best.

Val was the pinnacle of that ideal. She would be one of the most lucrative sales of any female permanent placement to date. It's what she had been born, trained and educated to do.

Specifically, she was slated for a wealthy widower. Where an older rich man hungered for class, elegance and beauty, Val worked to supply it… in irresistibly sensual spades.

Natural tone makeup, soft touchable hair and a fitted, but appropriate dress would complete the illusion. By the time Val saw her own reflection in the mirror, a woman who didn't belong in a box stared back at her.

"No sadness tonight Val," Alicia cautioned, catching her expression. "An older gentleman is more likely to be a kind companion and you could do much worse."

Yes, thought Val, much worse.

Unbidden, her mind flashed back to Bee. Stomach turning, she remembered how her friend had looked as they dragged her away, the dark tresses of her hair spreading out across the floor. She had been so lifeless just then.

Shaking her head to clear it, Val swallowed the sick sensation that gripped her. She could make it go away. With enough breathing and counting and trigger words, she could make the entire mess disappear.

Without further comment, Alicia scanned Val's forearm and released her back into the custody of Ronald. By the time Val returned to the safety of the box, she had mastered herself once more.

On the other side of the glass, the throng of business men and women pushed forward towards the far doors of the convention dinner. Standing straight and serene, Val kept her shoulders rolled back and her arms resting at her sides so as not to hide her figure.

She recalled the hours spent in training where thirty girls

stood perfectly still, observing nothing but a white wall. One slouch, one sigh, one eye roll and a thin wooden stick would come slapping down to punish the offender.

Bee had always harbored a fantasy of grabbing the stick and snapping it in half. Maybe she would have finally done it, too, Val thought, and it caused her unconsciously to beam.

"What a beautiful smile." A man's voice ventured, only a few feet away.

Val had been drifting again, for before her stood an older man of average height in an elegant suit. His graying hair and kind eyes twinkled at some memory of his own.

"You remind me very much of my late wife," he said with a touch of sadness lingering in his voice. "Her favorite color was green."

Val nodded, "What was her name?"

"Josephine," he answered, and seemed to think a moment, appraising her.

For several moments, Val let him look, keeping her eyes resting invitingly on his. Attracted by the silence, Ronald waddled over to engage the man in conversation. This wasn't the quick hard sell of the hourly girls, so he offered the gentleman a drink. Val suspected the man agreed simply to be rid of Ronald, but the salesman hustled off anyway.

"How long have you been without her?" Val asked. It was rare that she got to speak with free men.

"Oh my, must be coming on five years now. You wouldn't mind talking about her?" He inquired, eyebrows raised.

"Not at all, I'd like to hear about her life."

"Can you read and write?"

"Val has been educated to an Associates Degree level." Ronald had arrived back with the water and answered the gentleman's question for her.

Taking the cue, Val melted into silence once more. The Agency had discovered that a higher-end clientele wanted more from their D2 than originally thought. For this price, a warm bed was nice, but a partner whose intelligence and manner provided easy companionship was worth more.

"Tell me girl-" The gentleman addressed her directly. "Have they mistreated you?"

Again, Val flashed to the incident with Bee and everything that had followed it, but this time she kept her face clear and passive. Ronald stared at her, his small eyes almost bulging in anticipation of her answer. He knew what had happened. Everyone at Cambric knew.

"No, of course not." Val spoke easily. "The Cambric Agency is known for the finest treatment of all Domestic Captives, myself included."

Plastering a big smile on his face, Ronald turned to the gentleman who expressed interest in seeing Val again. They arranged a private interview for ten o'clock in the morning, but before moving to leave he nodded once at Val, smiling gently. She inclined her head in response and then watched as Ronald escorted him a few steps down the aisle, away towards the reception.

There was no rush of excitement, no sadness, no nerves. This was exactly in line with her instruction. She was devoid of any sentiment and that in itself was its own reward. *Nothingness is best.*

"Did he buy you?" A new voice whispered.

The sound was close. It had her jumping. Tilting forward on her toes, Val had to brace both hands on the glass to keep from falling over.

In front of her, a pair of blue eyes resonated not more than two feet away. He had returned. It was the same young man from before.

Stepping back, Val worried over her palm prints smudged along the glass before letting her gaze shift permanently back to him. He still had that look in his eyes from earlier and she felt even more uncomfortable under his stare now. But he had asked her something. What was it? Oh, yes, her buyer.

"He's going to." Val frowned.

Initially, she wanted to refuse to answer, but her training left her incapable of not responding to the direct question. This was a free man after all and he made a request, so she must make a reply. Her stomach flip flopped uneasily as she held his intelligent eyes with her own.

"Did he put down a deposit?"

"No, he did not." Val's brow furrowed deeper.

"Can I help you?" Ronald had returned, and for once Val felt relieved. "Need a date for tonight? Look over here." He pointed to the neighboring box. "See this girl with the brown hair? She looks a lot like Val and is hourly. I'll give you a discount."

"No, thanks." The man's careful eyes didn't leave her face as the salesman spoke. "I'll buy this one. Val is it?"

"Sorry, but she's permanent placement only." Ronald sighed.

"That's fine."

"You don't know how much she is," Ronald countered.

"I don't have to."

"Alright." Ronald squinted now. "What did you say your name was?"

"Jason Riggs."

"Of Riggs Oil?" Ronald's already beady eyes seemed to narrow even more.

"That's right."

"Riggs Oil is anti-captive." Taking a step back, Ronald glanced around. "Your family has spent a fortune trying to bring down the entire industry. Now you want me to believe you're going to buy a D2? Where's the hidden camera?"

"Let's just say Val here has changed my mind. I've heard Cambric is pretty good at keeping certain purchases quiet."

Turning to face Ronald for the first time, Jason pressed his hand into the wide palm of the salesman. They shook for perhaps a moment too long, staring at one another until Ronald finally blinked. Glancing down, Val noticed a green stack of bills curled tightly in his hand.

"Mr. Riggs, can I offer you a drink?"

"Sure."

"If you would just come with me I think we can arrange for escrow to open tomorrow. Closing typically lasts a few days depending on how fast you can fund our account."

The conversation continued, but Val wasn't privy to it. Side by side, the two men walked away together, neither of them bothered to look back. Slowly, a fresh set of nerves released in her body, sending prickles cruising through her blood stream. This was not the way things were supposed to go. This was not the owner she had envisioned.

For the past two decades her future had been mapped out before her. Each move she would be required to make was anticipated and prepared for. None of it included being kept a secret by a young man with power and a disapproving family.

No, it was supposed to be an older man. One she could have all to herself, one she might be able to convince. But then it was all over too fast and what could she do?

The deposit itself seemed to take only a few minutes. Once it was complete, Val forced herself to look over at the masculine figure that exited the booth. *He bought you. You belong to him, now.*

A black evening jacket covered his strong shoulders as he walked towards the dinner reception alone, hands tucked once more into his hip pockets. How would this change her plan? Would she be able to sway him the way she needed?

A faint click sounded behind her as the door code was punched into the electronic lock of the display case. With dogged practice, Val turned to exit. Though her whole life had been building up to this point, Val absorbed the change dumbly. It didn't feel real just yet.

Scanning her forearm, Ronald's cell phone gave its customary beep. It was the last sound to be exchanged between them. She would never see the salesman again. Two hulking guards from Cambric security were waiting to accept her into their possession. She recognized them as you would a vague acquaintance. They were free men. All of them were. You could never trust a captive to watch another captive, everyone knew that.

Walking between them without fuss, Val barely noticed the transition from the convention hall to the hotel portion of the building. The space itself was ultra-modern, with clean lines and blue cast lighting, but she had made the trip before so the click-click of her heels along the swirls of black marble flooring were all background.

The elevator though, that got her attention. Shaped like tubes they would shoot high up into the hotel, rising to the surrounding rooms as a tree trunk ascends into a burst of branches. She'd never experienced anything like it.

Her trip ended the same way it had the two previous nights, however. With the guards locking her in her room before lingering silently in the hallway. They would stay all night, monitoring the delivery of any food and restricting access to Cambric staff only. She had observed their listless pacing through the door's peep hole.

Tonight was no different, except that when her dinner arrived it was accompanied by one small orange pill. It was the suicide prevention drug. A requirement of her captivity.

There was a time when The Agency's rate of self-termination by D2s reached thirty percent. That was before the intensive personality screenings and docile breeding programs were initiated. After several decades of modification, The Agency's current rate was down to just one percent. A remarkable success, depending on how you looked at it.

As Val cupped the pill in the palm of her hand, she knew in her heart she could not kill herself. But whether she needed it or not, she would take it. Her training was just that strong. So like everything else they gave her, she swallowed the tiny oval shape without encouragement.

Aside from the pill, the tray contained an unusually massive amount of food. And unlike other times, she was expected to eat all of it. She would need the calories. She would need every bit of them because this particular drug wasn't something they gave you every day. In fact, you usually only ever got it the one time, right before you were sold.

Once swallowed, the medicine would swirl in your system until you succumbed to a mindless forty-eight hour sleep. So, Val ate the food. *Almost* every single bite. Because despite what they required of her, Val had a choice to make. After all, there was one persistent need that refused to leave her. And this could be her last chance to set the wheel in motion.

After she had done it, she lay down in the soft bed. Carefully, she arranged the white down comforter around her body before spreading her neatly brushed hair over her pillow. The drug was working now. She could feel it coming on.

As she stared at the ceiling, hands folded across her belly like a corpse, she let the heavy sensations fill her. Slowly, it crept up from the tips of her toes. Tingling. Blinding.

Her mind filled in first with opaque silver, then darkened to ash gray, then finally gave way to the shiny obsidian that is black.

CHAPTER 2

SHAKING, SHAKING, THE ROUGH SHAKING, IT WOULDN'T STOP. Leave me alone, she thought, but not out loud, never out loud.

"Wake up, Val." Alicia was stern, only inches from her ear.

Val opened her eyes in the hotel room and briefly wondered that the drug had not worked. It seemed only a minute ago that she had lost consciousness. But the sun pierced brightly through the now open pale-gold curtains. And so, Val realized that sleep had come to her and the days had indeed passed without her awareness.

"I'm awake," Val croaked.

When she moved her lips, barely any sound escaped them.

Blinking groggily, the room came slowly into focus. They were all alone in it, save for a solitary tray of food in the far corner. Well, that and the ever-present dress bag hanging in her small closet.

Holding out a cool glass of water, Alicia watched with something nearing boredom as Val reached for it. Her hand trembled, but stilled the moment she grasped the cup. Val wasn't sure if it was the lack of food or the drug that made her so unsteady. Perhaps a combination of the two.

Bracing herself up on one elbow, Val gulped at its contents greedily. Her throat was so dry.

"It's time for your final prep," Alicia told her, and moved off the side of the bed where she had been sitting.

Still a bit wobbly, Val attempted to stand as well, but quickly crumpled. Fortunately, Alicia hadn't gone far. The placid redhead came over to hoist her up by the arms, and was eventually forced to help Val get into the bathtub.

Soak, shampoo, scrub and shave, in that order. Always in that order.

Renewed by the process, Val shrugged into a terrycloth white robe and sat in a straight-backed chair to eat while Alicia combed through her mass of wet hair. The food was good, something the hotel kitchen had cooked up. She could tell the difference because of all the seasoning. The Agency never allowed for so much flavor.

After the first few bites, however, Val's stomach began to tie itself in knots. It was time, she thought. It was now or never.

"Alicia-" Val ventured. "Have you seen Bee?"

The brush that smoothed down Val's hair stilled momentarily. There was just a breath of hesitation before it continued on its path. It was so slight that anyone watching through a security camera would not notice. Studying Alicia's reflection in the mirror, Val saw a slight frown crease the other woman's face before her thin lips pressed together firmly. The next few seconds were filled with silence.

She would give no verbal answer. And in truth, Val couldn't blame her. This type of discussion was explicitly forbidden. Both women would face severe punishment if caught talking of anything deemed inappropriate. And what had happened to Bee definitely fell into that category.

"Is she alive? Can you pass a message?" Val rushed on, whisper quiet, eyes piercing the other woman's reflection.

This time Alicia did not stop brushing the dark mass of damp hair. She didn't miss another beat and she still wouldn't answer. Val's heart kicked painfully inside her chest before she continued.

"I can pay."

Alicia's eyes snapped to hers once, then back down. Brushing, always brushing, it was the first definite response Val had been given. *Bee is alive. Bee is alive.* Hope flashed like a beacon inside of her. But she couldn't let it get to her, she had to be smart about what happened next.

Ducking her head, Val resumed eating a few moments before she let herself whisper between bites.

"I saved three dinner rolls... *with* butter." Val's voice was hushed. "They're in the mini-fridge."

Food. It was the most common item of barter between captives. They didn't have money, could earn no wages. And food was scarce, there was never any extra on hand. The Agency controlled their portions, limited their intake. If you happened to have more, it was because you didn't eat it yourself, or you traded for it.

Butter, especially, was desirable. Now it all came down to whether Alicia felt it was worth the risk. Val nibbled at her bottom lip and waited.

Finally, Alicia nodded her head while reaching for the blow dryer. She would barter the food for information, but Val would have to do the talking.

Turning the dryer on low, the redhead waved it slowly back and forth. Back and forth. It's whirling sound covered any words that were exchanged. As Val's long chestnut locks rose and fell, she pushed on with her end of the bargain.

"Where is she?"

"Still in Isolation."

Val exhaled, her heart lurching with a mix of relief and sorrow.

"Tell her to follow the rules." Val squeezed her eyes shut, knowing she was making an impossible request as well as an impossible promise. "Tell her I will come for her, as soon as I can."

Despite Val's best efforts, a single tear brimmed and streaked down her cheek. Upon seeing it, Alicia clucked soothingly, but said no more. She would pass Bee the message… or not. It was out of Val's hands. But then again, that was nothing new.

The remaining hour passed quickly as Val's transformation proceeded in silence. Alicia applied her last bit of agency approved makeup before helping Val slip into a short ocean-blue sundress. Raising her eyebrows at the pair of flat sandals, Val couldn't recall the last time she hadn't worn heels.

"Your new owner requested they be comfortable," Alicia explained.

At the door, there were no goodbyes. No hug of affection passed between them though they'd known one another for many years. It was two o'clock in the afternoon and time to make the final exchange. Val couldn't afford to be late.

In the hallway, Cambric security scanned her arm before leading her to the elevator and down into the lobby. The bustle of people took no notice of the beautiful woman wedged between two hulking giants. At the front of the hotel, a large revolving door released them into the summer's air. It had been four days since she had last been outside.

Inhaling, Val breathed in the warmth of the breeze as it tickled across her face. Cars came and went in a circular driveway. Other people, free people, waited on the sidewalk. She heard them laughing in their little groups, saw them frowning down at their sleek phones. What was so mesmerizing about the tiny device? She had never held one.

A valet runner jogged by wearing a pressed red coat. He was busy collecting green dollars for vehicles fetched. She watched him for a moment before a glinting silver SUV caught her eye.

Pulling to a stop at the curb in front of her, she couldn't see who was inside, the windows were too dark. The driver, dressed in a black business suit, jumped out and walked around to open the rear passenger door. This was for her. She was about to leave the custody of the only owner she had ever known.

Presenting her right forearm to Agency security, Val listened to one final beep as Cambric scanned her release from custody. Should she be happy? Fearful? She wasn't quite sure and didn't have time to decide as the driver offered her his large hand.

Taking it, Val folded gracefully down onto a creamy leather seat. Immediately, the seductive scent of new car engulfed her. She could feel the soft material beneath her thighs, under her palms and pressing against her bare back. As the heavy door swung shut it snapped her suddenly back to her senses. There was a man seated beside her. She could *feel* his eyes dancing over her skin.

Turning her head, she met his steady gaze as a shot of adrenaline released to pour through her system. It sent uncomfortable tingles to the ends of her toes. Why hadn't she thought he would be the one to collect her?

Reclining against the comfortable seat, his arm propped along the window's edge, her new owner grinned. It was the first time she saw him be anything but serious and up close he was even more attractive than she initially realized.

Unlike any other time in her life, Val had to work to clamp down on her jitters. This lack of control wasn't like her and it had her missing the older man. He, at least, had left her feeling comfortably empty.

"Do you like the shoes?" Her new owner asked.

She glanced down at the shiny patent-blue sandals. They were a refreshing change from the too tall heels that seemed to plague her since high school.

"Yes." She forced herself to meet his gaze again. "Thank you."

"I'm Jason, by the way, I don't think we were ever formally introduced."

He stuck his hand out between them and she merely stared. After a beat, she reached out and took it. A strange warmth radiated up her arm before she could retract it back to the safety of her lap.

"I'm Val," she answered calmly. She refused to let her uncertainty appear on her face.

Looking down at his pocket, Jason retrieved a vibrating cell phone and studied the display.

"Sorry, I've got to take this one," he apologized.

In an attempt to give him privacy, Val shifted away to watch the skyscrapers pass by. For her, outings to the city had been rare. She marveled at the volume of people bustling hurriedly down the sidewalks. Their numbers were magnified in the reflection of the glass buildings as they walked along.

Were all of them free people? There were so many more than she had realized. In the background, Jason's conversation crept over her.

"Yeah, the conference went well. I'm heading back home now."

He paused, listening to the murmurs at the other end.

"I talked to them, yes. I explained what that sort of regulation would mean for us, but-"

The caller cut him off and he listened attentively once more.

"I agree, I'll take care of it. Let's talk more at the office tomorrow, okay? Sure. Sure, thanks. Yeah, bye."

He hung up the phone, but sat in silence, seemingly absorbed in his own thoughts.

"Where's home?" Val asked.

"Texas. Ever been to Austin?"

"I've never left New York."

"I take it you've never flown in a jet either," he commented.

Shaking her head, she let the conversation die and her gaze drift back out the window. Silence filled the space between them. The only sound came from the occasional buzz of his cell phone which he gave his full focus, thumbs working quickly across the screened keyboard.

Minutes later she noticed large planes overhead, landing and taking off in turn. The great booming noises they made had her pressing her face up close to the glass. Peering up, she did her best not to smudge her makeup. Somehow all the textbook photographs just didn't do the real thing justice.

When the SUV finally pulled to a stop, Jason slipped on a pair of dark sunglasses before reaching over and handing her a pair.

"Do me a favor," he said. "Don't talk to anyone, okay?"

Without waiting for an answer, he shoved his own door open and got out. The instruction not to speak wasn't an unusual request for her so she kept her lips together in a practiced pleasant expression. Putting on the glasses, she watched as the driver made his way around to open her passenger side door.

When she stepped out, Jason was waiting to take her hand firmly in his. The pressure of his touch was distracting, but soon faded as he led the way through the hustle and maze that was her first airport.

People, bags, noises, machines. The combined movement alone was overwhelming. Automatic doors slid open and closed, security wands were waved, people murmured and narrowly avoided bumping into one another. Without Jason in front of her, Val wasn't sure she could have managed it.

But then, as quickly as they entered the horde, they left. Buzzing through a small side door, Jason guided her into a serene and orderly space, leaving the throng of public behind them.

A trim woman wearing a uniform came over with a tray of drinks. Without encouragement, she handed a glass of champagne first to Val and then to Jason. Hesitating, Val waited until Jason took a sip first before she followed suit.

Agency rhetoric sounded in her head. *Alcohol consumption. Take only what is offered by your owner. Do not consume more than two.*

When they boarded the plane, it was much smaller than she had expected. The inside had several wide white leather seats and a small table near the back. Settling into one of the chairs, Val noticed that she and Jason were the only two passengers onboard.

A stewardess approached them, her raven-black hair smoothed neatly beneath a baby-blue cap. As Jason continued to work over his phone, the woman stopped in front of Val and asked what she would like to order for dinner.

The question could not have been a more difficult one. Never in her whole life had Val been allowed to make such a choice. The Agency served food and you ate food. You didn't get an option. You didn't make a request.

The stewardess blinked expectantly as Val sat frozen to the spot. What would they have her do in training? What was the protocol for this event? The seconds stretched out and she could tell it had attracted Jason's notice. His fingers stopped worrying over his phone. He was staring at the side of her head.

"I'll have what he's having," Val finally said, letting go a quiet breath as the stewardess nodded satisfactorily and looked over at Jason.

"The usual, Marcy, thank you," he said, but kept all his focus on Val.

Distract him. Divert his attention.

"This isn't what I thought a plane would look like." Val filled the awkward moment with the first thing that popped into her head.

"Oh. Well, no, this isn't an airplane like the ones you saw landing. This is a private jet. I prefer to use it when traveling. It's way better than pushing through all those people," he explained.

She gave him a vague nod before gripping the armrests as the jet pushed back to taxi along the runway. The movement was like riding in a car, but then again not. When the sound of the engines began to whir louder she closed her eyes tight and held her breath.

"The takeoff is the worst part." She felt him reach over and place his hand reassuringly over hers. "Once we're in the air it evens out."

But then the jet began its intense thrust forward. Faster and faster it went until she felt her insides pressed to the back of the seat. Fear gripped her, then exhilaration and a small sinking sensation.

Finally, when the plane evened out and began a gentle coasting, her nervousness gave way to embarrassment. She had failed to control herself. She allowed emotion to rule her features. What must he think of her? How odd she must seem to him.

Upon opening her eyes, Val's worry evaporated in an instant. Outside of her window, a wondrous misty white cloud had appeared. It was beautiful, like a morning fog without all the heaviness.

"The first takeoff can be a bit scary." Jason spoke just beside her as his hand left her own. Rubbing gently along her knee he gave her a soft smile before shifting away.

The moment he touched her, Val felt her confidence return. Finally, this was a cue she understood. Taking his hand in her own she placed it back on her leg and leaned over to kiss him. Her lips brushed seductively across his mouth causing him to stiffen momentarily in surprise. A knowing smile creased her mouth as she gripped his tie in her hands and pulled him in closer, deepening the connection.

Immediately, his hands rose to sweep the back of her neck, fingers twining through her hair. His mouth parted and he leaned into her. Everything was in line with her training. Everything except for the warm curl of sensation that spread within her. That was new, she had never felt anything quite like it before.

"Wait." Abruptly he broke the kiss and studied her. "Did you do that because you want me or because that's what you're trained to do when a man touches your leg?"

What a peculiar question, she thought. His arctic eyes darted back and forth, searching for an answer.

"Do you even know the difference?" He asked quietly, and appeared not to like the confused expression that crossed her face.

Untangling his fingers from her hair, Jason sat back in his seat and blew out a breath. Something had gone wrong, Val knew, but she wasn't sure what. Disquiet took over as he returned to his work without another word.

The question of why he had purchased her worked its way to the front of her mind. This was not how things were supposed to go, at least not at first.

When the stewardess appeared with a set of fresh drinks, Val accepted hers with relief. Conversation between them resumed for several minutes and was polite, but sparse. Eventually it faded into nothing. Ever distracted by his phone, Jason resumed his business calls.

And so, Val occupied herself in the way she always did. She let her mind wander. And it wandered inevitably back to Cambric.

They didn't have cell phones there. A D2 had no use for electronics. On rare occasions, more frequently as children, The Agency had allowed them to watch movies. What a treat it had been, curled up with Bee, giggling as the enormous screen filled with flashing colors and booming sound.

That sort of entertainment wasn't typical, however. In the small windowless bedroom they shared, Bee and Val had no blinking box to amuse them. Instead, they made up stories.

Letting their minds drift up and out of their bodies, they would go on pretend adventures. Like living dreams they could control, the girls would paint pictures inside their heads, then share them with one another. The freedom of spirit was a relief for Val, but in turn seemed a burden to Bee. She always longed to be free in body as well.

The little flame of hope that smoked and smoldered within Bee had been bred out of Val's disposition long ago. It was that very difference that had Val wondering if they were truly related. Bee's personality was just so out of touch with most of the girls around her. She was a fighter, always snappy and bright. It was beautiful to watch, until it wasn't.

In an unbeatable system, fighting did not always equal surviving. Val's ability to submit had served her well before. Now, though, it seemed she was immersed in a different game altogether. *No matter. A man is only a man after all.*

"Hungry?" Jason asked, as he set down his phone.

Blinking back into the present, Val nodded in response. An hour or more must have passed because the ice in her glass had melted. Its watery drips formed a ring on the sleek table.

Glancing up, Jason caught Marcy's eye. Soon after, porcelain white bowls filled with French onion soup gave way to pretty plates heaped generously with Caesar salad. This would be Val's first meal that Cambric had not approved. The idea gave her a slight rush.

Making no more effort at conversation, Val ate in delicate silence. Her bites were carefully measured and slow. Though

The Agency wasn't here in person, they still resided quite permanently in her mind. She would follow their rules, whether she realized it or not. They had warned her that free people often over-ate and so she must deliberately pace herself, making certain not to clear her plate. So of course, that's what Val did.

Marcy seemed to wait in some unseen area and when consumption slowed, she would appear. Clearing away used dishes, she presented the main course; a thick cut of ribeye steak, served rare, with an overloaded baked potato oozing melted cheese down the sides. Val had never seen so much food for one person in all her life.

Memories of hungry nights in her not so distant past urged her to keep taking more, but her training was stronger. The food was rich, full of seasonings and drowned in sauces.

Agency rhetoric echoed again. *Always leave food on your plate, always.*

And even when she obeyed, her stomach revolted at how much she had eaten.

"Look, Val." Jason broke the silence. "I'm sorry about earlier, I didn't mean to be so harsh with you. Cambric gave me this manual about D2s, it's almost like buying a car really." A light laugh escaped him, but seeming to think better of it, he composed his face into seriousness. "All I'm saying is that I'm going to read it so things will be better, okay?"

She wasn't sure what he meant, having never purchased a car, or anything else for that matter. Cambric sent all of their permanent placements home with an informational booklet to assist the owner in transitioning the D2 into their household. It was meant to help *him* get what *he* wanted, but his apparent frustration over their earlier encounter was still beyond her grasp.

The only thing she could figure was that the next time they kissed she should tell him verbally that she wanted him. Worry began to work itself inside her mind. Would that be enough? If he wasn't pleased, would he send her back? A tiny seed of doubt appeared and buried itself deep. What would The Agency do to her in the event of a return? She had to hold back a shudder at the thought.

Marcy swept back through the small cabin and cleared the last of their meal before indicating they should fasten their seat belts to prepare for landing. Val was determined that this time she would keep her eyes open and remain composed. Her whole life was on the line here. Both hers and Bee.

"Landing is quicker than takeoff." Jason cleared his throat. "There's sometimes just a quick bump when the wheels touch the runway, but often you don't feel anything at all."

Encouraging her to look out a window, his arm crossed close to her body without actually making contact. As the ground drew closer, Val gasped. Glancing over her shoulder at Jason, she saw him crack a quick smile. He wasn't upset at her reaction, that was good.

Buildings appeared, surrounded by streets full of cars as the earth rushed up to meet them. Holding her breath, Val managed to keep her eyes open, face flooding with a mix of trepidation and thrill. In the end though, he was right. When the jet's wheels hit the ground, she didn't feel a thing.

Sticky hot air clung to her skin as the cabin door opened onto her first taste of Texas. It was still light out in Austin, though the sun lay low in the western sky. The flight itself had been just over four hours and with the time change, daylight would last another two. They disembarked directly onto the tarmac with the heat radiating mercilessly up from the black asphalt. A red sports car awaited them.

This time there was no driver. No driver and no backseat. Jason settled himself behind the wheel and Val sat beside him. As they wove through traffic and past buildings, a persistent tension began to grow inside her. She knew absolutely nothing about this man.

"Do you have a family?" She ventured over the blast of rock music.

Reaching over, he turned it down.

"Well I'm the oldest of four kids. Angela and Theresa are my sisters, and Jeremy is our younger brother, he just turned sixteen."

"Do you live with them?"

"Oh, no. The girls are away at college and Jeremy lives with our parents in the city. When I took over the business after my dad retired, I moved into our summer house. It's just outside the city but I don't mind the commute. It's worth the quiet."

Val absorbed the information with no further comment and so he returned the blast of music to its previous volume. The Agency did let them listen to music, but it was pre-approved only. She wasn't even sure what they screened it for. Hidden messages maybe? Or perhaps talk of free life that was deemed too compelling.

Despite her best efforts, the words in Jason's music were impossible for her to follow and so she gave up trying. All around them, the city grew increasingly sparse. Tall structures gave way to shorter ones and the distance between them widened. Jason guided the car onto a freeway and accelerated, his right hand shifting expertly, his feet jamming against the pedals.

Val's breath caught in her throat and her fingers dug reflexively into the dark leather seat. Other vehicles traveled ahead of them, but the roar of their engine had them joining the race easily. Once she realized they weren't going to be run over, she relaxed. And if she really thought about it, the speed in and of itself did have a certain appeal.

With dusk steadily approaching, the flat landscape around them was cast in an opaque hue. When they finally exited the freeway, exhaustion licked at her senses. Thick trees and wide clean roads began to take over as the occasional massive house flashed down a distant avenue. They were winding through an expensive neighborhood.

As Jason steered them onto a cobblestone lane, Val's mouth dropped open slightly. The driveway was now flanked by a sweep of manicured lawns dotted with wispy trees. Making a final wide turn in the circular drive, Jason brought the car to a stop. The engine ceased its rumbling.

Tilting her face up, Val blinked at the magnificent white stone house with its green ivy clinging and wide windows twinkling in the fading light. Deliberately, she closed her mouth, but was unable to look away from the impressive beauty.

Unbidden, her door swung open and Jason reached for her. Keeping her hand loosely in his own, he led her to the massive front door. Its top was arched to match the curving stone.

"Pretty sweet right?" His face shone, sharing in her reaction.

"Yes," she breathed. "Only you live here?"

"Well, I keep a small staff, but they don't spend the night.

So I guess, yeah, just me." After thinking a moment, he added, "and now you."

Lingering in the entranceway, they watched as the deep brown wooden door swung open. A thin man in his forties with light skin and dark hair stood aside to admit them. If he was surprised by Val's presence, his expression did not reveal it.

"Welcome home," the man said, as he helped Jason to shrug out of his light suit jacket.

"Thanks Arthur. It's good to be here. Is Yvette around? I'd like her to meet Val."

Arthur retrieved his phone and typed quickly on its screen. Seemingly, he was summoning Yvette because within seconds a pretty woman in her fifties appeared. Her blonde hair was tucked up neatly, brown eyes blinking with interest.

"Jason, welcome home." Yvette extended her arms, and the two hugged warmly. "Is this the young woman you've messaged me about?"

"Yes, this is Val." Jason turned to make introductions. "And this is Yvette. She's run Summer House as long as I can remember. What, like over two decades now?"

"Since you were eight," she confirmed.

"I'd like to show Val around real quick and then I'm sure she'll want to rest. Is her room ready?"

"Yes, I've stocked it with some clothing in the sizes you sent over. The linens are fresh and turned down."

A moment of silence ensured in which Yvette studied Val. Her expression was veiled and so Val wasn't sure what she was thinking. But then Jason leaned in to give the older woman a quick peck on the cheek, whispering a hushed thank you that had her softening.

They've known each other a long time, Val realized. Over

twenty years would provide the bond of family, blood or no. When he reached back for Val's hand, Jason gave it a light squeeze, his eyes dancing as they exited the foyer.

Glancing around as they walked, Val noted that the entire house was filled with large paintings. There were pictures of lush fields and bright flowers in bloom everywhere. Her fingers itched to trace over each one but she followed demurely instead.

Their footfalls echoed against the marble flooring as he swept her through the formal living room. Its windows were left open over a small green garden. Outside, the sun was setting and darkness approached. They passed under stone archways and over plush carpeting as he showed her the dining room, guest bathroom, and the closed door to his office.

In the industrial sized kitchen, he asked if she was hungry. But after their meal on the plane, Val couldn't imagine eating another bite. Winding their way back to the front of the house he led her up a curving staircase just next to the foyer. Its old wood balustrade was smooth under her touch from years of use and attentive care.

"All the bedrooms are upstairs," he informed her, as they made their way up, passing painting after painting. "My bedroom is down the hallway to the left, just pass the library."

"You have a library?"

"Well, it's more of a study really. It has a decent collection of books, though. Do you like to read?"

He turned her body to the right with one hand while the other came to rest briefly on her hip. She felt his fingertips grasp at her quickly before they slid away.

"I've never had occasion to read for pleasure," she admitted. The Agency allowed only pre-selected books. Of those, there had been some she read over and over, and others never again.

"Well, you're welcome to read any that you want. You don't have to ask." He pointed to several closed doors as they walked, telling her they were guest bedrooms each with its own attached bath. There were six in total, including his master.

When they arrived at the end of the hall he opened the door and stood aside to let her enter. The room was large, bigger than any bedroom she had known. Wandering along the wall she ran her hand over polished dark wood furniture. There was a bureau and a side table with an antique stained-glass lamp.

Finally, she came to a stop in front of a large wall of windows. Like ones that actually opened. In *her* bedroom.

"You have a view of the side garden from here during the day." He stood next to her, taking in the darkness that had fallen. "I have to go to the office first thing in the morning so you won't see me for breakfast. Ask Yvette for anything you need, okay? I can't be sure I'll be home by dinner either but I'll try."

He hesitated, waiting for her to say something. Or, waiting for her to *do* something maybe. Edgy tingles started in her chest and spread quickly throughout her body.

All men were different, Cambric had instructed, yet all were basically the same. Some men might have particular desires or a specific way they wanted things to play out. It was her job to meet those expectations and the only way to discover was by doing.

Suddenly, she felt silly standing next to him filled with uncertainty and hesitation. It wasn't like she was a virgin. But then again, her trainer never had elicited quite this level of response. Trying to put it aside, she knew her future depended on pleasing this one man.

Turning to him she watched him carefully as she ran her hands up the front of his white collared shirt. She took her time, letting the feel of her palms on his chest draw his attention.

He was tall, but not overly so, and she rose up on the balls of her feet to reach his lips with her own.

Like before she could feel his immediate resistance. He held himself rigid, though he did not step back. Remembering their prior interaction, she broke the kiss and whispered how much she wanted him, her eyes flicking back up to lock with his, her mouth inches from his lips.

In an instant, his tension melted away. His arms wrapped around her waist, his body came down to press itself into her. She could feel his kisses travel down the side of her neck to her bare shoulder. As his lips traced over her skin, his fingers reached up to curve around one thin strap of her dress.

Slowly, he pulled it aside until it slipped loosely down and away. Keeping her whole body up tight against his, she slipped a hand into the leather belt at his waist.

It wasn't until she began to work the buckle loose, that he stepped back.

"I can't." He blinked down at her, rubbing one hand along the back of his neck.

"You can't?"

"I mean I can, but I shouldn't."

"You shouldn't?"

She watched dumbly as he turned to leave the room. What had she done wrong? The next steps were all so clear to her. Reviewing them in her mind, she couldn't imagine what mistake she had made.

The Agency's training discouraged questioning one's owner, but this was so far out of any situation that Val had prepped for that she couldn't help herself.

"Why did you buy me?" She called at his back.

He didn't turn, didn't acknowledge her words. He simply walked out, letting the door close behind him with a decided click.

CHAPTER 3

T HE NEXT TWO DAYS SHE SPENT HOLED UP IN HER ROOM. E ACH night she waited for him to visit her, and each morning she woke with a growing sense of dread. Why would a man purchase a D2 and not make use of her?

It was the morning of the third day and the question churned around her once more. Sitting in a comfortable barrel chair, Val gazed out over the expanse of lush gardens below her window. Her *open* window. When a polite knock sounded against her door, she knew it would be Yvette, wheeling in her breakfast.

"Come in," she called, and drew her bare legs up, tucking them underneath her plush cream robe.

The best part of the situation so far had been the wonderful variety of clothes. On her first day, Yvette had shown Val the walk-in closet attached to her bedroom. It was lined on both sides with countless hangers dripping with choices. Upon seeing it though, Val had blanched. The Agency kept them in uniforms, the only exception being when they were marketed for sale.

After Yvette had gone, Val spent several hours touching the different fabrics, pulling them out and holding them up against her body, only to put them back. On the second day, when Val still hadn't gotten dressed, Yvette seemed to sense her inability to make a choice. Though they never discussed it, Yvette had begun a routine of selecting and setting out her clothes.

But today when Yvette entered, there was no familiar light clinking of dishes being wheeled through the doorway. No. Instead, Yvette went straight to the closet, clucking softly to herself. Rising curiously, Val shadowed the older woman as she pushed several items aside. Hangers scraped along the railing lightly.

"Jason will have breakfast with you this morning in the dining room," Yvette informed her, while plucking out a pale green linen dress.

Val took it but waited until after Yvette had gone before changing. The revealing neckline and fitted bodice transitioned to a simple skirt that draped conservatively at her knees. It was classy but should still catch Jason's attention. At least Val hoped so.

Running a brush through her long hair, she decided to leave it down to flow over her shoulders. After a quick application of light makeup, she stepped into a pair of high heels and exited her room for the first time since she had entered it.

Unlike most people, staying inside for days on end did not bother her. At Cambric, after the disaster with Bee, she had been transferred to an observation room and locked up for several weeks. That chamber was constructed like a cell with empty gray walls and a slender mattress lying directly on the floor.

She was used to confinement. Had grown up with it. But

of course, back then she hadn't been entirely alone. No, she remembered the glass partition that had separated them. And the person on the other side? She couldn't forget him either.

The house was quiet as Val walked along the hallway and headed carefully down the stairs. She made a mental note to come back later and look at each painting that she passed. They were exquisite, beyond anything she had seen. Her heels clicked lightly as she moved through the bright living room and into the dining room.

Jason was already seated at the end of the dark walnut table, but he rose to his feet when she entered. Walking around to greet her, he pulled out the chair across from his and indicated she should sit. When he resumed his place, a young woman in her twenties approached them and set a plate of food in front of Val. Sliced cantaloupe, a bagel with cream cheese and extra crispy pieces of bacon were arranged to perfection on the large white platter.

"How are you liking your room?" Jason asked, as he cut into a chicken fried steak smothered in white gravy.

"It's wonderful, thank you."

"Yvette tells me you haven't left it. I hope you don't think you're stuck in there."

"Okay," Val ducked her head.

The vague response was all she could manage. It wasn't that she thought she was restricted to her room, but growing up, if you weren't instructed to be somewhere, you stayed put. That was the safe place to be and the feeling hadn't left her.

"This is your home now," he continued. "You can walk the grounds or visit the library. Do you swim? We have a pool."

"Yes," she replied. "I can swim."

She wasn't sure exactly why, but all of The Agency's children learned to swim at a young age. Thinking back, she supposed it had only been when they were kids. She hadn't been in the water in well over ten years.

"The office has kept me busy the past several days so I haven't been back by dinner, but if you'd be willing to wait until around seven I think I could make that time." He sipped his mug of coffee and swiped quietly at a tablet on the table.

"Seven would be fine," she answered. Truthfully, he could have chosen any time and her answer would always be a submissive yes.

The sound of silverware clinking gently against porcelain filled the room for several minutes. The bacon crunched deliciously in her mouth and she let her gaze travel out the wide bay window at the end of the room. Everywhere she looked in this house, beauty unfolded in dramatic fashion. Where there wasn't a window showcasing a softly drifting tree, a painting of wildflowers hung instead. She could spend days just studying the walls.

"Tell me how you came to be at Cambric Agency." Jason's voice broke through her reverie.

"I don't recall how I got there," she answered honestly. "From my earliest memory I lived at their boarding school. Maybe I was four or five by then."

"You don't remember your parents?"

"No." She thought a moment, then resumed. "There's always the fantasy of being held and loved by a mother, but I don't have a memory of it."

"I'm sorry." His look of remorse seemed real, but she couldn't share in it. How can you feel the loss of something you never experienced? She knew she should feel sad, but she didn't. "I've been reading through the booklet they provided. It doesn't detail how they acquired you. Do you know where you came from?"

"No." She wondered at his strange questions. "The Agency never tells us anything of parentage or family. We are all born into the program and that is all we need to know."

"They must keep track of your birth somewhere," he continued, almost to himself. "Maybe I can make a request for it."

At this, she put her fork carefully down on her plate. She wanted more food, but there was a small bite of fruit, bacon and bagel still left, and there they would remain. The sickening drop of fear had begun to fill her again.

He didn't visit her at night, refused her advances in the day and now he wanted to contact Cambric about her. If he returned her, surely the punishment would be severe. Fighting her instinct to question him, she tried desperately to remain silent. It was a battle she lost.

"Have I done something to displease you?" She asked suddenly, searching his face for some sign of her transgression.

"What? No." He shook his head.

"Are you considering returning me?" She held her breath.

"No, Val." His face lit with surprise. "Where is this coming from?"

"I thought maybe I had been too forward before and so I have waited. But the past days have gone by and you still haven't…"

She trailed off, not knowing quite how to phrase his lack of interest.

"Look." He reached across the table and put his hand over hers. "Let's not talk about it anymore. I want you to get comfortable living here. That's what you should focus on, alright?"

"Alright." She nodded, and he withdrew his hand.

Clearly this was an order and she would obey, although her insides tumbled about with unease. If she wasn't for him, then what was she for?

"I've got to go to work, but I'll see you at seven."

Rising from the table, he grabbed his tablet and walked coolly out. She was left to stare at her plate, then out the window, trying to calm her racing thoughts.

After listening to the rumble of his car engine fade down the drive, she too rose and exited the dining room. The house was shady and cool, but the sun shone brightly outside, and as she passed an open window she could feel heat on the slight breeze. Maybe she would go for a swim after all.

Several minutes later, Yvette discovered her standing dazzled in front of a large painting of impressionist vineyards.

"How do I get to the pool?" Val asked, as Yvette came to a halt beside her and looked up at the enchanting work.

"I'll show you to the pool house. There should be a bathing suit already stocked in your size."

Yvette turned briskly on her heel and clicked off along the marble. Weaving behind her, Val enjoyed the confident bounce of the older woman's perfect blonde hair. They left the house through wide open French doors and crossed a stone patio which ended at a rectangle of blue water. It was surrounded by evergreen shrubs and carved marble statues that mirrored the white stone of the house.

Set back down a wide gravel path sat the pool house. Yvette showed her inside, pointing out the bathroom, shower, lounge and changing room. Plush towels lined the cupboards and beside them hung a few robes. Pulling open several drawers, Yvette found a handful of swim suits that should fit.

"You may have lunch here if you would like," Yvette informed her. "There is a nice lounger alongside the pool where we can serve you. Would you like me to bring a book or perhaps a collection of magazines?"

"Okay." Val nodded as she surveyed the suits, reaching out to run her fingers along them.

Yvette turned to go, but then seemed to change her mind. Swinging back, she chose a deep-blue bikini with matching cover-up and set them neatly on a long bench. In that moment, Val realized this likely wouldn't be the last time she felt grateful towards the other woman.

Once she was alone, Val changed into the suit and carried the cover-up out to the lounge chair indicated. Tossing it aside, she stuck a careful toe down in the water. It was warm. They heated the pool.

Of all the luxuries, Val had never considered this one. Did all free people live this way? She thought probably not as she lowered herself in, bobbing happily up to her neck.

The outdoor pool at Cambric was filled with cold water, but back then they never seemed to feel it. When they were kids, she and Bee had run and jumped as high as they could before splashing crazily into the water. An instructor hired by The Agency taught them all how to swim and they were allowed to practice twice per week the entire length of summer. Girls were given a separate hour for play and then the boys had their turn.

Cambric Agency trained two types of Domestic Level

captives. Classification 1 was for basic household labor. A D1 captive might be a maid, a nanny, a butler or gardener. Though the market for a male D2 was not nearly so wide as for female, The Agency did stock them.

They produced captives you could rent by the hour, for special parties, or in a monthly membership. This worked for both D1s and D2s, though Cambric made the majority of their money on the sexual end of it.

A permanent placement male D2... now that was rare. In fact, there were only a handful. And Gabe had been one of them. Handsome, impulsive, tragic. Gabe.

Gabe with his dark eyes and quick laugh. Gabe and Bee. Bee and Gabe. Val tried to push the images of her old friends from her mind.

When Yvette returned, she brought a handful of fashion magazines and some iced tea with her. Val exited the water and lay down on the padded chaise surrounded by fluffy towels. Letting the warmth of the air dry her skin, Val flipped through page after page of photos as the cool drink soothed her inner ache.

The Agency had kept their Domestics 1 and 2, male and female together from preschool through sixth grade. At that point they had undergone their first sifting. This first round separated D1 category from D2, and isolated males from females. Temperament and appearance were the deciding factors.

A Domestic 1 then learned how to clean a house, cook, care for small children, manicure the yard, repair an automobile, things like that. Genders were kept separate until graduation from high school. That is when a final sift took place and D2 category was made permanent. This final phase hinged on intense personality screenings, aptitude tests and of course, looks.

From that point forward, D2s were all housed and trained together, male *and* female. Permanent placements received an Associates Degree on top of their traditional performance duties. They attended classes together, ate meals together, and sometimes even shared a trainer. Bee and Val had also shared a room.

Though trainee males were kept on a separate floor, by and large, Bee and Val had spent all of their days with Gabe. Gabe with his winning smile and golden hair. When Val shut her eyes, she could see him even now.

Just then Yvette returned wheeling a tray that clattered pleasantly with a plate of food. The interruption was welcome. Val was happy to be saved from the melancholy of her memories.

"Thank you, Yvette."

Val scooted to the edge of the lounge and lifted the plate down to settle it on the small teak table. It contained a chicken salad sandwich with curly French fries still hot from the fryer. The smells wafted deliciously on the air.

"When would you like to start choosing your own food?" Yvette asked, lingering a moment to watch Val pluck delicately at a fry. Blowing at the curl, Val cooled it before popping it into her mouth.

"I'm sorry, I just wouldn't know where to begin," Val explained.

"Well, how about I start by giving you two options to choose from and you can pick one or the other?" Yvette suggested. "I can lay out two clothing choices and offer two food choices. We can work up from there."

"That sounds good." Val smiled up at the woman she barely knew, but somehow trusted. "Are you a D1?"

"No Dear," Yvette answered, shaking her head just slightly. "The Riggs family does not own any captives. Well, except now I suppose they own one."

Turning, Yvette wheeled the empty cart back along the side of the sparkling pool. Once under the overhang of the second-floor terrace, she disappeared in its shade. Again, Val worried about the reason for her purchase. Not only was she the only captive here, but she wasn't being used for any purpose whatsoever. Well, at least not yet.

Consuming the sandwich slowly, Val sipped the cool refill of iced tea and traced droplets of condensation as they trickled down the outside of her glass. Somewhere off in the distance, her ears tuned to an odd sound. It was a peculiar rhythm that was like running, and then again not. It was so unusual, she had only ever heard it once, and never in person. The rapid thumping grew steadily louder and then distant again, fading to nothingness.

Her meal complete, she stood up on the lounge and turned to look behind her. Over the row of abundant emerald green shrubs, a small hillside gave way. Stretching down flat, it revealed a breathtaking landscape filled with white fenced pastures, a large stone barn, and a full size race track.

Gaping at the site, Val witnessed the distant stride that produced the strange sounds. A brown streak of horse strode effortlessly around the bend, its rider clinging to its back as he disappeared beyond the gray stable.

Glancing back at the house, Val noted there was no one else around. The Agency would have her stay put, but Jason's words from just that morning surfaced in her mind. He had told her that she could walk the grounds and so she would.

Hopping down from the lounge, she wriggled into the tiny cover-up before slipping on a pair of matching flip flops. The row of bushes that bordered the pool had a break near the end, which revealed a narrow walkway.

Keeping right, Val stood at the edge of the hillside and surveyed a small stepping stone path that cut down to the bottom before disappearing into a cluster of tall trees. Anticipation pumped within her chest. Was she really going to go down it? By herself?

Before she could change her mind, Val picked her way quickly down the slope, loose hair tangling over her shoulders. At the bottom, the tiny walkway merged with a well-maintained gravel road. She hurried along its curve which was lined by beautiful jacaranda trees in bloom. Their bright purple blossoms littered the ground beneath her feet.

Ahead of her, the sound of hoof beats grew louder, occasionally accented by the shouts of men. Suddenly, the protective trees ceased, and she drew up short to see the stables before her. Looming large, the scent of hay hung thickly in the air.

This was still Jason's property, she had crossed no fence, pushed through no doors or gates. But she was alone and without her owner's specific direction. Twining her fingers in front of her, Val hesitated. Should she go back?

But as she stood there, listening to the stamp of feet, her wariness was soon overpowered. She had never seen a horse in real life before, only in a movie. Making her way to the edge of the barn, Val wandered down the center aisle. At the far end, she spied an older man sweeping quietly but no one else.

The man didn't look up. Didn't pause or react and so she kept moving along the corridor, stopping to stare wide-eyed into each stall. Gray horses, black horses, brown horses, in all shades, greeted her. Some stuck out their heads, ears swiveling forward with interest. Some merely huffed a breath out of oversized nostrils and continued their steady chomping.

Pausing at one towering reddish face she tentatively extended her hand. An amazing warmth exhaled from its enormous nostrils. The tickle of soft hair felt smooth under her fingertips. Tentatively, she stroked the cheek of this mesmerizing beast as a clutch of inner yearning filled her chest. What would it be like to ride one?

As she neared the end of the barn a short young man with copper skin and dark hair exited one of the stalls. Starting upon seeing her, he spoke rapidly in a language she didn't understand. Val simply stared. His laugh was immediate and light as he began to walk towards her, a smile of approval playing across his lips. That's when the older man ceased his sweeping and spoke a few short words. Ducking his head, the young man doubled back and left.

At that moment, Val wished she understood them, but foreign language had never been her strong suit. The older man resumed his work, a pleasant hum emanating from his lips. Curiosity piqued, she walked over and watched as he finished the length of the aisle. When his work was complete, he looked over at her with kind brown eyes hidden under a faded blue ball cap.

"Would you like to watch the horses run?" His voice held a slight accent but was rich and smooth.

"Yes, I would." She returned his kind smile with one of her own.

Following him out of the barn they turned a corner and reached a long railing that ran the length of the track. A small wooden platform had been erected with a white plastic chair settled on top. The man shouted an instruction over his shoulder and soon the young man from before appeared, carrying another chair.

Lifting it up on the platform, he arranged the seats together, then left. Val followed the older man up the few steps and settled herself next to him. The arrangement guaranteed them a perfect view of the track with any horse and rider on it.

"What may I call you Señorita?"

"My name is Val," she answered, and watched as a rider entered the far end of the track.

"It is a pleasure to meet you Val, my name is Ignacio." His eyes focused on the horse as he spoke.

Several others materialized as well until a collection of four horses were walking, jogging and loping about. Occasionally, Ignacio would whisper into a tiny microphone he held clutched loosely in his work-worn hand. She assumed it transmitted his voice to an earpiece for each rider.

"When Jason was a young boy," Ignacio began conversationally. "He used to sneak down here without his parents knowing." Looking down he checked a cell phone in his pocket and then silenced it, ignoring the caller. "They fought him on it for a while, but every chance he had, all summer long, the boy haunted me."

Ignacio chuckled at the memory and had Val smiling along with him until one of the horses came thundering by. Hand covering her heart, Val exclaimed in wonder as the black horse and jockey made a fast pass by them. She could almost feel the animal's rapid breathing in her own chest. How she longed to experience it for herself.

"I can see how he would love it." She breathed the words, never taking her eyes from the animal.

Leaning forward, she edged ever closer to the rail, her chair tipping slightly with her.

"He almost had them convinced to let him train, as he is too big to ride," Ignacio informed her. "But then the Señor wanted to retire. Jason was forced to assume the role for which he was born. So in the end, the family got what it wanted. He's a talented rider, but even better with business. I still wonder about him, though."

The phone buzzed again, persisting in its request, but Ignacio didn't bother to glance at the screen.

Val listened absently to his words, but her attention remained riveted to the whoosh of horses that passed by. One by one they raced until a single rider pulled up short in front of them. Ignacio spoke rapidly in what Val figured must be Spanish. In response, the jockey rotated through a series of hand positions which Ignacio corrected. Once satisfied, the rider moved off to repeat the pass.

"But Jason has all of this." Val spoke in wonder at her surroundings, gesturing to the barn and the home beyond. Ignacio merely gave a sad shake of his head.

"He lacks the passion he showed before," Ignacio elaborated. "Since giving up the track, he is neither elated nor very angry."

With a final shrug, he put an end to their conversation. In silence they watched the rest of the horses run, each receiving instruction in turn.

As Ignacio's phone continued to buzz, Val looked over at him pointedly.

"They know I do not answer while I train," he explained,

blinking away a small smile that tugged at the corner of his mouth.

Completely absorbed in the rotation of horses, Val didn't notice the spin of tires on gravel speeding steadily closer. The large black stud had stopped in front of them and he had her full attention.

Drawn to the beautiful glisten of hide, Val leaned carefully forward over the railing until she could just reach him. Extending one hand to rest gently against the shoulder of the horse, she marveled at the feel of the warm hide slick with sweat.

"Val!"

Jason's voice boomed from just behind her, causing her to jump.

The horse spooked, dancing suddenly away at the unexpected motion. For a split second, Val's body hung precariously over the rail. Without the horse's shoulder to lean on, she tipped forward into the open air.

If Ignacio hadn't wrenched her back onto the platform, she would have tumbled face first onto the track. Instead of a fall to the earth, she was rocked back onto her butt, landing with an ungraceful thud. An embarrassed heat flushed her cheeks.

"My God." Jason was furious, eyes blazing as he spoke. "They've been searching for you everywhere. I had to come back from the office to find you."

"Such temper." Ignacio spoke quietly, his eyes holding a disapproving look. "You have spooked your best new prospect. Has it been so long since you trained?"

Bending over, Ignacio reached for Val and helped her to stand.

"And you." Jason turned on him. "Why haven't you picked up your phone?"

"You know I don't answer during runs," he replied, before turning to Val. "I apologize Señorita, I have not witnessed Jason this uncontrolled in many years. His manners have fled him."

Absorbing the last comment through gritted teeth, Jason bit his tongue and stepped forward to help Val down from the platform. He clutched her hand tightly, refusing to let go even as she followed him obediently to the small cart he had been driving.

It was still hot out, but the sun had started its downward arc in the sky. She must have been down here for hours because it was already late in the afternoon. The time had escaped her, she was so wrapped up in the moment.

In silence, they coasted down the barn aisle, then followed the gravel road back through the stand of trees. Keeping her eyes forward, Val dare not look over at him. The thrill of anticipation that had flooded her body when she first arrived at the barn now turned to a trembling fear. Survival at The Agency meant staying under the radar. She had failed in that ideal now.

"I'm sorry for yelling at you," he spoke finally. "I was just... concerned that you had run away."

He didn't look over at her, but kept his eyes focused on driving.

"I won't run away," she assured him, wondering at his apology.

Each time she thought she had him figured out, he went another way altogether. As to running away, the thought had never occurred to her, so thorough was her conditioning. Besides, she needed him. Needed his help.

"I should have told Yvette where I wanted to go. You are right to be angry. It's just... I've never seen a real horse. I don't know why but I had to go down there. I promise I won't go again."

"You've never seen a horse before?" He asked, shock registering in his tone. All the anger from before had evaporated.

"No, just pictures," she answered carefully, watching him.

When they reached the house, he stopped the cart and looked over at her, one arm strung out along the seat backs.

"Would you like to learn to ride one?" His face lit with a mischievous grin.

CHAPTER 4

THAT EVENING THEY DISCUSSED ARRANGEMENTS FOR HER TO begin riding lessons. Excitement at the prospect bubbled within her and Val was hard pressed to stamp down the rush of emotion. Even so, she tried.

The Agency made a practice of swiftly stopping any activity that provided a captive too much pleasure. One minute you could be riding a horse, and the next never see one again. They felt it wasn't good for a captive to become too dependent on anything other than the will of their owner. Was it possible Jason would feel the same?

Across the dimly lit dining table, Val examined him as he recounted stories from his childhood. He spoke easily of a much younger Ignacio and a barn full of grooms ready to help in a little boy's mischief. But it wasn't just the silly stories that had her wondering about him. It was Jason's charming manner that had her weakening as well.

Everything she had been taught about having an owner, *he* had proven false. When she expected punishment, he provided an apology. When she sought to draw him in, he pushed her away. Above all else, his motives baffled her.

Blue eyes dancing in the candlelight, Jason detailed how his parents had balked at the idea of his riding for competition. And even more so when he flourished under Ignacio's training. Something about the rebellion, though, gave him a spark. Val recognized that look all too well. Bee often had a similar twinkle when she bent a rule. Whenever Bee had walked the line at Cambric, however, Val's palms would break out in a sweat.

Dinner was exquisite as usual and for the first time, Val was able to make a choice between the two options offered her. Roast chicken, fingerling potatoes, and squash. The combination melted effortlessly in her mouth.

"May I ask you a question?" Val ventured, causing Jason to raise his eyebrows.

"Of course."

"Why don't you have an accent?"

"What?" Jason leaned back in his seat and chuckled. "You mean I don't sound Texan to you?"

Val shook her head, slightly embarrassed. She couldn't help but notice the difference in dialect. All the house staff aside from Yvette had some form of southern drawl or other.

"Two words," Jason held up his fingers. "Private school. My mother isn't from the south originally and she insisted none of us pick up the twang."

Rounding the corner of the table, Anne Marie filled Jason's wine glass yet again before moving towards Val. She was the same young woman who had served them breakfast. As apprentice to the cook, she had a hand in most meals.

The moment the wine touched her glass a churning started in Val's belly. This would be over the two drink maximum prescribed by The Agency. Though she wanted to say no, instinctively she felt it would be rude for her to wave off. Instead, she resolved to sip more slowly, letting the goblet remain full in order to avoid getting served more.

"So, did you get into any trouble as a kid?" Jason asked.

"Oh no, that was all Bee."

"Who's Bee?"

Immediately, Val wished she could swallow her words, but had to answer nonetheless. "She is, or was, my sister. Kind of."

"I didn't know you had a sister." He leaned forward, intrigued.

"Well, I don't really know if she is my sister by blood. It's just that everyone said how much we look alike. Same hair, same eyes, same face."

"Cambric never confirmed it?"

"No, they never tell you anything about family. Technically, there are no such relationships for a captive but Bee and I were together as long as I can remember. We shared a room all my life." That was before, Val thought, but she wasn't going to elaborate if she didn't have to.

"Do you know where she is now?"

"No."

It was a lie, potentially, and it sat heavily in her gut. Val let her eyes fall to her glass of wine. Changing her mind on the amount, she sipped deliberately at its contents.

"I'm sorry," he offered finally, and let the conversation die.

They went on that way for the next several weeks. Val rode almost daily, and spent each waking hour she could at the stables. Ignacio quickly conscripted her as a groom. He bade her wash, brush, and walk a selection of horses.

When she wasn't busy with that, she swept the floor, dusted at cobwebs and mucked stalls with the other workers. It was the first manual labor Val had ever performed and she found it strangely satisfying.

Every night at seven o'clock she was showered and dressed for dinner with Jason. They talked together for hours and she learned a great deal about him. At eighteen he used to sneak away from school to pull shifts as a roughneck in his father's oil company. It had worked fine for several years until a company man mentioned it to his parents. After that, he was banned from the platform.

She enjoyed discovering things about him, but inevitably the roles would reverse. Over dinner he would question her about her life at Cambric. He reviewed protocols, education, training and living conditions, but the information she provided never really seemed to satisfy.

He always probed for more. More details, more facts, more experiences. It was like he was searching for something and she could never give him what he wanted. Although, she did her best to be honest, Val held back certain details, especially what had occurred involving Bee. That was her own private torture and she resolved not to share it with him.

Physically, he seemed to be warming up to her. She often caught him staring when he didn't think she was paying any attention. The Agency had worked with them on subtlety and subconscious cues so she tried everything possible to encourage him. A twist of her hair, the look in her eye, the brush of her fingers against his hand.

After dinner, he would walk with her to the door of her bedroom. Backing her up against the wall, Jason would press his body against hers, letting his hands roam down her sides. No matter how hard she tried though, he refused to step foot over the threshold.

Everything about him told her he wanted more, but he always stopped short and made an excuse to leave. Nibbling uncertainly on her lower hip, she would watch him walk down the long hall to his bedroom alone. When he reached his door, he would turn back, glancing warily at her over his shoulder before pushing inside.

The feel of his kiss would linger on her lips, then. Sometimes for hours. But the weeks continued to pass that way and they seemed doomed to repeat the never-ending pattern. Tonight was no exception as she appraised him across the table.

Jason's gray tie lay tossed lazily next to his empty glass and his electric eyes glittered with an excessive amount of wine. When Val's gaze dropped to his clean-shaven face and strong jaw, he simply smiled. He was handsome, almost painfully so. The realization caused a warm pulling sensation to flood deep inside. It was coming more frequently now whenever she was with him.

"I have a short business trip that's just been scheduled and I can't get out of it," he was saying. Their meal had long since been cleared. She wasn't sure how much wine had been poured.

"How long will you be gone?"

"That's the thing. I want to take you with me." He laughed at the look of nervousness that crossed her face. "It's more of a working vacation really. Every few months a group of CEOs and their spouses go to a resort for a few days. A lot of important business gets done that way. We attend a few dinners, play a round of golf and when everyone is liquored-up, we make deals."

"I haven't been trained for that sort of thing," she admitted, circling the tip of her finger along the rim of her glass.

"You keep saying that. What exactly have you been trained for?"

"Well, they intended for me to be with an older gentleman. I would warm his bed and take the edge off his loneliness. Maybe cook him a few of his favorite meals. Remind him of his former wife, that sort of thing."

"Wait, you can cook?" He was incredulous.

"A little," she admitted. "Baking mostly. But anyway, I wasn't trained for business work. I wouldn't know the first thing to say or do."

"Don't worry about that." He leaned back in his chair and folded his hands behind his head, balancing precariously with a knee propped under the table's edge. "Half the ladies are second or third trophy wives and the other half are originals. There *is* one other D2, but no one cares about that."

"Alright." Val's heart leapt at the mention of another D2. "If it's what you want."

Good and drunk now, Jason pushed back from the table and let his fingers glide along its surface. Walking gingerly around to Val, he pulled her up to standing. She wobbled slightly on her feet, her head spinning just a little. Immediately, a giggle escaped her.

She'd never felt like this before. Her body sagged into him a moment before she gripped his arms in an attempt to steady herself. Jason looked down at her, an intense expression filling his face. But it was only for a moment.

Before she could react, his previous smile had returned and he had stepped away. Keeping hold of her hand, he pulled her along behind him, out the dining room door and off through the darkened house. All the staff had long since gone home.

On the stairs, they both of stumbled a few times. The sound of their laughter echoed off the walls.

"I guess I let the wine get away from me," Jason admitted, trying his best not to weave down the hall.

Beside him, she felt silly and carefree and light. When they arrived at her door she didn't turn to face him as was their custom. Instead, she pushed inside and dropped his hand before walking over to the bank of dark windows. Raising both of her hands, she placed them carefully against the cool glass.

Jason followed her inside, but said nothing. Standing next to her in silence, his eyes met hers in the reflection of the window pane. Reaching out, he covered her hand with his own and gently peeled it away from the glass. Eyes studying her, he brought it to his lips.

A shiver moved through her, causing goosebumps to travel up her arm. His blue eyes glinted at that.

Watching her for a reaction, his mouth traveled from her palm to her wrist, then up the inside of her arm. Closing her eyes, she absorbed the sensations he created, knowing soon it would come to an end. He would stop them, like he always did, leaving her at once empty and afraid.

Sucking in a breath, she pulled her arm from his grasp and walked away, heart hammering inside her chest.

"I shouldn't have pulled away from you," she said, keeping her back to him.

"Why did you?"

"Because I don't know how to please you."

"Val-"

"Every night you bring me here and you make me think

that you want me." Whirling to face him, she let the past month of uncertainty boil over. "And every night I do something wrong and you leave. Why did you buy me? What is it that you want from me?"

Releasing a long sigh, Jason ran a hand roughly over his face. Fear leaped immediately to fill her. The wine was making her say things she shouldn't. He was her owner, how dare she question him? Thoughts of Cambric, her trainer and the punishment she should be receiving flashed through her mind. But none of it even occurred to Jason.

Crossing the room, he wrapped his arms about her waist and pulled her up against him. He kissed the top of her head and whispered.

"I want you." He breathed into her hair. "I shouldn't want you, but I do. I wish I could tell you why."

Inside her head, a small warning bell sounded faintly, as if at a distance. But the wine was clouding her judgment, and what she would have questioned before was shoved aside now. Tilting her face up, she gripped the open collar of his shirt in both hands.

He said he wanted her. She had to act now. Brushing her lips over his neck, she trailed seductive kisses along his collarbone and down to his chest, working open the buttons as she went.

Letting out a small groan, Jason tipped his head back and looked up to the ceiling.

"You can tell me to stop, and I'll stop. You *know* that, right?"

Val ignored him. Reaching the final button, she smoothed her hands up his bare stomach. He took hold of her chin then, snapping his head back down and forcing her to look at him.

"You can say no to me if you want. Tell me you understand that," he insisted.

"I understand," she told him, knowing the truth would have him walking out her door.

She could never say *no* to him. But not saying anything… that was a choice in and of itself, right? And if she really thought about it, she did want to do this with him. Had wanted to for a while.

As he stared down at her, his fingers pulsed along her cheek. Whatever doubts he had, whatever reserve he held, seemed to break at that moment. Covering her mouth with his, Jason's hands slid down her sides to the end of her dress, then under it. His palms smoothed over her bare butt-cheeks, cupping and squeezing lightly before pressing her tighter in against him.

Val exhaled into his ear as he backed them towards the bed where they landed heavily together. Heart pounding, she wriggled and squirmed beneath him as he pulled her dress up and away.

His mouth came down to take hers, then moved to her jaw, along her neck and lower. She could feel the wrap of his fingers as he removed her lace thong, then the brush of his lips as he lingered over each breast. Arching into him, she let small plaintive whimpers escape her throat.

Cursing under his breath, Jason reached down to jerk at his belt. After a moment he was forced to stand, tugging it off along with his pants and shoes.

Sitting up to watch him, Val let her eyes roam over the muscles of his chest and stomach. With a knowing smile, she scooted to the edge of the bed and leaned forward to take him in her mouth. He gasped once, then groaned. His fingers stroked through her loose hair. Looking up at him, she enjoyed his reaction.

"I'm not going to last," he murmured after a few minutes, then pulled back and dropped to his knees in front of her.

His strong hands were firm as he pushed at her shoulders, encouraging her to tip back onto the bed. Crouching down, he spread her legs apart with his broad shoulders, then trailed his tongue slowly from her knee up the length of her thigh. Her eyes shot open in surprise at his contact. This had only ever happened once during training. They didn't want the girls getting too used to it.

Tingling pulses of pleasure built within her as she tried to lay still for him. But eventually it became too much. Her hips shifted and worked, tilting with each new crest, her fingers gripping the bedsheets tightly. Calling out to him finally, she whimpered, wanting more.

He raised up to crawl over her, letting the pressure of his body drag over her as he went. Blue eyes catching hers, he held her gaze as he sunk himself between her thighs. Squeezing her eyes shut then, she moaned. Her hands clutched at his shoulders, her heels dug into his back.

At first, his rhythm was almost torturously slow. But as he picked up the pace, he had her pulsing and gasping beneath him. His breathing grew ragged and shallow. She could feel the pant of air against her shoulder. His face was buried in her neck.

With each thrust, a wave of sensation built within her until she finally cried out, clenching tightly around him. She heard him bite back a groan before he let himself go, following her over the edge.

~

The next morning came early. Yvette entered Val's room only to discover them both still passed out in bed. Jason rolled onto his stomach and grumbled, covering himself with a half-hearted grab for the covers.

Embarrassed at being caught naked with him, Val immediately sat up. But then her head began to pound. A swift sickness swelled in her belly and she was forced to lay back down.

"Too much wine?" Yvette clucked softly as she walked across the room, searching the bathroom's medicine cabinets. "I saw the empty bottles you left on the table."

Tsking quietly under her breath, she placed a glass of water and three pills on each night stand. Jason lifted his head only high enough to get the drugs down, then was back to sleep. Val pressed a shaky hand to her forehead as she drank from the glass, gulping at the promise of relief. Before she left, Yvette set out two robes on the end of the bed then shut the door carefully behind her.

Sinking into the cool pillow, Val drifted back to sleep.

A few hours later they woke once more to Yvette's return. This time she was wheeling a tray piled high with plates of food. The smells at once enticed and revolted. Val's head was feeling better than before though, so she got up and slipped into the silk robe.

Their breakfast was placed on the small coffee table that was situated between two barrel chairs in the corner. There was hot tea and coffee, scrambled eggs with cheese, breakfast sausage, hash browns and bowls of fruit.

Propping her feet up on the edge of the table, Val carefully nibbled on a strawberry. She wanted so badly to eat it, but her stomach turned sour as she chewed. After a minute, Jason walked over and flopped in the chair next to her. Taking a plate, he filled it with every type of food available and dug in. Val watched him in mild horror.

"You have to eat the greasy stuff to settle your stomach." He advised her wisely between bites. "Once you get something down, then the rest is way easier, I promise."

She merely blinked disbelievingly at him.

"And get rid of that crappy fruit," he continued, batting the berry out of her hand.

She laughed at him then, noting the dark circles under his eyes. But then her head resumed its throbbing and she resolved to following his instructions. Tentatively, she took a few bites of the sausage. After keeping it down for a minute, she tried more.

"I really want to nap," he complained, as he downed the last of his coffee. "But we have to get on a plane and make that trip to the west."

Leaning over, he kissed her lightly on the cheek, his eyes flicking to hers briefly, then down to her mouth. Almost reluctantly, he stood up and turned to leave. She watched his casual stride as he passed through her door. This time, he didn't look back.

Strange feelings began shifting inside of her, but she had no time for reflection as Yvette swept back into the space.

"I'll pack your things while you freshen up," she announced, heading towards the closet.

Val's body was exhausted, her mind fuzzy from the hangover, but she pushed herself to move anyway. In her bathroom, she watched water pour from the faucet to swirl and fill the claw foot tub. Slipping into the warmth, she exhaled. This felt good. This felt so, so good. Head sinking below the water line, she let her hair soak before pushing smoothly back up to recline, eyes closed.

As much as she wanted to, she knew she couldn't linger there. Jason had a schedule to keep and now Val was on it. After washing herself thoroughly, she sat naked in front of the mirror as she dried her hair. Studying her figure critically, she tried to see herself how Jason would. Here he had kissed, here he had touched.

Sentiment welled inside her that she hadn't ever experienced, had no name for. Before this, she had worried about why he kept her. Now she worried about how long it would last. When would she become too old? Too routine? What would become of her when he moved on? She put the turmoil aside and applied a layer of practiced makeup.

Choosing between three outfits that Yvette set out, Val got dressed. She slipped on a flowing peasant skirt that swirled with muted red tones, matching it to a tight white crop top that revealed her flat belly. It provided just the right combination of comfort and sex appeal.

Following Yvette down the stairs, Val listened as the older woman lectured her on the contents of the suitcase. She reviewed what options Val would have for each event, though they should only be gone for four nights.

Outside, Jason was already reclining in the backseat of a black SUV. The driver stood waiting beside the rear passenger door, holding it open expectantly as Val approached. Slipping inside she settled in and listened to Jason talk on his cell phone.

"I'm telling you I don't know how they're making any money." He spoke seriously while gazing out his window. "No. The technology they sent over is great, but the price they quoted is way too low."

He paused, listening.

"If you could get me their financials maybe I could help with that. No. No, of course. I understand."

She let her mind drift off for a few minutes, watching the scenery as they passed. Despite the heavy breakfast, her stomach growled and churned. A slight headache persisted. Alcohol was evil, she decided and she was never going to drink that much again.

"You got it back? Finally." He glanced over his shoulder at her before turning to his window and lowering his voice. "I can listen. Tell me."

Murmurs sounded on the other end.

"What? Did you run it again? I don't believe it. I thought for sure-"

He pinched the bridge of his nose. Closing his eyes, he leaned against the seat and listened, tension settling into his jaw.

"Okay. Well… I'll move forward with that other thing we discussed, then. Yeah, bye."

Jason clicked off his phone and tossed it down onto the leather seat between them. He kept his eyes shut for the rest of the ride. A pit formed in her stomach. Why did she feel some of that was about her? Let it go, she coached herself, you aren't that important to discuss over a phone call.

When they arrived at the airport she trailed him obediently as before. The throng of people was now a more familiar sight. Once loaded onto the jet, she tilted her seat back to recline and shut her eyes. Sleep enveloped her. She didn't even last long enough for another takeoff.

∽

Rich meat, fragrant au jus sauce, hot bread. The smell of food brought her around. Opening her eyes, Val watched Jason take a huge bite of his steak sandwich. Leaning her seat up, she caught his easy smile and returned it. Whatever bad news he had received over the phone was apparently forgotten.

"Nice nap?" He asked, and signaled Marcy to come with her plate.

"Mmmm, that looks good." She stretched out her arms wide. Arching her back, she gave her sore neck a rub. Plane sleeping wasn't the most comfortable sleeping, she discovered.

While she ate, he told her about the group of people attending this "working" vacation. There were ten CEOs in total, each with a significant other. Jason was hoping to partner with a renewable energy company called Green Use in order to relieve pressure from the public concerning the ongoing use of fossil fuels.

He was also interested in a marketing firm called Clear Productions. They may be able to help Riggs Oil with some rebranding.

Keeping ahead of popular opinion was now crucial to long-term viability and success. Running a business wasn't the same as when his father formed the company. Riggs Oil was profitable, but if the public began to view them as detrimental to the environment, then they could take a serious hit. Jason wanted to get ahead of that possibility.

When they touched down in California it was still light out. But despite the brightly shinning sun, losing two hours on the time change had its effect. After checking into the upscale hotel, they both flopped groaning onto the bed. Reaching for his phone, Jason set the alarm so they wouldn't miss the first dinner, twined his fingers in her own, and then promptly passed out.

Val watched him breathe for a few moments, rubbing her thumb absently along the backside of his hand. She couldn't say why he had reached for her, why he wanted the contact, but she liked it. Eventually, the throbbing at her temples increased. Her hangover persisted until she too closed her eyes. Grateful for the cool room with its thick curtains drawn, Val dropped quickly into unconsciousness.

In her dream she was running. Although, in real life that's not what she had done. No. When they came for Bee, she hadn't lifted a finger. She sat frozen in shameful passivity instead. But the fantasy version of herself rose from her bed.

The dream Val chased them down the hallway, making a last grab for Bee's lifeless arms as they slid over the cold cement. She didn't quite touch them though, before security turned the final corner, and her best friend disappeared out of sight.

Shooting up in bed, Val sucked in a breath. Panting, she pressed the heels of her hands to her eyes in a vain attempt to stuff down the panic.

"You okay?" Jason's voice was soft, she must have woken him.

"Just a dream." Val's voice came out shaky, betraying her.

He propped himself up on one elbow to study her, so she covered her face. Tugging at her wrists, Jason murmured quietly. Though she couldn't see him, she could almost feel him frowning. This was a defiance of sorts, not doing what he so clearly wanted.

Reluctantly, she let him unmask her, but shifted her eyes away to stare at the foot of the bed. It was the best she could manage.

"Will you tell me?" His voice lifted with the question.

"I was running."

"Away?"

"No, not away." Her eyes popped up to his. "I won't ever run away from you."

Watching her for another beat, Jason finally reached out and pulled her down next to him. Without another word, he wrapped her body in his arms and kissed the top of her head. He wouldn't push her further. He wouldn't ask any more questions, though he had every right to. She didn't understand him. She just didn't understand.

Gently, he pressed her cheek to his chest where she listened to the steady thumping of his heart. After a few moments of quiet, his phone began to blare its warning tones. Dinner was in one hour. They couldn't be late.

Getting up together he suggested that she shower first. But when she did, he just stood by, watching her through the glass partition. She soaped her body, letting the suds slip down her skin as she glanced at him over her shoulder. The desire that rolled off him caused answers to echo throughout her body.

Trading places, she brushed by him on her way out of the stall. He called out to her in protest, but he didn't pursue her. Instead, he kept getting ready, and so she did the same.

Val wore a classic black evening dress, short and seductive. It fit just right, she thought, a perfect complement to Jason's sleek tailored suit. His brown hair was styled messily once more, blue eyes shining in a confident face. Ignacio was right, he was born for this role.

Despite having showered last, Jason was ready first.

Standing just behind her in the bathroom mirror, he observed her careful application of crimson lipstick. She caught his look, and couldn't help but offer him a flirtatious wink.

While she watched, he brought a strand of sparkling diamonds around from behind his back. Stepping forward, he looped them to dangle prettily about her neck. She clutched them impulsively in her hand, feeling the soft kiss he placed on her shoulder as he fastened the clasp. Never had she touched such exquisite jewels.

"These are yours to keep," he told her as she caressed the stones with light fingertips. "You can do what you like with them."

Understanding the implication, she felt grateful. If and when he broke off their arrangement, she would have something to sell. Would it be enough to save Bee?

"Thank you," she breathed.

CHAPTER 5

WHEN THEY ENTERED THE DINING ROOM, A HANDFUL OF PEOPLE stood milling about. Sophisticated people. Ones with custom clothing, expensive shoes and glittering jewelry. An expansive rectangular table stretched the length of the room. It was adorned with full dinner settings, heaping flower arrangements, candlelight and small white place cards.

The picture of cool, Jason pulled Val along beside him, his fingers entwined with hers as he introduced her around.

She met Mark and Audrey Linton of Green Use, the company Jason wanted to partner with. Then Rick and Amy Lowell of Lowell Oil, a competitor. Rick had grown up with Jason's father and inquired after him.

After a few minutes of small talk, they made their way to their seats. Jason held out Val's chair and then sat beside her before turning his attention to the woman on his right. He struck up a conversation without effort. This truly was his element. He made it all look so easy. But the truth was, this wasn't easy for Val. She hadn't been trained as a business asset, not the way some of the others had been.

Looking across the table, Val's mouth dropped in complete shock. It was the other D2, sitting directly opposite her, without a care in the world. And it was Gabe.

Her breath left her lungs. The last time she had seen him… well. She gave her head a little shake, it was so hard to think about still.

Letting her eyes drift over him, Val realized he must have been watching her for some time. Unlike her, he was able to keep his composure, allowing only a quiet smile to twist his lips. The woman seated next to him, she later found out, was his owner, Sharon Baine. An appealing woman in her early fifties, Sharon had lovely auburn hair and a curvy figure. The CEO of Work Tech, she was the power house and Gabe was the companion.

Slowly, Gabe brought one finger to his chin, motioning for Val to close her mouth. She snapped it shut, but couldn't stop her stare. It had been over six months since she had seen him. When a D2 was sold at Cambric, no information was given to their former friends. She hadn't known where he was or who he had been sold to. There were so many questions she had for him. Questions she would likely never get a chance to ask. Things she would never get a chance to say.

Finally, she forced herself to look away. Waiters began fluttering about, pouring drinks.

Sitting in silence, not daring to look across the table, Val picked at the salad on her plate. Cherry tomatoes popped juicily in her mouth while she listened to the conversations all around her. It took real effort to distract her mind.

Occasionally, Jason ran his hand reassuringly over her leg beneath the table. Surely he must think her manner was due to nervousness at the situation in general. He had no idea of her connection to the man he himself now spoke to.

Inevitably though, the conversation shifted, and Sharon addressed her directly. There was no avoiding it now, Val thought. Looking up, she held the powerful woman's gaze, taking in her dazzling smile.

"You're a D2 from Cambric Agency?" Sharon asked.

"Yes," Val responded.

"Well, isn't that something? Gabe is as well," she announced. "It's a large agency, but surely you must know one another."

Jason turned to examine Val more closely. His questioning eyes traveled the side of her face.

"Do you?" Jason asked, and she hesitated, wanting so badly to lie.

"As kids mostly," Gabe volunteered before she could say anything stupid. He had always tried to save her. "We haven't seen each other in a very long time."

Well, that was sort of true, Val thought, nodding her head in agreement. They had known each other as kids. And it had been a long time since they had seen one another. If six months was a long time.

Thankfully, Sharon jumped in to dominate the conversation after that. Val got the impression that she tended to dominate pretty much everything. Shifting the topic back to business, she inquired about the technology program that her company had recently delivered to Riggs Oil.

Jason soon became engrossed in the details of the program's implementation with Sharon answering his questions readily. Making use of the distraction, Val's eyes darted back to Gabe. She mouthed the words *thank you* and he briefly raised his glass before taking a drink. Same old charming Gabe, with his soft blonde hair and brown eyes.

He spent the rest of their dinner entertaining the gorgeous

trophy wife seated on his other side. Val watched the woman giggle and flush under his expert attention, drinking glass after glass of expensive champagne.

Surprisingly, Gabe seemed to drink just as much. Soon she observed the mild effects of his drunkenness. A slurred word here, a clattering fork there. He wasn't supposed to be drinking that much. Concern grew within her, but what could she say? Nothing at all.

~

At the end of the dinner they all rose and were ushered into a reception room. The business end of their group split off, while the companions were left to lounge in the comfort of the large space. The big boys, and girl, got down to their deals elsewhere.

The original wives, as Val liked to classify them, separated into their own corner. The trophy wives chose another, with waiters passing drinks evenly around to each. Val sat in a comfortable chair and crossed her legs, watching as Gabe interacted with each group.

He teased and smiled, fetched drinks and soon had all of the women giggling. Giggling and laughing. Laughing and yearning for more of his attention. This was exactly what he had been trained for. He was a sight to behold. He was the best. *Oh, Gabe.*

After an hour of getting all the women thoroughly drunk, he walked casually over and sat in the chair across from Val. His smile was still fixed to his face, but something else flashed in his eyes.

"God Val, you look just like her, you know that?" Gabe

started, leaning back in his chair. His prior drunkenness had seemed to dissipate. Was it all an act? She couldn't be sure.

"How are you, Gabey?"

"I'm great, can't you tell?" He laughed, but the sarcasm seeped through. "When you first walked in, my heart stopped. For a moment, I thought you were Bee."

"Have you heard from her?" She asked eagerly, tilting forward.

"Not a thing, you?"

"No," she admitted.

For several moments, a sad sort of stillness settled between them. But then Gabe seemed to shake it off.

"So, Jason Riggs, huh?" He resumed. "I've seen that guy nearly every month for the past six, and he's had a different woman with him every time, but never a D2. What's his angle?"

"I don't know." She shrugged.

"I'm just saying that the notorious playboy has bought himself a permanent," Gabe elaborated. Leaning in closer he spread his hand over her exposed thigh. The tips of his fingers played subtly against her skin. "You're gorgeous Val. Maybe I'm just a little jealous. Maybe I can't shake all those nights staring at you from behind glass."

"Come on, Gabey. You're going to get me in trouble again," she chided.

The burn of his hand against her leg for the first time unnerved her. He had always been with Bee, and Bee with him. It was *that* connection that had launched all three of them into a tumultuous darkness.

"Too late," he whispered. Withdrawing his hand, Gabe swore under his breath as he stood, adding a belated, *sorry,* under his breath.

With a big smile plastered back on his handsome face, her old friend sauntered away. Turning her head to watch, Val saw the reason for his hasty retreat. The working end of their group had just returned, bringing a giddy Sharon and sullen Jason along with it.

As Gabe swooped in to kiss Sharon's neck, she batted at him fondly before allowing him to fawn over her. The other women looked on. What a show, Val thought, but then again Gabe had always been exceptional at it. No one would ever know how completely miserable he was.

But to Val, it was obvious. Not only was he miserable but he was confused. That explained what he had said to her, and the touching. He had never touched her like that before.

Lost in her thoughts, Val didn't see Jason until he was standing right in front of her. When her eyes snapped up to his, she swallowed hard. He was angry. His brow was furrowed, his jaw clenching even as he looked down at her.

Without a word, he gripped her upper arm and lifted her quickly from the chair. His fingers dug into her skin, pulsing painfully, but he didn't seem to notice.

"You're hurting me," she whispered, as he swept her from the crowded room and out into the hall.

Weaving through the hotel corridors, he practically dragged her along beside him. The sky-high heels she wore made it difficult to keep up, but she managed to do so without falling. What had happened? What made him this way? She wracked her brain, trying to figure it out.

Once back in their room, he released her to stumble forward a few steps. Reaching out with her hands, she caught herself on the edge of their bed.

"How well do you know him?" Jason demanded, pacing the room.

"Who?" Val lowered herself to sitting, rubbing absently at her arm.

"Who?" Jason stopped and stared. "The guy whose hands were just all over you, Val. The one you hadn't seen since you were kids. That's what you said, right? You lied."

"I didn't-" Val started to protest, but then trailed off.

"They told me you've only been with one man... a trainer. Is that a lie, too?" His voice began to rise.

"No, that's the truth." Trying to reassure him, she reached out, but he backed a step, running his hands up through his hair.

"Was he your trainer?" Jason's voice was strained. "Have you slept with Gabe?"

"No, it wasn't Gabe. I've never been with him."

"You expect me to believe that? I know what I saw when I walked in. The way he looks at you, there's more to it. *What* is going on Val?"

"Nothing." Val stood up, holding out her arms placatingly. "Nothing is going on, I swear it."

Scrubbing his face roughly with his hands, Jason sat heavily on the bed. Sucking in a breath, he blew it out smoothly as he ran his fingers up through his thick hair.

Coming to sit beside him, she lay a hand tentatively on his arm. When he didn't push her away, they sat there a minute, letting the angry words dissipate around them.

"Tell me," he commanded. "I want to know everything."

Biting at her lip, Val focused on the geometric design of the carpet. She didn't want to share this part of her life with him. He had everything else, couldn't she keep just this? But her will was not her own, and he made the demand, so she must make a reply.

"I told you about Bee." Val swallowed before glancing up at

him. "She and I were always together, but then so was Gabe. As kids, Cambric houses both sexes together, so we knew Gabe then, that part is true."

Jason didn't say anything. His jaw remained tight, the muscle jumping slightly.

"Starting in middle school and through high school they separated us, for obvious reasons. It wasn't until we had our final sift that we saw Gabe again. The three of us were all chosen as permanent D2s which is so crazy because the number of us in that category is actually very small. Our class had maybe fifteen total."

She paused, twining her fingers together in her lap a moment before pushing on.

"Cambric moved us into the training section so we were all close. There were two D2s to each room. Me and Bee were in one and Gabe roomed with Charlie, they were the only males for our class."

In her mind, Val could picture it. They were young, innocent, teasing. Despite the circumstances, it was probably the best time of her life.

"Back then, things weren't so strict when you got up to that level. Sex between D2s was quite common. As long as you weren't a female permanent placement, it was okay. But Bee and I and the rest of our class, we had to keep ourselves only for our trainer.

The male D2s, though, and all hourly or party females… they didn't have the same restriction. Experience equaled higher quality for them so they were encouraged to have multiple lovers, as long as no serious relationships formed."

"And you followed that rule." Jason said it as a statement and Val nodded.

"A permanent female is allowed one trainer, one man, that's it. And Cambric chooses who it is, not us."

"But you lived with Gabe," Jason supplied. "Next to him."

"Until Bee, they never had a problem with a permanent female not following protocol. Maybe they should have seen it coming with her personality. But I think she was just so beautiful that they kept her there, hoping to make it work for the money. They said she was worth several million dollars."

"I paid three for you," Jason added.

She hadn't known the amount, and though she had been told it was a lot of money, it didn't mean much to her. Money itself didn't mean anything at all.

"We lived like that for years during training. And well, Gabe and Bee… they fell in love. He would sneak into our room at night and sleep with her."

Val sucked in a breath, seeing Bee so vibrant in her mind. Turning to Jason, she tried to make him understand. "She was my sister and I loved her so much. I just wanted her to be happy. Maybe I should have stopped it…"

"But you didn't."

"No," Val shook her head. "I didn't."

"So, what happened to her?"

"About eight months ago, Gabe overslept. Cambric security caught him in Bee's bed. It was awful."

Squeezing her eyes shut, Val battled at the memory. It was still so blindingly painful. The way the guards had come in. The shouting, them grabbing Bee. Then Gabe was losing it, throwing punches and they were on top of him, pinning him to the ground.

And Bee, she was screaming and screaming. If only she had just stopped screaming. But then that one guard lost his temper. Bee was knocked out. Her hair spread out on the floor, her eyes rolled up in the back of her head and they were dragging her away.

"I'm sorry," Jason said. Reaching out he rubbed his thumb at the silent tears that started to fall. "What did they do to her? To Gabe?"

"They beat her. They took her away." Val sniffed, then stuffed the feelings down where they belonged. "Then they took Gabe and locked him in Isolation. It's a sort of cell. Very small with a mattress on the floor and a toilet near the back.

They couldn't beat him like they did her. Nothing that would hurt his appearance in any way. Once he figured that out, he went on a hunger strike. He stopped eating, demanding to see Bee. Cambric must have panicked at that, Gabe was worth as much as Bee and I together. The way he looks and his... skill. They're rare."

"Sharon paid five million for him." Jason confirmed. "And he didn't look starved at the time."

"Well, they figured out a way to make him eat."

Jason frowned.

"Some of the Isolation rooms have a common wall. The wall has a large window cut into it, made of some kind of thick glass. They put me next to him. We could see each other through the glass, hear each other, too. So for every meal that Gabe refused to eat, they withheld one from me. He got to watch while I starved."

"Holy shit," Jason exhaled the words. When he looked at her, his eyes registered complete shock. It was like he couldn't quite believe it.

"Three days." Val said it simply. "It took me three days before I begged Gabe to eat."

"And he did?"

"Always." Val grimaced. "He would always save me. But

this time he gave up his leverage over seeing Bee. We remained in Isolation for about another week while they balanced out our nutrition.

It was long enough for Gabe to think of something else. Long enough for him to refuse his trainer. He demanded to see Bee, and he would not perform, no matter what woman they paraded in front of him. We both thought he had them beat that time. At night, we talked about how they would have to bring Bee back to us."

"What did they do to you, Val?" Jason guessed at the answer, his face grim, his mind working ahead.

"My trainer began to visit me at odd hours, waking me in the middle of the night. And he was… more rough, than ever before. Not violent exactly, just harsh. I've always been told Bee and I looked just alike so you can imagine how it was for Gabe to watch."

Jason glanced at the ceiling, then slowly closed his eyes.

"This time I was begging him to hold out. I could handle it. If he could just stay strong, then eventually we'd get Bee back."

"But he couldn't," Jason supplied, reaching out to take Val's hand.

"No." Val shook her head. "After a few more days he gave in."

Gave in, Val thought. More like he cracked, screaming and throwing himself against the glass. She remembered how it had looked, the glass, all splattered with blood from his split knuckles. He submitted to his trainer again, and all hope over Bee had gone.

"I'm sorry for doubting you." Jason's voice was low. "And for acting that way, it's not like me. And what they did to you…"

His words trailed off, dropping into the room.

She made no reply. Her shoulders sagged, her body felt suddenly incredibly heavy at the confession.

That night, sleep did not come easily. Thoughts of Bee, The Agency, and Gabe haunted her. Even with Jason's arm encircling her waist, she watched the digital clock on the night stand register one, then two, and finally three o'clock before she sank into nothingness.

When they woke the next morning, neither of them felt like leaving the room. Jason ordered room service for breakfast and their talk was benign. One arm slung over her shoulder, he sipped his coffee and talked quietly of the day's stock reports. Huddled against him, Val traced her fingers along his palm. The heavy topic of the night before was fading.

"We play a round of golf today. Tee time is at ten o'clock." Jason tapped steadily on his tablet. "They're serving mimosas on the terrace for you all, and when the round is over, we'll join up for lunch."

He didn't say it. Maybe he wanted to, but he didn't. Regardless, the unspoken request lingered in the air. Jason wanted her to stay away from Gabe. And of course, knowing Gabe, that wouldn't be easy, but Val promised herself she would try.

After jumping in the shower, Val noticed a light bruising on her upper arm. It looked like a series of fingerprints pressed into her skin. She hadn't thought Jason had held her that tight, but the discoloration was there just the same. When Jason joined her, he saw them and swore.

"Shit." He ran his fingers over the marks and shook his head. "I didn't mean to grab you so hard. Damn it."

One thing was for certain, Val thought, she needed to cover them up, either with makeup or clothes. After stepping out of the shower, she searched through the clothing options Yvette had sent with her.

Holding up a short blue dress, she judged that it just might work. It was tight from her waist down, form-fitting the way most of her outfits were, but the top was loose and flowing. The white sleeves were a see-through gauze-type material, but should work to conceal the area. No one would notice the marks, unless of course they were *really* looking.

Wriggling into it, she chose a pair of strappy flats to balance the exposed length of her legs. The dress ended abruptly just beneath her butt cheeks causing Jason to whistle appreciatively.

Standing beside him, she examined his figure in the full length mirror. His light blue golf shirt fit just right, revealing toned arms and bringing out the color of his eyes. Seeing her look of appreciation, his arms encircled her waist, drawing her up close against him.

He trailed affectionate kisses along her neck. She shifted against him invitingly. When he glanced at the time, he cursed under his breath before releasing her. Time to go.

Manicured green carpets of grass flanked by towering pines stretched out before them. The terrace of the resort's golf course provided a breathtaking view. Clinging to Jason's arm, Val let him lead her around for several minutes as they waited for everyone to arrive. Once assembled, the business end of the party departed for the course, leaving Val alone again with the array of spouses.

Sunshine beckoned from the far edge of the balcony and without anyone to talk to, Val moved towards it. Leaning her forearms on the thick stone railing she surveyed the golf course below with its players swinging clubs and pristine white carts gliding along. The game was so quiet, she thought.

A prickle formed at the back of her neck and she straightened her spine. Call it intuition, or perhaps years of familiarity, but whatever the reason, Val could feel Gabe's approach. She sensed him walking up behind her before he even said a word.

"Stay away, Gabey," she called, not bothering to look.

"I come bearing gifts," he answered smoothly, ignoring her request.

Coming to a halt, he stood beside her and gazed out over the course, drinks in hand.

"I don't want your gift," she countered, and had him grinning.

Placing one shimmering orange mimosa next to her hand, he sipped at his own and said nothing. After several moments of silence, however, he walked away.

Val sighed then, but her relief was short lived. Dragging a chair back over, Gabe placed it by her side and sat, his back leaned against the low stone wall.

In the quiet, she stood there, arms braced along the railing, doing her best to ignore him. But this was Gabe and he had made sure to be close. His shoulder was just barely an inch from her hip.

"Does he hit you?" Gabe asked finally.

"No, he doesn't hit me." She cringed, remembering the faint bruising on her arm. Only Gabe would look close enough to notice.

"Okay... does he grab you so hard that he leaves marks often?" Gabe downed his drink, signaling the waiter for another.

"Never, this was the first time. He didn't realize... oh why am I even talking to you about this?" She fumed.

"I wish it was different," he whispered, sounding suddenly helpless. "I wish I could do something."

"It's fine. He's fine."

A waiter approached. They both fell mute. He deposited the drink Gabe had ordered without comment and then left. After he had gone, Val reluctantly plucked up her glass and eyed it. Sipping at its contents, she frowned. Maybe she did need alcohol to complete this day.

A gentle breeze blew. It smelled of the ocean which wasn't too far off. It was then that she felt his touch. Whisper soft, Gabe's fingers brushed lightly against her leg, just below the edge of her dress. A dull ache bloomed within her body, she couldn't help it. Stepping quickly away, Val tried not to draw any attention. If someone saw them...

"I'll stop." Gabe chuckled quietly under his breath, holding up his hands. "I promise. It's just, all that time seeing you behind glass, and now here you are. I can't help but want to touch you."

"You're confusing me with Bee." Val cleared her throat, drank deeply from her glass.

"No, I know who you are." He grew serious. "It's just that Bee is long gone, and *you* are right here. We don't ever get to have anything we want. Why not steal a little of it while we can? Why not taste what it's like to make an actual choice, Val? To have freedom?"

"You're talking crazy," she hissed, wishing he would keep his voice down. Fear bubbled inside of her.

"Sharon is a decent owner, but sometimes I wonder if I'll ever have another woman that *I* choose."

Gabe turned his head to stare at her hip. Deliberately, he

let his eyes drop down the side of her leg. Enough, she thought. Enough of this.

Turning on her heel, Val pushed herself from the railing and strode back inside the terrace restaurant. She had to get away from him. She had to. After all the years of training together, Gabe knew exactly which buttons to push to get the reaction he wanted.

And for Val, it brought memories of them at Cambric swirling to haunt at her mind. Bee and Gabe and their constant talk of freedom. Something they would never have.

Finding a corner booth just inside the door, Val sat down. Scooting along the cool seat she tried to conceal herself from view but was unfortunately unsuccessful. Amy Lowell and Kiki Hallet had watched her enter and made the unusual decision to join her table.

She was a D2 and they were free women. Socially, the two classes rarely mixed. But being the second and third trophy wives of wealthy men, both women were young and strikingly beautiful. They didn't feel threatened by Val. No, in fact they were quite curious. Without asking permission both of them settled down across from her.

Up close, they were even more polished than from far away. Both had platinum blonde hair that drifted perfectly down to frame swollen fake breasts. Jewelry sparkled, expensive clothing was cut just so. Val could appreciate the work that went into their appearance.

"Val, is it?" Kiki asked, sticking out a hand to shake over the table. "How are you liking California?"

"What I've seen of it is lovely," Val responded.

Just then a waiter approached with a full service of tea. He brought the tray over to their table and set it down before handing Val a bouquet of fragrant flowers. Peonies, lilacs and roses. The women exclaimed in surprise.

Val wasn't sure what to make of it at first, until she discovered a small white card that read:

Val
Can't stop thinking of you.
Jason

A pink blush painted her cheeks. Ducking her head, Val tucked the card into her small clutch and smiled. As the waiter poured the tea, the three women watched. Amber liquid swirled to fill delicate porcelain cups. After he departed, they each sipped politely a moment before selecting from the array of fruited scones. Finally, Amy broke the silence.

"Honey, what exactly do they teach you over there in that agency?" Her sultry southern accent was accompanied by a good-natured wink.

Val couldn't help but share in the laughter that followed. It turned out both women were genuinely nice. Kiki had been raised in California and was happy to still be living just outside of Los Angeles. She was in her early twenties, her husband's third wife, though he was almost three times her age. Although a rich and powerful man, Val got the impression that Kiki was bored.

Amy wasn't too much older, maybe in her early thirties if Val was any judge. A born and bred Texan, the charming accent hadn't been schooled out of her like Jason. Unlike Kiki, she had married into the Lowell Oil family a few years previous, and seemed to have a sincere affection for her husband. Though Rick was still about twice her age.

For the next several hours Val sat with the other two women and talked. They debated the change in fashion from east coast to west, the latest techniques in makeup and complained about humidity and its effect on hair. Val enjoyed herself, actually. The topic of conversation was so mild, so frivolous, it almost made her forget herself.

And that's how Jason found her. Walking over with Rick and James, the men lingered while their women stood. Taking their place in the booth, Jason slid around until he was just next to Val. Waving them off, he promised they'd catch up in a minute and the other couples departed for lunch.

"Thank you for the flowers and tea." Val nibbled at her bottom lip as Jason reached out to tuck a loose strand of hair behind her ear, tugging on the end affectionately.

"You're welcome."

Leaning in Jason brushed his mouth over hers, let his hand travel along the length of her thigh. Scooting closer, he parted her lips with the gentle probe of his tongue and she welcomed him.

"Jason!" A female voice rang out, startling them.

Breaking contact, they turned to see Sharon approaching them from across the room. Gabe followed just behind. Val's gut dropped at the site of him, forcing her to glance away.

"Sharon." Jason motioned her over as he scooted out of the booth with Val in tow.

"That little trick you pulled with the flowers has all the ladies buzzing," Sharon commented. "What a charmer you are. I had no idea."

Smiling at this, Jason offered her his arm. Sharon took it with a light laugh and continued talking. The woman always had something to say. As Jason escorted her to the dining room for lunch, Val and Gabe were forced to follow along, side by side. Thankfully her old friend kept his hands to himself this time, but that didn't stop him from grinning knowingly. After a few minutes, he whispered.

"She likes younger men. What can I say?"

Val tried to maintain a straight face, determined not to get sucked back in by him, but old habits die hard. After a beat, she smiled at his joke, in spite of herself. Glancing over, she caught Gabe's eye. Had he really changed so much from before? Wasn't this the Gabe she knew? The one she and her sister both loved, if in different ways.

When they entered the dining room and found their seats, the order had been rearranged. She and Jason were on the far side of the table, away from Sharon and Gabe. It was a relief.

This time, lunch was pleasant. Wedged between Jason and Kiki's husband, James, Val actually enjoyed herself. Kiki kept leaning over her husband, regaling her with ridiculous stories of growing up in LA. The beach, the clubs, the nightlife. James merely rolled his eyes.

After the meal was complete, the men left their seats and moved out onto the veranda. Pulling out a box of cigars, they smoked and talked. Val listened to the flick of the lighter, then inhaled the sickly sweet drift of smoke. Kiki and Amy moved closer and the three of them chatted together for a time.

Everything was calm. Everything was measured and pleasant and controlled. Until Gabe. Always until Gabe. He switched seats from the far side of the table. Plunking down next to Amy, he positioned himself directly across from Val. She tilted her chin up a touch, purposefully keeping her expression plain.

"Hello ladies, what's the good gossip?" He was all smiles.

In that moment, Val realized that Kiki and Amy had spent the past six months at these events with him. The way they griped and teased one another, they were friends. And maybe Val had judged him too harshly. Maybe he had just been playing with her before.

Half an hour later she felt silly at her former concern. Gabe was just as relaxed and charming as he ever had been. Kiki and Amy made for easy companions, the four of them talking as if they had known one another for years.

"Ladies, you will have to excuse me. I need to find the restroom." Gabe cleared his throat before rising from his seat and departing.

After a beat Kiki stood, too.

"If James asks, let him know my tummy is a bit off," she said, then she hurried away.

"I hope she's feeling alright," Val commented, watching the pace with which Kiki scurried out the door.

At that, Amy laughed. Shaking her head once, she said nothing. Instead, she raised a delicate hand and signaled the waiter to bring another round of drinks. Fingers circling in the air, her diamond bracelets threw glints of light at the shake of her wrist. Val wondered at the amount of alcohol these people consumed, she couldn't keep up.

After about fifteen minutes, Gabe returned, taking his seat across from her. Reclining back in his chair she caught the look in his eye and her heart skipped a beat. No, she thought. He hasn't just been with Kiki in the bathroom.

Denial lingered only a moment longer while she appraised him. It was a look she had seen on him countless times before. Indeed, he had. Eyes shifting away, Gabe refused to meet her gaze any longer. He knew that she knew.

When Val looked over at Amy, she realized that Amy knew as well.

"What can I say, Honey?" Amy crooned in that lovely

southern drawl. "We all have our secrets here. We all do what is necessary to survive."

Just then James Hallet returned to the table. Inquiring after his wife, he grew concerned at her absence and decided to go check on her. The table was tense after he left. No one spoke. Amy excused herself politely, leaving to find Rick.

It was then that Gabe looked at Val. Then that he let her truly see him. And it was in his eyes. They were filled with a strange mix of defiance and sorrow. Forgetting where she was, Val leaned across the table.

Grabbing at Gabe's arm, she yanked him towards her.

"What the hell is going on with you, Gabey?" Her eyes blazed at his boldness. Cheating on your owner, it was like a death sentence.

"Don't you dare judge me," he whispered at her. "You don't know the half of it."

Glancing up, Gabe blanched.

Slowly, he withdrew his arm from under Val's grasp, his eyes fixed at the figure standing just behind her. Breaking eye contact she followed his stare to see Jason standing over them. He had been watching their exchange. And here she was, with her hands on another man. And a D2 at that.

CHAPTER 6

"I THINK IT'S TIME WE HAD A LITTLE TALK, GABE." JASON KEPT his voice low, the edge of fury barely resonating.

"Whatever you want." Gabe pushed up from his chair. "Just leave Val out of it."

"Sharon!" Jason tossed the word over his shoulder, causing Gabe to brace reflexively. "Val's had a little too much to drink. Can I borrow Gabe to help get her to bed?"

"Sure thing! Anything for you, Jason," Sharon called from the other end of the room where she remained absorbed in conversation.

Rising shakily, Val held her breath. The arm that encircled her waist was surprisingly gentle as Jason guided her towards the exit. On the other side of the long table, Gabe strode ahead, beating them to open the door. Then they were heading down the narrow hallways together, no one saying a word.

Stomach churning, Val's mind raced. Gabe was cheating on his owner, Val had upset hers, this was worst case scenario.

She had to do something this time. She couldn't let Gabe fight this battle alone.

Once inside their room, Val whirled to face Jason. Trying to head him off, her hands spread out over his chest. Placating. Pleading.

"There isn't anything going on between us, I swear it." She begged him to believe her, but he brushed her aside, his stare fixed entirely on Gabe.

"Does she really look that much like this Bee girl?" He asked.

"You told him about her?" Gabe lost it, his brown eyes searching Val's, his face filling with the shock of betrayal.

"I'm sorry, he asked and I- I-" Val stuttered, shame filling her.

"Well?" Jason pressed. "Does she?"

"Yeah, they look just alike." Gabe gritted his teeth. "Except Bee is shorter and their features aren't exactly the same. Why? You tired of Val already?"

"*You* don't get to talk about her." Jason stepped close to him, his finger poking into Gabe's chest.

"Oh, that's right," Gabe sneered. "Because I'm captive right? I do what you say. *She* does what you want."

Bypassing Jason, Gabe clutched at Val's arms, forcing her to look at him.

"Don't trust him, Val," he whispered.

"Back. Up." Jason's voice dropped, his jaw clenching.

"Or what?"

"Or, I'll tell Sharon about you and Kiki. You'll be out of here so fast-"

Gabe's mouth dropped a moment, then burst forth with harsh laughter. He threw his head back, his face shining and bright. "You think she doesn't *know* about that? You think that's not exactly where she orders me to go? Come on now Jason, I thought you knew better."

Shaking his head, Gabe's attention quickly returned to Val. His fingers gripped her arms still, his face turned suddenly serious.

"Gabey, what's going on?" Val's eyes darted over her old friend's face. Her heart breaking for him.

"Don't trust him, Val. Don't you ever trust any of them. You mean no more than his favorite dog or one of his fancy horses-"

"Get out!" Jason growled, his hands were between them now, shoving Gabe back.

"You're a pawn in their game!" Gabe called as Jason shoved him again, harder.

"Get out!" Jason yelled, his hands pushing at Gabe's chest.

Over and over he shoved, until Gabe's back hit the far wall. Val watched in horror as the anger between them grew. Gabe couldn't fight back. He wasn't allowed. But if he did? Val was frozen once more, helpless to stop it. Would she always stand back while her friends stood their ground?

Gabe's hands clenched and unclenched, but thankfully remained at his side. His captive training was too strong, he wouldn't cross that line. Managing a cocky grin, he eyed Jason for one last moment before turning for the door. When it slammed shut, Val cringed then a shudder ran through her.

Raising her eyes, she blinked at Jason. He kept his back to her, his shoulders heaving with each breath he took as he worked to calm himself down. She hadn't seen him like this. But maybe that wasn't quite true. Hadn't he lost his temper just the night before?

Her chest grew tight. Her breath shallowing out at the realization. Before he could recover, she bolted for the bathroom, locking herself inside. Backing away slowly, she came up against the far wall, then let her body slide down until she was sitting on the cold tile floor. She was a coward. Again. All she had ever been able to manage was to hide.

Tears welled up, collecting at the corners of her eyes. Days, months, years worth of tears that threatened to choke her if held any longer.

Remorse. Guilt. They ran so deep they were like a sink hole opening inside her chest. Bee was gone. Gabe was being used in some twisted game. And Jason, she thought, well he was a player in that very game.

She heard a gentle tapping on the bathroom door. Lifting her eyes, she watched as the handle jiggled, then held.

"Val," Jason called. "It's not true what he said. Come out, Val. Please."

Sobs bubbled up unbidden in her throat. Whimpering, she covered her face with both hands. She didn't want him to hear her cry. After all, she was defying him by staying in here. He had asked her to come out, and she should do what he asked.

Gasping, Val reached up and dragged a towel down to cover her face. She *would* come out, after she got herself under control. Unable to fight it, she cried, using the thick material to muffle her sounds. In the background, Jason continued to call for her, she didn't know for how long.

Eventually, though, his knock changed. It was brisk, more persistent than it had been before.

"Val," he called. "Come on out now, we're going home. I think we've both had enough."

Wiping at her face, Val stood, then crossed the few steps to the door before unlocking it. Immediately he pulled it open. It was as if he'd been waiting to hear the flip of the lock the entire time.

Glancing up at his face, she didn't know what to make of his worried expression. Though she knew he'd worry about his prize horses, too.

Taking her hand in his own, he drew her out then enfolded her in a heavy embrace. Per training, Val held on, but all the while, her heart revolted. Over his shoulder, she noticed their bags were already packed. He had been serious.

"Where are we going?" Her voice was thick from the crying.

"Home," he answered. "I booked our flight out. Let's go."

"What about your business?"

"I think I've got what I need for now."

Pulling back to look at her, Jason's eyes darted over her face. He didn't let go of her hand as he turned to lead them out, leaving their bags for a bell hop to collect.

Obediently, she followed him out to the waiting car. Once their baggage had been loaded, the driver pulled away from the hotel. Low music drifted out from the radio, Val couldn't tell what kind, classical maybe?

The streets were laden with traffic, so their trek to the airport was slow going. All the while, Jason stroked the knuckles of her hand. And all the while Val fought the impulse to pull away. When they came to a stop at the curb, Jason glanced out her window and swore.

"Shit." He grabbed for his sunglasses. "We've got company."

Outside, a group of people were milling around, holding cameras and looking watchful. Pulling her own sunglasses from her clutch, Val too, slipped them on. As soon as Jason stepped foot outside the vehicle, the crowd surged forward. Frowning, Val watched the driver hustle around to work open her door. What was all this?

Once it swung wide, she was bombarded with sound. Cameras flashed. People shouted.

"Is it true you're a D2 captive?!" A reporter cried.

"Has Riggs Oil changed their stance on slavery?!" Yelled another.

"What's your name?!"

"How long has he had you?!"

The questions hurled, one over another, until she couldn't distinguish them anymore.

The picture of cool, Jason ignored the press of people jostling for position just behind him. He stood still, unperturbed, and simply offered her his hand. Blinking at it, Val's eyes popped between his palm and his face. No matter what Gabe had said, she belonged to this man and if she wanted to survive, then she must rely on him.

Her hand snaked out quickly and grasped his. The corners of his mouth ticked up slightly before he tucked her up against his body. Ducking her head to avoid the cameras, Val kept close to Jason as he guided them inside. Once they passed through security, the throng was left to shout at them from a distance.

With her pulse still jumping unsteadily, Val marveled at Jason's unruffled demeanor. How could he be so relaxed when the mass of people had her skin crawling? Keeping quiet, they made their way to the private terminal and loaded directly onto his jet. Once settled, she removed her sunglasses to look over at him.

"What was that?" She asked.

"Someone snitched that I own a D2 to the media," he answered. "There isn't anything else going on right now, so my apparent hypocrisy is headline news."

"I don't understand," she said. "I'm legal. What's the big deal?"

"Riggs Oil is anti-captive. We've gone so far as to fund legislation trying to get rid of the practice. My buying you is a huge deal, it reflects poorly on the company," he admitted, sighing as his cell phone began to buzz incessantly.

The jet rolled back. The engines whirred. Marcy made her way through the cabin, depositing drinks, informing them they were ready for takeoff. Out the window the ground rushed faster and faster until they separated from it, lifting high into the air. Within minutes the airport was a miniature replica of itself. White puffs of mist surrounded them.

"It isn't true," Jason whispered. "What Gabe said. It isn't true and I've done something to prove it to you."

Blowing out a breath, Val battled for composure. What part wasn't true exactly? Jason owned her the same as his stable full of horses. It was as simple as that. Pinching her eyes shut she could still see the warning in Gabe's expression. He was scared. The desperate clutch of his hands on her skin lingered even now.

"I had my lawyer draw up paperwork," Jason continued. "When our arrangement ends, you will have your freedom. If I break it off with you or when I die, then you are free. Legally free."

Val's stomach dropped, her throat went dry. She had never, not once, pictured her life as a free person. Feelings she didn't know were there built and turned around inside of her. Did she want it? Yes. Was she afraid of it? Also, yes. What would she do to eat? Where would she live? Her level of unpreparedness was overwhelming.

"I don't know what to say."

"I'm not the monster, he thinks I am." Jason reached out,

ran his fingers through her hair, tugging gently on the ends. "You aren't just a horse or a dog to me, Val. I know you're a person, same as me."

Managing a slight nod, Val pursed her lips and let her gaze fall to her lap. So much had happened, she was confused, unsure. Maybe Jason was right, they both had enough and now it was time to go home.

With the photos of them at the airport being broadcast, Jason spent the duration of their flight putting out work-related fires. Marcy served them the usual dinner, but finding that she wasn't very hungry, Val picked over the salad moodily.

By the time they landed in Texas, the sun had long since set, but that didn't stop the sticky hot humidity that greeted them. Jason's sports car waited on the tarmac and thankfully, no reporters buzzed around it. The drive home was quiet, uneventful.

Val wasn't sure exactly when Summer House had begun to feel like home, but at the sight of it, her body sagged in relief. Yvette had lingered to welcome them inside; her familiar face offered some comfort.

"Will you stay in my room tonight?" Jason paused on their way up the stairs.

Ducking her head in acceptance, Val followed him to the master suite, a place she had never gone before. It was at least three times the size of her own room. Despite the oppressive heat outside, elevated ceilings and air conditioning worked to keep the space cool.

Discarding items as he went, Jason led her past a limestone

fireplace and massive bed. In one corner, a sunken tub was tucked into an alcove, flanked by tall windows that reached from the ceiling to the floor. Absently, he brushed a thumb along the inside her palm. She wasn't sure if he noticed the gesture.

Stopping in front of an oversized shower, he reached in to turn on the water. The walls were decorated with multi-colored stones swirling in an intricate circular design. It was pretty. There were so many shades of blue, more than she knew existed.

Unbidden, she began to undress, letting her clothes fall to her ankles on the cold marble floor. Raw emotions washed over her, then. Thoughts of Gabe, what he had said, and Jason's offer of eventual freedom.

Agency rhetoric came unbidden to her mind. *Do not feel, just follow the impulse to touch and be touched in return.*

Naked now, Val watched Jason undo his buttons then untuck his shirt. His steady blue eyes searched hers, the desire was clear in them.

Stepping into the hot spray, she inhaled the billowing steam. They took turns soaping each other, water dripping down slick skin. She chased the clear drops with her tongue as they fell along his shoulders, then reached down to clasp him in her slippery hands.

Keeping her eyes on his face, Val kept her strokes slow, bringing him steadily closer to the edge of his control. He groaned, then pushed her back against the stones of the shower wall. Bending down to her, he spread kisses along her neck.

Head tilted back, eyes closed, Val bit her lip and listened to his quiet panting. When he couldn't take much more, he reached for her legs and lifted her up, entering her on a moan.

Val clutched at his shoulders, wrapping her legs around him, feeling her own pleasure intensify. Stroke after stroke built until finally she cried out, clenching tightly around him.

Lowering her head, she nipped at his lower lip as he held her in place. He gasped. Her hands slid down his back. Her hips moved against him and then he was gone. Groaning into her neck, he found his release, but he wouldn't let her go.

Waking the next morning, she lay still, listening to the demands of his morning alarm. Reaching a hand out, she was surprised to find his side of the bed already cool to the touch. When she opened her eyes, he was crossing the room, working to silence the blare from his phone. He was already dressed for a day at the office.

"Have breakfast with me real quick?" He asked. She softened at his look of boyish chagrin.

"I'll meet you down there," she answered.

A sudden giddiness swept over her at the prospect of spending the afternoon in the stables. It was horse lesson day, so she better wear the usual jeans and t-shirt. Padding to her room on bare feet, she wore nothing but a discarded towel. Somehow the horses made her forget about her troubles. The horses made her forget everything.

Slipping into her supple brown leather boots, Val let an easy smile take over her face. They were the most comfortable, most wonderful thing she had ever worn.

Downstairs, Jason was busy swiping away on his tablet in the dining room. As she took her seat opposite him, the tantalizing aroma of fresh coffee filled the air. Pushing through the door, Anne Marie balanced a plate of hot sausage and Belgian waffles on her tray. She set them in front of Val, already doused in melted butter and rich maple syrup.

Listening half-heartedly to Jason complain about public opinion and market share, Val forked bite after delicious bite into her mouth. She didn't really understand most of what he was saying, but pretended to listen anyway. If they could only stay just like this, with the quiet meals and the empty house, then she would want for nothing else.

Bursting suddenly into the room, Yvette had both of them jumping.

"Have you seen my message?" She asked Jason, who looked down at his tablet and frowned. Swiping through screens he stopped to read.

"No." He sucked in a breath. "You've got to be kidding me."

Standing up, he took a few short strides to the large bay window. Pressing his face against the glass he looked to the left. Val sat perplexed, her heart kicking up a notch. What now?

"I'm afraid so." Yvette spun on her heal and clicked briskly away.

"What is it?" Val asked.

Jason pushed away from the window and stomped towards the end of the room. Just then the door swung open and a slight woman swept in, followed by an older version of Jason.

"Mama," Jason called to her, a strained smile covering his face. "It's so nice to see you. Glad you could swing by... unannounced." He added, in a mutter that did not go beyond her notice.

Though slight in figure, the woman was an absolute stick of dynamite. Her black hair and makeup were styled to perfection and she positively glowed with good looks.

"If you would answer your phone, then we wouldn't have to come by unannounced," she countered, beckoning for Jason to approach her.

Bending down to obey, he gave her a warm hug despite his words of protest. As he kissed her on the cheek, his mother's eyes roamed the room until they settled squarely on Val. The disapproval that lingered there was clear.

Dismissing her son with a pat, she pushed past him and strode confidently down the length of the table. Jason moved to greet his father next, whose tousled brown hair and bright blue eyes reflected those of his son. Val remembered that they shared a name as well.

"Oh, you brought the whole family along." Jason brightened as two young women in their twenties, and a boy of about sixteen appeared in the doorway. "What is this Dad? An intervention?"

The two men laughed at the joke, although there seemed to be a ring of truth to it. Val watched Jason hug his sisters, then shake hands with his younger brother. Her attention was so diverted, in fact, that she didn't notice his mother seat herself directly across the table. It was the sound of the other woman pushing the breakfast plate aside, fork clattering onto the table, that caused Val to shift her focus.

"Hello, my dear." The woman was even more intimidating up close. "My name is Elaine. I am Jason's mother."

"It's a pleasure to meet you," Val answered carefully, extending her hand to shake. But when Elaine made no move to reach for her, Val retracted it awkwardly. "My name is-"

"Val. Yes, we've read all about you in the blogs," Elaine snapped. "In fact, my phone has been positively ringing off the hook for the past twenty-four hours. Isn't that right, Darling?"

Jason Senior made his way over to his wife and stood

behind her, hands coming down to cover her shoulders. His eyes were kind, but worried. A stark contrast to the anger simmering quietly in his woman.

"That's right," he acknowledged.

"I was just about to head to the office but I'll stay if you're here for breakfast," Jason offered.

"No, no." Elaine answered him, keeping her gaze focused entirely on Val. "We don't want to get in the way of your day. We'll just stay for dinner instead… and maybe one or two overnights."

"Um, alright." Jason pushed at his phone distractedly. "I'll have Yvette prepare the guest rooms."

Wanting nothing more than to sink beneath the table, Val sat paralyzed under Elaine's withering look. This woman hated her. Glancing up from his phone, Jason noticed the tension and stepped in.

"Val, you better get going. You'll be late for your lesson."

Helping her to stand, Jason kept one hand firmly against the small of her back as they left the room. Once alone, he gave her a slow kiss before pressing his forehead to hers.

"They mean well." He sighed.

Val ducked her head in acknowledgement before he let her slip away. Hurrying out through the kitchen, she practically ran outside to the detached garage. The golf cart was waiting there for her, all white and clean.

She reversed smoothly out of the building before shifting forward into drive with practiced ease. Dipping down the gravel road that ran behind the house, she was soon out of sight in a tall stand of trees.

Learning to drive the cart had been an experience in itself. She had only backed into a fence twice while Jason sat cracking up in the seat beside her. When they were together like that, just the two of them, he made her almost forget she was his captive. Laughing with him, teasing and touching, she felt the closest to free she ever had.

All around her now, bald cypress and eastern red cedar grew. The road that connected the main house and barn was narrow, meant only for walking or small cart traffic. A separate, larger entrance to the stables was further down the main road. Coasting along in the shade of the trees, Val worried over the sudden appearance of Jason's parents. The Agency had groomed her to be an older man's companion, one without a living mother or father.

In that situation, her only potential concern would be the man's children. But she wouldn't be a threat to them because she was not a wife who would jeopardize their inheritance. Yet here she was in the exact opposite situation. How long would Jason hold out under the pressure of his family? When would he break things off? At least now she had his word that he would set her free.

Frowning, Val realized she would have to begin preparing for survival on her own. He had given her the one necklace, which she could sell, but how far would it get her?

Pulling to a stop at the stone barn, Val got out. The intoxicating aroma of alfalfa and horse greeted her. It had only been a few days, but she had really missed the animals. They had this relaxing effect. Worry seemed to lift off of her as she strolled down the aisle, enjoying the familiar greetings from the groom staff.

Maybe, when she was free, she could get a job at a stable somewhere. But how would she look for work? What would a free person do? She would have to ask Ignacio. He would help her. At least, she hoped that he would.

Hours spent with the horses and riding in her lesson absorbed her. All her heartache and uncertainty from the past few days blurred and grew quiet.

As late afternoon approached, Val lingered at the barn, watching Ignacio make training runs. The black stud from before still shied at the rail. Patience and practice, Ignacio told her. He would learn to trust again.

On any other day she would have already returned to the house, but today she knew what was waiting for her. It had her staying until dusk, when the last horse was fed and chomping contentedly in its stall. But as the sky filled in with dusty grays, she knew she could avoid it no longer.

After parking the cart in its garage, Val let herself quietly back inside the main house. Sneaking swiftly up the stairs, she made it to her bedroom and gratefully closed the door. A long sigh escaped her. She leaned back against the door. Oh, how she dreaded dinner.

Yvette had already come and gone, setting out a single dress with towering heels. Apparently there was no other option for tonight. Showering off the dusty grime from the barn, Val set about brushing through her wet hair, then took her time in blowing it dry. A pit formed in her stomach but she clicked through her makeup case calmly, as if nothing was wrong.

Working hard to breathe out the unwelcome feelings, she wondered at herself. Something about Jason made her emotions hard to control. It had always been so much easier to will everything away back at The Agency.

Leaning forward to gently stroke on her inky mascara, Val's robe slipped casually down one shoulder. Behind her,

her bedroom door clicked open. Jason's muted footsteps made their way over, the thick carpeting absorbed his sound. Coming to a stop just behind her, she observed his reflection in the mirror. How did he manage to smell so good? She had never noticed another man's scent before.

While she watched, his hand came down to rest on her bare shoulder. With a little push, he sent the robe further off her arm, just exposing her breast. Leaning down, he brushed his lips over her neck.

"*You* are so beautiful," he breathed, then dangled a pair of black pearl earrings in front of her face.

"Oh," she exclaimed, then reached back to touch them. "*These* are so beautiful."

He smiled and tilted his head to the side as he watched her put them on. Shaking her head delicately, she made them shimmer in the light.

When she got up, he helped her to slip into the emerald green satin gown. His strong hands worked slowly at the zipper, causing heat to flush her already warm skin. Turning to face him, she reached up to his neck, straightened his tie.

"Does your family always have formal dinners?" She questioned.

"Only when they have a point to make."

"Jason, I'm not trained for this," she warned, repeating The Agency's training out loud. "I'll never be able to say the right thing."

"Don't worry about it," he coaxed her. "I'll protect you."

She nodded as he took her hand, but puzzled at his words. Gabe's warning resonated, causing doubt to tug at her. *Don't trust any of them. You're only a pawn in their game.*

The dining room was dim. Candles flickered along the length of the old wood. China settings of which she had never seen shone in the trembling light. Crystal glasses gleamed.

At the far end of the room, Jason's mother and father sat next to one another, leaving the head of the table open for him. Val took her place on his right side, while his mother occupied the seat to his left. Jeremy and Theresa were beside Val, leaving Angela to nestle close to her father, across the table.

Soon, wine was being poured all around, even Jeremy got a small glass. Absently, Val listened to them talk of the weather, schooling and sports. The girls were both in college now, and had been called off campus by their mother for this family occasion. Jeremy excelled in baseball. His youthful face filled with pride when Jason promised he would attend a few more games.

Sipping politely at a tiny portion of lobster bisque soup, Val resolved to remain silent throughout the entire meal. She did her best to avoid Elaine's eyes and instead studied the way the flame wavered on the end of the nearest candle.

This behavior, however, was not to be tolerated. Eventually, Elaine's voice lifted over the divide to settle irrevocably on Val and there was nothing she could do but respond.

"Val dear, have you been educated?"

"I have an Associates Degree." Val set down her spoon, giving the other woman her full attention.

"Where did you study?"

"Cambric Agency has its own accredited program," Val answered, but glanced briefly at Jason when his mother huffed under her breath.

"Hardly worth three million dollars. Am I right, Darling?" She turned to her husband who was noncommittal in his answer.

"Mama," Jason warned, but she ignored him.

"Well, when I saw the withdrawal from your account I just didn't think anything of it at first. I told Senior, you know Jason must have found that next breeding stock race horse he has been talking about. Didn't I, Darling?"

Her husband nodded, his brows growing more furrowed.

"Remind me later to change my password," Jason grumbled.

"Imagine our surprise, when, come to find out, it wasn't a horse at all, but a real live girl! How our friends must be impressed."

"Mama, please." Jason reached across the table to her, but she waved him off with a flick of her wrist.

"And to think of all those gorgeous ladies I set you up with. Not one of them would cost nearly so much. In fact, more than a few would have brought money of their own to the bargain."

"Mama, stop." Jason gritted his teeth.

"You don't tell me to stop!" Elaine slammed her tiny hand down on the table, sending the crystal and china rattling. "This is about more than just you Jason. We are being positively dragged through the mud over this... this person you have purchased.

Senators have put their careers on the line to support our anti-captive legislation. And what's more, Riggs Oil is at stake. Your foolish actions, or desires, or whatever is going on with you, could cost this family everything we have worked so hard for!"

"I am handling the business end of it." Jason interrupted her sharply. "I've talked with every partner, every investor, every land owner that we work with. They're all good ole' boys who don't take all of this as seriously as everyone else seems to. We aren't losing any business. We won't lose any money."

"Is that what you want to be?!" His mother hissed. "Just some good ole' boy who buys a woman to use like some prostitute? Is that what you're bringing this family into?"

"Enough!" Jason shouted it, his control was slipping.

Shoving back from the table, Val stood abruptly. Around her, the argument ceased as all eyes swiveled up to watch.

"May I be excused?" Whisper quiet, her voice trembled. "I seem to have lost my appetite."

"Of course," Jason said, standing along with her, but she motioned him away.

Val's restrictive gown forced her to assume a normal pace as she turned towards the exit. Though her heart wanted to fly from the room, she slowly and deliberately walked. But before she made it completely out the door, she heard Elaine speak.

"She has to ask your permission before she can even leave? This is exactly what-"

His mother's words were cut off as the door swung shut at her back. Pulling up on her dress, Val rushed through the house, panted up the stairs and dove into her room. For the first time since arriving at Summer House, she locked the door.

CHAPTER 7

Late into the night Val's stomach grumbled. She had spent the entire day at the barn and only managed a few sips of the soup before fleeing dinner. Hunger gnawed at her insides, though it wasn't for the first time. But unlike at Cambric, there was a kitchen full of food just one floor below her. That little fact was hard to ignore.

Eyes flicking to the digital clock on her nightstand, she noted it was well past midnight. Jason and his family had to all be asleep by now. Shoving back the covers, she shrugged into her robe before carefully, slowly, un-clicking the lock on her bedroom door. The house beyond was cool and dark.

Tucking a strand of hair behind one ear, she walked along the hall, only noticing the sliver of light on the floor at the last minute. It was coming from the library. The door was open just a crack, so if she ducked down, she could almost certainly avoid being seen on the stairs.

As she creeped along, she heard male voices drift out. Pausing for a moment, she listened to their conversation. It was Jason and his father.

"Your mother isn't that far off base," Senior was saying.

"She's insulting and overbearing," Jason countered.

"Can you blame her? We raised you better than all this. How do you explain Val? Owning another person?" His father pressed him gently.

"What if I told you I'm in love with her?"

"I don't believe that," his father countered. "If you loved that girl, you'd have freed her already. Are you at least using protection when you sleep with her?"

"Dad," Jason protested. "Don't you think that's a little personal?"

"Son, if you get that girl pregnant, her first-born child goes straight back to that agency." Senior reminded him. "That's captive law and you can't get around it. Trust me, I've seen many rich men try. Now, I won't have a grandchild of mine born a slave. Do you understand me?"

"That's not going to happen," Jason hissed.

Val sucked in a breath and abruptly changed her course. Slinking quickly back to her room, she re-locked the door. The law, the law, the captive birth law. Why hadn't she ever thought it would apply to her? Why hadn't she ever worried about it?

All captives, whether freed or not, had to give their first-born child back to their original agency. This was to ensure that the captive population remained diverse and didn't drop substantially. The government was very strict about the captive trade. Free people could not be sold into captivity. And agencies could not import captives from out of country. The only way new captives were acquired, was by birth from a former or existing captive. So, in Val's case, even if Jason set her free, her first child would by law be a captive of Cambric.

Thinking back now, she realized that Jason had not been

careful about this. Actually, he had been rather reckless. She worried about when her last cycle was, vowing to press Jason for birth control the next time they were alone.

Tugging the large down comforter over her head, she curled into a tiny ball and tried to stamp out the ache of hunger in her stomach. It wasn't the first night she had gone without a meal. Something told her that it wouldn't be the last.

The next morning Yvette was forced to knock on Val's door. It had remained locked all night. Blinking up into the vaulted ceiling, Val realized that Yvette probably had a key, but was just too polite to use it. When she did let Yvette in, the first thing she noticed was the absence of a food tray.

"Can't I take breakfast in here this morning?" Val turned her sad eyes on Yvette who sighed in sympathy.

"Southern manners indicate that you should sit politely for a meal, even with your worst enemy," Yvette explained.

"But I'm from New York, and not a member of the family," Val protested weakly.

She hated southern manners, sweet one minute and scratch your eyes out the next. At least on the East Coast you knew what was coming for you.

While Val sat in front of the vanity, styling her hair, Yvette marched to the closet and began rummaging around. Again, there was no choice here, just a navy pencil skirt with professional white blouse.

"Will I get to ride today?" She asked hopefully.

"I'm afraid not, Dear."

Val's heart sank, but what could she do? Nothing. She could do nothing.

Yvette walked with her to the dining room, and held the door as Val entered. Stopping short, she was shocked to see that none of the men were present. It was just Elaine and the two girls enjoying breakfast with tea. *My worst nightmare,* Val thought ruefully, and sat in her old seat.

"Good morning." Elaine smiled, sipping delicately at her cup.

"Good morning," Val answered, as Anne Marie poured for her.

A plate of ripe strawberries along with a bagel spread thickly with cream cheese was placed in front of her. A meager breakfast, but it would have to do.

"I must start out by apologizing to you, Val," Elaine said. "My behavior last night was most… unwelcoming."

"Thank you." Val cleared her throat, waiting for the catch.

But Theresa and Angela just smiled at her sweetly, bobbing their heads in agreement.

"You must understand my initial reaction. Our family has a reputation to uphold, and Jason's unwise… impulse has put half the country in a tizzie. The balance of pro-captive and anti-captive is split quite closely down the middle of the voting block these days. To have a big player like Riggs Oil tip its hat the opposite way… well, that spells trouble beyond my son's current vision."

"I was not educated in the way of politics," Val was measured, choosing her words carefully.

"I imagine not," Elaine agreed, and then seemed to study her critically. "You *are* a lovely girl to look at really. I can see why Jason was so swept up by you. It's the eyes, don't you think girls?"

"Your eyes are beautiful," Theresa agreed, nibbling at her toast.

"Such an unusual shade of green," Angela added.

"Yes." Elaine continued to stare for a beat before resuming her breakfast.

They went on eating in silence for several minutes. The polite scraping of knives and clinking of forks filled the room. Normally, Val's nerves would have gotten in the way of this meal but she was still famished from the night before. Without really noticing, she made short work of everything on her plate.

Though she wanted to ask for more, she was simply too afraid. Instead, she gazed out the far window, longing for the stables.

"To make up for my unforgivably rude behavior, the girls and I would love to take you on a little outing today," Elaine offered.

The girls perked up at this, clasping their hands in expectation. Val's stomach sank even lower.

"Let's go for a bit of shopping, and then I have an old friend that I want you to meet. What do you say?"

"Of course," Val said, knowing she could never refuse such an offer.

Upon finishing breakfast, the women loaded into a flashy silver SUV. This day was going to be the ultimate punishment. Val's instinct told her that Elaine was up to something, but there was just no way of getting out of it.

Tucked into the back seat between Theresa and Angela, Val watched Elaine's perfect profile as she sat in the shotgun seat. A driver would take them wherever Jason's mother wanted to go.

As the ride progressed, though, Val found herself softening. Theresa and Angela seemed genuinely kind. Their manners were impeccable and they both had a sort of unaffected charm. In turns, they questioned her about her life, and shared stories of their own. Angela was the elder at twenty-two, and Theresa the younger at twenty. Both attended Baylor, with Angela set to graduate in the spring.

By the time the SUV pulled to a stop, Val's guard was slipping. Getting out, Elaine directed them to a section of high-end boutiques with Theresa linking her arm companionably in Val's. The gesture of female friendship was intimate, reminiscent of a childhood spent wrapped up with Bee.

When they entered the store, Val's eyebrows shot up in wonder. Custom drift wood railings lined the shop. Clothing was displayed sparingly, with an artist's eye to negative space. The colors and patterns were dazzling, reminding her of the things Yvette constantly unearthed from her closet.

Pushing past them, Angela wasted no time setting to work. She picked this thing and choose that. A store clerk followed her obligingly, her arms soon overloaded with the array of clothes.

Elaine took a seat on an antique daybed and sipped on a glass of champagne that had been offered to her. The staff seemed familiar with the Riggs women. Everyone was exceedingly comfortable in their role. Everyone but Val.

Beside her, Theresa urged Val to shop as well. She showed her a few items she thought might look good, but there were no price tags on anything. Though money was not a part of Val's education, The Agency had insisted she must never pick anything out for herself. Despite the other women's encouragement, she was hesitant to do so now.

Seeming to sense her discomfort, Theresa deposited her on the daybed next to Elaine, and then set about choosing clothes for herself. The fashion show that followed was a definite first. The two young women paraded about in outfits that ranged from ravishing to hilarious. Val sipped an offered champagne and managed to crack a smile once or twice when Angela showed off some crazy ensemble.

Several hours, and several shops later, the girls had collected a tower of bags that their driver had trouble stacking in the rear compartment. Elaine had discovered a few things for herself, and the sisters had chosen a new skirt and pair of sandals for Val.

On the drive to lunch they crossed a wide river, its rushing blue water tumbled beneath them. The land, though unbelievably flat, held its share of beauty.

When they arrived at a small tea shop, Val was surprised. She had expected something larger, more lavish, but the restaurant was cozy and private instead. The smiling hostess showed them all to a long table where a plump woman about Elaine's age already sat. When they took their seats, Val heard the woman gasp.

Keeping her expression plain and unassuming, Val merely nodded as Elaine introduced her to Mrs. Lillian Durand, wife of Bernard Durand. Later, she would find out the couple came from old money and had no profession. Their wealth grew by itself, thanks in part to good investing.

A perky waitress arrived to take their order. Maybe it was last night's hunger that propelled her, or perhaps she was getting used to this whole freedom of choice thing, because

Val had no problem choosing a turkey sandwich and side of cheddar soup.

Keeping her lips closed, Val sipped on an iced tea and absorbed the women's endless chatter about shopping and parties and charity auctions. Eventually, Elaine explained who Val actually was, and how she came to be with them. Lillian, for her part, was actually quite kind in her measured reaction, only pursing her lips uncomfortably twice.

Near the end of their meal, Lillian turned to address Val directly.

"You are truly a beautiful creature, my dear," she began. "I cannot fault our Jason for his rash decision. I only hope that he is able to correct his wrongs before inflicting further distress on his family... and business for that matter."

"Thank you," Val answered politely.

"You might have noticed my surprise when you first sat down," Lillian continued. "It's just that you look so very much like my daughter that I thought... just for a moment, that you were her. But then, of course I know that you are not. I just wanted to clarify my reaction."

"Oh, and where is your daughter now?" Val asked, but knew immediately that she said something wrong. The look that crossed Lillian's face was pained.

"She's dead, my dear," Lillian stated firmly.

Rising to her feet she excused herself from their lunch. Elaine stood to hug her, then stepped back, wringing her tiny hands together as she watched her friend go.

"I'm so sorry," Val told them all. "I didn't know."

"Of course not," Elaine assured her. "How could you?"

It was a simple explanation, but there was more to the story. Val saw the way Theresa gave Angela a quick questioning glance.

The ride home was considerably more sober than the drive to the tea shop had been. The mood was dampened. The spell broken.

It was late-afternoon when they pulled down the cobblestone driveway to Summer House and the heat of the day was upon them. Val's blouse clung to her uncomfortably in the humidity. Perspiration glistened along her skin in the minute it took to exit the vehicle and get inside.

The air conditioner had been blasting all day, so when the women entered the living room it was blessedly cool. Flopping down in one of the overstuffed chairs, Theresa reached for the television remote and clicked it on. Val wished she could run up to her room and hide, but instead she took a seat on the chocolate-brown leather sofa. Never having watched a television show before, Val was soon sucked in by the bright flash of colors and intense sound.

The movies Cambric allowed them as children had been limited to old classics, she hadn't even watched the news. And by the time Jason got home, he was too busy finishing up work, eating dinner and taking her to bed to bother with turning it on.

For an hour or more, the girls watched a show about people who were trying to buy a house. They were shown a series of homes in various locations and at the end, the couple had to choose one. For Val, it was absolutely fascinating. The world was full of different types of people, different homes, and different places. She began to realize just how limited her exposure to the free world was.

When the men returned from the office, the sound of their rough voices filled the foyer. Jason entered the living room, one arm slung over his brother's shoulders, their father shaking his head at some joke just behind them.

Growing bored with the house program, Theresa flipped channels endlessly. Her ruby red nails clicked constantly on the black remote. When the men joined them, Elaine chatted easily with her boys about their exploits. At her casual mention of lunch with Lillian, Jason scrutinized her carefully.

"You brought Val to meet Mrs. Durand?" He questioned. "Why would you do that, Mama?"

"Well, when I really looked hard at Val I was just so taken in by her eyes. I said to myself, Elaine, she resembles Veronica. But of course, she *isn't* Veronica, and Lillian knew so, too."

"No, Mama, she isn't Veronica." Jason scowled, his jaw clenching.

This change in Jason's tone caught Val's attention, but their southern style of polite speech with many levels of meaning was beyond her grasp. She couldn't decipher the implication behind their words, though she tried.

Just then, Theresa settled on a new show, one with loud introduction music and a wildly dressed host.

"Oh, not this gossip trash," Angela complained.

Waving the remote tauntingly in the air, Theresa smiled triumphantly from across the room.

The show was designed to grab your attention and Val easily succumbed. A series of photos flashed across the screen, showcasing different famous people. As the host poked fun at each, Angela made faces and Theresa laughed. Some of the reports were good, but mostly the host had bad things to say. When a picture of Jason and Val dodging cameras popped on the screen, Val's mouth went slack.

"Oh, God," Elaine murmured, looking up at her husband who closed his eyes.

"And of course, the headline of the week is still our favorite bachelor, Jason Riggs. Breaking with family tradition he has purchased himself his very own D2 captive! We laughed when he dated Heiress Trisha Wrightwood, we cried when his engagement to Actress Mae Starr fell through, and now we are angry that he has proven himself to be just another hypocritical elitist; putting his own selfish desires above the needs of the people. Shame. Shame on you Jason Riggs, and shame on Riggs Oil."

"Turn that crap off!" Jason shouted.

Stomping towards his sister, he glared as Theresa fumbled with the remote until the television turned dark.

"I can't believe they're still going on about that." Jason ran a hand back through his hair. "How many times do I have to say we were never engaged?! She's just some nut job actress who started to wear a ring for publicity."

"Well." Senior paused. "The other things are all true. So how are people to pick out that part as false?"

The room erupted in argument.

Voices were raised on all sides, leaving Val to sit meekly still, wishing she could disappear into the folds of the sofa. It was hard to follow really. Theresa and Angela seemed to be on Jason's side, with their parents gesturing wildly and shouting in turn. Only Jeremy watched in silence, but soon he was turning on his heel to walk out.

Val considered doing the same, but was concerned that she would never make it to standing before drawing someone's attention. So, she lingered there, letting her thoughts take her away. It was just like back in Cambric when things went south. Her mind flashed to Bee screaming. Then she saw Gabe's face as he twisted, restrained on the floor.

Banishing them from her mind, Val reached for something to replace them. Anything. The TV host's words echoed within her. Jason had been engaged. Jason the notorious playboy. She puzzled at the sharp pang of jealously that burst within her. Cambric was very strict in its dealings with jealously. It was the most abhorred emotion that a D2 could possess.

Lecture after lecture had centered around denial of this natural human reaction. A jealous D2 was a volatile captive. A volatile captive disobeyed. Besides, what right did a slave have to claim such feeling? How could you be jealous about someone that never belonged to you?

Sitting here now, she tasted the feeling. It was something new. Something she had never felt before and she struggled to resist its call now. Closing her eyes, she reminded herself that Jason was not hers. No, it was the opposite. She was the one who belonged to him. He could have as many women as he wanted. She had no claim on him.

All around her, the family disagreement continued full force. Ducking her head, Val made the decision to escape and stood before walking calmly away to her room. Once inside, she locked the door again. It felt like a new and necessary habit.

An hour later she watched the doorknob jiggle as Jason tried to open her door. When it held, she heard his gentle knock. Refusing to respond, Val merely sat, her feet propped up in the cushy barrel chair by the windows. The sky was so blue, it almost hurt to look at it.

His knock grew louder. She could hear his muffled voice through the door.

"Open up, Val."

Turning her head away, she gazed out over the gardens in

bloom and beyond. The property stretched for several acres before other expansive homes began to pop up amongst the clusters of mature trees. Hearing the handle rattle again, she didn't look back.

"I have a key! Do I really need to use it?!"

It doesn't matter what I want, or don't want, she thought. Let him force his way in.

The past six weeks had messed with her head. All of this illusion about choosing things for herself… it wasn't good. It had her longing for more. More of something or someone she could never have. Better to remind them both of their roles now. He called the shots, and she did what he wanted. Period. Truth. Reality.

After a minute the lock clicked and Jason stepped inside. She could see him out of her peripheral vision as he shut the door quietly behind him. When he crossed in front of her, she looked away. And that was all she had, really, the ability to look away. At Cambric, even that act was frowned upon.

Kneeling down before her, Jason took her chin in hand and turned her to face him.

In response, she closed her eyes.

"Val, please. Look at me," he whispered.

When she wouldn't, he kissed her, filling her senses with a swirl of confusion and lust. His body pressed closer, leaning against hers, pinning her to the chair. Why did she feel this way? This mix of anger, wanting to shove him away, then longing, wanting to pull him in. Finally, she returned his kiss, and he eased them to a stop, balancing his forehead lightly against hers.

"I feel like all I do is apologize to you," he began, and pulled her off the chair onto his lap. "I was never engaged to that crazy actress. We dated a few times, then she started wearing a ring to get attention. I broke it off, but the rumor stuck, I'm sorry."

"Why are you sorry? You don't owe me anything. We aren't dating like you say."

"Okay." He frowned. "What would you call what we are then?"

"You are my owner," she answered simply. "I do what you want me to do. I belong to you."

"So, all this time." He searched her face. "You've never wanted to sleep with me? When you told me you wanted me, that was just... what? Because you thought I wanted you to say it?"

Pushing off of his lap, Val walked a few paces away. If she told him the truth, if she admitted that she had feelings for him, then what? She was a D2, ruining his family's reputation and business. He would soon be on to the next actress or heiress or someone else. Not her.

This had to end at some point. If she lied, and told him she had never felt any desire for him, then maybe he would break it off sooner. She would be free. Her heart should fill with joy at the thought. But it didn't. Why did she feel such despair?

"You can't give me an answer?" Jason stood behind her, running his palms down her arms. Leaning in, he whispered in her ear. "My family's going home tonight. Let's go for a ride. I know you missed your lesson today."

Try as she might, Val was unable to fight the slow smile that filled her face. She wanted to do nothing more in the whole world.

Changing into riding gear, the two of them slipped out of the house without saying goodbye. Jason drove the cart, keeping one hand on the wheel and the other draped casually around her shoulders. Letting herself relax into him, Val exhaled and closed her eyes. Dusk was approaching, she could feel it on the air.

When they arrived at the barn, Jason took the time to greet each of the grooms by name. Shaking their hands, he asked after their families. She was surprised that he knew all of them so well.

Upon seeing Jason, Ignacio got the black stud out and tied him in the grooming racks.

"Maybe you can fix the last of the damage you did," Ignacio told him and strode away.

"Where's your horse, Val?" Jason asked, as he leaned over to clean the stud's feet. "I had Ignacio select him but never got around to seeing him for myself."

Leaving the rack, Val walked the length of the now familiar barn to the second stall from the end. She peeked over the half door eagerly and spied her horse, her Bud. A fit palomino quarter horse, his pale cream coat shown with her constant care. Letting herself into his stall, Val inhaled the huff of air he exhaled from his nostrils.

"Sorry, Bud. I know it's a little late today," she crooned, slipping the blue rope halter around his head. Ignacio had told her that he was about ten years old, a well-broke horse that would serve a beginning rider well. His placid disposition was a complement to her newness.

Jason let out a low appreciative whistle when she tied him up next to the stud. Not sure if he meant her or the horse, she smiled, thinking probably he meant her. But affection for the gelding filled her with pride. She groomed him efficiently, soon catching up with Jason, and they had both horses saddled at the same time.

Gaging by the position of the sun, they had maybe an hour of daylight left. She swung her leg up and over. Jason followed suit. Most days she would head for the arena just on the far side of the track, but when they got there Jason kept riding. Indicating a little dirt road that cut off through a thick stand of trees, he picked up to a jog and she joined him.

They trotted companionably in silence for a while, enjoying the puffing breath of the horses. From the trees, birds called to one another. The sound of their singing complimented the coolness promised by the late breeze. At the beginning of the tree line, Jason turned to her with a mischievous smile.

"Want to go for a little run?" He asked, and when she beamed excitedly in response he shouted. "Race ya!"

The stud moved off Jason's leg in a hurry, sending pieces of dirt flying. Bud danced in anticipation, his body loaded like a spring. Not a split second later Val gave him his head and was propelled forward by the piston pump of his haunches. Faster and faster she went, almost matching Jason for a few seconds before the thoroughbred kicked into high gear.

He left her decidedly in his dust.

Snaking through the trees, the worn dirt path had her horse ducking this way and that. Ahead of her, the stud's lead grew ever wider. The thudding of his hooves was like a relentless pounding. Never had Val felt such immense exhilaration. Her chest swelled, her heart hammering in time with her mount.

Leaning forward slightly, she egged him on until his reaching strides lengthened out beneath her. Suddenly the tree line gave way to a wide open pasture. They dashed along the fence line, dusty clouds rising off the road. Off in the distance, horses picked up their heads. Pausing in their monotonous grazing, ears swiveled to track them as they passed.

Finally, Jason pulled up. He began the process of slowing the great black stud. First, he dropped to a controlled lope, then down to a brisk jog and eventually into a purposeful walk. Val followed his lead, cooling her horse alongside him. Their great heaving lungs sucked in and shoved out air.

"That was amazing," she panted.

"Ignacio said he was fast." Jason grinned. "I guess I just forgot what it's like."

They followed the road as it bordered his property, rounding the edge of the far pasture. The white fences and tall grass were every bit what one would imagine in a dream. Overhead, the sky had built with towering clouds. The orange sunset reflected amongst them, casting everything in a warm glow.

"You're good on him," Jason told her.

"You say that to all your girls," she countered.

"Val, was that your first joke?"

They both laughed, maybe it was.

"But seriously, you've got a good seat, a lot of talent for being so new. You're a natural, like Ignacio said."

Had the serious stable master actually said that? Val's heart leapt at the thought, but she did not dare let the rush of pride show on her face.

"It flatters me to hear you say it," she replied, ducking her head. "Thank you."

"I want you to have him."

Stopping his horse, Jason waited as she took a few more steps ahead before coming to a halt. Twisting around in her saddle, Val stared back at him.

"What?"

"That horse," Jason answered evenly. "He's yours."

CHAPTER 8

THE NEXT TWO MONTHS WERE THE MOST BLISSFUL IN VAL'S life. Jason spent his days at the office. Val spent hers in the stable. She didn't venture beyond Summer House, and he didn't allow anyone to step foot inside of it.

Their dinners together were intimate and long, filled with rich foods, good wine and easy laughter. On the weekends, they might splash together in the pool, or take a quiet walk along the dirt road bordering the property.

At night, they lay tangled together in his bed. He had her clothes moved into his closet, her toothbrush was in a holder on his sink. More than once, she asked him for birth control. He dismissed her concerns, promising instead to be more careful, pulling out quickly at the last moment to avoid a pregnancy.

She didn't watch television and they didn't discuss politics. The swirling unrest that was slowly consuming the rest of the country went unnoticed by her, locked up safely under the protection of a wealthy man and his home. Her first taste of it came when Jason decided to break the monotony of their evening routine by taking her out to dinner.

Tucked into the darkened corner of an exclusive restaurant, Val sipped on her third glass of Chateau Lafite and watched Jason swirl his around a giant goblet of thin glass. Hors d'oeuvres of figs with bacon and chile had been a first for both of them. Surprisingly, the unusual combination of tastes had complimented the wine.

"Ignacio says Royal Outing is almost ready for his first race," Jason told her. The black stud had finally stopped spooking at the rail, his times growing even faster.

"That's wonderful."

"We should go to his first race together." He gave her thigh a light squeeze under the table. "Would you like that?"

"I would." She smiled, tracing a finger down the stem of her glass.

"It's settled then. I think we might start him at Lone Star Park. It's fairly close, in the Dallas area," he told her before looking down to flip through his phone.

Distracted, Jason didn't notice the woman approaching their table, but Val did. She was tall and thin, elegant in a simple white dress that cut abruptly at her knees. Her sandy blonde hair swept back to reveal a severe face. But maybe it only appeared that way due to the look of disgust that contorted it. Leaning in to get a closer look at them, the woman made no attempt to lower her voice.

"I thought that was you, Jason Riggs," she spat.

This caught Jason by surprise. Looking up from his phone, Val saw puzzlement fill his face. He didn't recognize this woman.

"Can I help you?" He ventured.

"You make me sick. It's people like you who are ruining our country. You talk a good game for all the little people, but when the chips are down it's different rules for the high and mighty. Is that it?"

As her anger increased, so did her volume. The restaurant around them dropped into silence.

"I'm sorry, but I don't understand-" Jason began, but she cut him off, pointing an accusing finger at Val.

"Your slave! This woman that you bought with all of your filthy money so you can use her like a whore!"

Pushing back from the table, Jason tried to stand, but the woman was quick. She grabbed his glass full of water and flung the contents into his face. At the commotion, the maître d' and a waiter rushed over and pulled the woman away. She was still hurling insults as they forced her out of the restaurant.

Embarrassment crept up Jason's neck in the form of a deep red blush. His light-blue collared shirt was soaked down the front. Water dripped from his face onto the table. Everyone was murmuring, then the maître d' rushed back over.

"Mr. Riggs," he said, dabbing at Jason with a white linen napkin. "I cannot offer you enough in the way of an apology. We have never had such a thing happen here. I assure you-"

"It's alright." Jason cleared his throat. Grasping the napkin himself, he wiped his face.

"Please, Sir." The man pushed on. "Allow me to make amends. Can we get you a fresh shirt from our office while we dry yours?"

"I guess I don't have any other choice." Jason sighed, and looking over at Val, he asked, "Are you alright? I'll be right back."

"Sure, I'm fine." She urged him, feeling a mixture of guilt and unease.

The patrons around them watched as Jason was led away towards the back of the restaurant. Their conversations resumed in hushed tones. Surely, they were discussing the entertainment of the evening. Val kept her eyes downcast, laying her fork aside. Not sure what to do with her hands now, she carefully folded and unfolded them in her lap.

"Hi."

A man's voice just beside her had Val peering up into an unfamiliar face.

"You're a D2 right?"

Not knowing what to say, she just stared at him blankly.

A silly smile spread across his face then, as he crouched down next to her. Tilting his head to touch hers he swung his phone around and snapped a picture of them together.

Before she could protest, before she could do anything at all, another hand crossed into her field of vision. Plucking the phone from the silly man's grasp, a man in a dark suit flipped expertly through it and deleted the photo.

"Hey!" The silly one shouted, rising to his feet to grab for the phone.

"Get the hell out of here." The suit shoved him once, hard.

The silly man stumbled a few steps but then quickly righted himself and fled out the door. Jason returned just in time to see the exchange, his brow furrowed, his jaw clenching. The frantic maître d' rushed past him to click the lock on the front door.

"What the hell?" Jason whispered to the suit. "You following me now?"

"Looks like you need following," the suit responded.

At once both men glanced over at Val, who realized they must know one another. Jason grabbed the suit by the arm and moved him a few steps further away. She couldn't hear what passed between them, but it was intense and brief. Without looking back, the man with the suit walked to the front door and waited a beat while the maître d' let him out.

"Who was that?" Val asked.

"That's John Finn," Jason answered evenly. "He's an old friend."

"Where do you know him from?" Val pressed, but Jason cleared his throat.

"Are you still hungry? Or do you want to get out of here?"

"What about your shirt?" She questioned. The replacement he was wearing was a spare from the kitchen staff, white and a size or two too small.

"I can buy twenty more just like it," he answered. "Let's go."

She nodded, brushing at the red silk of her tiny dress and rose to stand. Placing the white linen napkin carefully back on the table, Val grabbed her clutch purse and let Jason lead her to the front of the restaurant. Through the tinted glass of the windows, Val watched a crowd of people that had gathered on the sidewalk.

"Who are they?" She whispered. Jason stood next to her, surveying them.

"Reporters… protestors…"

"Why are they all here?"

"Me," he huffed a laugh. "I'm a bad man, don't you know?"

"You aren't a bad man," she insisted. Rotating to face him, she wrapped her arms around his waist, pulling him close.

"They think so." He spoke into her hair, rubbed his hands over her bare shoulders.

Finally, Jason's sports car screeched up to the curb. The valet, in his black shirt and bow-tie, jumped out to run around and open the passenger door. All around him, the throng of people began to swirl and push, shouting. They recognized the car, and who would be coming out to drive it.

Inside, the maître d' grew worried and asked Jason if he would like to call the police. But Jason shook his head no. For whatever reason, he was determined to face the mob himself.

"Ready to make a break for it?" He asked.

Val tore her eyes from the angry crowd and caught Jason's eye. Some sort of perverse excitement danced in him, he wanted to do this. Pushing her trepidation aside, Val placed her trust in him and nodded.

As the door of the restaurant flew open Jason and Val rushed out into the horde. Fingers grasped at her arms, her hair and her dress. People yelled and cursed. Cameras flashed.

In the few yards that separated the car from the restaurant, Val filled with the sick primal fear of being crushed. But then they were at the passenger side of the car and Jason was shoving her down inside. Together, Jason and the valet fought to shut the car door.

Stuck there inside, Val lay her palms against the window, watching in horror as the crowd grabbed at Jason and the valet, pinning them against the vehicle.

Just when she wanted to scream, the two men broke free. Climbing up and over the top of the car, the valet leapt off the hood and scrambled away. Jason made it to the driver side and managed to pry open his door and slip inside. Revving the engine, he quickly slammed the car into gear.

It was raw instinct alone that had the crowd parting in front of him because Jason did not pause and he did not brake. Just as he whipped away from the curb, a rock sailed through the air and splintered the glass of the rear window.

"Are you alright?" He glanced over at her. Grabbing gears and changing lanes, he worked to put distance between them and what they had left behind.

"Yes, yes," she answered shakily. "Are you?"

"Yeah."

After a few seconds of silence, he burst out laughing.

Dumbfounded, Val stared at the side of his head. They had almost died, she thought. Well, maybe that was being a bit over-dramatic. Then she found herself smiling. A grin spread across her face.

The rush of adrenaline that had sent uncomfortable tingles from her fingers to her toes was ebbing away. And the flight down from the terror left her strangely high. Suddenly, she was laughing along with him. They were both hysterical. Tears ran down her face and she wiped at them with her fingertips.

"Jason, that was insane," she told him, once they were both back in control.

"It was," he agreed.

"Aren't you afraid for your family? Why do you still own me? Why not put an end to all of this now?"

"I wish I could tell you why," he answered her quietly, turning down the darkened cobblestone of his driveway. "Let's just forget all of them, Val. Can't it be just you and me? Together, for just a little while longer?"

They pulled to a stop and she turned to him, wondering at the small expression of sadness she saw there. Her heart filled with emotion for this man. He was not a bad person. If anything, she was grateful to have been purchased by him.

The world he had shown her in the past several months was an amazing and thrilling place. She didn't understand why other people hated him so much. She didn't hate him at all, quite the opposite.

Reaching out to hold the sides of his face with her hands, she pressed her lips to his. In her mind she answered his question. Yes. Yes, they could be together for as long as he wanted her. If she had been the one to decide, if the roles had been reversed, she would never let him go.

He broke their kiss only long enough to drag her across the gear shifter and onto his lap. She giggled as her back bumped uncomfortably against the leather steering wheel.

"On second thought," he said, and shoved open his car door.

Entangled together, they tumbled out. She laughed and he swore. His back absorbed the brunt of their fall.

Getting up, he pulled her along behind him. Her heels tapped against his stone steps, then along his marble floor, then up his wooden staircase. Upon reaching his bedroom, she fell forward into his arms, shoving his back against the wall.

Then she was pouring kisses all over him.

He hiked up her dress, groaning into her mouth as his hands traveled underneath it. Pausing, he let one hand stroke lazily over her lace panties. She gasped then and reached down to loosen his pants.

Hands spread across butt cheeks and breasts. Lips traveled down necks and across shoulders. Their clothes soon lay discarded on the floor.

In one swift move, he picked her up and switched their positions. Now he was holding her back against the wall. She wrapped her legs around his waist, whispering encouragement in his ear as he entered her. Shudders of pleasure caused goose bumps to tickle along her skin. He tilted his forehead against the wall just beside her head. His hands gripped impulsively at her thighs as he held her in place.

Rhythmically, he moved against her, in her, until she grew dizzy. Letting her feet down, she slipped away from him on a laugh. He chased her to the bed where they tumbled over one another and she pinned him beneath her, a smile playing across her lips.

Sitting astride, she lowered herself on top of him. He hissed out a breath, hands reaching up to cup her breasts while she rocked back and forth, building steadily faster.

The sensations were strong now, pulsing and demanding and burning all at once. She came in a rush, pressing her body down against his, she whimpered her release into his neck. Beneath her, she felt him clutch at her hips, taking over their movement until he was groaning into her hair.

Pulling her off him at the last moment, he let himself go, cursing under his breath as she wrapped her hand around him and stroked softly.

Laying her head against his chest, she listened as his heartbeat slowed and his breathing became regular. The darkness of the room surrounded them. What had happened only hours before seemed to be a dream, and this right here, this was reality.

Absently, she wondered what he wasn't able to tell her. Although she had successfully avoided it until now, she knew him well enough to understand that he was hiding something. To put his family and business on the line like this, it must be something big.

"I love you." He breathed the words, barely audible, into the air.

He must have thought she had fallen asleep, she realized, just like she had thought that of him. In the safety of unconsciousness, he could tell her how he felt. She didn't stir, not wanting to violate his trust. Instead, she took his words and stored them deep in her mind, to treasure them always. For a time was coming, when all of this would be over, of that she was certain.

Waking the next morning, rays of sunlight shone through the windows, casting an aura of peace throughout the large room. Jason was already gone, off to work by now, as was his routine. She lingered in bed, burying her face in his pillow, sliding her hand along his empty side. Yvette did not bring breakfast to this room like she had the last. If Val wanted to eat in the master suite, then she had to call down for it.

And the truth was, she had nothing to call down with. Jason had tried to get her a cell phone, but Val was resistant. It seemed that the tiny electronic box had a special power all its own. Everyone who held one was unable to put it down. In her life, she had already been slave to far too many things. She didn't want to add another.

Dressing in her favorite jeans, t-shirt, and worn leather boots she jogged her way down to the dining room to eat alone.

When Anne Marie came in with breakfast, Val thought she saw an expression of concern cross the young woman's face. Val waited, but the other woman said nothing, merely poured a cup of coffee and then left. Filling her cup with honey and heavy whipping cream, Val transformed the bitter caffeine into a sweet treat.

Out the bay window, the first fall leaves were beginning to turn. They were brilliant. All oranges and soft yellows mixing and blending with the lingering pale-green leaves. Soon they would take over entirely, then fall. Their crumpling cracking shapes would litter the ground. For now though, it was still warm during the day. Perfect weather for riding.

Movement, of a kind she hadn't seen out this particular window, caught Val's eye. Standing up, she gaped as a strange man walked through the garden outside, carrying a ladder. Rushing to the window, she held her face against the glass and peered to the left. There were several strange men walking along together actually. Turning, she called for Yvette, and found her just beyond the dining room door.

"Is everything alright?" Yvette asked.

"Who are all of those men outside?"

"Jason is having a security gate and fence installed on the property. Those men are here to do the work."

"Why would he do that?"

"I shouldn't tell you, Val. He wouldn't want me to," Yvette replied, but her eyes held hesitation.

"What's going on Yvette? Please." Reaching out, she took Yvette's hands in her own.

"Over the past month, Jason has received some death threats." Yvette shushed Val's exclamation, and continued on. "None of us took it very seriously until after what happened to you last night. Maybe five years ago none of this would matter so much, but the state that the country has gotten to, well…"

"Well, what Yvette?"

"Buying you was like throwing a match on kindling. It's

ignited a fervor. People are upset, and it's not going away. There is nothing people can band together to hate more than a wealthy man preaching to people for years about how wrong something is, only to turn around and do it himself. Jason used to give speeches in college about ending the captive industry. Now here he is... owning you."

"I think I'm beginning to understand." Val ducked her head, eyes studying the floor.

She was afraid for Jason now. Afraid like she hadn't been before. But what could she do? What power did she have to stop this? None. None at all. Briefly, Val fought with her natural impulse to hide. She needed to clear her head. She needed to think and the only sure way to do that was to head for the stables.

Ignacio met her when she pulled up to the barn. His brown eyes were troubled underneath his ball cap but he said nothing. Getting out, she walked quietly alongside him. The horses poked their heads out of the stalls as they passed. Occasionally a favorite would call to him, nickering a greeting. Unlike other times, Ignacio did not stop.

When Val arrived at her horse's stall, Ignacio lingered, watching her enter and fit the halter over Bud's caramel colored ears.

"What is it?" She asked finally from inside the stall.

"I was watching the television this morning. I saw the footage of you and Jason being attacked last night."

"I wouldn't call it attacking exactly."

"Pushing and shoving. A rock breaking the car window? What would you call it?"

"I don't know." Val's shoulders sagged momentarily.

Pushing past him, she led Bud out of the stall and over to the grooming racks. Ignacio followed on her heels.

Grabbing up a curry comb, he worked down one side of Bud while she did the other. They didn't speak, though tension hung in the air between them. Frowning, she focused on the task at hand.

"There may come a time," Ignacio murmured, working at Bud's shoulder with firm strokes. "That you will need to run away. Have you thought of it?"

Her stomach churned. Of course she had thought of it. She'd wanted to ask Ignacio for advice, in fact. But now that he was the one coming to her, she was uncertain. Could she trust him? She didn't *want* to run away, didn't want to leave Jason. But with the turmoil that surrounded them now, how much longer could she stay?

Ignacio waited patiently. As with a horse, he wanted her to make the choice to trust him and so finally, she did.

"Yes," she whispered. "I have thought of it."

"I have a brother, Javier." He stopped brushing to glance about, making sure no one was around. "He has his own ranch in Wyoming. His daughter, Camila, runs it now, but he still does all of the hiring. They always have room for a quiet person who is good with horses. A bed and food is usually included."

"That sounds peaceful," she said wistfully, letting her hand rest on Bud's soft coat. "But I would miss him."

Ignacio snorted, the corner of his mouth tipping up in a slight smile. "Do you mean Jason or the horse?"

Val smiled then. Thinking it over, she knew she meant both. Leaving Jason would be an awful emptiness, like losing Bee or Gabe. And Bud was her first animal. A loving companion, a true friend. Her heart would ache for him too, in a different way, of course.

Ignacio carried her saddle over as she fitted Bud with his pads. Swinging it onto his back, she adjusted the cinch, sliding her hand between his silky belly and the strap to make sure it wasn't too tight. Next came his bridle. He took the bit easily, ears relaxed, tail swishing at the occasional fly.

Ignacio walked him forward for her and she hopped up, sending her leg over to sit carefully in the saddle. When she turned to look down at him, Val dipped her head in gratitude at the older man.

"Thank you, Ignacio. I don't know what to say."

"You're welcome, Señorita," he answered evenly. "I will pass your name along discreetly. And if I ever get a postcard from that address, well then I may find a way to send Bud there. To work, of course."

Nodding at that, she had to avert her eyes. Tears brimmed at his kindness. He was a free man. He owed her nothing.

Urging Bud forward she walked down the aisle of the barn and out into the air. A warm wind was beginning to blow. The leaves of the trees around her rustled. Up high in the saddle, her heart slowly eased as she breathed in.

When she arrived at the arena, she entered the ring and urged Bud into a trot, jogging big round circles in the freshly graded earth. Circling wider and wider she had them both puffing out breath before turning to close tighter and tighter. He was supple and giving under her legs.

Kissing to him once, she tilted forward and felt him pick up the pace, reaching out with his legs into a controlled lope. Around and around they went, making patterns. Figure eights, four corners, zig zags, until both were sucking air from the exertion. Sitting down, she pressed her backside into the saddle and asked him for a walk on their way out of the arena.

There was still plenty of daylight left, and for some reason she just didn't feel done yet, so they meandered along the dirt road towards the far stand of trees. Her mind flashed back to that day racing along with Jason. The thrill. The speed. His eyes dancing at her. His cocky grin.

Beneath her, Bud's steps were light and she was lulled by his casual rocking motion. Once through the grove, she watched the pastures stretch out to her left. They were filled with horses, just like in the old movie that The Agency had let them watch as children. It had been about a black horse, a beautiful one. The animal had been sold around to a variety of owners before finally coming back to his original person. She forgot what it was called.

Though it had been one of Val's favorites, Bee absolutely hated it. That horse is *us*, she had said, scowling. And where was her Bee now? It had been too long since Val had thought of her. Guilt swamped her suddenly, then overflowed into a sick sadness at the time and distance that was now between them.

She couldn't let herself forget the promise she had made, and what she had told Alicia that final day. Had she given Bee the message? Was Bee waiting for her somewhere, hoping each day that Val would come? Looking back, Val could see why Bee felt as if she were like the horse from the movie. Bee's heart had always rebelled against their confinement.

Why hadn't Val felt the same rage? Even Gabe dealt with his captivity better, but then again, he had more freedom within the system. He could have multiple partners and walk about the halls of their dormitory at night. Even when he had been caught with Bee, she was the one who had been taken away. His value hadn't diminished.

What had become of her friend? What would Cambric do with a permanent placement they could no longer sell as having only one prior lover? Did they put her in the breeding program? Demote her to a monthly subscription? Private parties? Hourly? Val wasn't sure she wanted to know.

Her thoughts and Bud's feet had taken her full circle. Arriving back at the stables, Val dismounted and handed her horse off to one of the grooms. Normally she would have taken care of him herself, but a sort of melancholy had crept over her.

The feeling persisted, clinging to her damply as she drove the cart back to Summer House. Beneath her, gravel crunched under the churning tires.

Back at the house, she let herself in quietly and climbed the stairs to the master suite. It was early still. Jason wouldn't be back from the office for an hour or more.

Showering off the layer of dust from the stables, Val traced a finger along the stone pattern that twisted in circles over the wall. Were they forcing Bee to shower? Maybe she was facing the gray cement walls even now, letting the icy cold water pour over her skin. Cambric didn't bother to heat it.

Stepping out, Val brushed roughly through her wet tangle of hair. Her eyes fell to the travertine counter of the bathroom sink. A glint of light caught her attention. It was Jason's watch. He never left for work without it.

The gleaming gold of the wristband winked at her in the fading light as dusk touched at the windows. It was an heirloom piece, passed down for generations amongst the Riggs men. If that watch was here, that meant Jason was here as well.

He was home early. That was unusual these days, but Val brightened at the thought of seeing him. Rushing through her routine, she blew her hair dry and left it loose. She forgot about the makeup, moving to select a soft sundress from the closet instead. Barefoot, she skipped hurriedly down the winding stairs and into the foyer.

There was no sign of him.

Her brow furrowed. Hands on hips, Val turned a small circle in the hall. He wasn't in the kitchen. He wasn't in the living room or dining room. Then she heard him. It was his low voice, muffled behind a closed door. The sound traveled out from his home office. She hadn't been in there before.

Hesitating in front of the entry for a moment she listened to his voice murmuring. He was on the phone with someone. Training had her backing a step, but intuition urged her to place her hand on the knob. It wasn't like he had told her that she was forbidden from entering, but the door was always kept shut.

She stood there a moment, fighting with herself. Then sucking in a breath, she twisted the handle and pushed the door wide.

Poised in front of a wide window, Jason stood behind an expansive mahogany desk. His back was to her. He was absorbed in his conversation and hadn't heard her come in.

Taking a few steps forward, Val's attention was soon captured by a picture lying flat on his desk. Peering over at it, she froze.

It was a little girl, maybe about three or four-years-old. The soft brown hair framed a child's round smooth face. And the eyes, the unmistakably unusual green eyes, they glittered back at her even then.

Snatching at the picture, Val brought it greedily up to her

face, crumpling the edges in both of her hands. She knew this child. She would know her anywhere.

"*What* are you doing with a picture of Bee?" Val hissed it, her teeth gritting, her nerves spiking.

Jason whirled at the sound of her voice, his blue eyes registering surprise, then an unmistakable flash of guilt.

CHAPTER 9

"I'VE GOT TO GO, FINN."

Cutting the call short, Jason slipped his cell into the pocket of his navy slacks. Val's eyes darted from his face to the picture of Bee, and then back again. Chest heaving, her throat tight, she didn't know what to think.

"Why do you have this picture of Bee?" She demanded, further crinkling the edges of the photo.

"Shut the door." Frowning, he pointed at the opening behind her.

"No." Flipping the picture to face him, she waved it in the air deliberately.

Grimacing, he skirted the edge of his massive desk and brushed by her. She didn't turn to watch him, but she heard the click of the door being locked into place. The sound was like a lightning bolt at her back. For the first time in a long time she did not feel safe.

"How do you know that's not a picture of you?" He asked quietly from behind her. "When I first saw you, I swore for certain that it was."

"Is that why you bought me?"

"Yes," he admitted.

Approaching carefully, he reached out to touch her arm, but she shied away, so he let his hand drop back to his side.

"This is a picture of Bee. I would know her anywhere," she insisted.

He crossed back to his desk, pulling aside the brown leather chair and resuming his seat. Without a word, he reached into a drawer and pulled out a single bottle of whiskey. Two crystal tumblers followed them, clinking. She watched him open the bottle and carefully pour them both a drink.

He set hers on the table top and slid it over to her before looking up into her face. The glass scraped along the wood.

"Will you sit?" Eyebrows raised, he waited a beat before drinking deeply. She complied, but left her glass untouched.

"*Where* is Bee?" She asked.

"I wish I knew," he answered honestly, and then took another long swallow. "And her name isn't Bee, it's Veronica Durand. She's the daughter of Lillian Durand. Do you remember meeting her?"

"Mrs. Durand said that her daughter had died." Still gripping the photo, Val held it against her thudding heart.

"No," Jason corrected. "Veronica Durand went missing. She disappeared when she was about three, while her nanny had her back turned at The Texas Zoo. It was believed she had been kidnapped. I was about ten at the time, but I'll never forget my parents talking about it."

"So, when you saw me in New York..." Val's resolve broke, she reached for the whiskey.

"It was everything about you really, especially your eyes, they're remarkably similar. God Val, how I wished you were her. For weeks when you first lived here I was tortured by it, but then the DNA came back and-"

"I'm not her."

"No." Shaking his head, he polished off his glass. Tipping the bottle, he filled it again.

"Those first weeks when you wouldn't sleep with me, it wasn't anything that I did or didn't do. You thought maybe I was a free girl, and you had no right to me." Val's heart pinched uncomfortably at the truth.

"It wasn't as simple as that." Shoving up to standing, he turned away from her and examined the setting sun through his wide window. "Free or not, I wanted it to be consensual. I wanted you to feel like I did. To want me the way that I wanted you."

The walls around them turned pink as the sun slowly disappeared in the west. It was quiet. Quiet and heavy and painful. Why was it so painful?

She studied him, hung up on the idea that all this time, he had been wishing she was someone else, some*thing* else. How disappointed he must have been when it turned out that she wasn't the woman he sought.

Suddenly, her arm dropped, and she slapped her empty glass loudly on the edge of the desk.

"On the way to the airport, right?" She asked. "That's when you found out the DNA wasn't a match."

Turning around to face her, Jason's face contorted with misery. He sat purposefully then, as if trying to stuff down any reaction. Gripping the bottle, he reached across the desk to pour her a refill.

"We thought we were finally so close," he explained. "I never meant to hurt you in all this, Val. Everything that has gone on between us is real. I want you to know that."

"We. Who is we?"

Blowing out a breath he tilted back in his chair and shut his eyes, pinching the bridge of his nose between stressed fingers. She waited for him to collect his thoughts while her heart shattered into a million pieces that ricocheted around her chest.

"The FBI has had an investigation open into the kidnapping of Veronica Durand for almost two decades now. They felt that she fit into a certain profile of victim: a child under four, naturally beautiful, a female. These types of abductions have been going on for years with little to no clues.

But then a decade back, they got a break. Someone on the inside wanted to make a deal for immunity and rolled. These little girls were being kidnapped and sold illegally into the D2 captive trade. The industry was suffering from an apparent lack of supply and needed a hit of fresh genetics."

He paused to sit forward, palms spreading across the surface of his desk. But she glanced away, so he continued.

"Only problem was, they had no evidence to prove it. The guy got cold feet at the last minute so they couldn't push any further."

"Did he say who was behind it?"

"Yes, he did give a name. But it's a big name, so the FBI has to be careful about how they move forward."

"That's where you come in?"

"Well, they let it sit for a few years. Then I was approached by an agent at a business conference."

"John Finn?"

"Yeah, Finn. He recruited me. Said they were desperate, needed someone to go on the inside to help. Someone with money and connections. I couldn't refuse, I knew Veronica.

My mom and hers are still friends. But the catch was that I couldn't tell anyone about it."

"So, you were at the conference in New York…" she began, but trailed off, could feel his eyes piercing her.

"I would have been there for work regardless. But every time I got a chance to look over captive girls, I did. God, Val, when I saw you behind that glass…"

Pausing, he seemed to swallow his thoughts. "If we could find Veronica, and have her DNA match, then the FBI would be able to prove without a doubt that she had been illegally trafficked. They could subpoena business records. Demand DNA tests on all captives. It would bust the whole thing wide open."

"But I'm not her, and Bee or Veronica is long gone. What now?"

"Finn has been working on a few things, but I haven't agreed to them yet."

"All this time, despite the threat to your family, to your business, even to your life, you've been working for the FBI?"

"Yes."

"All of those other people are losing their minds over your anti-captive hypocrisy, and you're actually just trying to… what? Expose an illegal kidnapping ring?"

"Yeah, I guess." He swallowed before adding, "But it's gotten more complicated."

"Oh, and by that you mean me. I'm the complication."

"Val." Jason reached for her but she jerked back, her whiskey careening to the floor.

"You bought me hoping that I was someone else. Then when I wasn't her, you… what? What are we doing? Your parents are losing it. Your mother paraded me around in front of Lillian Durand for pure shock value! You've lied to me and you've used me."

Her voice was escalating along with her claims as her mind raced in a thousand directions at once.

"I didn't want to lie to you," he pleaded.

"You've given me things. Moved me into your bed. You made me believe that you- that you-"

She couldn't bring herself to say it. Standing abruptly, she swiped at the tears that threatened to take over. Shooting to his feet in response, Jason moved swiftly around to her and yanked her against him. Lungs burning, her attempt to resist was pitiful and half-hearted. Giving in, she buried her face in her hands and let his arms encircle her.

He whispered into her ear, his voice at once pleading and soothing and desperate. But all she could hear was the one truth that remained. You aren't free. You aren't free. *You aren't.*

Slowly, she regained her composure as the realization set in. Agency rhetoric sounded in her head, reminding her to submit her will in exchange for his. After all she was a D2, born and bred. No getting out of that now.

A light knock on the door had them separating. He took the picture of Bee from her and locked it back in the top drawer of his desk. How she longed to keep it for herself.

Dinner was ready and although utterly exhausted, her stomach worked to convince her to attend. He opened the door for her. He stood aside as she made her way to the dining room. He pulled out her chair while she took a seat. All the usual niceties remained. All of the things he did to help her pretend she was free.

Anne Marie swept in and began pouring a crisp white wine into each glass. Val sipped hers demurely, contemplating the vapid darkness outside the bay window. Perhaps she had gotten used to southern manners after all. Sharing a meal with a complete stranger, someone you thought that you knew so well. Someone who had complete control of your life, though he made you feel otherwise.

Fresh bread was placed between them, accompanied by an array of spreads. Jason tore off a piece and handed it over to her. She took it from him, feeling the warmth of it spread over her palm. Selecting the pesto, she smoothed it on using a miniature silver knife. She tried her best to clear her mind. She failed.

The picture kept coming back around to haunt her. What about Bee? All those years of fighting the system and maybe, just maybe she never belonged there in the first place. Bee's spirit knew that she wasn't meant for captivity.

And what did that say about Val? Clearly her spirit knew better. It had always been so much easier for her to acquiesce. It explained her cowardice. It explained her compliance.

Looking up finally she caught Jason's eye. She sat there for several minutes, just looking at him in wonder. Questions threaded themselves in and out. Who was this man? The handsome playboy? The successful businessman? The FBI informant? The generous benefactor? The sinful lover? Why did he still own her?

"Release me," she demanded, then held her breath.

Across the table, Anne Marie was just setting a Caesar salad in front of Jason when the sentence rolled unthinkingly out of Val's mouth. Straightening, the young woman tried desperately to fade into the background of the room before making fast tracks towards the exit.

"I can't do that," he managed through gritted teeth.

Val exhaled, she hadn't really known how she wanted him

to answer. Jason's jaw clenched, the muscle jumping the way they so often did.

The door to the dining room swung shut behind Anne Marie, but the ripple that went through the staff must have been intense. Seconds later, Yvette came pushing in. She made her way towards them, holding an open bottle of wine, making a slow show of refilling their glasses. Val ducked her head, picking at her salad a moment, but then Jason shoved his plate sharply away.

"So, you want to leave me, now. Is that it?"

"What more could you possibly want from me?" Val cried, standing to lean against the table.

"Damn it, Val!" He smacked his hand down before pushing back to pace. "Isn't it obvious? Isn't it obvious how I feel about you? Look around! Come on, it's still me!"

"I'm not who you wanted! Why keep me? I have no control over this. I have no say."

"Don't you play that card with me." He stopped his pacing to face her. "Don't tell me you haven't made your own choices. Don't try to say that you didn't want *everything* I've given you."

"That's enough!" Yvette shouted.

Her voice turned the air to silence. They hadn't realized she was still in the room. Val's face burned with embarrassment. Jason swore under his breath.

"Now, both of you will sit to have a civilized dinner. Take this dispute back with you upstairs." Sweeping by them both she plucked up their glasses, leaving them with water. "And no more alcohol."

A heavy meal of prime rib, au jus, horseradish and garlic mashed potatoes was served. They ate quietly. Jason's shoulders were taut, Val kept her face downcast. When they finished, Val stood, her nearly empty plate rested off to one side on the table. The staff had already fled, leaving them alone in the darkened house.

She didn't make eye contact. She didn't look at him or speak to him or acknowledge him in any way. She was determined to sleep in her own room tonight and if she was going to be successful she would have to be fast.

Just before her hand reached the door of the dining room, she heard his chair scrape across the floor. He was coming after her and her lead wasn't nearly as big as she'd have liked.

Winding up the stairs, fresh anger built within her as she attempted to maintain a blank face. She wouldn't be sucked into another confrontation with him. She couldn't keep fighting with him this way. But his presence was constant, a looming shadow at her back. Cresting the landing, she veered immediately right, but felt the quick grab of his hand on her wrist.

"Oh no you don't," he hissed.

In one fluid movement he flipped her easily over his shoulder.

"Put me down!" She raged.

Hair tangling in her face, she braced herself awkwardly against his back. A quick about-face had them closing the distance to the master suite. Once through the door, he kicked it closed with his foot and strode over to the bed where he tossed her unceremoniously down onto the mattress.

"You don't have to sleep with me ever again if you don't want to." Jason stood over her, handsome as he burned with frustration. "But you *are* going to hear me out. Tomorrow, I will contact Finn and arrange a meeting. You need to listen to what he has to say."

She began to protest, sitting up on his bed, brimming with

a mixture of outrage and longing. He cut her off with a wave of his hand, and continued.

"You thought Bee was your sister. You act like you love her and now here is your chance to save her. Has anything really changed now that she might be Veronica?"

They stared at one another a moment but Val was the first to look away. She heard Jason sigh, then he left her to alone sit in the middle of his expansive bed. Water sprayed from the shower. She could hear the open and shut of the glass door as he got in.

Throwing her face down on the pillow, she sobbed. Great heaving gasps shook her until sleep gathered, clouding the edges of her senses. The last thing she remembered was Jason coming to bed. He pulled the blankets up around them, his arm circled her waist, and he pulled her in close.

The next morning, she reached instinctively for him, but grasped empty bed sheets instead. Sitting up, she braced herself back against the mountain of pillows. The shock from yesterday worked its way gradually back in. Bee could be free, *if* Bee was Veronica.

Jason crossed into her field of vision. She was surprised to see him still there. He was dressed in a gray suit with a deep blue tie that held a tiny paisley pattern. Scrutinizing him from across the room, she watched him tug to straighten it.

"Finn cleared his day, we're going to see him first thing," he announced.

"What about breakfast?"

"We'll take it to go."

Glancing down, Val realized she was still wearing her

dress from the night before. She had slept in it without noticing. Getting up, she purposefully slipped it off, letting the wrinkled fabric fall to the floor. Her eyes on Jason, she shimmied out of her tiny panties and kicked them aside. Completely naked, she sauntered past him, and headed for their shared closet.

Let him look, she thought ruefully, wanting to punish him still. A small lick of power surged within her, knowing he stood in the doorway, watching and wanting.

Taking her time, she touched the different items of clothing, moving the hangers aside to look critically at each piece. Something classic? Or, maybe something ridiculously revealing? Finally, she settled on a short black skirt with an unusual white pattern that bordered the bottom. It would go well with a soft linen blouse, the tiny buttons of which cascaded down the front. From the nearby drawer she grabbed a lace thong and matching bra.

Dressed now, Val passed Jason at the entrance to the closet as she tucked in the shirt, then sat at her vanity in the bathroom. Purposefully making him wait, she took her time in brushing and then curling the ends of her hair. She worked to apply a carefully reserved palette of makeup.

"Done yet?" He demanded, impatience tapping out a rhythm with his foot.

"All set." She smiled.

Out front, a driver pulled a shining black SUV to a stop on the cobbled circle of driveway. The windows were heavily tinted. She couldn't see inside.

When Jason pulled open her door she slid onto the seat

and reached for her belt. The driver had gotten out to open Jason's side, his hulking figure standing just within her narrow view. She didn't recognize him. Once they were rolling forward down the drive, Val leaned over, whispering to Jason.

"New driver?" She asked.

"No, this is Agent Schipp with the FBI. They thought it would be best to have an escort, make sure no one follows us."

"You get followed to the office now?"

"Occasionally," he admitted with a shrug.

The ride was long and confusing. They got onto freeways and then back off, crossed a river twice, and wound through surface streets. After a while she gave up trying to figure out where they were. Staring out the window, Val remembered her life once lived behind glass.

Eventually, they entered a business district with moderately sized office buildings lining the narrow street. The area reminded her vaguely of the reflective high rises in New York, but on a much smaller scale. She wasn't surprised when they turned into an underground parking garage.

Winding down, down, down, her head began to spin on the slow carousel ride. When they reached the bottom level it was nearly empty. Pulling into a slot next to an elevator, the SUV stopped. Overhead, fluorescent lights set everything in the concrete structure to glow in odd purplish tones.

Agent Schipp swiped at his cell phone before exiting the vehicle. He came around to open Val's door, reaching a massive hand in for her to grasp. Jason got out by himself. Together, the three of them walked to the elevator and took it up to the lobby. This doesn't look like an FBI office, she thought. A few women dressed in business attire walked by, chatting about customer service and an awful boss.

A far bank of elevators gleamed with gold colored trim and they waited a minute or more for an empty one. Agent Schipp waved his badge over an electronic pad before the elevator began its ascent. Val watched the numbered circles light up in sequence. It was this way at Cambric. So much beeping and scanning and waiting. When they got to floor twelve, the doors binged open and they walked out.

Bare white walls greeted them, highlighting a lone security desk, its sleek rectangular shape revealed nothing. The face of a young man watched them coolly from behind a computer screen. As they approached, the man rose to his feet and stepped around the side of the check-in area. Val noticed a matte black handgun secured in a holster at his hip.

As the man checked Jason's driver license, Agent Schipp said nothing. His eyes scrutinized the ID before giving it back and proceeding with a brief pat down. Jason held his arms out to the side and made no comment. When the agent approached Val, his serious expression did not waiver.

"Ma'am," the young agent said. "I'm going to need to see your identification, and check for any weapons."

"She doesn't have any ID," Agent Schipp told him. "And no weapons."

"Protocol says that I need to do a quick check, nothing personal," the young agent countered. When Jason seemed ready to protest, Val waved him off.

"Let him check me," she said, then fixed her eyes on his, letting a knowing smile creep across her face.

Pat downs were a common practice at Cambric. She and Bee used to make a game of it, seeing who could get security to blush first. When they were in training it had been good fun. They got just a tiny taste of power every time they made a guard feel weak.

The young agent frowned at Val's expression but pushed forward regardless. Indicating that she should lift her arms, he reached under her hair, brushed his fingers behind her neck. Blinking at him, Val leaned in a bit closer as he swept his hands professionally down to feel under her armpits, grazing along her sides to her waist.

As his hand passed over the side of her breast, she bit her lip, moving into him just a fraction. This had him hesitating for a moment, a break in stride. His brow furrowed. Determined to do his job, he reached for her again, this time sticking the tips of his fingers just inside the waist of her skirt to feel around the lining. At this she let out a tiny gasp, shifting her hips.

A rose-colored flush began to creep around the collar of his starched shirt. He leaned back uncomfortably. Val's smile broadened and she gave him a wink. Shaking his head slightly, he bent forward, and quickly grazed the sides of her hips, hands traveling along the outside of her thighs.

Then his hands went still. They both knew the last step was for him to check the inside of her legs, to make sure she wasn't concealing anything there.

When he crouched down, she kept her legs pressed together. He would have to ask her to spread them in order to proceed. He didn't want to ask her. He didn't want to say it. Finally straightening up, his cheeks rosy, he sighed.

"I can't do it," he admitted.

Agent Schipp cleared his throat, eyes dancing over to Jason whose jaw was locked tight, fists balled at his sides. Val kept her gaze fixed on the young agent and nibbled at her lower lip.

"She's a D2." Agent Schipp shrugged. "No weapons, I promise."

The hallway that lead away from the reception area was narrow, with closed dark wooden doors lining both sides. When they drew near to the end, Agent Schipp came to a stop and knocked briefly on one door. There was no answer.

Standing aside, he pushed the door open and gestured for Val to walk through first. Jason followed close behind, but Schipp did not enter. He stepped back into the hallway and closed the door softly instead.

The small room was reminiscent of the entranceway. Stark white walls contained a single window situated behind an L shaped wooden desk. Val recognized the figure of a man in a dark tailored suit that rose to greet them. It was John Finn, the man from the restaurant.

His well-muscled shoulders and short crop of black hair screamed ex-military, while his appraising brown eyes gleamed with intelligence. He wasn't so much older than them really, maybe in his early-thirties at most. Sticking out his right hand to shake hers, Val found it to be strong, his expression serious.

"Val, this is Agent Finn." Jason made introductions. "And Finn, this is Val."

"The suit from the restaurant," she said, and sat in an uncomfortable wooden chair opposite his desk.

Jason folded down into the seat next to her. She crossed her legs away from him. The two men exchanged a brief look.

"That's right," Agent Finn acknowledged. "I'm sorry that I wasn't able to help you get to your car that night. I couldn't risk being seen on camera. Jason here was supposed to have called the local police, as we had discussed."

"Oh, that's what you two were whispering about," she intoned, keeping her face carefully devoid of emotion.

"Jason tells me that you discovered a photo of Veronica

Durand in his office yesterday," Finn began. "He tells me you are pretty certain she's the same woman you grew up with called Bee."

"It *is* Bee," she said.

"How can you be sure?"

"Because I stared at that little girl's face all day long, every day for my entire life. Because I wiped tears from her eyes, rocked her when she was sick, and listened to her sing herself to sleep at night. Because we believed we were sisters. Because she's in every memory inside my head and I can see her even now. I am *telling* you, that is my Bee. But I don't know anything about Veronica Durand."

"Do you know where Bee is now?" Finn asked.

"I was hoping you did."

"Tell me what happened to her," he said.

"Didn't Jason tell you? I figured he's been reporting our every conversation to you," she snipped, and felt Jason shift uncomfortably in the chair next to her.

"I want to hear it from you," Finn replied.

"The last time I saw Bee, she was standing in our bedroom screaming at the top of her lungs so the whole damn floor could hear her. The last time I saw her, a security guard knocked her out. Her eyes rolled up in her head and I did nothing while they dragged her out."

"Do you think she's dead?"

"No, she's not dead."

"You seem sure, how do you know?"

"Because I know."

"You aren't going to tell me?" Finn's eyebrows raised.

"Who owns me? You guys or him?" She asked, indicating Jason.

"Val!" Jason whirled on her, but Agent Finn waved him off.

"No, it's a valid question. Jason bought you with his own money. You legally belong to him."

Val folded into silence, letting her own thoughts consume her while the two men sat, waiting. Who was this new person she felt inside her? It had always been her way to submit, to give in, to survive. Bee had been the voice that questioned, that rebelled, that raged. Anger at Jason was consuming her now, getting in the way of her ultimate goal. The goal of rescuing Bee.

"Are you ordering me to answer his questions?" Wanting to make a point, she turned to Jason, searching his eyes that now blazed with anger.

"Yes," Jason responded through gritted teeth. "Answer the man's questions, Val."

"What the hell do you care about Bee for?!" Violent outrage sliced in her words. "Both of you are only asking because you think she is Veronica, a *free* girl. When it was just a captive getting slapped around, or starved, or coerced into sex then it was all okay, right?"

"Val-"

"You only bought me because you thought I was her. If I didn't look like this Veronica Durand then you would have left me standing in that glass box."

"That's not-" Jason tried.

"It's the damn truth, Jason! You aren't here to save Bee. You're here to save a missing free girl. If the DNA comes back wrong, well... look at me. I'm not free, am I?"

CHAPTER 10

Folding her arms across her chest, Val sat up straight in the stiff-backed chair. Jason had long since stood. Facing away from her, he stared out the solitary window, hands shoved into the hip pockets of his slacks. Still at his desk, Agent Finn studied the wooden surface quietly. Clutching a black ball point pen in his hand, he tapped lightly at the table top with it. With a quick nod, Finn finally broke the silence.

"I want to show you some photos," he said.

Deliberately, he placed picture after picture in neat rows, covering the top of his desk. There were over thirty little faces shining up at Val when he was done. All girls. Some had blue eyes, some brown. Some had red hair, some black. All were pretty. All were under the age of four. All had been free.

Some vanished from a park or the beach. Some were snatched from their front yards or while waiting in front of their school. Blinking, Val studied each and every one. Occasionally, a flicker would catch fire in her mind and pointing shakily she would utter the name of the girl that she grew up with. That's Suze. That's Brenda. That's Candace.

And plucking the photo from the desk, Finn would collect them, making notes. He echoed their free names back to her. That's Emma Reynolds. That's Olivia Smith. That's Ava Thomas. None that she recognized had made permanent placement. Most were hourly, party or monthly, she didn't remember which.

Her heart sank for each of these little girls, but she didn't really know why. What made them so special that they didn't deserve the life she led? In fact, they were lucky. At least they had felt three years of love from a mother and a family; something Val now knew for sure she hadn't.

But as conflicted and angry as it made her, if she ever wanted to see Bee again, then she would have to cooperate fully with Agent Finn. Despite his motives, Finn was the only way that Val could make good on her promise to rescue her friend.

"If the DNA comes back negative, and Bee isn't Veronica, will you commit to buying her out of captivity?" Her question was aimed at Jason. Agent Finn would have a hard time getting that kind of authorization.

"Yes," Jason agreed.

"Alright. I'll tell you everything you want to know. I'll do everything you ask me to do."

Clearing his desk of the remaining photos, Agent Finn filed them carefully away. He pulled out a note pad of yellow lined paper and scribbled something at the top, the date maybe?

"Let's start with why you don't think Bee is dead," he began.

"They wouldn't have killed Bee. She was still worth some money to them. Keeping her alive and making her work would be the only way to recoup some of the value she lost," Val explained.

"Why did she lose value?" Finn questioned, jotting down notes as they talked.

"She fell in love with another D2 and they carried on a secret affair. When Cambric caught her with him, they couldn't sell her as having only been with her original trainer. She wasn't agent quality anymore."

"Why does one or two lovers matter?"

"Cambric does a lot of market research. Bee and I were selected for an older wealthy widower. Those kind of men mostly miss their late wives. They don't want a virgin, but they don't want to feel like they are with a whore either. One lover only is the magic number when you are talking about several million dollars."

"I see. What do you think they could have done with her?"

"They could have demoted her to a monthly member subscription. Or even lower, to doing weekends, parties or even hourly. Knowing her personality, I'm not sure she would do well in any of those positions."

"What would happen if she couldn't last doing that?"

"They could commit her to their breeding program."

"What happens then?"

"The Agency has a strict selection process. I'm not quite sure what they look for other than the girls have to be healthy and marginally pretty. Usually the breeding program is for the ones that were a success at monthly subscriptions until they got a little too old. That's when they try to breed them back as many times as possible, until they start miscarrying or producing unhealthy babies."

"Where is the program housed?"

"I don't know if it was on site with us or not. Gabe would

know. They used him a lot in it because of his looks. He's probably got more kids than-"

Val swallowed hard, never having thought of it before.

"Gabe. Sharon Baine's D2?"

"Yeah, that's him," Jason confirmed.

"Come on Jason, this guy is even more critical a piece than we realized." Agent Finn shifted his attention to Jason, who shook his head and swore.

"No." Jason's face grew cloudy, he answered an unspoken question that passed between them. It made Val wonder at the layers going on here.

"What if she was sold to another agency, or they did find a permanent placement who paid a little less because of her transgression?" Finn resumed his line of questioning.

"Cambric still owns her," Val said. "At least they did the day Jason bought me."

"How do you know that?" Finn asked, his interest piqued.

"Because I snuck a message to her. They wouldn't have even bothered if she was sold or dead."

"How did you get her this message?"

"A Cambric C1 agreed to give it to her. She does our sales prep."

"Why haven't you included this in your prior reports, Jason?" Finn asked.

"Because she didn't tell me." Jason sighed.

The interview went on like that for several hours. Val answered all of Finn's questions to the best of her ability. Details of The Agency's intake method, boarding school, educational programs and sexual training were not easy for her to discuss. When she got to a difficult part, she pushed past it for Bee.

The process was arduous and her stomach grumbled unhappily. The breakfast to-go that Jason had promised never came to fruition. At some point Agent Schipp made an appearance. He supplied them with a couple of stale sandwiches wrapped in plastic.

Val ate hers more easily than Jason who was used to only the best quality food. Gulping at a bottle of water, she passed on the offer of coffee, figuring it was probably as stale as the sandwich. By the look on Jason's face when he sipped at it, she had been right.

Finally exhausting himself, Agent Finn ended his relentless questions and began filing his notes away. Fingers flexing involuntarily, Val decided to ask a few of her own. This might be her only opportunity.

"Who do you think is at the top of this thing?" She asked.

Jason and Finn exchanged a look. Whatever it was they wanted to say, they couldn't do it with her sitting here. With a sigh, Val realized it would be necessary to give them a chance to talk. Standing, she excused herself to the restroom.

Agent Schipp escorted her there and back, but made no remarks. Upon her return, Jason had resumed his former stance. Looking out the window, he didn't turn when she took her seat.

"Sharon Baine," Finn said simply. "She's at the top."

"Gabe's Sharon?" Val was shocked. "Why? How? It doesn't make any sense."

"We can't prove it," Finn said, then added. "Yet."

She listened as he talked. The informant from ten years ago had indicated that Sharon was the mastermind behind the entire scheme. She had inherited money from her father at a young age, but blew it all trying to get her company, Work Tech, up and running. Unable to make the numbers compute, Sharon had allegedly used the last of her funds to buy out The Cambric Agency.

Though the FBI was still unable to follow the paper trail to date, the informant swore that through the use of several shell corporations Sharon Baine was the actual owner. Now straddled between two large businesses, she had turned to the illegals market.

Human trafficking, drug trafficking, kidnapping. She used Cambric to process the girls and Work Tech to launder the dirty money. Everything came out squeaky clean on the other side.

"You see," Finn concluded. "What we really need now is a subpoena for all of her business records. We need to be able to tie her to The Agency."

"But you can't get that without some evidence big enough to convince a judge, right?" Val could see where this was heading.

"We need to know the areas to target. We need copies of the records before we can request legal ones, if you know what I mean."

"Where does Bee come into this?" Val asked.

"Well, we're working two sides of the same coin here. If we can get Bee's DNA, and prove that she's Veronica, then we can show that Cambric is trafficking these girls illegally. If we get the documents that prove Sharon is the owner then-"

"Then you can connect her to the kidnappings, in effect shutting the whole thing down."

"Yes. We could get a subpoena issued to run DNA on every single captive. We could rescue all of these girls, Val."

"Yeah, all of the free ones, right?"

Her mind twisted uncomfortably. What about the rest of us? Do we mean so little?

All of this time Jason had stood detached. His hands were stuffed once more into the side pockets of his slacks, he remained uninvolved in the conversation. Something was going on with him.

"So, how do you get the documents? You need an insider or something, right?" Val asked.

As soon as the words left her mouth, the name dawned on her, clear as day.

"Gabe." Finn's voice stated what now echoed in her mind. "We need you to convince him to give Sharon up. We need you to persuade him to download all of the business documents that he possibly can on a memory drive and return it to us."

"That sounds dangerous," Val remarked, thinking aloud. "He would give up the stability of the only owner he's known. If she really is the mastermind behind all of this illegal activity, then he could be risking his life. How do you expect me to get him to-"

Out of the corner of her eye, Val saw Jason's shoulders stiffen. He had turned to watch her face. Some emotion passed over him, but in an instant, it was gone. Anger? Regret? She wasn't sure. What she did understand clearly was that they intended for her to seduce Gabe into betraying his mistress.

Finn remained silent, his eyes traveled her face closely, watching her process.

"You want me to sleep with Gabe and make him turn on Sharon."

"That's the first step," Finn acknowledged. "Then once we have the documents we want to send you back to into

Cambric with Jason. You'll have to find Bee, get a DNA sample, and sneak it back out."

It was crazy. Val huffed a breath. It was crazy *and* dangerous, but it just might work. Her mind clicked through the angles. How could a judge ignore the DNA when it was there before him? What if Bee really was Veronica? Then she would indeed be free. She could return to her family. How could Val say that she loved her almost sister, if she wasn't willing to put her life out there to save Bee?

"Jason." Val lifted her voice to him as he stood a few steps behind Finn. He gave her a look full of utter misery. "You want me to do this? You want me to seduce Gabe?"

"Yeah." He looked away from her. "We need this."

Some still small part of her splintered at that. He could give her away so effortlessly. All of this whirl of life that he had wrapped her up in over the past few months, it was only an intoxicating illusion. One that, like alcohol, left you sore and aching when it was over. No more, she thought, I don't want anymore.

"One last thing," Finn continued. "Jason has mentioned wanting to free you several times and I have to admit that I am the one that's been holding him back. If you are legally free, then it will raise suspicion within The Agency. I am afraid that they would not admit you or Jason at that point. If you are still his captive, however, then we can pitch a better story about why you want to find Bee. Do you understand?"

She only nodded. Sure, what did it matter now?

"When this is all over, Jason has assured us that you will gain your freedom. He has even provided me with a copy of the legal documents. You can be certain I will hold him to his word."

"Thank you," Val whispered, ducking her head.

Before the interview was over, an FBI tech specialist came in to take a scan of the tracker injected in her arm. They wouldn't remove it, they weren't willing to risk any potential alarm it might send back to Cambric. They were hopeful that with the scan alone, they might gain further insight into The Agency's digital database.

Suddenly, the weight of the day came crashing down upon her. Val slumped slightly in the chair, her body was numb. Everything was numb.

"We've had enough, Finn." Jason stepped close to her, his arm encircling her waist. It was the first time he had touched her since the night before. She didn't push him away, she didn't have the strength. All of her fight had fled.

Agent Schipp escorted them out of the office and down through the building to the waiting SUV. Its dark tinted windows offered welcome protection from the outside world. But what of her companion inside? How could Val hide from him?

The ride home was quiet. Night had fallen.

The vehicle made its winding, back-tracking course home. Out the windows, lights flashed by in muted reds, yellows, and whites. Her mind was a blank page, having emptied it all in front of the two men. She had poured out its scandalous contents for Finn and Jason to pick through. She hated them for it, and then again, she didn't.

Nearing Summer House, the passing lights became more infrequent. It was only when the cobblestone rumbled beneath the tires, that Val finally sighed with relief. Once inside, she and Jason sat together for dinner. Heaping plates of lasagna saturated her senses, the ricotta cheese oozed out from between saucy layers.

"Anne Marie." Jason stopped her. "Please tell the rest of the staff that you are all to go home. Take a few days off. It's been a long couple of months."

Ducking her head, Anne Marie scurried out. Val could hear the clinking of dishes and the gentle tap of closing doors. Lights that shone out onto the garden, were one by one switched off. Summer House was being shut down. All save for her and Jason, who lingered in the dim glow of the dining room, sharing a meal.

"Do you pay them when they aren't here?" Val inquired. "How does getting paid work?"

"I pay the staff a set salary. They receive the same amount whether I tell them to go home or not. It's not like that in every job, though. Mostly you get paid when you work. If you aren't working, then you aren't getting paid."

Mulling it over in her mind, Val wondered how much money she would need to buy things like free people did. How long would she have to work to earn a home, food and clothing. How much was a car? Did she need anything else?

She knew enough about the world to realize that Jason's lifestyle was far out of her reach. And Ignacio had mentioned the ranch in Wyoming. It had a place to stay included in the work arrangement. Truthfully, all she wanted was a small house, a quiet kitchen, her own bedroom maybe. But how would she get as far as Wyoming? She didn't own a car, had no license.

"Will you teach me to drive?" She asked the question cautiously, keeping her eyes fixed on the forkful of lasagna she held in waiting.

"Planning your escape?" He whispered, fingers clenching tightly around his water glass. "Of course, I'll teach you to drive. I'll even give you your own car."

"Thank you." She exhaled.

Once she got to Wyoming, maybe she could arrange to have the car sent back. She didn't want to take anything more from him than she had to.

Nearing the end of the meal, she heard the snap of his fork as he placed it carefully on the table top. When she looked up to watch him, she could tell he was fighting with himself. Shifting in his seat uncomfortably, he leaned back in his chair, then forward over the table. Elbows braced, head bent. There was something he wanted to say, but was trying not to.

It was time for her to leave, she thought. Before he said something neither of them could take back. The sound of her chair scraping against the floor seemed overly loud in the constricted space but she stood anyway.

"I think I should move back into my own room now," she said.

The words dropped from her lips to roll over him like a wave. And the moment they hit him, it was as if they had set off a bomb.

"You'll need money, too." His blue eyes pierced hers now, imploring. "I can open you an account. And a house... I can buy you a house if you refuse to live here. Is that what you want? What do you want? I can give it to you. More clothes? Another horse?"

"No, I don't want to take anything more from you." She put her hands up in defense as he skirted the table, closing the gap between them.

"All that stuff? It's nothing. It *means* nothing." He reached out tentatively, touching her arms before pulling her against him. "Please, Val, am I such a bad man?"

"You're not a bad man," she whispered, breathing into his neck.

The smell of his skin filled her senses. Holding her there,

his hands stroked up the small of her back, cruised along the swell of her hips. Desire curled tightly within her. Starting low, the feeling built and spread, reaching up to her chest, where her heart beat faster. Conflict reigned. A battle between her body and her mind.

He had said that he loved her, but never to her face. And what did she really know about being in love? If she gave herself over to him, if she stayed after he set her free, how long would it be until he grew tired of her? At some point, she would have to watch him find a suitable wife. His duty to the business and his family could not be met with her alone. She didn't think she could stay to live through that. It was better to leave and be free, not knowing.

Cupping her chin with his wide palm he pressed his lips down onto hers. Gently at first, testing for her reaction. Unable to stop it, a low moan crawled out of her throat and she returned his affection. Her hands curled in the front of his shirt. His grip grew tighter, his mouth bruising as he held on.

"We have to stop." Val broke their contact abruptly, pushing back from him.

His chest heaved, hands clenching and unclenching at his sides. Those arctic eyes didn't want to stop and they called to her.

Legs aching with unfulfilled want for him, she tried to turn and hurry away, but he caught her hand with his own. Keeping his grip firm, he strode by her, leading her past the table, and out into the living room.

"You want to move into your own room tonight?" He asked, but didn't give her time to answer.

They traversed the foyer and ascended the stairs. She didn't yank her hand from his grasp, but instead held on, her thirst for his contact was too great. At the top of the stairs he turned to the right, guiding them down the hall by moonlight cast from a nearby window. The door to her former bedroom had remained open, but once they crossed the threshold, he shut them both inside.

"There." He pulled her tightly against him once more. "We're back in your room, just like you wanted."

"Jas-"

"Tell me to leave now and I will."

Seconds ticked by, then a minute. Somehow, she just couldn't get those words to pass from her lips.

Finally, turning her head to the side, she succumbed to the inevitable. This connection they had forged was one she didn't fully understand, but it burned hot, she couldn't stop it. And that was all the answer he required. Greedily he gathered her to him, laying frantic kisses along the line of her jaw, then down her throat to her collar bone.

Inside, her need for him grew, vibrating within her. Arching her body, she brushed her chest against his, heard him groan. His fingers shot up from her waist to fumble at the buttons of her blouse. Her skirt was next. Then his clothes.

Quickly, he walked her back towards the bed. Working the clasp of her lace bra with one hand, he dipped thick fingers into the waist of her panties with the other. When they reached the mattress, her thong had slipped down low on her hips and her bra lay discarded a few feet away.

Wriggling, she lowered her panties to her ankles before stepping out of them. Eyes wide, she watched as he cupped and kissed her breasts. His tongue drew lazy circles over their swell.

One of his hands left to travel down, brushing gently between her legs. Murmuring against her skin, he entered her with his finger and hissed, she was already damp and ready for him.

Raising his head, he watched her while continuing his steady work. He kept at it until she was biting her lip and pulling him closer. Then he was pushing her down onto the bed and climbing on top of her. His mouth was on hers, hot and demanding. His hips pushed between her thighs, spreading her legs.

He slid inside, then pulled back. She gasped into his mouth and felt him smile. Their pace quickened. The weight of his body restricted her breathing, leaving her panting her pleasure into his neck. Her fingers scraped at his back and he groaned. Then she was contracting around him, calling for him, coming for him, and he was too. With a last pulse he stilled inside her, then collapsed down. Her heart beat almost painfully in her chest.

"I want you to be free," he said finally. Rolling to the side, he kept one arm thrown possessively across her waist. "But I don't want you to leave me. Is that so wrong?"

"No," she answered him. Moonlight shifted the shapes inside her room. "It's not wrong."

CHAPTER 11

OPENING HER EYES TO A POWDERY GRAY SKY, VAL TURNED OVER in bed to watch the sunrise through the windows of her bedroom. It was rare for her to wake so early here. The house was utterly quiet. Her room faced east, so the new sun's rays came inside here first, painting her walls with their warm yellow hue. She loved it. She loved witnessing it.

Outside, birds began their morning song, the notes strung together were halting and short. Jason did not stir beside her. The soft huff of his breathing was shallow and regular. She couldn't help but smile down at him when he was like this. His sleep mussed brown hair and the stubble from his five o'clock shadow were so appealing.

Stomach rumbling, she remembered there was no staff today. Getting up she padded to her closet but upon opening the door, she only found a few empty hangers. All of her things were still in Jason's room.

Leaving him behind to sleep, Val walked naked down the hall to retrieve her silky robe. She wrapped it around her body before cruising barefoot down the stairs and into the kitchen. Flipping on the lights she looked around at the over-sized industrial grade equipment and gleaming white granite countertops. She hadn't had a chance to cook since leaving The Agency and even then, her skill was limited mostly to baking.

Perusing the dark walnut cabinets, she searched for the utensils and ingredients for her old favorite, blueberry muffins. She collected everything together on the counter, arranging measuring spoons, cups, a large wooden stirring spoon, and stainless-steel mixing bowl, then switched on the oven.

Busying herself with mixing and pouring, measuring and tasting, Val lost track of the time. Maybe it had been half an hour, or perhaps a little more. Scraping the batter into the muffin tin, she slipped it easily into the hot oven before turning her attention to the coffee maker.

For a long while she studied it critically. She knew that this thing would produce the much-desired drink for her, but she had never used one, and hesitated now. That's when she heard the sound of his footsteps coming down the stairs.

A smile of anticipation filled her face, accented by a twinge of nervousness, though she couldn't say why. Maybe it was because this is how she had imagined a free life to be. Cooking in the kitchen. A wife and a husband, alone in their home together early in the morning. But that could never be them, she reminded herself.

"What smells so good?" He appeared in the doorway, hair still tousled, wearing a pair of loose sweats and faded shirt.

"Blueberry muffins," she answered, then turned back to peer at the coffee machine once more.

Coming up behind her, Jason wrapped his arms around her waist and kissed playfully at her neck. She batted at him absently, before reaching for the cord of the machine and plugging it in. He watched quietly over her shoulder as she tested buttons and lifted the lid to look inside. Finally taking pity, he laughed and pushed her gently aside to take over.

"You've never made coffee before but you can make muffins from scratch?" He asked, surveying the carnage of dishes.

"I told you Cambric trained us to make a few comfort foods. Which is mostly baked goods, I guess."

"Hey, I'm not complaining." He held up his hands, a teasing smile played on his lips.

Showing her how to remove the coffee pot, he filled it first with water. Then he poured the contents into the machine, inserted a filter, then coffee, and *then* he pushed a series of buttons.

"That's way harder than it should be," she sighed.

Shaking her head as the machine hissed and puffed, Val watched it spit drips of dark liquid from its spout. Her comment had Jason throwing his head back to laugh. Striding around the kitchen island, he slid onto a barstool to wait.

The buzz of the oven timer went off and she donned thick mittens to remove the first tray. Despite her warning glare, he leaned forward and grabbed one.

"Ow, so hot." He mouthed, blowing bits of muffin out of his mouth in tiny puffs. "But so good." He gulped finally. "So good."

"You're supposed to wait until they cool a few minutes."

"Can't wait. Not good at waiting."

He charmed her with a casual grin while reaching for another. Pausing, he blew on this one first.

They spent the next hour there together, eating muffins and sipping coffee on barstools at the kitchen island. Keeping the conversation light, they discussed his work plans for the day, and the progress of her horseback riding lessons. Although left unsaid, they both felt the pressure of yesterday's meeting with Agent Finn. They would not be able to avoid the next steps forever.

When he left to get ready for his day, she stared at the dishwashing machine for a while. There was no way that this thing was easier than the coffee pot. Rolling her shoulders, Val set about washing the entire mess in the sink. The chore was almost cathartic. She lost herself in the scrubbing and rinsing. It was just too easy to forget that this was not her kitchen, not her house, and not her husband.

Never would be.

The rest of the day passed without much notice. Jason went to work. Val went to the barn. At seven, they were back in the dining room eating takeout from one of Jason's favorite restaurants. White Styrofoam containers filled with red beans and rice, Andouille pork sausage, chicken taquitos and Cajun Jambalaya littered the dark old wood of the table.

Val had never tasted anything like it. Cambric's limited menu was focused on complete nutrition for the least possible cost. They didn't have sauces and spices and seasonings, not like this. Every bite that she took was an explosion of flavor. And this time, training be damned, she didn't leave a single thing on her plate.

"The next business vacation that Sharon will be attending starts in two weeks," Jason began, after pushing the last of his meal away.

"Where will it be?"

"Ever heard of the Virgin Islands?"

"Vaguely."

"The Hallets are hosting this one. Kiki loves St. Croix. The plan is to fly in, then charter a yacht to accommodate the entire group. It will be a bit of a long trip, about seven days before we fly home."

"I've never sailed," she said nervously.

"It's a motorized yacht with a full crew, so *you* won't be doing any actual sailing. Do you get motion sick?"

"I don't know, I've never been on a boat."

"I'll bring some medication just in case." Jason tensed visibly, his foot tapping lightly under the table. "So, I guess we should talk over our strategy."

"Alright." Val sucked in a breath.

"We need any and all business records related to Work Tech and Sharon Baine that we can get. Gabe will need to download everything he can onto this small memory drive."

Jason pulled a plastic rectangle no bigger than a quarter from his pocket and slid it across the table to Val. Picking it up she noted that it was light and easily concealed in a clutch purse or even in her bra. Laying it back down on the table with a light click, she slid it back over to Jason.

"So, you want me to seduce Gabe, then blackmail him into getting us the information?"

"Yes." He glanced away from her briefly, the muscle in his jaw ticking.

"How will I be able to do that without Sharon noticing?"

The reality of the danger involved to both Gabe and herself was becoming clear. If caught, Gabe could suffer any number of punishments. Val was only marginally at risk because of Jason's approval. A new sort of guilt began to weigh heavily on her. She was sacrificing one lifelong friend for the potential rescue of another. The choice was not an easy one to make.

"I'll keep her distracted and drunk. Late in the evening would be easier than during the day."

"What if he doesn't want me?" She thought of Bee, and the three of them together back at Cambric.

"I've seen the way he looks at you. Trust me, he'll do it."

"But, Bee-"

"To him, Bee is unreachable and you're the next best thing. This is what you've trained for right? When I first bought you, I promised myself that I would never sleep with you. That didn't last more than a month."

He rose to his feet then, pacing a few steps before turning back towards her.

"Let's not talk of this anymore tonight," she offered.

"I'll do one better. Let's not talk of it ever again. Can't we pretend a little longer? Can't we just spend the next few weeks like we did today?"

"I liked today." She reached out a hand.

"Me too." He took it.

But the next weeks were gone too fast. Before either of them realized it, they were seated on his private jet, heading for St. Croix on a six hour flight. They talked of the mild weather, the risk of hurricane season, and the large group of CEOs and political leaders that would be in attendance. Though she didn't say it out loud, Val knew that the more people who were swirling around the yacht, the easier it would be for her to find time to slip away with Gabe.

For the trip Jason had lavished her with more jewelry,

explaining that the other women would be wearing it even while swimming. Brilliant bracelets, platinum rings, dripping necklaces and dangling earrings filled her luggage.

Even now, circling her neck was the first diamond necklace he had given her. She loved it by far the best. Clutching at the cold glittering stones she leaned over, letting her forehead rest against the window.

Jason was telling her about a new series of government regulations that were slated to become law soon. He didn't like them. No one in the oil industry did. He said they would cripple production and increase costs to the consumer. So while Val was working on enticing Gabe, Jason would be cornering a politician or two on the trip. He was hopeful they would be able to put a stop to the pending legislation.

As his fingers worked across his computer, she puzzled at his ability to manage Riggs Oil while at the same time working the FBI investigation. At home he was up early and back late. Often times he still handled his tablet throughout dinner. Work consumed his waking hours, but his drive and focus were admirable. Surely the success of his company spoke for itself. And she didn't mind his physical absence from her days. The stables kept her plenty busy, plus she always had him to warm her bed at night.

Glancing out the window, her eyes opened wide. Far below them, the water was changing. Shifting from the depths of midnight blue to mix and twirl, it grew lighter in shade as they made their approach. In the distance, she could see the pop of mountainous green islands peeking up from the surrounding ocean.

Turquoise water traced around them in a breathtaking outline, its fluorescent hue separating the land from the deep-ness of the sea. It was even more beautiful than the photos Jason had shown her.

When they touched down and disembarked, a private car was waiting for them. The floral scent of the island dominated the air.

Luggage loaded, cocktail in hand, Val raised her eyebrows at Jason. He just sipped his Mai Tai and quirked a knowing smile.

"This is pure Kiki," he explained. "She really knows how to make a business trip into a party."

"I'll say." Val reclined in the seat and brought the drink to her lips.

The car took them straight to the dock where they walked along a paved roadway flanked by glittering water and enormous sleek yachts. Warm winds licked at her legs, swirling the ends of the loose gingham skirt she wore. Fitted through her hips, its black and white check pattern flared out in folds above the knee.

This was the one that Jason's sisters had picked out months ago when they were shopping boutiques. Val hadn't heard about his family since the night they left. Jason's pull with his parents must be greater than she originally suspected.

Gripping her hand to steady her, Jason and a crew member helped her to traverse the shifting plank that connected the dock to the ship. The incredible three story vessel had eighteen cabins and would be accommodating thirty-six passengers this trip. Where she had envisioned small and dark, there was only open space and light.

Vast windows lined every wall and they were left open, letting the ocean's breeze sweep through the space. Sheer blue curtains floated in the air. People laughed. Glasses clinked.

Kiki skimmed over to them, a vision of class in her pressed white dress.

Its high neckline was an unusual choice for such dynamite curves, but when she turned to escort them to the reception area, Val noted the dress plunged into a V shape, dipping down low to reveal the small of her back. Smiling to herself, Val ducked her head. That was more like the blonde bombshell she remembered.

The large central room was lined with elegant white leather sofas where men and women gathered in small groups. A pool table, the felt lining a cool blue, stood empty in one corner. A full service bar bustled with activity in another. Val kept her hand resting loosely on Jason's arm. His hand was tucked into his hip pocket casually.

For a few minutes, Kiki introduced them around to a few couples they hadn't met. There was Representative Peter Higgins and his wife, Tawny, who were in their early forties and new to the political scene. Where he was tall and broad, she was petite. An attractive man, Representative Higgins' deep brown skin and appealing chocolate eyes were filled with intelligence and easy humor.

Mrs. Higgins matched him. She shone with an outward beauty, like so many garnets that twinkled around her wrist. But after taking one look at Val, a sneer of revulsion transformed her face. It was impossible to know whether she objected to the state of captivity or the sexual aspect, perhaps both.

Val kept her face composed. This was just another turn in the glass box.

David and Carol Chen were considerably more polite. They owned an investment firm and were *extremely* interested in gaining Riggs Oil as a new client. Val did her best to listen attentively but their banking buzz words soon had her eyes drifting away. Asset management, bull market, commodities.

Hiding a sigh, Val blinked and smiled, smiled and blinked. Kiki had abandoned them to greet additional guests long ago, so Val was relieved when they finally found their way to a familiar couple. Seated comfortably on one of the leather couches, Rick and Amy Lowell rose to welcome them.

"You look stunning Amy, as usual," Jason remarked, giving her a kiss on the cheek.

"Have you seen your cabin yet?" Amy asked excitedly. "They are out of this world. I guess Clear Productions really wants to show what they can do, right?"

"Oh, they'll get a few more clients after this show." Rick nodded, clinking a champagne glass lightly against his wife's. "Did you meet Representative Higgins?"

"Yeah, but-" Jason glanced over his shoulder furtively. "I think I might have hurt our chances with him."

"Why's that?" Rick asked, suddenly concerned.

"Val," Jason explained. "Mrs. Higgins seemed pretty upset. My research didn't reveal any anti-captive history, but-"

"That's alright," Rick assured him. "We've got to push forward anyhow. We'll come up with a work around. Hey, Riggs Oil is still anti-captive right?"

"Right." Jason nodded.

Val shifted uncomfortably at this. If only Mrs. Higgins knew the truth about Jason.

"We can push that angle, then," Rick continued.

Taking a seat next to Amy, Val listened as the other woman pointed out people in the crowd. She detailed their social transgressions and highlighted their business accomplishments. The whole group was a veritable soap opera when seen through her eyes. Soon, between Amy's sarcastic descriptions and the beauty of their surroundings, Val forgot the real reason they were there.

But she wouldn't be allowed to forget for long. Her reminder came strolling up just then, dressed in cream colored slacks and a pale green button up shirt. His golden blonde hair shone in the light, his tan skin already looked sun kissed.

Val's stomach did a small flip, yearning to betray her. But years of poised practice helped her to keep her expression friendly and open. Sharon was all smiles standing next to Gabe. Val swore the woman radiated power.

"I guess we are the last aboard," Sharon remarked. "Kiki said we'll be getting underway shortly. Magnificent vessel isn't it? They call it the Moonlight View."

Murmurs of agreement were passed around. The crew had become scarce as they made ready to depart. Amy pouted then, swinging her empty glass side to side in the air. And Gabe, ever the attentive charmer, offered to grab them a round of drinks from the bar.

As she watched him, Val fought the influx of nerves that gathered in her belly. Glancing over at Jason, she noted he was the picture of cool. She resolved to get into character fast, forcefully exhaling her jitters. Just like back at The Agency with her trainer, it was time to step up.

"Feeling okay?" Amy patted her leg affectionately. "Do you get sea sick?"

"Oh." Val smiled at the woman she so wished she could call a friend. "I'm not sure, I've never been on a boat before."

"It's okay to be nervous," Amy soothed, as Gabe returned to dole out the champagne.

"Nervous?" Gabe repeated. He took a seat on the couch next to Val.

"Val's never been on a boat before," Amy offered.

"You'll love it," Gabe assured her with a wink.

Val's heart softened for her old friend. What was she about to do to him? She only hoped he wouldn't get hurt.

A quick jolt from the ship had Amy rocking roughly into Val who in turn pitched forward onto Gabe. He grinned at that, using one hand to keep his drink aloft, and the other to support her. Amy straightened herself with a subdued giggle and brushed at her dress.

Using her free hand against Gabe's knee Val too sat back against the couch. But she let her hand linger a moment longer than usual, adding pressure before withdrawing it slowly. Reaching up, she tucked a loose strand of her hair behind one ear and then flicked her eyes up to lock with Gabe.

The touch wasn't lost on him, nor was the glance. After all he understood the art of D2 work well. His eyes searched hers, questioning, unsure. She pressed her teeth down into her lower lip, then looked away.

Conversation continued around them. Amy remarked on her plans to visit the hot tub on deck later. Gabe readily agreed, with Val nodding her interest.

"There's supposed to be a little poker game tomorrow night," Sharon remarked to the group. "Any players here?"

"Rick loves that stuff." Amy slurred slightly, the drinks were sinking in.

"I'll play," Jason volunteered. Sharon beamed.

"Count me in, too," Rick agreed.

When Sharon shifted away to quiz Rick on his past poker exploits, Gabe leaned across Val to whisper with Amy. Drunk now, she gossiped with him readily, giggling at each one of his silly jokes.

All the while, well concealed by his body, Gabe let his fingers brush against Val's hip. He was testing her, wondering if what her actions told him earlier were true. The last time they had seen each other she had been upset, and would have walked away from him by now.

Val tilted her head closer and joined in the whispering. Keeping her lips close to Gabe's ear, she let her soft murmuring be his answer. After a few more moments Gabe sat back, withdrawing his hand. They were still D2s and nothing could be done in the open, or for very long.

Amy's head dropped lightly against Val's shoulder, her lashes fluttering. This attracted the attention of her husband, who rolled his eyes and made a grab for her. It was time to retire to their cabins, take a nap maybe, then get ready for dinner.

The crowd around them began to disperse. Gabe rose to escort Sharon away, leaving Val all alone. Looking around for Jason, she saw him standing at the corner bar. When she walked up beside him, he shied away from her touch, moving his arm just out of reach.

Immediately, she retracted her hand, keeping it poised at her side. It was the first time since they had slept together that he had refused her touch. She swallowed then, at once unsure and confused, but these weren't things she could communicate easily.

Instead, she waited patiently while he spoke to the bartender and gulped at his whiskey. Only when he set his empty glass on the bar and turned to go, did she follow him, keeping a step behind.

As they exited the reception area, a crew member intercepted them and escorted them to their cabin. The room was larger than she had expected, but not expansive. It had an attached bathroom with a stone basin sink and matching shower. Their luggage had already been unpacked, and was hanging neatly in the closet. Even her cosmetics bag had been set out on the counter.

The bed was a queen size with brass lamps set atop tiny night stands of dark wood. One large window ran the length of the room, its heavy blue curtains were left open to reveal the endless expanse of waves beyond.

Alone once more, Jason flopped heavily on the bed and closed his eyes. The motion of the yacht could barely be felt as it cut through the water. Taking a seat on the edge of the soft mattress, Val surveyed the ocean out the window. The sun glinting on the water was mesmerizing. She drank it in for a while.

"You're mad at me," she said finally.

"No."

She let his answer sit in the air. They both knew how false it was hanging there.

"It's just harder to watch than I thought. That's all," he admitted.

"You want me to do this," she reminded him.

"No, we just got to the point where you have to do this."

He sat up then, scrubbing a hand roughly over his face. Glancing sideways at her, he scooted close and looped his arm around her waist. She leaned her head on his shoulder. Together, they looked out at the sea.

Dinner was served at one long central table. It started inside, ran the length of the room and then ended under a covered veranda. Rich wood paneling covered the walls with intricate nautical carvings that were repeated on the surface of the table. Fine china rimmed in gold marked each place setting. Everything gleamed. Overhead, light poured down from several ornate chandeliers.

Jason and Val were seated near the middle of the table, with the Chens on one side, and the Hallets on the other. Sharon and Gabe, of course, were directly across. Jason spent the entire time deeply involved in a discussion with Carol Chen. Sharon too, soon became wrapped up in the promise of higher yields and lower risk.

That left Val stuck next to a shamelessly flirtatious Kiki and a mildly amused Gabe. Poor James Hallet was so distracted by the guests on his other side that he didn't seem to notice. This small fact only served to rev Kiki up all the more. She wanted attention. Desperately. And now, not only was her husband ignoring her, but Gabe was too.

Steak, lobster tail, baked potato, and asparagus made up the main course. All of it was divine. The lobster melted in Val's mouth, doused in butter, parmesan cheese and capers. Unbelievable explosions of flavor, paired with a crisp white wine, were followed by a bold red. She pushed her plate away early, sipping instead on her glass, and surveyed the spectacle before her.

Gabe was charming, but reserved. He kept his comments polite and above reproach, but all the while his eyes danced with good humor. Kiki was simply audacious. She had changed into a low-cut dress that left the swell of her breasts heaving with each breath she took. Finally thinking she got what she was after, Kiki rose from the table and excused herself to the restroom. Her husband nodded vaguely at her as she patted his arm to go.

Val remained silent.

As she watched, Gabe glanced briefly at Sharon, who shook her head *no* almost imperceptibly. So, it was true then. She had ordered Gabe to seduce Kiki previously. And now for some reason, his attentions were being withheld. Frowning, Val became concerned that her ability to lure Gabe into bed might be more challenging than she had originally thought. It would depend on how beholden he was to his mistress.

"No bathroom this time?" Val asked quietly when she was sure Sharon's attention was diverted.

"Nope. I've got all the company I want right here," Gabe replied.

Out of the corner of her eye, Val saw Jason flinch, he had been listening after all. Lifting his glass to signal the waiter, Jason motioned for more wine. Amy's words from a few months ago crossed her mind. *We all have our secrets. We all do what we have to in order to survive.* Val guessed that Jason would be surviving on alcohol tonight.

Kiki returned a few minutes later and sat in a huff, refusing to look at Gabe. Instead, she spoke too loudly to Val. Raising her voice, she made sure others knew what a good time she was having. Thankfully, Val didn't have to participate much in the conversation. She only had to utter the occasional *yes* and Kiki would take over.

As the meal wound down, people rose from the table and spread throughout the yacht. A game of pool began on the lower level. Music thrummed out by the spa on the front deck. People drank profusely, lounged on sofas, and reclined in chairs that dotted the decks of the ship.

Rising with David Chen, Jason moved outside to smoke a cigar. He didn't look back at Val as he left. Sharon took Gabe's arm next, leading him away. This left Val to comfort a very drunk Kiki who sat staring forlornly into her glass.

Eventually, Amy made her way over to help. Between the two of them they were able to get Kiki upright and staggering on four-inch heels towards her cabin. Seeing the spectacle, a crew member came over to assist. Working together they returned her to her room and tucked her safely into bed.

"I'm calling it a night," Amy commented.

"Me, too." Val nodded as they stood over Kiki, listening to her steady snore.

CHAPTER 12

IN THE MIDDLE OF THE NIGHT VAL HEARD JASON stumble into their room and fall drunkenly into bed. He had ignored her throughout dinner and left without a backwards glance. Maybe she was feeling a bit bitter but she didn't move to undress him, let alone tuck him in. Rolling away from him, she let herself drift back to sleep, listening to the sound of the waves on the other side of the window.

Breakfast the next morning was served buffet style. Silver dishes overflowing with waffles, pancakes, sausage, bacon, scrambled eggs, hash browns, and bagels were on display. There were bowls of fresh fruit, an array of cereals, coffee, orange juice and of course mimosas. Jason donned sunglasses, as did more than half of the guests milling about the deck.

He sipped conservatively at a mimosa and nibbled on a piece of crispy bacon. Val smiled to herself. Serves him right, she thought. She hadn't seen him that drunk, maybe ever.

Kiki had yet to make an appearance, but James Hallet was in high spirits. They had a group of scuba divers going out today, and he was among them. The plan was to drop anchor on a dive spot, then take small boats of guests to a nearby island where they would spend the day on the white sandy beach. A picnic lunch was to be served, and there was even a small local bar right on the water.

Already dressed in her sheer cover up and emerald green bikini, Val was looking forward to a day spent on the sand. Leaning against the rail, she stared out at the island that lay in front of them. Its lush hillsides were not as mountainous as that of St. Croix. This was a small neighboring island, with a strip of inviting beach that ran along its curving shoreline.

The crew busied themselves readying the shore boats and grouping together the scuba party. Val watched them with interest. It looked like Sharon was diving, too. That woman didn't let any event go by that she wasn't a part of.

As always, Val felt Gabe's approach long before she saw him. Call it instinct or familiarity. He came up beside her and leaned his back against the rail. As she gazed out at the water, he looked into the ship. Or at least that's what someone would think if they were watching.

"How's our pal Kiki?" He asked.

"Poor thing is still passed out I assume," Val answered, not looking over at him.

"So, what gives, Val?"

"What do you mean?"

"You know what I mean. Tired of our playboy already?"

"Does it matter?" She asked.

"It's me Val, of course it matters." He kept his voice low, but looked straight ahead, chewing nonchalantly on a tooth pick.

"I guess I just miss you," she said honestly, but not the way she implied it.

At this he exhaled, teeth still clenched around the toothpick. He stood upright then, letting his arms hang casually at his sides. Reaching out with one hand, he brushed at her hip with his fingertips. A dull ache bloomed within her body as she stirred in response to him.

Regardless of how her heart might feel, she and Gabe had been conditioned their whole lives together. Where he touched, her body wanted more. Purposefully, she bit her lip and shifted her leg, leaning into him for a split second before retreating. *The answer is yes, Gabe.* She spoke with her body, the only way she could communicate out here.

Turning around, he faced the rail next to her and braced his elbows against it. In silence, they watched the shore boats, the crew, the sparkling water, and the sand.

"I miss you too, Val," he murmured quietly before strolling away. "I miss you, too."

The short ride to the beach was exciting. Val enjoyed the spray of ocean water on her face, and the warmth of the sand spreading beneath her toes when they arrived. Plush towels were doled out generously before Amy led their little group down the shoreline to select a cabana lounger. The shade overhead was made of woven palm leaf material.

While Amy situated herself in the sun, Rick made the walk to the beachside bar. Removing his white polo shirt, Jason tossed it on the daybed, then grabbed Val's hand.

"Let's go for a swim," he said.

Hesitating at the water's edge, Val stuck in a tentative toe while Jason took a few running steps and dove in. The water was delightfully warm and she soon waded in to follow him. When he surfaced, the water dripped from his shoulders, ran down his muscled arms and over his toned chest. Shaking his head, the spray from his hair splattered her body. He cracked up at her squeal of protest before encircling her in his arms and holding her body against his.

"Feeling better?" She asked.

"Yes." He sighed. "The water has healing powers. I'm sure I heard that somewhere."

Bobbing together for a while they watched as Kiki finally made an appearance. She was stunning in her tiny black sequin bikini and positively glowed now that Gabe walked alongside her. They stopped every few feet to speak with various guests on their meandering journey towards Amy and Rick in the cabana. Watching them, you could almost forget that it was James Hallet's money that had provided all of this.

As they drew closer, Val felt Jason pull her in tighter, kissing her shoulders as they peeked up from the water. Then all at once he released her. Making no comment, he took off for a swim. Her heart ached after him, but she knew that she had to let him go.

From up on the beach, Kiki spotted Val and waved excitedly. She took a seat beside Amy whose prone body was positioned to get the optimum amount of sun. Waving back, Val had to smile. She really was a nice woman, except for the cheating part of course.

After a bit of obvious convincing, Gabe and Rick walked Kiki down to the water. Amy staunchly refused. Without her, the rest of them joined Val in the shallows.

"This beach thing isn't really my deal," complained Rick half-heartedly as he sipped a rum and Coke.

"But the drinking thing is," Gabe countered, and had Rick shrugging with a sly smile playing on his lips.

Careful not to get her blonde locks wet, Kiki shimmied

and dipped, making sure the water poured off her body in just the right way. The men largely ignored her, which drove Kiki to even more demonstrative measures.

Finally taking pity, Val intervened, pulling Kiki out of the water to sit with her in the warmth of the sand. The fine white grains stuck to her wet skin and had Val rolling the substance between her fingers in fascination. Beside her, Kiki whispered her angst mixed up with desire. The last two trips Gabe had cut things off with her, refusing to continue on in their affair. She was distraught and needy, unsure of what to do to renew his affections.

Val tried her best to talk Kiki off the ledge. It was hard to explain to a free person the way a D2 handled sex. When you are raised to provide it on command, there is an emotional separation that forms. For a D2, sex was supposed to be just another skill or game, like playing tennis. It was a physical act that you could perform without caring too much about the other person involved.

Kiki just couldn't make the connection, pouting as Gabe and Rick left the water to join Jason at the bar. After a while, Kiki left Val to go lay beside Amy, who refused to leave her spot. Val could hear her sigh as Kiki blubbered to a new ear that would listen.

Returning her gaze to the sea, Val marveled at the sleek white yacht as it towered over the water. Around it, the crystal ocean had turned a miraculous shade of vibrant blue that Val couldn't quite name. Who knew such a stunning place existed?

Just then, a shadow passed over her and came to a stop, covering Val's legs with a single slash of shade. Lifting a hand to block the sun, Val tilted her face up to survey the at once beautiful and severe Tawny Higgins.

"May I sit with you?" She asked. Val did her best not to let her mouth hang open in shock.

"Of course, Mrs. Higgins, please sit," Val responded.

"Call me Tawny. Val, right?" Her voice was rather subdued now, almost kind. It was a stark contrast to yesterday's introduction.

"How are you enjoying the beach?" Val asked.

"Oh, it's great. You?"

"It's lovely."

Val waited while Tawny inhaled, then pursed her lips.

"Listen, I wanted to apologize to you," she said. "I didn't mean to have such a strong reaction. It's not you, just the idea of captivity that bothers me."

Val nodded her head, but offered nothing in return. These were murky waters they were entering. She had been coached time and again at The Agency not to verbalize any distaste for the industry.

"May I ask you a few questions? I promise it will stay between us," Tawny ventured.

Yeah right, Val thought, but nodded once more.

"What do you think of Jason Riggs?"

This got Val's attention. Jason needed Representative Higgins' help to protect his family's business. Maybe Val could assist after all.

"He is a wonderful man, truly." Val looked steadily into Tawny's eyes, letting the truth show in them.

"Do you think that he intends to purchase additional captives? Do you think he is going to turn Riggs Oil into a captive-work business?"

"He would never do that," Val assured her.

"So, you're the only one?" Tawny pressed.

"I'm the only one."

"Do you ever wish to be free?"

"No captive of Cambric Agency ever wants to be free," Gabe announced from behind them.

Both women jumped, they hadn't heard him come up. Reaching down he handed them each a drink, then crouched in the sand. His answer was perfect agency speech. They were the words she *should* have said. Val's insides summersaulted.

"You would never wish to be free of Sharon Baine?" Tawny appraised him, eyebrow raised in question.

"Never." Gabe's face remained calm and pleasant. No one would know if his true feelings were different. "And I know that Val feels the same way about her owner. We have all of our needs met right here. Look around, who could hope for a better life?"

"That's right," Val agreed, looking away from Tawny's searching eyes. "I don't know of any captive who would seek to be a free person. Our fulfillment comes in the pleasure we provide to our owner."

"Of course," Tawny said finally and reaching out a hand, Gabe stood to help her up.

Once Mrs. Higgins had retreated far enough down the beach, Gabe turned on Val. Lowering himself to her level, he shook his head slightly.

"What the hell are you doing?" He was whisper quiet.

"Jason needs the Higgins, I was just-"

"Just. Stop. Are you trying to get yourself hurt?" Gabe was positively boiling with anger. "You think she's going to help Jason? You think she's going to help you? No. She's going to slam Jason for buying you, probably publicly. Then what's he going to do you, huh? Slap you around? Send you back to Cambric? We both know what happens to you then."

"I'm sorry." Val bit back tears. "I forgot myself."

"Damn right you forgot yourself." Gabe glanced around quickly, and then resumed. "I already lost Bee. Damn if I'm going to let you go, too."

Rising to his feet, Gabe walked casually off down the beach like nothing had happened. Val wiped at her tears, marveling at Gabe's ability to play the game. He was right. Of course he was right. This was a dangerous world they found themselves in. Much more complicated and serious than she had ever thought possible.

Getting up, she turned back to the cabana and froze. Jason was watching her. He sat propped up next to Amy who hummed happily into the air, lying on her back now, cooking slowly. Taking a seat with them, Val listened as Amy recounted Kiki's one too many margaritas. Rick had been forced to escort her back to the yacht.

After several more minutes of basking, Amy excused herself to find the ladies room, leaving Jason and Val alone.

"What did he say to you?" Jason asked.

"I don't want to talk about it."

"Planning your little tryst?" His voice took on an edge.

"Stop it, Jason," she warned.

"Is that why he's not with poor Kiki anymore? He's got a shot at you now?"

"I don't know why he cut things off with Kiki, and it doesn't work like that anyway," she hissed at him.

"How exactly does it work? You guys can just screw as many people as possible and not care? Is that it?"

He was saying these things now out of hurt, she tried to remind herself, but she was raw too, and couldn't help but snap back.

"That's right. What do you think most D2s are bought for?

You think Gabe even knows how many women he's been with? I can assure you that he does not."

"My God, Val, how do you do it?" Face filling with disgust, Jason shoved up and stormed off.

Crawling into the far shade of the cabana, Val covered her face with a towel and held back tears. When Amy returned, she just rubbed comfortingly at Val's back. She asked no questions and Val was grateful. They spent the rest of the day lost in silence, lying in the sunshine together.

Back on the ship, Val showered before dinner. Jason had already dressed and left their room, he wasn't speaking to her. Val let the water clean the salt from her hair before lathering in fragrant shampoo and conditioner. Taking her time, she made sure to shave. The dress she would wear tonight revealed nearly every inch of her legs.

Standing over the stone basin sink, she carefully styled her hair. Soft curls held in place with ample spray, cascaded down her back. Opening the small safe in their room, Val picked through bits of precious stones strung along chains of white gold. When done, her wrists glittered with sapphire laden brackets. Around her neck looped strands of black pearls.

The short midnight blue dress clung through her sides and waist, flaring out in soft pleats of chiffon to stop haltingly, barely covering her butt cheeks. Slipping into three-inch heels, she surveyed herself in the bathroom mirror. No matter how she had felt today, tonight she would show them what she was capable of.

Before leaving the room, she grabbed her clutch and slipped the memory drive inside, just in case.

Climbing the short flight of stairs to the middle deck, Val joined the mass of people already there. Drinks in hand, they were enjoying a live band before the meal was served. A waiter offered her a glass of chardonnay which she took, pressing her crimson lips against the rim until it left a mark. Amy approached her then with a triumphant smile.

"That's my girl," she whispered into Val's ear. "I don't know *what* is going on with Jason, but sometimes a girl has to remind a man just what he's dealing with."

Arms linked, they paced companionably around the edge of the room. Eyes shifted to look at them as they passed. Val's chin tipped up a notch higher. She may have felt confident before, but when James Hallet came over to ask for a dance she knew she'd hit her mark.

A space cleared in the center of the room. James swayed along with her, spreading a firm hand over the small of her back. He was an excellent dancer. She enjoyed his style as he smoothly twirled her out, then gathered her back in close.

Other couples were inspired to join as James spoke charmingly in her ear, telling her how beautiful she looked.

"If you weren't owned by someone else I'd be trying real hard to make you my fourth wife," he told her slyly. Her head tilted back in an easy laugh.

When the song was over James returned her to Jason. He had been watching them from a distance, his back propped against the corner bar. A now familiar glass of whiskey was clutched loosely in his hand.

"Ever considered sharing?" James teased lightly. "I've got money to spare."

"Not a chance, Hallet." Jason joked.

He kept the edge of emotion from his voice, but Val saw the discomfort layered in his eyes. When James faded back into the crowd, Jason turned away from Val and asked the bartender for a refill. She was just about to leave, when he spoke.

"You're going to put poor Kiki out of a job," he chided under his breath.

"Maybe we all just need a little reminder of what position we're in," she countered, frustrated at her own situation.

"Yeah." Jason swirled his glass, sending the ice cubes to clinking. "Maybe."

Turning to her, he took her hand and pulled her out onto the floor. With his glass still sitting on the bar, his hands traveled boldly over her body as they swayed to the music. His purpose was clear. This belongs to me, he told them without saying it.

Keeping her hands on his chest, Val didn't fight him as he drew her in close, one hand firm in the middle of her back. He let the other stroke seductively down her hip until it tugged teasingly at the edge of her dress. Lifting the hem ever so slightly, he revealed even more of her leg.

His body was taut, like a drawn bow, filled with unspent energy. The breathing in her ear, however, was controlled. Over his shoulder, she saw Gabe standing with Sharon. Ever the picture of relaxation, this was his element. He raised his glass to her as she made eye contact... kept it.

Something powerful stirred within her then. Val returned his knowing smile, then looked away, pressing her cheek against Jason's shoulder. When the song was over Jason leaned into her for an extra beat.

"I could take you back to my room right now." He exhaled into her ear.

She ached silently in response before speaking.

"You could," she acknowledged.

He released her then and strode off towards the bar alone.

⌇

The seating arrangement at dinner had shifted again. Tonight, Val was next to James Hallet, who turned his back on his wife and flirted shamelessly. Now it was Kiki's turn to be nervous. Lamely, she vied for his attention without much success. Perhaps she had remembered that her position as hostess on this yacht was not the doing of her lover, but of her powerful husband. Val hoped for her friend's sake that she wasn't too late.

Representative and Mrs. Higgins were positioned directly across from Jason. Their conversation began politely enough, with Tawny forgoing any probing questions in front of so many witnesses. Still, Val felt her measured gaze throughout the dinner. It was obvious that she had much more to say.

Without Gabe to distract him, Jason gradually came back to himself. He talked companionably with Representative Higgins who asked to be called by his first name, Peter. The two seemed to have a lot in common. Both graduated from Duke University, both were first sons of large families, and both owned race horses.

Towards the end of the meal Jason absentmindedly let his hand rest on Val's thigh. The reminder of a once easy connection struck at her heart, making her question what they were doing. That question ended abruptly, however, along with dinner.

Sharon made her way over to remind Jason of his promise to play in the poker game. Mr. Chen and Rick suggested a smoke on the upper deck first. Jason rose to go, taking his gentle touch with him. His former standoffishness returned full force.

"Amy, Val." Sharon leaned over the table in invitation. "Would you ladies like to play, too?"

Stopping short, protests arose from the men nearby who grumbled about maintaining a serious game. Sharon waved them off with a flick of her jeweled wrist.

"Nonsense." She laughed at them. "What are you worried about Rick? That Amy will be better than you?"

"I'm worried that you'll take all her money," Rick responded. "Which is actually *my* money."

"Sorry, but I don't know how to play," Val interjected.

"Oh, Gabe is a fantastic teacher," Sharon countered. "He'd be happy to sit with you! Won't you, Dear?"

"Absolutely." Gabe grinned over Sharon's shoulder as he popped an olive into his mouth.

Jason remained silent, watching the exchange. He kept his face neutral, hands shoved into the pockets of his beige slacks. Maybe no one else noticed the way his jaw clenched, but Val did.

"I'd love to play a round or two." Amy glared in mock anger at Rick. "Thank you for including me, Sharon."

Rick rolled his eyes and then made a big show of reaching into his pocket to shell out hundred dollar bills into his wife's open palm.

The group made their way down a level from the expansive dining hall to the reception area. A long poker table had been set up with several other people gathered around it already, sipping cocktails and puffing on cigars.

Sharon counted in ten players, with Gabe and Val grouped as one. He positioned his chair just behind her at the table so he could read her cards and whisper instruction in her ear.

Sharon sat on Val's left, and Amy on her right. Pointedly, Jason chose a spot on the far end of the table.

When the crew member who doubled as a dealer flipped out the first round of cards, Gabe showed Val how to hold them, checking what she had without anyone else seeing. Quietly, he explained how the betting system worked and talked about the possible reasons why each person would bet the way they did.

Soon she forgot herself in the fun of the game. Amy was throwing Rick's money away with reckless abandon and he groaned audibly before turning to goad Sharon. Val pulled up a pair of Kings that had Gabe breathing in her ear to keep her face plain. It was a simple request after so many years of practice. She was back in the display box once more, not reacting to gestures, stares or requests.

Another round of bets had some folding. Gabe urged her to match bets, but not exceed. When the flop came, another King appeared. Gabe remained silent. She knew what to do. They worked together until only she and Carol Chen remained. The final round of betting commenced.

Through the opening in her high-backed chair, Gabe placed the tips of his fingers against her lower back. In this way, he applied pressure to encourage more betting, and withdrew to signal an end. When the river card was exposed, Carol threw her pair of Aces in defeat.

Val's three Kings took the pot, an amount of which she hadn't bothered to count. Erupting in cheers of excitement the other players at the table congratulated Val on her first win. Smiling broadly, she scooped up the chips and brought them in towards her. Gabe quietly helped her to stack them as she beamed.

"Come now," Sharon teased. "My Gabe was helping you somehow. Tell us!"

"I didn't say a thing," he protested.

"I know from experience you don't have to use your mouth to get your point across," Sharon commented, and had every woman at the table hooting in delight.

Val laughed along too, caught up in the banter. But when her eyes settled on Jason, his jaw clenched and he averted his gaze. Suddenly, she didn't want to play anymore.

Turning to Gabe, she asked him to take her place. He nodded happily for everyone to see, but let his hand travel up her thigh beneath table. Giving her a gentle squeeze, he released her before he stood to let her by.

"Well, I'm all out of money," Amy complained, and rose to join Val who retreated to a plush leather sofa that sat against the wall only a few feet away.

Over the next several hours, Val and Amy drank while player after player fell to defeat. Eventually, Gabe came over to join them. Sitting in between the two women he put an arm around the shoulders of each. Rick, Sharon, both Chens and Jason were still heavily into the game. Thousands of dollars in chips shifted possession with each hand.

At one point, Kiki and James made an appearance. She clung to her husband, not leaving his side as he walked around, engaging in conversation with the remaining players. Rick was the next to lose out. He didn't linger long before hauling Amy back to their room.

For a bit longer Gabe and Val sat. He retracted his arm, but kept the closeness, his leg pressed along the length of hers. From time to time he would lean in to whisper to her, but never for very long. He was an expert at this game of walking the line of impropriety. With every glancing touch, she felt him kindle desire within her. Biting her lip, she finally nudged him with her shoulder, muttering for him to back up under her breath.

"What's the matter, Val?" His voice barely audible through the relaxed look of boredom that framed his face.

"You're driving me crazy." She glanced down, feigning indifference.

"Just say the word, and I'll do more than that." Giving up the requested space, he shifted his body away from her to recline.

Standing, Val yawned, covering her mouth prettily. Making her excuses to the room, she headed for the exit. Just inside the doorway, she turned and caught Gabe's eye. He had been watching from his laid-back pose on the sofa.

One look was all she needed to give him before disappearing down the stairs toward her bedroom. She didn't know what he would say to the room, if anything at all, but she knew he would find his way down to her.

Pacing nervously, Val waited. Some ten minutes later, the door handle jiggled and Gabe stepped inside, twisting the lock behind him. They stood there alone for a moment, just looking at one another from across the room.

"Is this really happening?" Gabe asked. "Are we actually alone in a room together?"

"Yes." She exhaled.

He crossed to her quickly, but then stopped short. Reaching out a single hand he hesitated before tracing his fingers along the side of her face. His eyes focused on where his hand brushed her skin, traveling down her neck then out over her shoulder.

Taking a thin dress strap in hand, he slipped it off to droop loosely. She trembled slightly under his touch. Longing worked its way down to curl just below her belly.

"Remember all those weeks of watching each other through glass?" He asked, not meeting her eyes.

Instead his gaze followed the path of his hand down the length of her dress to tickle against her bare thigh. She swallowed down her jumping nerves. He glanced up briefly at her, testing to make sure his next move was okay.

Using both hands now, he worked up her legs underneath her dress. Curling his fingers into the tiny straps of her lace thong, she felt her need quicken. Pulling gently, he tugged her panties down. Slowly scooting them off of her hips, over her thighs and finally letting go, they fell to her ankles where she stepped out.

"Every time your trainer came for you-" He breathed into her hair now as he drew her close. Wrapping his arms around her body, he trapped her in an intimate embrace. "I wanted to murder him. Every time I had to hear him with you… I swear, if I ever see that man again, I *will* kill him."

"Shhh." She soothed, bringing her hands to cup his face. "He never hurt me, it's okay."

Gradually she worked to undo the white buttons of his shirt, revealing his toned chest and smooth tan skin just underneath. She trailed kisses along his chest until he blew out a breath.

Shrugging out of his shirt, he tossed it onto the bed. She closed her eyes and let him kiss her. He explored her mouth with his gently probing tongue. In her mind, she almost forgot she wasn't with Jason. Almost.

When Gabe pulled back to look at her, she avoided his searching eyes, not wanting him to see her guilt. Instead she threaded her fingers into his belt, casually working to undo the buckle.

"Wait, Val." Voice raspy, he moved to still her hands. "Look at me."

Dropping hastily to her knees, she continued to tug at the front of his trousers. Buckle open, button undone, he let her unzip him, but then backed a step away.

"Val, stop," he commanded, and reached to pull her up to standing. "This is text book training. I need you to look at me. I need you to know who you're doing this with."

When she brought her eyes up to lock with his, he searched her face carefully. She couldn't hide from him, this man she had known all her life.

"You don't want to do this," he said finally. "You're in love with him, aren't you? Val, why are we here?"

"What if I told you there was a way for us to get Bee back?" She opened her eyes wide, letting him see the truth of possibility there.

Running his fingers through his hair he rotated away from her. Knowing him well, she gave him time to think. When he came back around he was ready to hear what she had to say. She grabbed his hands and pulled him down to sit next to her on the bed. That's when she let the tale of her last few months unwind before him.

Sparing no details, she explained Jason's purchase, the photo of Bee, and the FBI investigation into Veronica Durand. He peppered her with questions that she answered as best she could. Seething with anger at Sharon's involvement, he agreed to get all of the files that he could. Val passed him the memory card and watched him shove the tiny plastic rectangle into his pocket.

Wrapping her arms around him, they clung to one another. Two last soldiers in a small band of three, their quest for the missing member grew more perilous by the minute. Hanging on, they breathed together, never having come so close to getting Bee back than at this moment.

The slide of the door lock sliced through the quiet. Not a split second later, the door swung violently open, causing them to jump.

Their arms still entangled, Val watched Jason enter the room and slam the door shut behind him.

CHAPTER 13

"Done yet?" Jason smoldered, his face full of dark misery.

Shooting to her feet, Val disentangled herself from Gabe. Jason's furious eyes filled themselves with her, making her realize how she must look. Grabbing at her dress strap she pushed it back up on her shoulder. His gaze left her and traveled to the floor where they came to rest on the crumpled panties that lay discarded there.

"Jason, we were just-"

"Yeah, we're all finished up." Gabe spoke out, not letting Val finish with her excuses.

Rising from the bed, he shrugged into his shirt, fingers working at the buttons.

"I'll get the files you want, but I'm going to need a few more things first."

"Gabe!" Whirling to face him, Val stopped short. Her old friend shot her a look that had her mouth snapping shut. This was one of his cons, like back at Cambric.

"What else do you want?" Jason took the bait.

"I want immunity from all of the blackmail schemes that Sharon has me tied up in."

"Okay." Jason gritted his teeth.

"I want five million dollars. That's *my* sale price, in one of those fancy offshore accounts that you rich bastards use to hide money."

"Done." Jason nodded.

"*And*, I want my freedom."

Finished with the buttons, Gabe began to tuck his shirt into his pants. Jason's eyes darted to the hanging belt and open fly. Pausing for a moment, Gabe watched him, then seemed to reconsider.

"One last thing," he said.

"The list is getting pretty long," Jason countered.

"I want Val again… twice." Gabe stood straighter. Facing Jason, he dared him to disagree.

Don't agree to it. The words were strained but locked firmly inside Val's mind. She wanted to intervene. Wanted to fly to Jason and tell him that they hadn't slept together. Wanted to warn him that Gabe was testing him, but outwardly she remained perfectly still.

More than all of that, Val wanted to know the truth. What would Jason do with her if she really had slept with Gabe, as he had commanded? In limbo, she awaited his decision.

Rotating away from them both, Jason's shoulders tensed. Seconds dragged like hours in the atmosphere, thick with tension. Purposefully, his fists clenched, then at once relaxed limply at his sides. She never heard a verbal response from him, only saw his quick nod of acceptance.

"This is your hero, Val?" Gabe sneered, finished with his dressing. "You're actually in love with this piece of shit?"

Spinning back around, Jason closed the distance between

them and gripped Gabe's shirt in both fists. Gabe didn't flinch. Holding eye contact he stood his ground, unafraid. It was only his training that kept his arms at his sides.

"What?" Gabe taunted. "You hit guys for telling the truth? You get yourself into a tight spot with this investigation and your first instinct is to whore her out. You're nothing but a glorified pimp. She might as well be back at The Agency."

"Gabe, stop!" Val cried.

"No." Gabe kept his eyes trained on Jason. "Let him suffer. Let this rich prick see what it feels like to wonder what another man did with his woman. That's right. I want you to picture everything I did to her. I want you to hear what she sounded like as she begged me for more."

On the edge, Jason yanked at Gabe's shirt collar, bringing their faces within inches. Hovering there, they puffed out adrenaline with each breath. But Gabe couldn't return to his mistress with a black eye, it would ruin everything they had accomplished thus far.

Haltingly, Jason forced himself to let go. Cocky victory had Gabe brushing at his shirt to smooth it. With a final shining smile, he strode out the door.

Alone in the room now, Val's pulse smoothed out. It hadn't come to blows after all. The plan would move forward like before. Approaching Jason cautiously, she examined the side of his face. Stress deepened every line.

She reached out to touch his arm, but he jerked angrily away. A part of her longed to tell him the truth, put an end to his suffering. But another part, the new part, tripped over what Gabe had said.

Jason had just sold her to another man, again. This time he had done it without consulting her. It didn't matter the things he had said to her in the past. Right now he had just traded her out. Betrayal gnawed at her insides. Not wanting him to see her reaction, she hurried her steps to their bathroom.

She could feel his presence like a shadow at her back. When she slipped through the doorway, he came after her. Closing them inside, he grabbed her arms, pushing her back against the sink. Their bodies filled the narrow space. His breathing was short, ragged.

Those arctic eyes brimmed with agony. She knew he pictured her as Gabe had suggested, entwined passionately with another lover. Whatever anger she had built against him softened at the scrutiny of his pain.

Reaching up, she stroked her hands down the sides of his face, ran her thumbs comfortingly across his cheeks. Pulling his face close to hers, she pressed red lips to his, seeking to soothe his hurt along with her own.

Her touch crushed through the barrier of restraint he had worked hard to maintain. Hot and clutching, his hand slid up her thigh. When his finger entered her, she gasped. Already wet from hours of teasing, she froze, feeling him work within her.

Rubbing her expertly with his thumb, he curled his finger in and then out. Unable to fight her inner aching response, she moaned lowly, looking away from his fascinated stare.

Close to climax now she arched to meet him, but he withdrew his hand at the last moment and turned her roughly around. Bending her down over the sink he hiked up her dress and fumbled with his pants. Though she held still for him, he spread one hand over the back of her neck. The side of her face rested against the cool of the mirror above the sink.

Pushing himself inside of her she could hear him bite back a groan. His free hand was a weight, laying firmly on the small of her back. He held her down, and pumped slowly at first, then faster. Thick strokes sent waves of sensation throughout her body. Whimpering her pleasure, she bit her lip and closed her eyes.

"Who's inside of you now?" He panted his desperation close to her ear.

"You are." She gasped as he pushed even harder.

"Open your eyes," he demanded.

When she did, he eased the hold on her neck just enough for her to shift, catching his reflection in the mirror. Forehead held against the glass, she cried out, clenching around him in tight waves. Not bothering to pull back, he released himself inside her, following her over the edge.

Immediately, he stepped back to catch his breath, relinquishing his hold on her body. She watched his movements in the mirror, recognizing his expression pinched tightly with temper. Her hands braced against the stone sink. He said nothing.

Wiping at himself with a hand towel, Jason tossed it carelessly onto the counter. When she reached for it, he shook his head.

"I want you to feel me dripping down your thighs," he told her. "We're going back out to finish my poker game."

Straightening, she smoothed at the material of her dress. If she felt shock at his treatment of her, it was only because it came from Jason. The act and request themselves were not outside of her background. It didn't bother her the way it might a free woman.

Complying with his order, she walked past her thong still discarded on the floor and trailed him obediently back to the game room. He returned to his seat at the table as if nothing were amiss.

The players had been reduced to Sharon and Mr. Chen. Val felt Gabe's presence hover on the outskirts of her vision, but she dare not look over at him now. Standing demurely behind Jason, she observed him win round after round, clearing Sharon easily of her money. That left Mr. Chen.

The two men spent several rounds folding bad cards, testing one another on relatively small pots. Sharon fluttered excitedly. She loved competition, announcing it to the remaining few observers. Val noticed that she also loved to talk.

"Aren't you dead on your feet, Val?" Sharon asked. "Please, go have a seat on the couch with my Gabe. He'll get you another drink."

Val hesitated, awaiting direction from Jason. She knew that he wanted to force her to remain standing next to him, but if he refused Sharon's offer, it might raise suspicion. Quickly he ducked his head in agreement and resumed play. Val smiled her thanks to Sharon who waved her away.

When Val approached Gabe and took a seat next to him, she felt the cool leather beneath her. They sat in silence for a beat before Gabe rose to fetch her a drink. The martini that dangled in front of her vision was a lifeline. She took it shakily, lips sipping hungrily at the bite of liquor.

"I'm sorry." Gabe whispered in her ear, leaning back to avoid notice. "Like always, my actions have been taken out on you. I shouldn't have taunted him."

"It's okay." She exhaled. Gulping now, she polished off the martini. "Nothing I haven't experienced before."

"Did he hurt you?" Gabe questioned, taking her empty glass.

"No, but he's upset." She gestured for Gabe to bring her another, which he did.

Fingers clutching the fresh drink, she sucked on an olive, trying to make this one last.

"He's trying to erase me." Gabe attempted to hold back his expression of triumph. "I'm sorry that you're enduring it, but that prick seriously needs this."

"Fuck you, Gabe." She shoved the now empty glass at him.

"Gladly. Twice more remember?" He chuckled conspiratorially. "Seriously though, you need to slow down on the drinks. I'm going to get you a water."

"Bring me a water, and I'll cut you," she countered.

They both cracked up. This time it was loud enough to attract notice.

Sharon swaggered over. Half-crocked herself, she wedged down in between them. With a flick of her wrist she had Gabe jumping to fetch another round. Val kept herself easy and unassuming, though her insides rolled at the woman beside her. Sharon didn't feel threatened in any way by Val, and it showed.

By the time Jason claimed victory at the poker table, the two women could hardly see. As he supported a sagging Sharon under one arm, Gabe offered to help tuck Val into bed. Flipping Gabe the bird, Jason dragged Val off by himself.

When they reached their cabin, she collapsed on the mattress. The room spun in lazy rotations around her. After a few moments, her vision blurred and she passed out.

The following morning, or was it afternoon, greeted her with a pounding headache and roiled stomach. Jason was long gone. As she bent to vomit repeatedly in the toilet, Val noticed that she was still wearing her dress from the night before. It took all of her strength to creep up the side of the bathroom sink and greedily gulp water straight from the tap.

Melting back onto the floor, she hugged the cold tile against her hot face. Absorbing its calming energy, she let herself drift in and out of sleep.

The next time she woke it was to the bubbling sounds of Amy and Kiki sweeping into the room. Together, the women clucked and hovered, helping her to get up and into the shower.

"I could just strangle that man," Amy shouted through the shower door. "Jason told us you were fine, just sleeping the day away."

"Yeah," Kiki added, as she distractedly perused Val's makeup bag. The clicking of eye shadow cases snapped in the air.

"Thanks ladies," Val muttered. Her head was much improved, but her stomach had turned ravenous.

After slipping into a blue swimsuit with matching crochet coverup, Val and the women wandered up onto the middle deck. Choosing three lounge chairs, they sat and looked out over the railing.

The yacht was anchored in the rays of the sun, just off the coast of yet another spot of sand. Turquoise water vibrated around its border, reflecting bits of the brightness back in their eyes. A waiter brought around drinks for the girls, and a pesto turkey panini for Val. Amy and Kiki had already eaten their lunch hours before.

Reclining in the shade afforded by the second level, they watched as other guests played around on ultra-fast jet skis below. Towards the end of her meal, Val noticed Jason zoom by with a pretty redhead clutching excitedly at his back. Her squeals of delight could be heard from the deck.

Launching off of small waves, he sent the jet ski twisting in tight corkscrews. The twinge of jealousy that fired off within Val was tamped down by force of habit. Sighing, she blew away her emotions, replacing them with calm nothingness. Pinching her drink straw between her fingers, she placed it into her mouth and sipped at her water through lipstick red lips.

"I'm sorry sweetie." Amy gave her leg an affectionate pat. "He's been at it all morning with that crew girl."

"Don't be sorry," Val responded. "It's okay."

"Well, he's here with you, isn't he?" Amy pressed.

"No, he doesn't belong to me," Val reminded her. "I belong to him."

"I guess I sort of forgot." Amy appeared shocked. "Rick was under the impression that you all had some kind of agreement."

"No." Val shook her head.

How she longed to confess the truth. Wanted to explain that what they did have was far more complicated than Rick or Amy could imagine. It involved kidnapping, blackmail, illicit sex and undercover work. But of course, she couldn't.

Besides, Cambric had worked very hard to prepare Val for the inevitability that most D2s face. The reality was that they were rarely the only woman.

Trying to look away from Jason now proved more difficult than she would have thought, but Val persevered. Bringing her training to mind, she repeated over and over that she had no right to judge if he sought comfort elsewhere.

～

The next three days, Jason immersed himself in drinking, gambling, and ignoring Val. By avoiding him, Val was able to remain outwardly unperturbed. Spending her days arm in arm with Amy and Kiki, they indulged in many activities free women were accustomed to enjoying.

They visited the onboard spa for pedicures, were taken to St. Croix for a day of shopping, and laid out by the hot tub at all hours. The more reserved and at peace Val appeared, the more outlandish Jason's behavior became.

At night she was left alone in their room. He had stopped returning to their cabin. Val didn't know for sure where he slept, but everyone else seemed to be well aware of it.

The final night onboard the yacht, Val sat reclining on a leather sofa with Amy after dinner. They watched disinterestedly as Rick and Peter Higgins played their fifth round of pool. While Jason was off getting smashed, Rick had been building a steady rapport with the Representative.

Even Tawny Higgins had loosened up considerably. She now sat on the other side of Amy, chatting comfortably about her life as a high-powered spouse.

As the game came to an end, Rick moved to shake hands with Peter. That's when Jason came bounding up, dragging the curvy redhead along with him. Plopping down on the couch next to Val, he pulled the other woman onto his lap. She giggled sweetly in her fitted red dress which set off her lovely hair and pale skin perfectly.

Tawny sneered in revulsion before glaring at her husband. Peter quickly made their excuses and helped her to stand. The couple nodded politely at Rick and Amy, then wandered off, blending with the crowd.

"Come on Val." Amy pulled at her arm. "Let's go take a little walk."

"No," Jason said, all smiles. "*She* stays right here."

Val remained seated, as directed.

Straining to keep her face impassive, she felt hot embarrassment build inside her throat. Jason's hand moved to caress her exposed knee, then stroke gently along Val's thigh to the edge of her black dress. The redhead crossed her legs seductively, still poised on his lap. His arm was looped casually around her waist.

Amy sucked in a sharp breath. Imploringly, she looked to her husband whose eyes flashed with a sudden anger. Crossing close to the couch, Rick bent down and whispered vehemently.

"Will you excuse us for a few minutes?" He stared at the redhead. "Uh, what's your name again?"

"Genevieve," she replied giddily.

Rising then, she sauntered off, looking over her shoulder to give Jason a last wink.

"What in the holy hell do you think you're doing here, Son?" Rick fumed.

"Give me a break Rick-"

"You know something? Half of the people in here couldn't give a hot damn if you own a D2 or not." Rick sucked in a breath and glanced around. "But the other half are an entirely different story. Those folks seemed to be able to overlook you *owning* Val as long as you helped them to forget just what she actually was."

"Come on," Jason interjected.

"No!" Rick's voice raised before he purposefully lowered it. "No. You will *listen* to me boy. Now you've gone and, for some reason that I can't ascertain, are shoving the fact that she's nothing but your damn sex slave in everyone's faces… including hers.

Although I don't like it myself, I might have been able to ignore it, if not for Peter Higgins and his *very* anti-captive wife. You are supposed to be helping me to convince them to stop that new legislation."

"I *will* help."

"You *will* help? You know something? You may be your parent's prodigy, doubling profits and all that, but if your daddy could only see you now. What a shameful waste."

Rick straightened and tugged at his shirt. Looking down his nose at Jason, he extended his hand to Amy, who rose reluctantly. Obviously, she wanted to take Val along, but after a split second, she let herself be escorted away.

Left side by side, Jason and Val occupied a bubble of silence in the crowded room. His jaw clenched, the muscle ticking before he got up to walk away. He didn't look back.

Val had just decided to follow suit, when Peter Higgins appeared. Strolling casually back over to her, he took a seat. Clearly, he had something to say.

Glancing around, Val noted that his wife was nowhere in sight. The crowd had dissipated, shifting in such a way as to leave them decidedly alone. Well-practiced in the art of men, Val remained silent, merely looking into his eyes. Peter had an open, friendly demeanor, she could see why he had been elected.

"Val. May I call you Val?" He began, so formal.

"I don't have any other name." She gave him a dazzling smile. The tension eased.

"My wife spoke with you several days ago but you were interrupted. She felt that you couldn't be honest with her after that." Peter paused.

"We spoke, yes," Val answered, non-committal. He gave a knowing smile.

"You see, my wife is a strong and outspoken woman. I'm sure you are aware of her anti-captive ideals?"

"She's made her position plain."

"Well, she has that luxury. *I* am not able to draw lines quite so clearly. This is the beginning of my political career, and unfortunately, I must work both sides to remain in play at this time."

"I see." Val wondered where this was heading.

"We've watched you this trip, Val. My wife and I have seen the position you are in. To be honest, it seems to be unraveling rather quickly."

He slid her a business card. Keeping it low along the line of the sofa, it came to rest just next to her hip. Taking it in her palm she didn't look at it, but snapped it shut inside her clutch.

"What was that?" She asked.

"A life line," he answered. "On the back of that card is my personal cell number. If at any point you want out, just call. It doesn't matter the day or time, I will send someone to get you. There is a network of sorts. We can get you out of the country. You could start a free life."

"Have you offered this to Gabe?"

"No." He was taken aback by her question.

"Is that because he's male?"

"I suppose so, yes."

"Don't offer it to him, he won't take it. But I do want to point out your bias. You think that I'm in a worse situation, but you are very wrong."

"Thank you for calling me out," he said honestly. "We just don't know enough about what captive lives are like."

"I will keep your card, but on one condition." She leaned closer.

"Tell me," he said.

"I want you and your wife to go to an agency. It doesn't matter which one. Order up an hourly girl. Try to choose the oldest one that you can. When you get into a room with her, give her this same life line. She will answer all of your questions then, but you may not like what you hear. Will you do that?"

"Yes, I promise that we will." He nodded, eyes following her as she moved to go.

CHAPTER 14

Their flight home was tense and quiet. Short of exchanging a few necessary words, Jason and Val had no meaningful conversation. Upon arriving home, the silence grew worse, blooming to fill a void that widened between them. He broke it only to inform her that she would be moving back to her own bedroom.

That first night she sat on the edge of her bed, watching as Anne Marie and Yvette carried armfuls of clothing, shoes, makeup and jewelry down the hallway from the master suite. How had she accumulated it all? No matter, she thought. When they found Bee, she wouldn't need any of it anymore.

She got into the habit of carrying Peter Higgins' card with her at all times. It was like a get out of jail pass. It made her feel more secure to have it.

After that first week back, Jason began to bring other women home with him. Banishing Val to her bedroom, he and his date would enjoy late dinners together downstairs. Yvette would mutter under her breath when she would bring Val's meal up to her on a tray.

One such evening, after finishing her dinner, Val stood leaning against the expansive windows of her room. She liked to admire the twinkle of lights from far off houses that dotted the landscape. Smoothing her fingers over the glass, she flashed to those days spent in the display box. How had she watched the free people move by and not felt the call to experience their lives? Well, for whatever it was worth, she did now.

Movement in the darkened garden below caught her eye. A brunette with lovely long hair walked along, followed by the all too familiar figure of a man. The lights from inside the first story of the house shone out through the windows, offering some dim illumination to the surrounding green of manicured bushes and trimmed trees.

Val's stomach sank as she observed the pair, exchanging flirtatious conversation that would lead to more. Taking the woman by the hand, the man pulled her close in an intimate embrace. Glancing up for the briefest moment, he revealed his face to her. Val covered her mouth with her hand.

Retreating from the window, she could no longer pretend that it wasn't Jason. Had he wanted her to see him? What a tortured game they were playing.

Sinking down to her knees, she bowed her head in the cast of moonlight that creeped along the floor. So, this was how Gabe and Bee felt that whole year they snuck around together. She tried to recall all of the things that Bee had confided to her then. How she wanted to throw up each time they sent Gabe to the breeding program. How difficult it was to continue on with her own training.

At the time, Val hadn't understood why Bee couldn't just keep her mouth shut. Why did she throw curses at her trainer? Often, she had become angry with Bee for talking back or refusing certain tasks. After all, it was Val who had to watch them carry out Bee's punishments.

Breathing in through her nose, Val inhaled precious clean oxygen and held it. Counting in her head, she reached the number four. Slowly, she exhaled the tainted carbon dioxide, pushing it out through her mouth. Just as The Agency had coached her, she piled up all of her unwarranted emotion, cleaning it out of her system with each released breath.

She didn't have the right to feel as she did. This sharp pain, so exquisite as it pierced inside her, belonged to a free person. There was no room for it here, in the body of a captive.

After several minutes her head began to clear. The ache in her heart gave way to a vast unfeeling emptiness. Rising from her position of prayer on the floor, Val was able to scrub her mind of any lingering impulse. Today did not belong to her. Tomorrow did not belong to her. The next day did not belong to her.

She let them go.

In time, Val became a ghost in Summer House. She woke late, after Jason had gone. Eating dinner early, she would retreat upstairs before he returned home from work. For several weeks, she did not see him at all.

Her days became devoted to constant toil in the barn. Once soft hands grew small calluses against the work of shoveling stalls and cleaning leather tack. When she glanced at her face in a passing mirror, she hardly recognized the woman who stared back. A loose pony tail hung where carefully curled locks had drifted before.

Her routine became so set that she lost track of the days.

The warm air from a month ago chilled with the change in season.

One afternoon, she found herself immersed in a new stable activity. Ignacio had let her groom Royal Outing after his workout from early in the morning. Perhaps she had finally shown enough experience to lead the stud around, or maybe the keen trainer had taken pity on a lonely girl. Whatever the reason, Val was determined not to care. All she knew was that Ignacio trusted her to take care of his prize.

Full of exhilaration around the magnificent horse, Val worked for over an hour until his coat shined like black satin. Because of the unexpected opportunity, she was forced to bend her rigid schedule, riding Bud much later in the day than was her custom. After her ride, she tied him in the grooming racks inside the barn, out of the cold wind that threatened to spook and bluster.

Taking her time, she picked out his hooves and scratched the familiar itchy spots behind his golden ears. As she brushed along his back, smoothing the hairs of his yellow hide, she heard voices float down the length of the barn aisle. In a world of Spanish-speaking grooms, the southern drawl of English had her stomach tightening uncomfortably.

The male voice definitely belonged to Jason, but the female accompaniment was unfamiliar. Never in her life had Val wished to hide more than at this moment. Short of bolting from the racks to run for cover, there was nothing that she could do. So, she let them come on.

Purposefully, she relaxed the muscles of her face then slowed down her breathing. She didn't have control over much, but she refused to let them see her react. Continuing in her grooming she ducked under Bud's neck and began to work his other side.

Out of the corner of her eye she saw them approach, listening as their conversation dropped suddenly away. The figure of the woman stopped short to stare. Jason took a few steps past before turning back reluctantly. Val did not look over, but kept brushing.

"My God, Jason is that her?" The woman asked.

At this Val shifted to look, soft bristle brush poised in her hand. The woman was petite, with ample breasts and a slender waist. Her golden blonde hair cascaded over her shoulders. Large blue eyes blinked prettily. She wasn't the same woman from the garden, so many weeks ago.

Could this be his future wife? Val thought. Surely this was the type of mate his mother had in mind. Diamonds winked from every available surface.

"She's more ravishing in the photos, though."

The woman critiqued Val as if she weren't standing there. Jason cringed. Remaining silent, Val merely ducked her head before returning to Bud. She wished the woman would just walk away.

"Val, right?" The blonde addressed her, curious. "Tell me, do you work as a groom here now that your services are no longer required?"

Val's heart jumped painfully in her chest.

"I help in the stables," she answered, and couldn't stop herself from peering past the woman into Jason's face. She wanted to search his eyes for the answer but he looked away, not able to meet her gaze.

"Jason, you have positively turned her into a real life Cinderella, except in reverse. Why don't you sell her, or let the poor thing go free already?"

"I'm sorry, I don't understand," Val ventured. "Who is Cinderella?"

"How shocking," the blonde commented, glancing over her shoulder at Jason who registered surprise before closing his expression. "They really don't teach you girls anything aside from how to have good sex. Scandalous."

"Enough," Jason finally spoke. "Renee, let me show you Royal Outing. He's just down this way."

Taking her elbow, Jason led the woman off. They strolled down the aisle and out the side of the barn. Once they had gone, Val unhooked Bud shakily. Leading him the few yards to his stall, she let him inside and released him to munch his leftover alfalfa.

Swinging the half door shut behind them, she backed herself into the far corner. Slowly, she slid down to sit in the soft bedding. One hand clutched at her stomach while the other covered her mouth. Hot tears came in full drops that streaked a trail down her cheeks. There was no makeup painted on her face, though. She had long since stopped getting dressed up to work with the horses.

Her long brown hair was pulled back simply, and she wore only blue jeans with a comfortable long-sleeve shirt. No wonder Renee had thought her plain. She didn't compare to the photos of herself all made up. But what did it matter anymore? So what, she was stupid as well as plain.

"Cinderella was a beautiful orphan girl." Ignacio's low voice drifted down to rest on her ears.

Glancing up, she saw him leaning over the half door of Bud's stall. He had heard everything, apparently.

"She was forced to be a servant in her own home by her stepmother. Each day she endured abuse, until finally her fairy God-mother took pity on her. Cinderella was transformed into a stunning princess so that she could attend a fancy party, but the magic spell would only last for one night.

There, she met a handsome prince who fell hopelessly in love with her. But she ran from him, afraid he would see her for the servant that she really was. The prince pursued her, finally uncovering the truth. He rescued her then, bringing her to live with him as his wife, forever after."

"It's a lovely story." Val whispered, wiping the tears from her eyes.

"It's called a fairy-tale," Ignacio explained. "There are many different stories that we tell our little children, to give them hope. I suppose there is no need for hope in this agency you came from."

"Hope of escape is the most dangerous thing The Agency could think of."

"Jason is punishing you," Ignacio said wisely. "He is also running from himself. Are you deserving of this punishment?"

"No," Val admitted. "But he doesn't know that."

"Why don't you tell him?"

"It's complicated." She averted her eyes. "Ignacio, how would I get to your brother's ranch in Wyoming, if I ever had the chance to go?"

Nodding acceptance, Ignacio let himself inside the stall. He sat down in the deep shavings next to her and whispered the directions over and over. He made her repeat them back to him, until she had them burned into her heart.

That evening, Val ran her fingers over each and every book binding in the library. Jason was downstairs taking his dinner with Renee. She could hear the seductive female laughter filter up the stairs.

When Val's finger paused on the right one, she pulled out

the thick leather book and flipped through it greedily. There were pages upon pages of the children's stories that Ignacio had spoken of. Tucking the heavy rectangle under one arm, Val tiptoed down the hall to her room.

When Yvette came wheeling in a tray of food, she found Val sitting comfortably in one overstuffed barrel chair, reading through the whispery pages. The two women hadn't said much to each other of late. Yvette seemed very loyal to Jason and the Riggs family that way, but Val did get the impression she disapproved of his current behavior.

After setting out a plate of roast chicken over a bed of rice, Yvette lingered a second longer than usual. Val paused in her reading to look up.

"I am sorry," Yvette said. Her eyes were filled with compassion. "I don't know what has come over him. His parents did raise him better than this."

"Better than owning me, or better than having all of these other women?" Val was curious.

"Both." Yvette admitted before wheeling the empty cart out.

Absorbed in her book, Val ate the food absently with one hand. She didn't recall tasting a single bite but when darkness came, her plate was empty. Exhaustion licked at the edges of her consciousness and as much as she longed to read everything in one night, she put the book aside.

Flicking off the lights, she crawled into bed and rotated to watch the moon as it hovered in her window. The Agency hadn't allowed windows in their bedrooms, too much temptation. When the nights at Summer House had been warmer, Val had left all of them wide open, welcoming the freshness of the free air. It had been such a beautiful experience. But now it had grown too cold. The windows were sealed up tight.

The house had fallen into silence without her notice. It seemed almost empty. Heart leaping once, Val listened as a hand came to rest on her bedroom doorknob. She hadn't once locked it during the past month. Something deep inside her had wanted him to find it open when he eventually came looking.

Slowly it rotated, the sound was a metal twisting in the moonlight. Jason pushed the door wide then, his silhouette filling the frame. Pausing there, he seemed to second guess himself. She waited in silence, watching.

"I thought I saw your light," he began.

"I'm awake," she answered, sitting up in bed.

"I haven't seen you in weeks." He paused a moment before continuing. "Until today."

Entering the room, he swayed slightly as he turned to close the door behind him. When he sat down on the bed next to her, she could smell the whiskey permeating his skin. She judged him to be fairly drunk.

Hesitating at first, he lifted his hand then ran his fingers through her loose hair to tug gently at the ends.

"She's wrong you know." He sighed. "You are even more beautiful than any photo they ever took of you."

Bringing his hand up to cup her face, he let his thumb brush back and forth over her lips. She parted them for him, closing her eyes, trying to absorb the feeling he created inside her.

"I've tried." His voice cracked. "God knows that I've tried. But every time I'm with them, all I see is you. I just can't do it anymore. I just can't stay away from you."

His eyes begged her silently. She would answer his need. Welcoming him into her bed, she clung to his body as he moaned into her hair. He rocked, pressing her beneath him in a consuming embrace. When it was over, he lingered beside her. The alcohol having loosened his tongue, he poured out his agony.

"I hate myself," he confessed. "It's my fault you slept with him."

"It's alright," she soothed, running her hand over his bare back.

"I can't stop thinking of what he's done with you," he groaned. "I want to break him."

"Jason, I need to tell you something about me and Gabe-"

"Don't." He shoved away from her. "Don't ever talk to me about him again."

He left then. Walking out of her room, he retreated back into the darkness.

Waking late the following morning, she knew Jason had already gone to the office. The smell of breakfast cooking wafted up the stairs. It seemed unusually strong.

Sniffing, she lay in bed. She recognized the scent of bacon and eggs. Eggs, she thought. Saliva flooded her mouth unexpectedly. Suddenly, her stomach turned. Flinging the covers off the bed, she made a mad dash for the toilet. She barely got the lid up before retching violently.

After a few minutes, the feeling passed, leaving as quickly as it had come on. Strange, she thought, she hadn't had anything to drink. Maybe the chicken from the night before was bad. Walking to the sink, she grabbed her pink toothbrush.

Gripping the toothpaste, she found that she had squeezed the last bit from the tube the day before. She bent over, opening cupboards, searching for more. Stopping short she blanched.

Boxes and boxes of tampons, unopened, were stored there. Her heart sank. When exactly was the last time she had needed to use these?

Flipping back through her mind she couldn't remember when she had her last period. It was sometime before the trip to St. Croix. Her legs wobbled once, then gave out. She sat back heavily on her bottom, panic bursting forth like a flood. She could feel its angry tingles spike through her blood stream all the way to the ends of her toes.

There was no way to be sure if she was actually pregnant. It wasn't like she could go to Yvette or even Jason and ask for a test.

Damn him, she thought. She had begged for birth control. Why had he withheld it from her? Now here she was potentially carrying his child. No, that wasn't right, she corrected herself. She was carrying Cambric's child.

It was at that moment she knew she would rather die than give her own baby over to those monsters.

Shoving up from the ground, Val paced the room and entered her closet. She didn't want Yvette coming in to find her on the floor and start asking questions. How long did a woman have before she started showing her pregnancy? Was it three months? Or maybe four? Val couldn't recall.

Now there was a time limit on her search for Bee. She would have to conceal this possible pregnancy, hide it from absolutely everyone. When and if her body began to betray her, then it would be time to make the call.

Grabbing her favorite clutch from the shelf in her closet, Val opened it and plucked at the card from Peter Higgins.

Running her fingers over its smooth surface, she blew out a long breath. *You have a way out. This is going to be okay.*

Slipping into her riding jeans, Val stuffed the card deep in her pocket. She sniffed the air tentatively with her nose as she eased her way down the staircase. No nausea rose up to claim her, that was good.

Feeling a small spark of hope that she had been overreacting, and wasn't in fact pregnant, Val made her way confidently to the dining room.

There on the table in front of her usual spot was the largest arrangement of flowers she had ever seen. Soft purple lilacs, fragrant gardenias, pale pink roses and many others she couldn't name. They overflowed in colorful abundance out of a blue glass vase.

Sitting down heavily in front of them she reached for the simple white card and read:

Val

Have dinner with me?

Jason

She pressed the card to her chest, felt the heating creep of pleasure fill her cheeks. But a moment later, reality began to nudge its way back to the forefront of her mind. Did she really want to go around on this carousel with him again? When Jason was pleased with her, everything was amazing. Falling out of favor though, that's when the darkness consumed. She had spent the entire last month in that ghostly abandon.

Still, her heart beat for him strong inside her chest. Maybe Gabe had been right when he said she was in love with Jason.

"My those are pretty," Anne Marie commented, before setting Val's plate on the table.

"Yes," Val agreed, eyeing the mass of yellow eggs. "I'm sure you've seen so many lately."

"Why, no." Anne Marie gave a slight shake of her head. "These are the first flowers he's ordered."

"Oh." Was all Val could manage.

"Will you be having dinner with him tonight then?"

Val bit her lip in concentration. If she wasn't pregnant, then she could carry on with him this way for as long as possible. When she risked only herself, then it didn't really matter. But if she was pregnant, then being around Jason put her secret at risk for discovery. It would only be a matter of time before The Agency tracked her down. It just wasn't worth it.

"No," Val answered simply, and managed to keep a straight face as Anne Marie gasped.

VAL RODE THE FOLLOWING WEEK ON A TIDE OF HOPEFUL DENIAL. She woke late in the morning and worked in the stables all day. Before Jason returned home, she would retreat to an early dinner in her room. No more bouts of vomiting plagued her, so she clung to the possibility that she was not, in fact, pregnant.

But as each day passed without the start of her cycle, a new sort of fear built itself steadily in. Eventually all that hope and denial were replaced by the simple truth. She was no longer in this alone.

Sheer exhaustion dropped about her like a heavy blanket, making her body achy and her eyes hunger for sleep. All she wanted to do was go back to bed. But that was a luxury that she could no longer afford. She had to be careful not to show any outward signs.

Forcing herself to get up in the morning, she ate breakfast at the long table alone. That was when Jason began leaving progressively more outrageous gifts for her to discover. Diamond earrings, keys to a car, and finally a bank statement in her name with more money in it than she knew what to do with. All of them were accompanied by little white rectangular cards. All of the pieces of paper asked the same question.

Inside her, a battle raged. She was flattered by the gifts, but more so it was the tiny little question mark that accompanied each line. At any point he could have removed the symbol, turning the question into a demand which she would have been unable to deny. It was the freedom to choose whether or not she had dinner with him that made it so hard to continue in her refusal.

But each time her heart yearned to say yes, her body reminded her why she had to say no. Pushing the gifts to the side, she resolved not to take anything more. In the back of her mind she was aware that this dance between them would not last forever. At some point he would change tactics and force her to face him.

So, she shouldn't have been surprised on the morning of the seventh day when she walked through the door of the dining room and found Jason waiting for her, instead of a card. But the thing of it was, it *did* surprise her.

Pausing on the threshold for only a moment, she blinked back the nerves that shot instantly to her fingertips. Her hand fluttered up momentarily, wanting to rub protectively across her belly, but she stopped short. Calmly, deliberately, she took her seat opposite him.

"Good morning," he said, sipping at his white mug of coffee.

"Good morning," she responded, avoiding his searching blue eyes.

Anne Marie entered the room, carrying a wide plate laden with breakfast. Setting it before Val, she moved to pour orange juice before sweeping back out the door. It was late in the morning, perhaps somewhere around ten o'clock. Jason should have been at the office hours ago. He must have been working downstairs, she realized, only ducking in a few minutes before because Yvette or Anne Marie had told him when she normally took breakfast.

"You're upset with me." Jason set down his cup.

"No," she answered honestly, then chided herself. She couldn't tell him the real reason for her avoidance.

"You won't have dinner with me. You won't accept my gifts." He watched as she began to eat, taking small bites of her omelet and chewing quietly. "I want you to know that it won't happen again. I want you to know that I'm sorry."

"Why are you sorry?" Her fork stopped halfway to her mouth, she didn't understand where this was coming from.

"For bringing those other women around. For betraying you. I'm asking for just one more chance, Val." He was earnest now.

"You haven't betrayed me. We have no relationship." She shook her head at him, but her body tensed, she wanted to leave. Wanted to escape him right now.

"Alright." Jason sat back, scrutinizing her. "Let's start a relationship, then."

"That's not possible," she countered, letting her fork clatter to the plate below. He wasn't going to make this running away thing easy on her.

"Why not?"

"I'm a captive. We don't have relationships."

"When you're free then."

Impulsively, she shoved back from the table and stood up. The legs of her chair scraped against the stone floor. She couldn't look at him. Couldn't manage a straight face in front of him so she turned away.

Why this? Why now? Didn't he know it was too late? No. Of course he didn't. How could he?

Then Jason was behind her, tentatively wrapping his arms around her, drawing her in. He soothed and stroked, pressing his face into the back of her shoulder.

"I didn't mean to push so hard," he murmured. "This isn't why I even stayed to see you this morning. It's just that when I saw you, I couldn't help myself."

"Why are you here then?"

"Finn called. They're sending Agent Schipp over to pick us up."

Rotating her around to face him, he held her at arm's length, studying her expression for a few moments before releasing her.

"What do they want? Did they find Bee?"

"He didn't say. Just that we're needed today for something that came up. It wasn't planned."

"When will he be here?"

"Any minute." Jason surveyed her worn jeans and casual shirt. "Better go change."

Taking the steps two at a time, her stomach tumbled into a decided knot. Thoughts of Bee and what condition she might have been found in brewed in her mind. When she reached her closet, she ran her fingers down the hangers filled with clothes. It was fall now, and cold outside.

Choosing a simple black knee-length dress, she stepped into it before cinching a thin leather belt just above her waist. Slipping into a pair of matching pumps she surveyed the plunging neckline before shrugging into a large cream-colored jacket. Rubbing her fingers along the cashmere soft trench coat, she descended the stairs. She was confident about her outfit, if nothing else.

Jason waited for her in the foyer, looking handsome as ever in his dark business suit and heavy wool coat. Without thinking, she took the arm that he offered and he opened the front door. Another indistinct black sedan waited for them in the curve of the cobblestone driveway. Agent Schipp got out and moved to open her door. He and Jason shook hands briefly before it swung shut, closing her in.

When they pulled out of the electric gate, she noticed two men dressed in uniforms standing next to a small guard stand that hadn't been there before. Pulling past them, Val saw the bulge of a holster on one man's hip as he raised his hand to wave them through.

She asked Jason about it, but he merely shrugged as if it was no big deal. When pressed, he admitted the armed security guards had been working for him for over a month now. Blinking, Val realized it had been longer than that since she had stepped foot outside of Summer House. A prickle of concern formed, taking up residence in her mind alongside all of the other worries that collected there.

The drive to the FBI building was shorter this time, but just as confusing. When they reached the underground parking garage, Agent Schipp led the way back up through the lobby and into the elevator.

After swiping his card, they rose once more and were admitted to the nondescript clean walls of the FBI office. Obligingly this time, Val submitted to an uneventful pat down at the check-in desk. Her nerves about Bee had taken all the fight out of her.

Agent Schipp's oversized figure filled the narrow hallway ahead of them as he led them back to Finn's office. Val gripped Jason's offered hand but he trailed just behind her, letting her go first. Near the end, they stopped at the familiar door and were admitted inside.

The room had been practically empty before. But not now. Now it was lined with whiteboards. They were covered with large photos of little girls, the ones who had gone missing.

And it wasn't just Agent Finn standing inside, looking at the missing. There was another man with him. When the new man turned to look over his shoulder, Val's heart skipped a beat. Dropping Jason's hand, she rushed for him.

"Gabe!"

Breathless, she closed the short distance between them. Gabe reached for her, dragging her into his arms and holding her tight against him.

"Everything okay with you?" He whispered into her ear, then pulled back, eyes darting over her face.

"Yeah. Yes, I'm fine." She nodded, eyes brimming with relief. She hadn't known how much she missed him. "What are you doing here?"

"Our friend Gabe has been in town with Sharon on business for the past week." Agent Finn spoke from just behind him. "He's been given a lot of leeway with his days, so was able to make contact to arrange this meeting at the last minute. He tells me he has the documents that we requested and is ready to sign his deal."

"I wanted to see you," Gabe continued. "Before I signed everything. I wanted to make sure you're guaranteed your freedom, too. I need to hear it from you in person."

"Thank you." She ducked her head. "I am getting my freedom… after we get Bee."

"As you can see, I've enlarged all the photos of the missing girls." Finn gestured to the boards. "While we were waiting for you, Gabe recognized quite a few more."

Val left Gabe's side then, wandering the perimeter of the room. He followed her, pointing first to a pretty black-haired, dark-eyed girl, saying that her agency name was Mia. Under the photo, Finn had written carefully in green ink the number four.

They moved on to another photo of a brunette with large blue eyes and long lashes. Her agency name was Angelina. The same writing under the picture depicted the number two. Around the room there were eight more girls, each with a different number in the range of one to four.

"I don't recognize any of these girls." Val studied each photo critically, letting her hand drift over their young faces. "They weren't at our boarding school and we didn't train with them. How do you know them, Gabey?"

"These are breeding program girls." Gabe cleared his throat and stood quietly beside her as she let her hand linger over the last face. "You'd never have met them. They were raised at the Havana Agency."

"And the numbers?" She asked, not looking over at him.

"These are the number of children Gabe has by each woman," Finn answered for him. "The ones he is aware of at least."

"My God." She breathed it.

"They started me in the program at sixteen-"

"That's two years before the regulation for consent." Val cut in. It shocked her. Even agencies were supposed to abide by certain age restrictions.

"Believe me, at sixteen I didn't care where they sent me. It was all fun and games the first few years. I just didn't realize the scope of it until much later." Gabe laughed then, shaking his head at her sadly.

"Until Bee?" She ventured.

"Yeah." He nodded solemnly. "Until I didn't want to do it anymore."

"Do they tell you how many children you've fathered?"

"No, I started asking the mothers whenever I was brought back in." Gabe studied the floor. "They remember each one, even if they don't get to keep them."

"How many do you have?"

Gabe's jaw snapped shut, he cleared his throat once more before muttering, "I don't want to talk about it."

"All of the children born to these girls will likely be considered free." Finn stepped in, his voice sounding almost hopeful. "Only Gabe's first born would legally be required to remain a captive. The rest is sort of a gray area because the girls were kidnapped. I think we could release all of them."

"What about the rest?" Gabe asked suddenly, anger getting the best of him.

"What do you mean?" Finn's brow furrowed.

"What about the rest of my children? Why are the ones had by these girls so different from the captive born? It's like you only want to save them because of bloodlines. It's sick."

"I'm sorry Gabe," Finn tried to explain. "It's not that I don't sympathize with your situation. We just have to start somewhere."

"Tell that to Val." Gabe turned to look at Jason then. "Why is Bee worth saving, but not Val? DNA? You guys are a bunch of pricks."

"Gabe." Val stopped him, wrapping her arms around his waist she drew him against her. Sucking in a breath, he buried his face in her coat. "These are good men. They are doing the best that they can."

"Okay. Alright." Gabe got ahold of himself and stepped back. Running his hands through his mass of golden hair, he looked to Finn. "I don't have much time. Let's review the contract."

Ducking his head, Agent Finn took his position behind the long wooden desk and pulled a stack of papers from his drawer. Gabe sat with Val next to him and began reading through each line of the document carefully.

Jason walked over to the lone window and stood with his back to them, looking out. He hadn't said anything since entering the room. He was consumed by his own thoughts.

The language in the document was simple enough, and appeared correct. When they got to the line guaranteeing Gabe two more nights with Val, he gave her a playful wink and crossed it out, applying his initials to the mark.

Finn watched, his face plain, and said nothing.

"What's this line about testifying in court?" Gabe scrutinized the wording again.

"When we put Sharon on trial," Finn explained. "We need your testimony. You have to appear in court or the deal is off."

"That is the biggest bunch of bullshit!" Gabe raised his voice. "She runs an international drug smuggling and kidnapping ring. You think she isn't going to have me whacked the second she knows I've turned on her? I'm as good as dead. I might as well stay like I am now."

"We'll protect you." Finn tried to appease him. "Keep you in witness protection until after the trial. Look, I'll have my best guys on it. This is a huge case. We can't risk not having you testify. She won't be able to get to you, I swear it."

Rocking back in his chair, Gabe groaned and closed his eyes.

Val watched him mull over his options. Though she wanted desperately for him to sign, she wouldn't try to sway him. It was a dangerous mess they were wrapped up in, and this decision was his alone.

Finally, snapping back to attention, Gabe leaned forward and briskly signed his name on the bottom of the document. Once done, he shoved it at Finn.

"Take it before I change my mind." Gabe stood. "I better get going."

At this, Jason turned from his post at the window. His face twisted with some mix of anger and dread.

"When are you going to want your next night with Val?" Jason asked. His frown only increased as Gabe's face filled with delight.

"Well, I said I wanted the man to suffer, Val, but I never thought you wouldn't tell him." A smile of admiration played across his lips.

"Tell me what?" Jason's eyes darted to her once, then back to Gabe.

"I never had sex with Val. Let me guess, you've been treating her like a whore ever since, right?" Gabe turned to Val. "I told you this guy was nothing but a piece of shit."

In a blink, Jason rounded the corner of Finn's desk and headed straight for Gabe.

"Don't do it, Jason," Finn cautioned, shooting to his feet, poised to break up a fight.

"He's right." Jason gritted his teeth and stopped short. "I am what he says."

Gabe's face registered surprise at the admission. His mouth opened, then closed again. He appeared to bite back what he had been about to say. Instead, he turned to Val and gave her a light kiss on the cheek.

"You know where to find me right?" His voice barely audible. "Do you remember?"

Of course she remembered. How could she forget? Gabe and Bee had talked of nothing else. All those nights the three of them had been tucked into her room with Gabe making his endless plans. Plans for freedom. The where was the easiest part. Maybe he would show up to trial, she thought, maybe not.

"I remember," she whispered and he released her to go.

"What about the memory card?" Finn asked.

"I slipped it into Val's pocket," Gabe called over his shoulder as he cruised out.

Jason stepped to her then, unable to meet her eyes, and dipped his hands into the pockets of her jacket. Distracted by their exchange, Val forgot until the last second why she didn't want his hands searching there. Grabbing Jason's wrist, she managed to stop just short of wrenching his hand away.

When he looked at her, she knew that he gripped the memory card, and much more than that.

"What is this, Val?" Jason asked.

Holding up the business card from Peter Higgins, he examined the hand-written number on the back. *That's my backup plan. That's my get out of jail card. That's my escape.* All of the phrases passed quickly through her mind as desperation filled her soul. She was unable to speak.

Instead of pushing her about it, Jason pocketed the small rectangle himself, then set the memory card gently on Finn's desk.

"Now that Gabe's gone-" Finn moved to take his seat once more, gesturing for them both to join him. "I would like to go over the next phase of our plan. We'll have our tech team start working on these documents immediately but I may need to send some your way to help point us in the right direction."

"Sounds good." Jason nodded.

"The next step is going to be the most risky so far. We need you to reach out to Cambric Agency and request an hourly session with Bee," Finn said.

"How do you know she's there?" Val asked.

"We've sent a few undercover guys in. The girls that they have ended up with have confirmed that Bee is hourly, and she still resides at Cambric."

"Why don't you send one of those guys in to get her DNA?"

"Because we need the best, most clean sample that we can get. We'll only get one crack at this and it has to be perfect. You need to get a mouth swab from her and I can't risk her trusting a stranger to do that. If she told Cambric, then they'd know something was up."

"You want me to request her by name?" Jason asked.

"Not exactly," Finn cautioned. "This has to be really delicate. We don't want to tip our hand. I need you to make contact, explain that you're bored with Val. She mentioned she was raised with a girl that looks just like her, and you want to try her out. Maybe offer to buy her permanent placement eventually, something like that."

"Okay." Jason nodded.

"Make an hourly appointment, but bring Val. You will have to find some way to smuggle in the DNA swab kit. Val, do you think you can get her to take the test and not tell?"

"She'll do it. We won't have to smuggle anything in. Just say you want her delivered to your hotel suite. They do that," Val offered.

"Great." Finn brightened. "Once you get the appointment, then let me know. Things are getting pretty thick these days. Agent Schipp and I will tail you both in New York. Maybe you could find some excuse to be there. Any conventions soon?"

"I'll find out," Jason agreed.

"And you've got to hire at least one private bodyguard for the trip. I'd prefer that you hire two."

"I'll think about it," Jason acknowledged.

They went round and round like that for another hour. Hashing out details and working through possible scenarios until Val's head spun. Lunch had come and gone with no stale sandwich offered. Val's stomach grumbled unpleasantly, making her feel suddenly weak.

Slumping in her chair a little, she worked to loosen the heavy winter coat. It was hot in here. Had someone turned on the heater? Noticing her discomfort, Jason ended the session and told Finn he would be in touch. Agent Finn nodded his acceptance, but scrutinized Val a moment in silence. She could feel his eyes following her on her way out the door.

Their ride home with Agent Schipp was the same as on the way there. Silence reigned. Closing her eyes, Val tilted her head against the rear window. She thought of Gabe and those agency girls. Then of all the children he was forced to leave without a father. What about her own parents? Had they experienced a similar fate?

Sighing, she tried to blow out the heavy weight of her sadness. It was hard to reconcile doing so much for all of these girls, even for Bee, but stopping short when the blood didn't match. How could they point to one and lift them up out of captivity, but leave the rest?

When they arrived home, Jason helped her from the car. She clung to his arm gratefully as he walked her inside. Her knees felt wobbly. Maybe it was from the lack of food, or the roller coaster of events. Perhaps both.

Sitting for an early dinner, Val blinked at her surroundings. It was as if she was seeing the magnificent dining room for the first time. The white crown-molding, the endless blue walls, the travertine floor, and the paintings. Oh, the masterpiece paintings that hung on every single wall.

She didn't belong here.

Yvette's arm crossed her vision then as she poured a heavy red wine into Val's crystal glass. The rich garnet color swirled in the bottom of the goblet, filling gradually until just halfway. She would have to drink some of this, Val realized. A few sips of it would be worth the risk of refusing altogether.

Raising the cup in her hand she applied the cool rim to her lips and let the liquid play along her tongue. When she set it back down, she had hardly drunk any at all.

Quietly, Jason removed Peter Higgins card from his pocket and examined it closely. He flipped it over, frowning at the handwritten numbers. Placing it down on the table, he locked eyes with Val.

Slowly, he slid the small slip of paper across the surface of the table until it was staring up at her. Lifting her hand from her lap, Val covered the card completely. Curling her itchy fingers around it, she retracted it back to the safety of her body.

"What is that, Val?" Jason asked quietly, not breaking eye contact. "Are you talking to Higgins? Does he know about the investigation?"

"No," she assured him in a rush. "He doesn't know anything about the investigation. I'm not talking to him."

"Then why did he give you his cell number? Why would you have it on you?"

"That card..." She swallowed hard. Try as she might, she couldn't think of any explanation except for the truth. "That card is my back up plan. Representative Higgins offered to smuggle me out of the country. Give me a free life, if I ever just called."

Nodding, Jason tilted back in his chair. Blowing out a breath, he reached for his wine and downed it in several long gulps. Shifting uncomfortably, he seemed to battle himself. She watched him struggle, not knowing what else to say. Another time, when she was a different person, she would have gone to him. But not now.

"You never slept with Gabe," he began.

"I tried to tell you-"

Jason held up his hand to cut her off, shaking his head in slow defeat.

"I trotted out every single woman that I could think of, for over a month, in front of you. And you're telling me that the whole time you could have just called that number and disappeared?"

His eyes snapped up to search hers, the wretched shame in them was clear.

"Yes," she admitted.

"Why didn't you make the call?"

"I don't know."

"You really didn't care about all the other women? You don't feel anything for me? You're just waiting to save Bee, and then you're gone? What is it? I know I don't have a right, but I need to know. Please," he begged.

"I'm not supposed to care about the other women. We've been trained for that, to accept it. But yes, I admit that it hurt me."

Nibbling on her lip, Val wondered how much more to say.

He had given her back the card, but could he prevent her from leaving? If things had played out differently, then she would have stayed, but they hadn't.

The dining room door opened. Anne Marie walked in and set down their plates. Prime rib, roasted red potatoes, creamy spinach, more wine. Moving about deftly, she refilled Jason's glass before leaving them alone.

Despite the topic of conversation, Val could not stop herself from eating. She was hungry in a way she never had been before, so she cut and scooped and ate with a singular focus. It wasn't until she was halfway through that she noticed Jason watching her. His food was untouched.

Reluctantly, she put down her fork, and resolved to answer his questions.

"Yes, of course I have feelings for you," she admitted, holding his gaze for a few moments again before glancing down. "And no, I won't leave after we save Bee. I'll stay with you."

Crossing to her, Jason knelt next to her chair and pulled her down onto his lap. His hands snaked around her waist, his lips brushed her forehead. He caressed her with his words, making desperate promises. He was sorry about what happened with Gabe and with the other women. He would make it up to her. He could make her happy. She would see.

Placing tender kisses on her cheeks, lips and neck, Jason refused to stop. Refused to let her go. She could feel his love radiating from within him and her heart shattered then.

Because she knew now that her lie would hurt them both in the end. The first part had been true. She was in love with this man. But the second part was not.

After Bee was safe, Val would make that call and be gone with their baby, forever.

CHAPTER 16

THEY HAD TO WAIT THREE WEEKS FOR THE NEXT BUSINESS
convention in Manhattan. Val spent the time on pins and
needles. Her nerves ran high during the day, fluctuating
between worry for Bee, and anxiety over keeping her own
precious secret. At night, after dinner with Jason, when the
cold wind blew the heavy trees outside Summer House, she
let his love overtake her.

He had moved her back into the master suite and she
never felt such peace as the first few moments of unreality
each morning when she woke. Blinking in the light of the sun,
her awareness of the truth would gradually come back into
focus. She was certain that Jason had no idea.

But all that was over now. They were finally on his private
jet heading for New York. For Val, a sense of everlasting calm-
ness had set in. They were on their way to see Bee. Her best
and oldest friend.

Jason had contacted The Cambric Agency, and after some
persistence, they relented in booking her for a half day
appointment. They had worked hard to persuade Jason to try

someone else. Claiming they had prettier, younger girls that looked even more like Val, than Val herself.

But he had used his charm and years of business experience to adjust the situation in his favor. He could have Bee for half a day, but would then be required to return her. When he mentioned a possible permanent placement if things went well, they hesitated, agreeing that it could be negotiated after a thirty day waiting period.

Val had wracked her brain at that time frame. It was not typical of Cambric policy. The only reason for it that she and Jason could come up with was that Bee was on a heavy drug regimen. The thirty days would be the right amount of time for a detox and it fit Bee's personality to have to medicate her to keep her working. When she first found out, Val had been sick over it.

But that was a week ago now and the moment they lifted into the air, all of the stress and worry and regret had melted into the ground, staying behind her in Texas.

Instead, Val counted the hours in her head until she would see Bee again. It was an early morning flight with touchdown in New York scheduled for noon, adjusted for the time change. Then there was the ride from the airport to The Plaza in Manhattan. It shouldn't take more than an hour, probably less. Jason had made Bee's appointment for two o'clock, so even now her old friend was probably prepping for her trip into the city.

Staring out the side of the jet, Val watched the ground move far beneath them. Sporadic clouds covered the earth. Every now and again a glimpse of farmland would flash. Then the next time there would be a network of roads, or the sprawl of suburbia.

Feeling him gently rub her back, Val turned to smile into

Jason's tense face. Where she had blossomed with confidence at the task ahead, he had gathered her former burdens and carried them heavily. Halfway through, Marcy brought them breakfast burritos. It was a childhood favorite of Jason's and Val sprinkled hers liberally with salsa.

Taking a large bite, she glanced across the aisle and eyed their newest addition. He was an absolute monster. Relenting to Finn's demands, Jason had finally hired a personal security guard. At six-foot-five and easily two-hundred-fifty pounds, the man was exactly what Val pictured a bodyguard to be.

His name was Calvin T. Beckett, but he preferred to go by CT. A slick shaved head was a stark contrast to his thick black beard. Calculating brown eyes, forever scanning ahead, were almost always hidden behind sunglasses.

Marcy had brought him two burritos instead of one, and he munched happily.

"Need another burrito, CT?" Jason asked, after the first two disappeared easily.

"No, Boss," CT replied, wiping his fingers on the warm damp towel Marcy offered.

He was a man of few words. It made Val smile.

He had come highly recommended from a business associate of Riggs Oil. CT had no political affiliations, no moral qualms about captive status, affairs, gambling, or drug use. He showed up, did his job, took his paycheck, and went home quietly. It was just what they needed.

When the jet landed safely on New York soil and taxied to a stop, a private car service was already waiting. Jason and CT had run through scenarios for exiting and entering vehicles a handful of times, but occasionally still clashed. Upon leaving the jet, CT descended first and opened the door of the vehicle, glancing briefly inside. He then returned to shadow Val and Jason on their way in.

"CT," Jason huffed. "Stay with Val. Get her inside first. I can handle myself."

"Yes, Boss." CT ducked his head, shifting positions to protect Val alone while letting Jason walk well out of his zone of influence.

Riding shotgun on the way to the hotel, CT remained silent, sunglasses on, observing the surroundings as they passed. Val spoke to Jason in hushed tones.

"Take it easy on the guy," she admonished. "He was hired to protect you, not me. Let him do his job."

"*I* hired him," Jason hissed. "He does what I say. I want you safe first, then me."

"I'm not the one with the death threats," she replied, but resolved to let it go. The ego of a Texan man was about the same size as the state itself.

Weaving through the streets of Manhattan, the sedan approached a castle-like hotel. Its massive white stone structure was trimmed in an almost mint color of light green. It was not the tallest building around, but something about its architecture lent it an air of imposing weight. On the sidewalk, just outside the red-carpeted entrance, a swarm of people lingered.

"I guess I should have booked under an assumed name," Jason muttered to himself, as the sedan pulled to a stop at the curb.

CT exited first and opened the door for Val. As soon as her leg made its first tentative step onto concrete, the push of people rushed forward. Cameras flashed, voices shouted, but she felt safe in the protective bubble that a man the size of CT could create.

"Why are you back in New York?!"

"Is it true you're forced to work in the stables?!"

"How do you feel about Jason's other lovers?!"

The questions were designed to draw a reaction, she knew, but that didn't mean they weren't effective. Keeping her head tilted to the ground and large sunglasses firmly in place, Val let CT lead her up the steps and into the lobby.

Once through the doors, peace resumed. The hotel staff stood guard to prevent the reporters following them any further.

Glancing back through the glass doors, Jason could be seen amongst the group, answering several questions. He even posed for a few photos. Calm and confident, the tension that had plagued him recently didn't show. He excelled at this game. If anyone at Cambric had concerns, they need only look at his public persona. Jason Riggs, rich playboy, mixing a business trip with a bit of pleasure. She wasn't the only one who could act the part.

A slight man in his forties came to flutter about her. Offering his apologies for the swarm outside, he beckoned her further into the lobby. Its massive marble columns and vaulted ceiling made for a breathtaking room full of luxury and light.

She declined a glass of champagne but accepted a bottle of sparkling water. Sipping it, she listened to the echo of voices as other patrons strolled carelessly through the space. Heading out to the street or in towards the bank of elevators, they lived life unhindered.

As CT went back out to retrieve his boss, Val stood for a few minutes alone. What sort of life had Jason lived before purchasing her? He had been a public figure, yes, but the captive controversy had thrust him into a much brighter light. One that was casting an incredibly long shadow.

Was all this worth it? He was sacrificing his personal security and putting his family legacy in jeopardy. If only all the people who loathed him knew what his true motive was. Would they be the first to apologize when they found out? Somehow she didn't think it was likely.

When Jason and CT finally came inside, she exhaled a breath she didn't know she'd held. Time with him was running out.

Balancing on her four-inch heels, she waited while Jason checked them in and confirmed his acceptance of an appointment with Cambric for two o'clock. They were then shown to their one bedroom suite located on the nineteenth floor. CT was set up in an adjoining room.

"Are you alright?" Jason asked, as he settled himself into a blue suede sofa at the center of the room.

"I'm fine." She slipped out of her heels.

The carpet was plush between her toes as she walked the space. The decor was a mix of old-style wood furniture covered in brash blue patterns, with modern abstract art hanging sporadically on the walls. Pausing at the window, she took in the view of Central Park. Its deep green expanse caused a strange void in the middle of the skyscrapers and paved streets.

"I'm going to order lunch. What do you feel like?" Jason crossed the room to a small desk and picked up a sleek silver hotel phone.

"What do they have?"

"I'm sure they'll make anything that you want."

He waited.

"Pasta sounds delicious right now." She turned to glance at

him over her shoulder, stealing her eyes from the bustle below. "Maybe a chicken alfredo?"

"Sure." He depressed a button on the phone before muttering under his breath, "You really do have an appetite lately."

Biting back a knowing smile, she returned her gaze to the streets below. Food was like a new obsession for her. Though she didn't have any unusual cravings, the quantity never seemed to satisfy. Consciously, she tried to keep from placing a comforting hand over her belly.

Bittersweet feelings filled her throat. She was a liar. Ducking her head, she excused herself to the restroom.

Lunch arrived a half hour later, but Jason hardly touched a bite. When seated, his leg tapped out a nervous dance. When standing, he paced relentlessly. Val watched him alternate between positions as she polished off her heaping plate of noodles. Eyes cruising over to his plate, she held herself back from eating his sandwich.

For Jason, this was the culmination of over five years of investigative work. All the risks that he had taken now hinged on the DNA of one person. And that one person was about to walk through the door.

Val could understand his level of stress but her experience was quite the opposite. A queer excitement had taken over. She was about to see her sister again for the first time in almost a year. It didn't matter what the DNA results were, to Val, this was Bee. She would always be her family. And besides, if the DNA didn't match, then Jason had still committed to purchasing Bee out of captivity. For Val, this was a win-win.

The knock that finally sounded on the door took them both by surprise. Jason had been sitting, holding Val's hand. At the sound, he jumped immediately to his feet. She rose as well. Nodding to him then, Val retreated into the bedroom and shut the door behind her.

It wasn't that The Agency didn't know she was with Jason. It was that Val wanted to avoid seeing them herself. Any possible tell that could play across her face would be potentially dangerous for both Bee and Jason. So, they agreed she should remain hidden.

Keeping her ear against the closed door, Val listened as Jason let Cambric Security and Bee into the room. He laughed easily with the guard while signing the necessary paperwork. Guess the nerves had finally left him.

It wasn't until Val heard the faint beep of the arm scanner, that her heart began to pound a furious pace in her chest. The heavy front door swung shut, and with the click of the lock, the room dropped into silence.

This was her cue. This was when Val was supposed to emerge. But as she reached for the door handle, Val's hand shook. All the steady sense that had boosted her the entire day had fled with that scanner's beep. Glancing at her own forearm she trembled with a renewed fear. Her safety, and that of her unborn baby, were merely an illusion.

"Come on out, Val." Jason raised his voice slightly from the other room, but Val remained frozen in place.

Footsteps approached.

She managed to step back as Jason twisted the knob and pushed the door inwards. His eyes found hers through the six-inch opening created by the door and his face fell. They had traded positions again. The burdens, the stress, the nerves. They had all been transferred back over to her, and she struggled under their weight.

The warmth of his hand clasped hers gently. He coaxed her out of hiding.

"Bee," Val whispered.

The woman who stood in the center of the room, tipping slightly on too tall heels, was a thin shadow of the devastating beauty she had once been. Cambric had cropped her brown hair short. The sleek bob ended abruptly along the line of her chin. It framed a gaunt face, drawn from lack of sleep, or inadequate food, or perhaps excessive drug use. The short red dress she wore revealed thin legs, pale from months without sunlight. But the unusual green eyes... they still glittered shockingly. A touch jaded maybe, but it was the same person underneath.

"Val?" Bee questioned, eyes registering surprise.

"It's me, Bee." Val crossed to her then, wrapping the waif-like body in her own healthy arms. "I was afraid I'd never see you again."

"Me too," Bee managed, before they both broke down, crying together as they swayed on their feet.

Tipping unsteadily, Jason guided them to sit on the couch. He chose a chair across from them and handed Bee his uneaten sandwich. Glancing to Val first for confirmation, Bee consumed it ravenously, taking big bites, barely stopping to swallow.

"Don't they feed you?" Val asked.

"When I'm not on discipline, yes." Bee managed to rush through the answer before resuming her meal.

"How often are you on discipline?" Jason interjected.

"Often," Bee answered, then seemed to remember herself.

Looking up at Jason, she blanched and sat up straighter. "But I have a strong desire for improvement, and can accommodate any requests you may have of me."

"Bee." Val rubbed comfortingly at her sister's back while peering into her face. "It's alright, you can trust him."

Bee's brown hair fell forward to cover her expression. She kept her gaze focused on the floor. Jason reached for the other half of his sandwich and placed it carefully on Bee's plate, but she made no move to grab it. Val continued to stroke her back, but knew that her sister was suffering in fear. Jason seemed to sense it, too. Leaving them alone, he shut himself firmly into the bedroom.

"Is he your owner?" Bee whispered then.

"Yes," Val admitted. "But he is a kind man. A very good man, in fact. There is so much that I have to tell you."

And the story unraveled itself for the next two hours. When Val got to the part about Veronica Durand, Bee shook her head no, firmly denying she was anything but a captive born. Maybe it was too much to think that by rights she shouldn't have had to endure any of the awful things that had been done to her.

Jason came back out to join in the discussion and between the two of them, they were able to convince Bee to submit to the DNA test. Mouth open, Bee held still as Val inserted the cotton swab. Gently, Val swiped it along the inside of her cheek, then around her gums. Sealing everything up in its plastic package, Val and Jason both initialed it, including the date and time. Then it went straight into the small safe located inside the closet of their bedroom.

Whatever the results, they assured Bee that Jason would buy her and subsequently set her free. Once the kidnapping ring was brought down, of course.

"The thirty day waiting period," Bee admitted. "Is for the detox program. Cambric placed me on a drug regimen after I started failing my monthly clients."

"I thought you were hourly now."

"Well, after the whole thing with Gabe, they removed me to Isolation for six months. I suspect that's how long it took to prep and sell both of you."

"That's about right," Val cringed.

"When I was phased back in, they marketed me as monthly membership. But I was only able to play that part for a few months before it became too much." Bee shrugged once, then cleared her throat. "A few of my clients complained so I was demoted to parties. Before each gig they hand out a little series of pills for the all girls and that made it okay. When you take them, the whole thing isn't really so bad."

"But you don't do parties anymore?" Jason asked.

"No. A lot of the party girls can handle the drugs well. I just liked them way too much. I started trading extra food and client tips for more pills. Eventually they caught on to me. I've been stepped off a lot of it, but to do hourly appointments they still have to give me some. It's never enough though." Bee blew out a breath.

"I'll put in the request to start the purchase process today." Jason told her. "I'll make sure they don't book you anymore appointments during the waiting period."

"Thank you." Tears formed at the corners of Bee's eyes.

"If the DNA comes back as a match, then the FBI will be able to secure a warrant to remove you right away," Jason added. "And I think it will be a match, Bee. Even Gabe thought so when he saw Veronica's picture."

"Gabe? You've seen him?" Bee's face lit up, eyes bouncing from Jason to Val.

"Yes," Val confirmed. "He's risked a lot to help us get to this point. Jason has, too. That's why we need you to make sure you don't breathe a word of this to anyone."

"I won't," Bee assured them. "Tell me about him. Is he okay?"

"Bee." Val was serious now. "If you change anything about yourself, if they even begin to suspect that something is up, then Gabe could very well be killed. I'm dead serious."

"Why? How? I swear it, they won't know anything."

Jason and Val shared a quick glance. How much should they tell her? Gesturing to his wrist, Jason indicated they were running short of time. Dusk had arrived without Val noticing. Its shadowy grayness filled the wide windows of their suite.

In the time they had left, Val did her best to fill Bee in on Gabe's involvement without getting into too much detail. By the time the knock came again at their door, the women clutched each other in a last embrace. Val's lips brushed Bee's cheek before she faded back into the bedroom.

She had done it. Val had kept her promise. They found Bee and she was going to get out, one way or another. The realization should have been comforting, but the distant sound of one final scanner beep had Val collapsing to her knees. They had accepted Bee back into Cambric custody, she was under their control again, it was just that easy.

Trembling on the floor in a puddle of weakness. That is where Jason found her. With a grimace, he sank down next to her and listened quietly to her hysterics. She shoved her right forearm in front of his face. She screamed at him.

"Take it out! Cut it out of me now!"

Shaking his head pityingly side to side, he reminded her they would have to wait for FBI approval. Just having the thing living underneath her skin filled her with a sickly raw fear. What could they know about her aside from her location? Did they monitor every breath? Every heartbeat? Did they know if there were two?

Getting up she rushed to the bathroom and vomited in the toilet.

"They can't touch you, Val." Jason came up behind her. "I will protect you. I promise."

Swiping the back of her hand across her mouth, she rocked back on her feet and stood slowly upright. The woman in the mirror who stared back at her was a frightened, but robust, version of the sickly drug addict who had just left.

Blinking at her own reflection, Val couldn't help but think how easy it would've been for the roles to be reversed. Of course Jason thought he could protect her, he owned her, she belonged legally to him. But the truth she was hiding from him changed everything. No one could protect her baby. No one could offer her what she so desperately needed. No one except Peter Higgins.

"The convention dinner starts in another hour." Jason hovered, leaning against the frame of the bathroom doorway. "We have to make the drop to Finn tonight. Can you be ready?"

"Yeah." Val turned on the shower. "How do we get it to him?"

"He and Agent Schipp have been in New York for the past few days setting everything up. Finn will be our driver tonight. All we have to do is bring the DNA kit down in your purse and leave it with him in the car when we get out for dinner."

"That sounds simple enough." She agreed.

As she undressed, Val worked to shed the overwhelming fear that resided in her body. When she stepped into the shower, the hot spray of water stung her skin. The bright pain was distracting and welcome. She let the water cascade over her shoulders. An hour wasn't much time to get made up, so she would need to skip a full wash on her hair.

Bee's visit had thrown Val off course, leaving her at once empty and desperate. If she was going to survive this, if she was going to save her baby, then she had to strengthen her resolve now. Losing focus was not an option.

Cutting the shower short, she passed Jason as he shaved carefully in the mirror. A path of tiny drips followed her as she moved to the closet and appraised her gown for tonight. Full length, formal, fitted satin in a remarkable shade of sapphire blue. Val fretted at the tightness of the fabric, it wouldn't be long until she could no longer wear this size.

Makeup, a curling iron, and lots of hair spray later, Jason looped her favorite strand of diamonds around her neck. They were the first gift he had given to her, and she let the memory ease the stress in her face.

"Val." Jason stood behind her, his hands resting on her bare shoulders. She studied his face in the mirror. "I meant what I said before. I'll never let them touch you. And... I know I haven't said it before, but... I love you. I mean. I'm *in* love with you."

"I'm in love with you, too."

She echoed his words, responding easily because it was the truth. At once a look of relief and peace crossed his face. He exhaled then, before swallowing hard and clearing his throat.

Offering him her purse, she waited as he opened the safe, and placed the sealed DNA test into her bag. He handed it back before helping to drape a black mink shawl over her shoulders. Stroking the incredible softness, she fretted briefly about the animals that had made it.

"Is it real?" She asked.

"I'm from Texas," Jason countered. "Of course it's real."

Taking his arm, she tucked her body close against him, as if trying to absorb the safety from his contact. CT waited for them in the hall, his hulking figure was outlined smartly in a formal suit.

During the ride down in the elevator, Val blinked at their reflection in the ornate gold-tinted glass. The panels were framed with a rich dark wood that covered the entire interior of the small box. All she could think of was how it made for the most lovely of cages. When the muted ding of arrival sounded, the doors slid open to reveal the expanse of luxurious lobby.

"Mr. Riggs." It was the slight gentleman that had checked them in hours before. He rushed over upon seeing them. "Your driver waits for you just outside, but I'm afraid that a rather disorderly crowd has gathered. Will you wait until I can call the NYPD to disperse them?"

"No." Jason looked to CT. "I think we can handle a few steps to the car. Anyway, they weren't that bad a few hours ago."

"Yes." The man nodded, as if to give in, but then he persisted. Following them towards the exit, he added, "This crowd seems to be made up of protestors as well as reporters, Sir."

"Thank you." Jason dismissed him. "We'll be fine."

But as they reached the spread of tall glass exit doors, Val caught her breath. Illuminated by the light from the hotel, stood a mass of people, maybe fifty or more. Some had signs waving in the air. Some yelled, chanting words that she couldn't quite hear. It was obvious they were anti-captive, and Jason had become the scapegoat for all that encompassed.

"The car should be just past them." Jason turned to CT whose face was set in a grim line.

With a nod to the doorman the glass swung outward. CT pushed his bulk through first, creating a small void for Val to follow. She felt Jason's hand resting firmly at the small of her back. Noise overwhelmed her other senses, the crowd gained in momentum at their arrival.

At once, all organized chanting was replaced by screams of anger.

"You're disgusting!"

"Hypocrite!"

"Free all people!"

"Let her go!"

She tried not to look at the faces that rushed up to shove and jostle them. Terror rocketed through her as strange hands tore at her hair, her arms, and her clothing. Clinging to CT's back with one hand, and her purse with the other, she couldn't see how far they were from the car.

Suddenly, large fingers closed around her left arm, wrenching her grasp from CT. Gasping, she was yanked sideways, her shawl tumbled to the ground.

"Get back!" Jason shouted.

Darting forward he wrapped a protective arm around her middle and tried to pull her away. The other man wouldn't let go. Quickly Jason maneuvered between them. And cocking back he landed a fist in the other man's face.

The impact caused the thick fingers to briefly lose their

grip. Val staggered back and away as Jason soon became overrun with retaliation. CT whirled to envelope her. Like a linebacker he shoved through the crowd with her tucked under one arm. Chaos ensued.

"Jason!" Val screamed.

She had lost sight of him in the flurry of fists and bodies. Had he been knocked to the ground? Were they stomping on him now? Agent Finn met them at the passenger door. Flashing his badge at CT, he shoved her inside and slammed the door. Through the glass, she heard Finn shouting.

"Go save your boss! I've got her!"

Flinging open the front passenger door, Agent Finn darted inside. Yanking it shut behind him, he crawled over to the driver seat. Val pressed her face against the car window, watching in horror as CT joined the fray. Picking whole people up bodily, he cast them aside.

"Go help him!" Val yelled at Finn. She heard him click the door locks.

"Do you have the DNA?!" He shouted back.

"Go help him Finn!" Val screamed again. The car sat in park.

"Do you have it?" He persisted.

"Yes, I have it! Now go help him. Please!"

As Finn put the car in drive, she began to cry.

Yanking violently at the door handle, she shouted her fury, but was unable to unlock it. The push of bodies faded quickly behind them as they pulled away. Tears streamed down her face, but anger readily replaced them.

Finn was talking hurriedly into his cell phone, she listened intently.

"Send black and whites to The Plaza immediately," Finn

demanded. "Assault in progress on Jason Riggs and his personal security guard. Keep me updated."

He hung up. Tossing the phone in the center console, he ran a hand over his face.

"Why didn't you help him?" She dragged the words out of her lungs, aching now with a strange agony.

"I'm sorry, Val." Finn glanced at her in the rearview mirror. "The investigation is priority. I couldn't blow my cover."

"He's getting the shit beaten out of him by a huge mob, and all you can think of is the DNA? After everything he's scarified for you guys? This is how you leave him? It's wrong. It's so, so wrong!"

"I begged him to get two guards!" Finn bit back, showing the first emotion she had seen from him. "He knew what the risks were when he signed up for this. Damn it. Sometimes you have to sacrifice a few people to save many more. Right now, that's you and Jason."

"I hate you," she breathed it out, letting the tears fall to streak the makeup she had so carefully applied only a short time before.

City lights and other cars crowded at her window. She placed her hands subconsciously on her belly, mourning for the fragile life that grew there.

"It *is* just you and Jason." Finn stared at her in the mirror. "Isn't it, Val?"

CHAPTER 17

Not able to meet his gaze, she kept her eyes focused on the passing buildings in downtown. Her throat was constricted, burning all the way down into her stomach. Blinking through tears, she opened her clutch and tossed the DNA kit into the front seat. Let him have what he came for.

"Does he know you're pregnant?" Finn asked quietly.

"I don't even know if I'm pregnant."

The car rocked then. She let her shoulders sway slightly with the movement. Braking for traffic, then accelerating in uneven bursts, several minutes passed. Finally, his cell phone rang. Scooping it up, he answered immediately. She clung desperately to his one-sided conversation.

"What's his status?" Finn asked, waiting a beat for the answer. "Do you know what hospital? No, I don't think you can risk going. Do you still have that buddy in the NYPD? Okay, yeah. Let me know the second you hear back. Also, Schipp? I need a Witness Protection Kit. Bring me a pregnancy test, too. Thanks."

Clicking off, he tossed the phone down on the center

console and switched on his blinker. Maneuvering through traffic, he made first one turn, and then another. Gradually, the high-rises of downtown spread out before ceasing altogether.

"Where are we going?" She asked, not sure if she could handle hearing about Jason's injuries. It meant he was alive though, right?

"Jason's in serious condition, and being taken to the hospital now. His injuries are non-life threatening. The NYPD will provide him with protection." Finn answered the question she hadn't asked. "The way I see it, you have two options."

"Oh yeah?" She spat, still not meeting his eyes.

"You can return to Jason once he's out of the hospital. You can live your life with him, try to hide the baby. Eventually, The Agency will find out and take what belongs to them. You and I both know that."

"Sounds about right." Applying the heels of her palms to her eyes, she exhaled.

"Or, I can put you in witness protection. No one will ever know that you're pregnant. When you have the baby, it will be under your new identity as a free person, making the baby free. You won't be able to live a life with Jason, but you can give the gift of a free life to his child."

"So I have to choose between abandoning Jason, and saving the baby he knows nothing about?"

For weeks she had already made this choice, but when confronted with the reality of leaving, her heart wanted to explode.

"I will pass you off to a handler. They won't know who you are. They'll think you're just another woman running from an abusive boyfriend. They'll place you in another state, in another home that's safe. Even I won't know where you are. But you must stay there until the trial," he cautioned her.

"Right the precious trial."

"After you testify," he ignored her remark. "Then we'll place you back where you were. You can move on with your life. With your *free* life, and free baby. Imagine, never having to look over your shoulder wondering when Cambric would catch up."

"It's not even a question," she muttered into her hands. Then looking at his reflection in the rearview mirror, she asked, "Will you tell him? About the baby?"

"No," he answered. "If he knew, he wouldn't stop until he found you."

"Alright then. I'll do it."

The car worked its way through darkened streets for a few more minutes before they ducked into an underground parking garage. Finding a corner with one black SUV parked alone, Finn pulled to a stop. They waited there in silence. Agent Schipp exited the other vehicle, leaving the driver door wide, and strode around to open Val's door.

"Get out," Finn instructed. "Leave the purse."

Doing as she was told, she teetered across the distance in her strappy heels. The clicking echoed against the enclosed concrete walls. Getting in the front passenger seat, she was momentarily surprised as Schipp knelt down next to her. He removed a small shrink-wrapped packet from his pocket and tore it open.

"Turn your ahead away," Schipp instructed.

She did, biting her lip as the slap of latex gloves encased

his large hands. Grabbing her right forearm, he felt along her skin. Pressing down every once in a while, he tried to locate the tiny tracker that lay just beneath.

When he found it, she felt the cold wipe of a sterile pad, then a deep, piercing pain. Her left hand shot up to slap heavily over her own mouth, trying to muffle the scream of pain that wanted to erupt. After he was finished, a dull ache throbbed along the incision site. Deftly, he bound her arm with gauze.

"Let's hope this doesn't set off any alarm bells at Cambric," Finn commented as Schipp swung her door shut.

Closing her eyes, Val leaned back against the seat and listened to the men's exchange through the open driver side door.

"He's going to be okay, just a couple of broken bones is all," Schipp stated.

"Thank God," Finn replied. "Did you get the stuff I asked for?"

"Yeah, it's all there. I tossed in some burgers, too. Safe-house location is a few hours from here. I sent the details to your phone."

"Thanks, man. DNA kit is in the front seat. Get on that ASAP."

"Will do. The case handler should show up first thing tomorrow morning to pick her up."

"We'll be ready," Finn affirmed.

She heard the two men clasp hands briefly before Finn slid inside and slammed the door shut behind him. Once out of the parking garage, he guided the SUV onto the highway. The tantalizing smell of greasy hamburgers filled the cab, but Val refused to ask for them. Mouth watering, she clamped her teeth together, and instead stared sullenly out the window.

At least Jason was okay, for the most part. Her mind struggled with the idea that all of this was worth it. In the broad light of day, she would have to say yes, of course. Saving Bee and any other captives had to be placed first in line. But here in the darkness of the night, her heart rebelled. While Jason lay in a hospital bed somewhere as she made off with his baby, down low here, that's when her answer changed to a no.

"You win." Finn broke her reverie.

Reaching behind him, he brought forth two heaping fast food bags. Snatching hers greedily, she dug through and shoveled soggy French fries into her mouth. Stale or not, it was food and she was famished.

Paper crinkled as they both unwrapped their lukewarm cheeseburgers. Finn lost his grip momentarily on the wheel. Instinctively, Val reached out to keep them straight. When he took back control, he ducked his head. Sadly, as if in apology for all that had transpired, but she refused to acknowledge him.

Her focus settled on consumption. It was the only thing keeping her from losing it.

With a full belly, heavy heart, and desperate thoughts, Val reclined her seat back and tried to drift off. Her head swayed gently in time with the rhythm of the road that passed beneath them. Staring out, she saw the lights of the city be replaced by the twinkle of countless stars. No moon. There was no moon tonight. It was her last thought as she finally surrendered to the mindless empty chasm of sleep.

It was the shift of the vehicle into park that woke her. Sitting up, Val blinked at the brightness of a dimly lit garage.

"Where are we?" She asked, as Finn moved to exit.

"Pennsylvania."

Pushing out the passenger door, she watched him retrieve

a few bags before shoving through the doorway into the house. She trailed him obediently. It was dark inside and hard to make out any details, but she found herself in a small kitchen.

Setting the bags on the counter, Finn moved about, shutting blinds and checking rooms. When he returned, he flipped on a light switch. The clock on the wall registered a quarter to midnight.

"The house is clear. There's only one bedroom, which you can have. I won't be sleeping," Finn announced.

"Okay."

"This bag contains a change of clothes, shoes, hair dye, and colored contacts. You will either need to cut your hair short to leave it brown, or streak it blonde if you want to keep the length. The colored eye contacts are *not* optional. You must wear them at all times, even when you are placed. Understand?"

"Yes, I understand."

"In the morning, I will hand you over to your witness protection case worker. She will know you only as Katrina. She won't ask you for a last name. Don't volunteer one."

"Okay."

"In fact, the less detail you provide to anyone for the rest of your life, the better. Stick as close to the truth as possible. You never knew your parents. Don't invent any."

"I get it." She stopped him, a wave of exhaustion washed over her, causing her to sag.

"It's a lot to take in." He moved to support her. They walked together into the bedroom where she sat heavily on the edge of the double bed. "I'll wake you a few hours before your handler arrives. That should give you time to get ready."

Backing out, he closed the thin white wooden door behind

him. In a daze, she glanced around the tiny room, running her hand absently over the simple cotton sheets and faded quilt that covered the bed. Her eyes were drawn to the small wooden dresser pushed up against one wall. Over it hung a watercolor of a blue vase filled with yellow sunflowers.

She slipped out of her elegant evening gown and kicked off her heels. They would likely be the last she'd ever wear. Crawling nude under the covers, she leaned up to switch off the lonely bedside lamp. Sleep came easier than she would have imagined.

"Val." Finn's gruff voice woke her through the closed bedroom door. "Time to get up."

"I'm up," she called groggily, then groaned as the awareness of her surroundings crept back in.

Jason was hurt, she had fled, and her life was still not her own. Walking naked on the thin carpeting, she cracked the door and called to Finn for the change of clothes and witness protection bag. Moments later, he slid them inside.

The room had a small adjoining bathroom, and so she retreated in there. Rifling through the contents, she found the pregnancy test. Shakily, she unwrapped it first. Just pee on the tip of the little white stick and lay it flat for two minutes, the instructions read.

While she waited, she dressed in the ill-fitting denim jeans and oversized black shirt. Yanking a thick brown hoodie over her head, she tried to stop the trembling. She gripped the square of speckled Formica counter, and peered down at the test.

Two solid blue lines stared back at her, definitely pregnant. A mixture of elation and forlorn longing filled her. This baby would be free, but this baby would also never know its father. Blowing out a breath, she resumed her rummaging through the large brown paper bag. Finding the box of Golden Sunset Hair Dye Number Seventy-Three she decided she'd rather color the full length then have to cut it off.

She set to work brushing in the blonde streaks of dye, following the how-to directions on the box. After rinsing the last of it out, she used a thin towel to wick out the majority of the moisture. No hair dryer here. Now for the contact lenses.

She huffed out a determined breath. Never having applied one before it took her multiple tries. Several tears were shed in frustration before the startling green of her eyes was concealed behind a coffee-colored brown. Examining the finished results in the small mirror, Val was surprised at the scope of her transformation. Without makeup, brown hair, or green eyes, she resembled her former self only vaguely.

"How's it going in there?" She heard Finn lean heavily against the wall next to the bedroom door. You could hear everything in this small house.

"All done," she answered, pushing through to the living room.

"Wow," he commented. "Any last words?"

"Tell him that I'm sorry." She hesitated, biting her lip to keep from tearing up. "That I wanted to be with him in the hospital. Can you tell him that?"

"I will." He nodded.

Sitting next to each other on the lumpy brown couch, they waited for her handler to arrive. Nothing more needed to be said between them. Val let her hand's play across her lower belly. She wouldn't have to hide her pregnancy anymore. That was the only upside to any of this.

When her case worker arrived in a red minivan, Val experienced a flood of relief. The days of covert dark sedans were at an end, for now.

Her handler's name was Jeanine Lucio. She was an employee of the FBI, but specialized in witness protection placement for abused women and children. Auburn hair fell from her head in thick waves, framing a round face dotted with freckles.

On the ride out of Pennsylvania, she did her best to put Val, or Katrina as she knew her, at ease. They would be driving all day long, hoping to arrive in Indiana by six o'clock in the evening.

"I brought along some breakfast." Jeanine spoke out happily, keeping both plump hands securely on the wheel. "Do you like cinnamon rolls?"

"Yes." Val kept her answers guarded and brief.

Her right forearm still ached. She hadn't examined it underneath the bandage. The warm gooey icing on the roll melted in her mouth, but after a few hours, Val's stomach grumbled unhappily. Back in Cambric, she could tolerate small meals and the almost constant pangs of hunger, but her pregnancy had taken on an urgency all its own.

"Can we get something more to eat?" Val broke the silence this time. Poor Jeanine seemed to have given up.

"Of course, Dear." Jeanine flicked on the minivan's blinker to move towards the next exit.

They pulled off the highway and cruised down small surface streets. Val noticed various buildings that had become somewhat familiar to her in Texas. There were gas stations, small strip malls with stores and fast food restaurants. Jeanine selected one of these, stopping short of the speaker box in the drive thru.

"Have you ever eaten here? I love the chicken club sandwich," Jeanine volunteered.

"I'll get one of those, too," Val answered, overwhelmed by the red and white menu board that listed countless chicken-centered options.

When Jeanine got out her plastic credit card to offer payment, Val's gut did a small twist. The Agency had supported her since childhood. In turn, that obligation had transferred over to Jason, who clearly didn't have to worry about money.

Val wasn't sure how to go about offering a contribution here. She had no money of her own, just the cold strand of diamonds tucked carefully into her pocket. Remaining silent as Jeanine handed over her food and a drink, Val waited politely for them to make their way back onto the road.

"How does the money thing work?" Val asked, after Jeanine began chomping on her own sandwich, one hand balanced on the wheel.

"We have a budget for your transition. But once you're placed, you'll have to find work. Actually, Agent Finn slipped me an extra five hundred dollars to go towards your placement. It's not typically done, but I wouldn't look a gift horse in the mouth. We can use it to buy you some better clothes."

"Thank you." Val whispered it, feeling eternally grateful to Finn.

Once Jason recovered and was released from the hospital, he would corner Finn about her whereabouts. Maybe he would offer to pay Finn back then. Scrunching up her face, Val tried to stave off the flood of emotion. It was hard to picture how Jason would react when he realized she was gone.

How long would it take for him to move on? She pushed

the question aside, purposefully biting the inside of her mouth. The shock of pain helped to clear her head.

"Do you feel up to discussing your new identity?" Jeanine ventured, licking French fry salt from the last of her fingertips.

"Sure." Val set about crumpling empty wrappers, shoving all of the trash into one of the bags.

"There's a small stack of papers in the back. You should read them while we drive. Try your best to commit them to memory because you won't be able to take them with you."

"Okay." Val reached around to grab the white sheets.

"Your new name is Kelly Martin. There is a birth certificate for you already and I will finish up your passport before the end of today. Those two items you will keep. Your parents are deceased. You never knew them. You were raised in an orphanage in Upstate New York."

Jeanine went on that way for nearly half an hour. Finn was right when he said they would try to keep it as close to the truth as possible. Things were easier to remember that way. From then on Jeanine would call her Kelly to help her get used to the new name. She must condition herself to answer to it.

Val confirmed that she was indeed pregnant, although she wasn't sure how far along. Jeanine coached her on how to go about setting up an OB appointment once she was situated in her placement home. She made her swear to list the father as "unknown" on the baby's birth certificate, and to avoid naming the child anything that would link it to him.

Of course, Jeanine was under the impression that Val was fleeing a severely abusive ex-boyfriend. It was a good cover story since she didn't know how to use money or function without direction in society. An overbearing man was a convincing explanation as to why Val lacked worldly confidence. Jeanine was her first step in breaking that cycle, or so she believed.

After another hour, they stopped to get gas and use the bathroom. As Val stood in the convenience store, she waited for the bathroom to become available. A television hung in one corner over the head of the desk clerk. It blared out commercial ads for bar soap and dog food.

Shifting from one foot to the other, Val decided that her bladder had taken over her entire abdomen. But then the serious voice of a male news anchor caught her attention. Glancing over at the flat screen, her mouth dropped open in rapt amazement.

Footage of last night rolled freely across the black framed box. She saw herself being carried away by CT. Then a jostled camera focused on Jason as he went down swinging. Bodies jammed in close, blocking out the view as he was smothered by unknown people. They stomped him repeatedly until the camera cut away.

When the door of the bathroom opened, Val darted inside. Despite the unclean conditions, she bent over and retched in the soiled white toilet. It's disgusting stink barely registered in her consciousness. Feeling lightheaded, she thought she may just pass out. She staggered to the sink, splashing cold water over her face until the tingles faded.

Hearing a knock at the door, she flushed the tank using her foot, then let herself out.

"Morning sickness?" It was Jeanine waiting for her.

"Yeah." Val glanced up at the television, but the news had shifted to another story.

"I know just the thing to brighten you up." Jeanine smiled

conspiratorially. "Shopping. But first let's take your passport picture and get that sewn up."

Back in the car, Val's fake smile creased her lips as Jeanine snapped a quick photo. Printing it out like magic in her hand, she affixed the perfectly sized picture page into the passport book and handed the document over to Val.

Shopping with Jeanine was nothing like the boutique experience of Austin with Jason's mother and sisters. The store they entered was huge, sprawling with merchandise as far as Val could see. It wasn't limited to just clothing, either, that was only a section. Following Jeanine closely, Val noted kitchen items, toys, electronics, and even food.

"It's a superstore," Jeanine explained.

Taking her cues from the other woman, Val ran her hand along the numerous racks of clothing. They were all shoved so close together that you could barely tell what was there.

After a cursory stroll through the entire department, Jeanine circled back. Selecting items, she flung them across Val's open arms. It was coming on winter so she would need long pants, warm shirts, a sweater and big jacket.

Being pregnant, she should try to choose loose fitting clothes that would last for several months. Maybe even buy a pair of maternity pants with elastic around the waist. Then it was on to the shoe section. She would need thick socks, a pack of underwear, a few bras, and a large purse.

Val's head spun, her lower back aching by the time she tried everything on, rotating through various sizes. Before they got to the register to check out, Jeanine made Val count up the price on each item and add tax. She explained the idea behind a budget, and staying within your limits. A life in witness protection could be a good one, but never lavish. She needed to stay under the radar.

Flopping back into the minivan, Val fastened her safety belt and reclined back as far as the seat would go. If she had been alone, she could have given in to the overwhelming sorrow. Instead, Val let her mind fly away from her body. Like back at The Agency, surrounded by locked doors and white walls, she released her soul to be free.

A few raw tears squeezed out anyway, but turning her face to the door panel, Val let the past disappear on the road behind her.

When they finally pulled to a stop in front of a small wooden house, night had fallen. The white trim and red brick chimney could just be seen in the glow from a million stars and sliver of moon.

A solitary light shone down from the small front porch, illuminating an old brick walkway and carefully pruned evergreen bushes. Val was thankful for the large jacket. The temperature hovered just below freezing. If there had been clouds in the sky, perhaps she would have witnessed snowfall.

"Welcome to Patriot, Indiana." Jeanine picked her way along the stone path next to Val. "This will be your new home."

The sound of their footfalls cresting the three small steps to the porch could be heard all along the empty street. Still, Val jumped when the front door swung open just before Jeanine went to knock.

Standing in the door frame was a slight woman of about eighty-years-old. Her short fluff of gray hair was combed to perfection, and she smiled kindly up into their travel worn faces.

"You're late!" The older woman piped happily, not a trace of anger in her voice. "But I've kept supper warm for you. Come in, come in."

Jeanine took the first step. Val followed doggedly, thinking of how this journey was not yet over, wondering if it ever would be.

The hallway was cramped but clean, with several hooks lining one wall for coats and hats. Val shrugged hers off and hung it next to Jeanine's. The tight corridor gave way to a small living room where Val observed a tiny television. It was positioned in the corner across from one pink love-seat and an accompanying rocking chair.

A fire burned neatly inside an old iron wood stove. The flames could be seen leaping behind tiny slats in the front grate.

"Kelly." Jeanine looked at Val, then turned to face the older woman. "This is Mrs. Ida Abraham. She has agreed to take you in, and help you to transition into your new life. She's done this successfully with countless women before you, and I'm sure you will find her to be a devoted friend."

"It's a pleasure to meet you," Val answered, shaking hands with Mrs. Abraham. "I appreciate your kindness."

"Oh girl." Mrs. Abraham shook her head easily. "Call me Granny Ida."

CHAPTER 18

THE FIRST SEVERAL WEEKS WERE SPENT GETTING TO KNOW Granny Ida's unique quirks. Ever an early riser, she liked to shower first thing. Singing in the morning, her voice would echo throughout the tiny house. She believed that each day had to be met with the same warrior-like gusto of the day before.

With the energy of a four-year-old, Granny Ida tackled every task set before her, insisting the floors remain swept and the kitchen counters wiped, even when no apparent dirt could be found. They weren't hard requests to maintain and Val soon discovered herself falling quite in love with the older woman. She was, underneath everything, a generous and patient soul.

Every meal was made from scratch and Val was expected to assist. In this way, Granny taught her to cook healthy, homemade meals that were typically much less expensive than most store bought items.

She even began to show Val how to drive her impressively heavy old blue Cadillac. Though the size of the small town didn't really require a lot of driving, winter was upon them, and it was more convenient to stay out of the snow.

There was one long main street, which Granny's house was only two blocks away from. Patriot had a small church, a grocery market, a single screen cinema, one bank, two restaurants and a handful of shops. In the quaint town, everyone knew everybody else. They greeted each other on the street, and stopped to talk for an hour together when they met in the store.

If they looked curiously at Val, it was only in appraisal of another one of "Granny's girls." When it took longer than usual for her to answer to the name Kelly, no one seemed to mind.

Back at home, Granny didn't believe in a lot of television nonsense. Before dinner they would sit together in the cozy living room, fire crackling, and watch precisely one half hour of broadcast news. At that time, Granny would enjoy a single tinkling glass of gin while Val sipped hot herbal tea. That was how Val found out about the DNA match of Bee to Veronica Durand.

One evening, the anchor began with a breaking news alert and proceeded to detail the raid on Cambric Agency. Val's heart leapt in her throat as she watched footage of a ragged Bee being reunited with her mother and father on a runway somewhere in Texas. Tears stung her eyes as Jason was finally outed as an FBI informant and hero, having been released from the hospital a week before.

Not one to break with tradition, Granny rose to shut off the program after exactly thirty minutes. It didn't matter to her that the story wasn't complete. As the screen faded to a dull empty gray, Val snapped suddenly back to her new life.

She would never see those people again. Somehow, she managed to push down her heartache for another day.

Once a week, Granny Ida attended a bible study. It was Val's job to drive her there and back. Sitting quietly, she would listen to the women discuss the word of God as they lifted their voices in prayer to their Jesus. Never having been involved in religion of any kind, Val wondered at the things they said, all so new to her. The Agency didn't allow such teachings, leaving each captive to decide on their own what would happen when they died.

On Sundays, Val drove Granny to church. She flipped eagerly through the bible that rested on the back of the small wooden pew. Apparently, the town of Patriot was filled with Baptists, whatever that meant. Regardless, Val thoroughly enjoyed the signing.

It was there that Pastor Thompson and his wife approached Val with an offer of a part-time job. His brother, Ryan, owned the small diner on Main, and needed a new waitress. As long as Val was physically capable of the work, the position would be hers. She nodded gratefully. Was there no end to the kindness of these strange people?

Her first month of training was a challenge. Dropping platters of hot food on the floor, tripping over customer's outstretched boots, and dumping a pitcher of water in Mrs. Jenning's lap, were just some of the highlights. But Ryan was a patient boss and the other girls working with her did their best to improve her performance.

As Val's belly grew in size, so did her proficiency. After a while, she actually began to enjoy the work. The locals grew to accept her, sometimes they even made seating requests for her section. For the first time in a long time, Val felt pride of a job well done.

When Granny Ida stumbled upon her stack of paychecks one day, the old woman huffed in surprise. Together, she and Val walked the frigid two blocks to Main Street and entered the local bank. The manager coached Val through the opening of her first account, showed her how to deposit checks, and retrieve money back out. It was the first time Val signed her new name, Kelly Martin.

During the following months her bank account slowly grew as her ankles swelled and her body took on a new shape. She made monthly visits to her doctor's office about an hour's drive from Patriot. He assured her that the baby was very healthy, meeting all of its desired size measurements. Val burst into joyful tears when the doctor informed her that she was having a boy. Damn them all, she knew just what she'd name him.

Despite the cold weather, and occasional bluster of snow, Val often times insisted on walking the short distance to her shift at the diner. She loved the comforting quiet of the small old town. Each house she passed had an owner she now recognized. Despite Granny's occasional protest, Val persisted, pointing out that the doctor had told her physical activity was important for the baby.

~

On one gloomy day, she arrived for her Tuesday brunch shift and unwound the crocheted blue scarf the bible group had made for her. Work progressed without incident. She waited on a handful of regulars who came in to sip coffee and exchange old gossip.

When super time approached, she was hit with a slight rush. Consumed with filling glasses, placing orders and delivering heaping plates of spaghetti, she didn't glance up as the old sleigh bell on the front door chimed invitingly.

The new customers made their way to a booth and took seats across from each other. Val spied them out of the corner of her eye. Slowly, she looped around to scoop up menus and plop them on their table. It wasn't until she looked up into the eyes of the women before her, that she stopped short, mouth hanging.

Sparkling green eyes blinked back at her, framed by brown hair grown shoulder length over the past six months. It was Bee. Bee and Jeanine.

"Kelly." Bee peered at Val's name tag, then back up into her face. "Will you be serving us today?"

"Yes," Val croaked, then cleared her parched throat. "Do you know what you'd like?"

"We aren't in any rush," Jeanine intervened. "Serve your customers and come back to us."

Val left them then, trying to hide the shaking of her hand while waddling her heavy frame over to the next table. Thankfully, her regulars didn't notice anything was off. Swallowing her nerves, Val pushed through the rest of her shift. Although treating Bee and Jeanine like she didn't know them was difficult, Val persevered.

When her co-worker came to take over the night shift, Val completed her side duty tasks, then let Bee and Jeanine follow her out into the crisp air.

"Can we give you a ride home?" Jeanine asked. Val nodded, slipping into the backseat of the red minivan.

When they arrived at Granny Ida's house, Jeanine kept the car running, the heater at full blast. She got out unceremoniously and left the two women alone. Val watched out the window as she navigated the cobbled brick path to Granny's front door and let herself inside.

Bee turned around in the front seat and openly stared into the back at Val. Letting her eyes travel down, they rested heavily on the swell of her belly.

"Take your contacts out," Bee commanded. "I want to see my sister."

Blinking, Val complied. Plucking each brown circle from her eyes, Val observed Bee's careful study of her face. Angry lines softened as water brimmed Bee's eyes. Her tears drew moist lines down her flushed cheeks. Her old friend's former beauty had returned full force during the last months of freedom. The drug drawn face had filled in with healthy flesh. Her skin positively glowed in the dim light from the car.

"I've missed you." Val offered her hand, and was rewarded with Bee's tight return squeeze.

"You know… I've missed you, too," Bee stammered. "When they raided Cambric, the first person I thought that I'd see was you. Only half done with detox, I was nearly out of my mind. They took me to see my parents instead."

"I'm so sorry I wasn't there." Val too began to cry, listening to the heartache permeate Bee's voice.

"They're strangers to me. I wanted my family, but you were gone."

"What about Gabe?"

"He got grabbed up by the FBI, too. Protective custody has him until after the trial."

"Oh, I didn't know."

"We thought both of you were together for the first few

months, Jason and I did. Our parents and the reporters, they all wanted us to have a huge reunion. They planned it where Jason and I would see each other again after the raid, and like run to each other and be so happy together.

After I finished detox, and Jason didn't look so bad, they set up cameras at his house, and brought me over there. When he hugged me, the first question he whispered in my ear was if I knew where you were. He came unhinged when he realized that I had no idea."

"Finn was supposed to tell him I was okay," Val interjected, wondering how everything got so mixed up.

"Oh, Finn has been pretty tight lipped about the whole thing. He said he didn't want to upset either of us so soon after recovery. Anyway, Jason and I complied with the media tour. We spent a lot of time together. It all made more sense when we thought you and Gabe were together, but then the letters started coming."

"Gabe wrote to you?"

"Yeah, it became pretty obvious you weren't with him. That's when Jason began to make demands. He refused the media tour, and stopped taking Finn's calls. There was even a private investigator that he hired to try to retrace your steps, but they never got anywhere with it. Once the Feds got you, it was like our Val ceased to exist. And I guess she did."

"Something like that," Val admitted, looking away, her palms slick with perspiration.

"It made me so angry to think that Gabe would write and you wouldn't. Jason began to think maybe you were hurt somewhere, and Agent Finn was hiding it to make sure we all testified. He's really crazy about you, Val." Bee shook her head, wiping at her smudged mascara.

Val didn't know what to say. Her heart thudded painfully

in her chest as she thought of the agony both Jason and Bee had gone through. Tucked safely away in Patriot, she had been spared at least that much. The baby shifted inside her belly then, reminding her just why she had chosen to run.

"How did you get here, Bee?" Val asked finally, rubbing the tiny feet that prodded against her ribcage.

"Jason convinced Gabe and I to refuse to testify without contact from you. The FBI has been in negotiations with Jason ever since. They finally came to terms yesterday, and I was sent out," Bee explained.

"Will you tell him?" Val asked, eyes darting back and forth, searching Bee for the truth.

"They blindfolded me for the majority of the ride out here, but I promised Jason to give him every single detail that I could. You have to understand, I was so angry with you for abandoning us, but that was before..." Bee trailed off, glancing down, she let her gaze land on Val's protruding belly.

"Before what?" Val whispered.

"Before I walked into that restaurant and saw the real reason you had to disappear." Bee looked back up to hold Val's eyes. "I don't blame you anymore."

"You have to swear to me that you won't tell Jason where I am. You have to promise you won't tell him about his baby." Val grabbed both of Bee's wrists, holding tightly when she tried to pull away.

"He saved my life, Val. I owe him something."

"No." Val squeezed harder now. "*I* saved your life. I told him about you. It was me. You owe *me*. Swear it."

"Fine... I swear it." Bee wrenched her arms away, rubbing at her wrists absently. "What do you want me to tell him?"

"The only thing that makes sense." Val pressed her eyes

shut and tried to sound calm. "The only thing that will help him to move on."

"What's that?"

"Tell him that I've met someone else. Tell him that I've left him for another man." Val's voice kept level, even if her insides quaked.

Bee grimaced. After a beat, she nodded reluctantly before reaching into her large purse and pulling out a small white card and tiny black velvet box. Placing them carefully on the center console she pushed them over to Val.

"I already know what your answer will be. But I can't lie and tell him that I gave these to you," Bee said finally.

Eyeing the items as if at a distance, Val fought with herself. On the one hand she desperately wanted to grab them up and hold them close to her heart. But on the other hand, the one based in cold reality, she knew she should push the items away. She should push them away unopened, less she risk being tempted to trade her baby for a life with the man she loved.

In the end, Bee made the decision for her. She ripped open the tiny white envelope, and held the black writing close up to Val's wretched face.

Val

Will you marry me?

Love Jason

Gently slipping the card back in the torn envelope, Bee opened the square box to reveal an exquisite diamond ring. Its round cut solitaire sparkled from every angle, shedding light like raindrops splattered against a window.

Val leaned in, but kept her hands firmly in her lap. Placing a light kiss on the ring, she pulled back then looked down. The box snapped shut with a decided pop. Val felt her heart fracture, flying into a million tiny pieces that fell away from her on the floor.

"The trial date has been set for another six months. I assume you'll be attending without the baby. When are you due?"

"In the spring. It's a boy." Val patted her belly in distracted anticipation. Only six more weeks to go.

~

When Jeanine came outside an hour later, she discovered the two women had fallen asleep. Bee had crawled into the backseat with Val. They held each other loosely. Long blonde streaks mixed with gentle waves of chestnut, as their two heads tilted inward together.

Waking with a jolt, Val crept quietly away, scooting her bulk out the sliding side door and into the bite of wind. She watched as Jeanine drove away with her best friend, the closest thing to a sister she would ever have. A piece of her soul went along with her.

Upon entering the cramped hallway of the house, Granny Ida called her into the kitchen. She had kept a thick broccoli cheddar soup warm on the stove and spooned it happily into an antique bowl. No questions were asked while Val sipped appreciatively. Perhaps these occasional visits from the past weren't so out of the ordinary.

After Bee's departure, Val fell into a pit of melancholy. Going through the motions, she kept up on her household chores, worked hard during her shift, and prayed hard while at church. Granny Ida soothed her, telling her that this late term of her pregnancy was usually plagued by a flood of mixed emotions.

As her doctor's visits increased, Val's work scheduled decreased. Finally one day Ryan shooed her out of the diner the moment she waddled in.

"I won't have your water breaking on my floor." He laughed heartily at her dismay. "You'll have a job here waiting for you when you get back on your feet."

"Thank you, Ryan." She gave up trying to fight the sway that had taken over the movement of her body.

Bickering back and forth, Val and Granny disagreed on what extent to limit the rest of Val's activities. Granny wanted to prop her up with pillows, and Val wanted to scrub the floor of the shower on her hands and knees. She was so tired of being too plump to see her toes, or even to roll over in bed. The countdown to baby boy's arrival had begun.

Spring time in Indiana was a mix of weather. Just when it seemed that the sun was warming the air for good, a cold snap would roll through, smashing the tiny green flower buds back into the hard earth. Val had grown sullen, tired of the perpetual bleakness. Maybe she was overrun by feeling tired in general, and just looked for somewhere to place the blame.

During bible study one evening, she sat idly by as the women took turns reading. Listening absentmindedly, she noticed an increased flutter in her chest, then a low ache that spread itself warmly across her belly. After a few minutes she was forced to lean back, trying to give her tummy the extra room it seemed to always be demanding lately.

That worked for a while, but then the slow creep of burning crossed her abdomen again. She shifted uncomfortably. Granny Ida took notice.

"Feeling alright, Dear?" She asked. All heads swiveled to watch.

"Yes, just a little tightness." Val exhaled, and the pain left her.

"Tightness you say?"

"Well it's gone now…" Val stiffened again, as the pressure returned.

"Back again?"

"Yes." Val's knees began to knock together in trepidation.

"You ladies will have to excuse us." Granny Ida stood, smiling brilliantly. "I think we need to take a drive to the hospital."

Aside from the fear that captivated her mind, the drive to the hospital was smooth and without much distress. The burning pain would come and spread, then leave her at peace for minutes at a time. It was tolerable. Val watched out the windshield as Granny navigated swiftly down the two lane highway. Its barren enveloping darkness seemed perfectly serene. Val tried to absorb the energy.

Upon arrival, a nurse checked her, then recommended she take a walk around the birthing floor to keep things moving. Granny Ida settled in the waiting room. Taking out her latest crochet project, a sky-blue blanket for the newest addition, she told Val that it would be complete by the time the little guy filled his lungs with his first breath of Indiana air.

The hours progressed, and so did Val's pain level. Her ability to walk upright ceased. She sat hunched on the side of the hospital bed, legs dangling loosely towards the floor. With each contraction she moaned her agony into a thick white pillow. A nurse fluttered around, gently offering comfort when possible, but in truth Val had never felt so alone. When the suffering gripped her, she could think of nothing else.

In the few moments of relief in between, her mind filled with Jason. The way he looked when he smiled, the sound of his laughter, the smell of his skin. When they offered her an epidural, she refused, knowing that she would rather endure the blinding contraction than face the memories of the man who deserved to be there.

After two hours of pushing, her son was born. Healthy and screaming his outrage, he was nothing if not completely free. Val wept over him, praising God for saving her son.

On the birth certificate, she averted her eyes as she checked the box listing the father as "unknown."

"Do you swear to tell the truth, the whole truth, and nothing but the truth, so help you God?" The court clerk's serious hazel eyes waited for a response.

"I do," Val intoned. Her left palm grew damp against the old leather binding of the court's bible.

"You may be seated." The clerk removed the thick book.

Swallowing nervously, Val lowered her right hand to tug at the tight fabric of her new business skirt. She hoped no one in the overstuffed room noticed when she casually wiped the sweat of her palms against the gray material.

After almost five months she had lost most of the baby weight, but a nagging ten pounds made her feel uncomfortable as the lights of the court room shone down. The conservative outfit was nothing compared to the expensive clothing she had once worn, but it was the best that she could afford on a waitress's salary.

Watching the lawyers conferring in low tones together, she worked hard to keep her eyes decidedly away from those most familiar in the room. The trial of Sharon Baine had been going on for weeks now. Bee, or Veronica Durand, had given five days of sworn testimony already. Val had seen bits of it over the evening news while tucked in her sanctuary at Granny Ida's house.

Back in the city now for almost forty-eight hours, Val had been brought in early for testimony preparation. It was the longest amount of time that she had been without her son since she had given birth. The need to flee back to him was like a panic attack lying in wait just under the surface of still waters.

"Will you please state and spell your full name for the record?" The prim defense attorney asked.

Sharon had amassed a team of hot-shot legal minds. No less than four hovered around her now. Despite the mountain of evidence, the national media claimed she had a good chance of walking away. *That* could not be allowed to happen.

"Val. V-A-L."

"Is that your only legal name?" The defense pressed.

"Objection, your Honor." The prosecution stood. "This witness is under Federal Protection. Any other identities are privileged and not relevant to this case."

"Sustained." The hefty balding judge agreed. "Stick within the lines counselor," he cautioned.

During her hours of prep, the prosecution team had warned her that the defense strategy would be to shift the focus away from any negative captive conditions. Instead, they would make Val's testimony about the personal relation-ship between she and Jason. The initial DNA test for Bee had been witnessed by them alone. The defense sought to discredit it.

"Can you tell us how you came to be owned by Jason Riggs?"

"He purchased me while I was on display at a business convention in New York."

Val's voice sounded small in the hushed atmosphere. She could feel Jason's eyes boring into her. It was the first time that they had shared a room since the night of the mob attack.

"Did you find him to be attractive at that time?"

"I did." Her heart fluttered.

"When did he first seek for you to perform your trained duties?"

"Objection." The prosecution stood again.

"Overruled. She may answer." The judge responded.

"It was several weeks later." Val focused on the ornate antique desk of the defense attorney. Memories of Jason's arms encircling her floated at the edge of her consciousness.

"Was it something you enjoyed?"

"Objection!" The prosecution shot once more to his feet. "Relevance? This is a highly inappropriate line of questioning."

"It goes to the nature of their captive-owner relationship. If you'll give me a bit of leeway, your Honor." The defense responded.

"I'll allow it." The judge decided. "You may answer the question."

"I did," Val admitted, a blush creeping into her cheeks. She wrung her hands together, hiding them in her lap just below the line of the witness box.

"What about the next encounter?" The defense pressed.

"I always enjoyed my time with Jason." Val sought to cut the line of questioning short, feeling the burn of humiliation as cameras rolled silently in the reporter section of the gallery.

"Was his treatment of you more like that of a girlfriend, and less like that of a D2 captive?"

"Yes."

"So, his ownership was a good experience for you?"

"Yes."

"Life in captivity was much better than most free people experience, is that right?"

"I'm not sure how to answer that." Val was confused.

"You didn't have to work. Everything was taken care of. You spent his money, lived a lavish lifestyle, got everything you asked for. Is that right?"

"Yes, that's right."

"Did you ever feel indebted to him?"

"I did," Val admitted, knowing instinctively a trap was being laid.

"If he asked you to do something for him, then you would have done it, right?"

"I would have."

"So, when he asked you to help him fake a fellow D2 captive's DNA test, you did it, right?"

"No." Val was firm.

"But this is the man that gave you everything you wanted. You couldn't help him with his FBI investigation? Make him look like a hero?"

"I helped him with the investigation, but I never-" Val wanted to elaborate. She couldn't let the defense make it seem like Jason faked that test.

"Just answer the question with a yes or no, please." The attorney cut her off. Val was forced to bite her tongue.

~

For over an hour, they went around and around. Working hard, the defense managed to twist what happened in that hotel room. In turn, they also highlighted the positive aspects of Val's particular captivity, avoiding the truth of her training, and utter lack of control.

At times she felt outrage, at others, despair. Her prep team had warned her that it would feel one-sided when the defense had their turn to question. Above all, her goal was to be truthful, and to keep from having any emotional outbursts. The jury must not only like her, they must also believe her to be sincere.

The defense attorney was poised over her desk while Sharon blinked, unruffled in the seat next to her. Val wondered if any of this even phased the powerful woman. During the past hour, Sharon had appeared relaxed, even bored at times. The thought of her walking away from the charges was terrifying.

What would that mean for Gabe? For all of them? It sent a shiver of fear down Val's spine. This intelligent sociopath must never uncover Val's secret.

"Just a few last questions. Did you fall in love with Jason?" The defense attorney had moved from behind her desk to approach the witness box. Val shifted uneasily, not wanting to answer.

"Yes," she whispered finally.

"Do you love him still?"

Val swore she could feel the entire courtroom lean in towards her. Keeping her eyes downcast, she fidgeted desperately with her hands, squeezing so tightly that alternating fingers turned white.

She wanted to lie, but was under oath. Afraid that the jury might see through her, and dismiss her entire testimony, Val resolved to remain honest. Blowing out a controlled breath, she worked to calm the loud thumping of her heart.

Glancing up, she caught Jason's face in the crowd. Those same arctic-blue eyes pierced her. Even after all this time, her heart beat harder just for him. She was forced to break the connection.

"Yes."

"And people will do anything for the ones they love, right?"

"Objection!"

"Sustained."

"I have no further questions, your Honor." A smug smile illuminated the defense attorney's face as she turned her back to the jury and resumed her seat next to Sharon.

It was the prosecution's turn to cross-examine next. Val provided the ugly details of her training with Cambric. They talked openly about the common practice of withholding meals, refusing to adjust room temperatures, corporal punishment, and other coercive tactics.

Admittedly, Val had it relatively easy in comparison. Tales of the breeding program, and Bee's forced drug use were beyond her ability to speak about. Her testimony was limited to her own experiences, or those witnessed directly by her.

The prosecution walked her through the period of time after Bee's removal. Forcing her to re-live the weeks of hunger, isolation, and sexual manipulation that she had shared with Gabe. The attorney was relentless in his pursuit of detail and it was the first time that Bee had heard anything about it. She wept openly in court.

Watching her friend sitting in the gallery, Val endured

pangs of longing as Jason kept his arms wrapped protectively around Bee. Sobbing together, the Durand family flanked her other side. But… where was Gabe? A pin prick of worry moved through Val when she didn't see his face anywhere. He was scheduled to testify next.

Moving on, they covered the night of the DNA test for Bee, who turned out to be the missing child, Veronica Durand. Val explained how she administered the swab, then carefully sealed it in the package provided. She swore to its validity, confirming that both she and Jason had signed across the seal and never reopened it.

"What happened to the DNA kit once it was sealed and Bee left the room?" The prosecutor questioned.

"I watched Jason lock it in the safe," Val said.

"Did he ever reopen the safe and remove it?"

"Only when we left for the convention dinner."

"Was he ever out of your sight? Could he have opened the safe without your knowledge?"

"No."

"Did you witness when he removed the package?"

"Yes."

"What did he do with it?"

"I handed him my clutch and he put the DNA inside."

"And then you left the hotel together?"

"We tried."

"Is that when the mob attacked you?"

"Yes."

"I'd like to submit the surveillance video of the attack into evidence at this time."

The prosecution crossed to the judge, who beckoned the defense team forward also. As they argued in hushed tones, a wave of panic coursed through Val's blood stream. Would she really be made to watch the whole horrid thing over again? The prep team hadn't mentioned it the day before. Maybe they wanted to get her honest reaction.

Hate built itself into a burning flame that flickered, pushing away her fear. No one had warned her. Instead, they used her. Used her for whatever purpose suited them, with no thought to how she would feel. The defense. The prosecution. All of them.

Frame by frame, the attorney walked Val through the events of that night. She observed herself walking arm in arm with Jason, so secure in her ignorance. Saw CT's bulk do its best to shield her from the reaching arms and thrashing bodies.

Averting her gaze from the next moments, she caught Jason's eye for the second time in the crowd. He nodded once, trying to steady her. His eyes glittered as if to say, they didn't get me, I'm right here. Turning back to the monitor she pressed on.

At the end of the evidence reel, the prosecutor was able to prove that the purse which contained the DNA kit had remained intact and in Val's possession. The FBI agent that had awaited her in the car accepted chain of custody at that time.

Val thought back to the real life version. She wished she could play the sounds of her screaming at Finn to the court. They accepted custody and abandoned Jason all in one moment. That was a truth she would never forget.

"You've been talking to us for a long time now, Val. I appreciate how hard this has been for you." The prosecutor was nearing the end of his questioning.

"Thank you." Val's hand trembled as she grasped a water glass from the edge of the witness box.

"What is your reaction to finding out that the woman whom you thought of as a sister, was actually a free girl, kidnapped from her loving home?"

"My reaction?"

"Yes."

"Confusion," Val responded honestly.

The prosecutor missed a step, face growing pale. It wasn't the answer they had practiced.

"Can you explain?"

"Confusion as to why all of you have been so outraged at how Bee was treated only when you realized she had been born free. Confusion as to why it suddenly mattered that she went hungry, or cold, or was forced to have sex with countless strange men for money she didn't even get to keep.

Confusion as to why the public chose Jason as their vile scapegoat when each and every one of them is responsible for allowing captives to remain as they are. Confusion as to why you would promise to rescue half of Gabe's children, and leave the rest to rot in a lifetime of servitude jail.

You! Each of you here… are the biggest most guilty of all hypocrites that ever walked. Shame on you. Shame on this nation. You all disgust me."

Like the moments after a bomb explodes, the first few seconds in that court were filled with an eerie silence. Then with one certain blast the room erupted with sound.

People stood, shouting their opinions into the air. Reporters shifted camera angles. Attorney's from both sides yelled their objections. The judge banged his gavel repeatedly, calling for order where none was to be found.

Amongst the chaos, Val sought Bee's eyes and held them. She was rewarded by her sister's old rebellious smile. *You're not the only one who can cause a stir anymore.*

Standing up carefully in the witness box, Val smoothed at the wrinkles in her skirt, and fluffed her fitted white blouse. She pushed open the tiny wooden swing door and stepped down the two steps to the floor. Not making eye contact, she wove through the bodies that had spilled out into the aisle and left the courtroom behind her.

Agent Finn met her just outside the doors. Grabbing her arm firmly, they walked together down the cool of the air-conditioned hallway. Passing through long tile corridors aglow with garish fluorescent lighting, he led her to an unmarked room.

Once inside he blew out a breath. She allowed herself to grin openly at him.

"What in the hell did you do in there?" Finn asked.

"What happened?" Gabe's voice sounded from behind her.

Turning, Val looked upon the handsome face of her old friend. His brown eyes glittered at her with concern.

Running the few steps to him, she flung her body against his. They held on, rocking slightly. She ran her hand through his golden locks, relieved to see him alive and well.

"Gabe, you're okay," Val breathed.

"Yeah, I should say the same about you." He held her at arm's length, scrutinizing.

"What's going on with you, Val?"

"Bee hasn't told you?"

"She gave me some line about a new man, but I can see right through both of you." His eyes darted across her face.

"I wish I could tell you, Gabe, but I can't."

"Just tell me that whatever it is, *you* are the one who made the choice."

"I did."

Yanking her back against his chest he hugged her, rubbing

an affectionate hand across her upper back. Just then they heard shouting outside the door. Agent Finn opened it a crack, but was shaking his head a determined *no*.

It was Jason and Bee. Their mix of angry voices resonated deeply within her.

"Let them in, Finn," Val spoke quietly. "Give us just a minute, okay?"

Finn glanced over his shoulder at her. His heavy foot still kept the door mostly closed. They exchanged a knowing look. His eyes told her to tread carefully, and she silently promised him that she would.

Stepping back, he swung the door wide which caused Jason to tumble roughly forward with Bee pushing at his back. Before either of them recovered, Finn stepped around them and let himself out, clicking the door closed behind him.

Gabe moved to help Bee off the floor. Swiping at her expensive dress, she laughed almost giddily into his frowning face.

"You should have heard her in there!" Bee squealed in delight. "It was like our Val finally spoke up after all this time. I wish you got to see it, Gabe."

"I wish I did, too." Gabe couldn't help but be swept up by Bee's personality, he grinned.

Val listened to them banter together like old times, but only with half her attention. Unable to move, she locked eyes with Jason. He was on his knees on the ugly brown carpeted floor, and there he stayed.

He was thinner, where she had thickened out. Although still handsome, she noted dark circles beneath his eyes. They swept over her, seeming to drink in her presence. Heart pounding, she resisted the urge to run.

"I haven't seen you in over a year," he said quietly. Then brushing at his thighs, he rose from the ground.

"How are you?" She asked and observed him shake his head in wonder.

"How am *I*? I've been right here the whole time. The real question is… what *happened* to you?"

"I never meant to abandon you like that. I wanted to be with you in the hospital. Finn was supposed to tell you." Val took one retreating step, not able to endure the flames while his heart burned in front of her.

"Yes, he told me. But that is all he ever told me." Jason stepped forward, closing the gap between them until he could reach out. Hesitant at first, he traced one finger down the side of her cheek.

"It killed me not to be there. You have to know that."

She felt his fingertips travel lightly through her hair, then tug gently at the ends. She had returned it to its natural color for the trial.

"Why? Why couldn't you be there? Can't you even look at me?" His voice had grown quiet.

"Please." She kept her face averted, trembling under his touch.

"I searched for you," Jason continued, his fingers moving to trace lines along her jaw. "I couldn't hardly sleep. Still can't. Then Finn agreed that Bee could see you."

"Finn shouldn't have done that." Val was harsh.

"Tell me about him." Jason's voice shifted to match hers.

"Stop."

Val tried to push away, but Jason gripped her arms.

"You just told the whole world that you still love me, is that true?"

"Stop it, Jason." Val's voice raised.

"Do you love this other guy, too? What's he like? Is he good to you? I have to know!" Jason demanded.

Gabe moved to step in, but Bee crossed in front of his body. She tried to hold him back, but was too tiny against his fit form. He brushed her aside easily with a sweep of his hand.

"That's enough, Jason," Gabe said, reaching to separate them.

"Don't touch me." Jason didn't shift his focus from Val.

"He's not going to hurt her," Bee protested, tugging at Gabe's back. "They need to hash this out."

"I'm not going to stand here and listen while she tells him to stop. Maybe that's why she chose the other guy," Gabe responded.

Instantly, Jason released his hold. Val stumbled back, only regaining her balance on the edge of a nearby desk. Sucking in air, she stared at him. The hurt was raw all over his face. Her heart broke, knowing that she owed him so much, but could give him so little.

"It's okay." Val nodded.

Gabe gathered a still nagging Bee in his arms, and retreated to a far corner of the room. Whispering their differences heatedly, Val realized that some things never changed. But other things did. Covering her face in both hands, she breathed in, trying to gather her thoughts.

"What we had–" Val met Jason's eyes. "Was the most wonderful time of my life. It was real, every bit of it, and yes, I still love you. But–"

"No buts–" Jason interrupted, closing the distance between them.

Hungry arms encircled her waist. Greedy lips pressed down firmly against hers. He poured out a year's worth of heartache into her soul, filling it with the depth of his longing. After a moment's resistance, she let him sweep her away.

Parting her lips, she returned his kiss with the truth of her own passion. For those few seconds she allowed herself to forget their circumstance. Heart throbbing its desperate ache in her chest she traded his fire with her own.

But re-living what they shared brought on an exquisite pain. One that forced her to break their connection. Eyes frantic, Jason cupped her face, ran his thumbs across her lips.

"I'm asking you to let me go." Val watched him squeeze his eyes shut.

"You can't tell me that you don't love me," he whispered.

"I just love someone else more."

The honesty in her answer made him step aside. He let her pass.

Not looking back, Val made a break for the door. Flinging it open she saw Agent Finn leaning against a wall, waiting.

If she hesitated now, she might go back and tell Jason the truth. She might tell him that the person she loved more than him was his very own son. If she let him hold her one more minute, confessions would pour from her mouth. The only other man in her life was a five-month-old baby, but she *did* love him more than anyone else in the world.

"Get me out of here," Val warned.

Their hurried steps echoed down the corridor. This time she gripped Finn's arm tightly as they ducked down hallways and into obscure elevators. They were sneaking out the same way they had creeped in. Down into the underbelly of the courthouse and out a prisoner's entrance. Perhaps this would be the last dark sedan she ever had to ride in, she thought, as Finn helped her to settle into the backseat.

"Guess this is goodbye," he said, almost sadly. "Hell of a

thing you told the world in there. I watched the replay. Just might start a war."

"I hope so." She smiled to herself as he shut the heavy door and tapped on the roof.

Agent Schipp put the car in drive. She watched in silence as he maneuvered the vehicle further and further out of the city.

Because she had to look like Val for the trial, the FBI hadn't felt it was safe for her to fly. They assured her that once things settled down, and she resumed her new appearance, that Kelly Martin would be free to choose her own mode of transportation. For now though, she was limited to escorted drives.

Jeanine picked her up at a truck stop on the Pennsylvania border. Val put her brown contacts back in and had dyed her hair back to blonde in a gas station restroom a few miles previous. If Jeanine was curious about the still damp locks, it was her job not to say anything. And she was good at her job.

Agent Schipp's parting words still lingered in Val's mind. *Don't go anywhere until after the verdict is announced. We may need you to come back for more testimony.* At the time, Val had assured him she wasn't going anywhere. They could get ahold of her anytime they needed at Granny Ida's in Indiana.

But her real response, the one she kept hidden inside, echoed ever louder as Jeanine drove safely away. *Just give me a week, and you'll never find me.*

CHAPTER 20

"MUM!" HIS BABBLING SHOUT HAD HER OPENING ONE TIRED eye. "Mum, mum, mum, mum."

Groaning, Val rolled over and covered her head with a thick cotton pillow. They had spent too much time with Granny Ida when he was tiny, she thought. He insisted on beginning each day with a cheery song… at five-thirty.

Trying to keep him up later seemed to have no effect on the timing of his morning wake up call. From experience she knew his demands would only increase in fervor, so reluctantly Val tossed aside the pillow and sat up in bed.

Jace gripped the edge of his wooden crib rail in both chubby hands. Seeing his success, he bounced with delight, showing her the whites of his three tiny teeth. Just over one-year-old now he stood with confidence on the tip toes of one foot, lifting his other leg daringly over the railing.

"Oh, no you don't." Val swung her legs over the edge of the bed and reached in to grab up her dynamic child.

Lifting him easily to the floor she released him to totter away. She shrugged into her thick flannel robe, then shivered once in the cold morning air of the one bedroom ranch house. It was spring in Wyoming, but the temperature still plummeted into the teens at night.

Padding in thick socks, she followed the sound of giggles into the perfectly square living room and stepped over toy trucks and plastic horses alike. Moving aside a baby fence, she stooped to shove more split logs into the black wood burning stove. It would heat up in no time.

Doling out cheerios and sliced blueberries for her son, Val sighed. She knew half of it would become hopelessly smashed into the old wooden floor. But that's what time and a broom was for, she figured, and left him to munch happily. Sunrise would come in under an hour and then her real work would begin up at the main house.

In the bathroom, she splashed icy water on her face, then ran a brush through her hair. She had kept the length and natural color now, feeling secure within the borders of the property. It was a rare day that she had to leave. Even then it was only to venture into the small neighboring town to buy groceries.

Coming here had been the perfect escape. Eight months ago, she had arrived back in Indiana only long enough to drain her bank account and say her goodbyes. Hopping a bus with her infant, she spent forty-eight hours riding halfway to various destinations. At random moments she would disembark, then choose another bus, and head in the opposite direction, always paying cash.

When she was sure that no one could have tracked her, she headed directly to Ignacio's brother's place in Wyoming. The directions were burned into her memory, after all. Hitching a ride from the bus stop with a kind-faced old cowboy, she had arrived on Señora Camila's front porch. Southern hospitality had nothing on Spanish familia when Val had dropped Ignacio's name.

No questions were asked. Val and her son were admitted into the tight family circle of the isolated prairie. And the vast beauty of her surroundings hadn't yet ceased to take her breath away. The property was situated in a valley of just over forty-thousand acres that sprawled along the base of the mountains before reaching fingers up the still snowy sides.

Hustling out of the bathroom now, Val peeked in on Jace who sat slamming a toy truck repeatedly into the rickety old kitchen table. Stepping into well-worn blue jeans, she stood vacantly in front of the three foot closet and surveyed her relatively clean thermal shirts.

Green, her favorite, she thought, slipping it comfortably over her head. The soft material fit snugly across her chest. Patting her flat tummy contentedly, Val smiled as the hard ranch work had quickly shaved off that last ten pounds.

"Time to get you dressed, Baby." Lifting her voice, she was rewarded with an answering squeal.

In return for their room and board, Val cooked a large meal for the cowboys each morning, and again at the end of the day. When an extra hand was needed moving cattle or fixing fence, Val would step in. Camila always volunteered to watch Jace, saying how much she missed her own grandchildren who had moved to North Carolina.

Dressing Jace was a marathon in itself. He squirmed and screamed while she buttoned his shirt. Val tackled the task with grit, coaxing kicking legs into miniature jeans. This got easier at some point, right?

Finally ready, Val balanced her son on her hip as she pushed out the front door and into the blast of chill air. Her fleece-lined canvas jacket kept most of the cold at bay, but she hustled the hundred yards to the main house.

The sun was just cresting the mountains in the east as she let herself inside and set Jace down to run. Javier had already been up and at the fire. The large home radiated warmth. Hanging her coat in the entranceway, Val kicked out of her boots and made for the open kitchen.

"Good morning, Señorita," Javier intoned, sipping comfortably at his black coffee.

"Hola, Javier," she replied, giving the older gentleman a wink.

It wasn't long after Val began working for him, that the Señor made a habit of watching her cook breakfast in his grand kitchen. He would sit quietly on an old barstool, and observe her mix pancake batter, scramble eggs, and fry bacon. Occasionally, Jace would toddle by, yelling incoherently. At these moments the older gentleman would slip the small child pieces of soft toast, running his fingers affectionately through the thick mane of brown hair.

"I mailed the postcard last week, like you asked," Javier said, between bites of crisp bacon.

"You didn't include a name?" Val paused in her cooking but didn't turn around.

"No," he assured her. "I would expect the horse to be delivered any day. My brother does not waste time."

"Thank you." She handed him another piece of the coveted bacon.

"You two!" Camila caught them red-handed, making her father jump. "The doctor said no more bacon."

"My apologies Camila." Val smiled sweetly at the old man's scowl. "Señor Javi's charms are impossible for me to resist."

At this Camila cackled and Javier grinned. He couldn't stay

angry with his overprotective daughter for long. And as always Val's easy flattery helped.

The cowboys came drifting in now, stomping their boots along the well cared for wood flooring. After they had gone, Val would sweep up the pieces of mud and debris left scattered in their wake.

"It's real good, Kelly," Dylan commented, as he sat amongst half a dozen cowboys at the long table.

"Yeah, real fine work Miss." The others echoed.

"Thank you, boys."

Val took her seat with them and Dylan's eyes followed. She tried not to notice.

For the past few months, his attentions had become steadily more apparent. He was in his mid-twenties, tall, with black hair and brown eyes, a good-looking man. Always willing to give her extra help, he would linger to walk with her by the house, or offer to saddle her horse when she got a chance to ride. He was good with Jace, kind, and patient.

The first time he kissed her, he didn't get upset when she pushed him gently away. The only problem was that she didn't feel anything for him at all. At this point she just didn't know what to say, though she supposed she should give him more of a chance.

Months of watching the gossip shows with Camila had assured her that Jason had finally moved on. That was the only reason Val felt comfortable enough to send for Bud.

In the evenings, Camila would flip through the stations on the big screen television in the spacious living room of the ranch house. Tucked deep in comfortable leather sofas, she and Val would watch with rapt attention. Camila loved the drama, saying it was like a real-life novella. Val simply wanted to catch a glimpse of her old friends.

Those first weeks before the final outcome of the trial had been intense. Val wasn't sure what the future would hold. But when the guilty verdict was finally announced, and Sharon Baine was convicted on all counts for illegal kidnapping and drug trafficking, Val saw the light at the end of a very long tunnel.

Cambric Agency was forcibly shut down. There was an on-going debate over what to do with its population of captives. In the confusion, Val knew that her son's chance of slipping through the cracks grew ever brighter.

At first, Jason and Bee made a media circuit together. Appearing on talk shows and news programs, they called for the complete dismantling of the captive system. Unrest rippled through the nation, some saying they were on the brink of civil war.

But Bee was only able to play that part for a short while. Her natural rebellious nature could not be stifled for long. Now that she was Veronica Durand, wealthy heiress and overnight socialite, her antics were an almost constant source of media frenzy. Val often times had to stifle a laugh while watching the programs with Camila, who exclaimed in shock when Bee was seen dancing on top of a table in some fancy bar.

Reportedly, the Durand family had spent quite a lot of money on therapists and family counseling. Even so they couldn't seem to make Bee conform to their ideal. Occasionally, she was seen attending a lavish affair with Jason, but most often she was reported to have run off with some golden-haired hottie the media couldn't name.

When Val peered closely at a picture of Bee in the passenger seat of a speed boat somewhere, she swore that she recognized Gabe as the driver. Maybe they *had* made it to his perfect spot after all. She hoped so.

"Please clear your plates, fellas," Camila announced as wooden chairs scraped back from the table.

Val crossed to the white porcelain sink and poured soap into the hot running water for dishes. Dylan handed her his cleared plate, first. Just then Jace ran by unsteadily as Camila pretended to chase him. Her son squealed in delight and Dylan only smiled more broadly.

Val made herself give Dylan a genuine smile in return. Another cowboy elbowed him aside in order to set down his own dish, muttering grumpily under his breath. Val couldn't help but giggle as the next man and the next all kept pushing at Dylan until the last one finally pretended to drag him away by the ear.

"He's a nice boy," Javier said, after they had gone.

"I know." She kept scrubbing.

"You cannot blame him for trying. After all, you are a beautiful young woman."

"Thank you Javi, but you know that I just can't get over you." Val smiled as Javier shook his head.

"Believe me Señorita, if I was fifty years younger, you would be speaking the truth!"

Javier left then, to ride out with the others. He rarely let the cowboys range far without him. Despite his daughter's protests, he insisted that it kept him young. During their quiet mornings together, Javier told Val that he would die the day he could no longer step foot in the saddle.

"Somebody has a dirty diaper." Camila handed a wriggling Jace over to Val who dried her hands on a red-checked kitchen towel.

After changing Jace, she finished the dishes and cleaned up

the kitchen. Wiping at the massive granite counters in long strokes, the smell of white vinegar lifted into the air. Camila shut herself in the downstairs office while Val swept the entire floor. Stopping every so often to play with Jace, Val threw in a few loads of laundry and was about to start in on the bathrooms, when Camila poked her head out.

"I just got a call from town. That horse from Tio Ignacio just passed through."

"Oh, awesome." Val's heart leapt with joy at the thought of seeing Bud today.

"I can take Jace over to your place and put him down for a nap, but I'll need to come back here in another hour or so. Why don't you go out and get a stall ready?"

"Okay. Thanks, Camila," Val called.

Grabbing her tan jacket off the hook, she pulled on her dirty leather boots. Outside, the air was still cold, but the sun blazing in the vast sky lifted the temperature into the high fifties. Though a stiff breeze blew, the cluster of ranch buildings were surrounded by huge old growth trees. The thick evergreens provided a break for the majority of whipping winds that swept across the vast rolling plain.

Val stepped along the worn dirt path that weaved just past her little red house on its way toward the large covered barn. When she entered the wood structure, she inhaled the aroma of alfalfa hay and horse. There was no better scent in all the world.

Reaching out to touch a warm nose here, tickle a testing lip there, Val made her way to a section of empty stalls. Peering in, she found them to be in good condition. Whomever had used them last left them free of old shavings.

Finding a wheelbarrow, Val slipped on her gloves and pushed it over to the shed piled high with dry bedding.

Making five separate trips, she dumped load after load into the soft dirt of the twelve by twelve box stall. Next, she used a pitchfork to spread the shavings around evenly. Her Bud would have a welcoming soft bed when he arrived.

Making a last push to the end of the barn she grabbed a few flakes of hay and tossed them inside the feeder of the stall. Standing back a moment, she removed her gloves and surveyed her work.

It wasn't the brass and polish of the Summer House stable, but the patina of the old barn wood had a charm all its own. The cowboys kept the place in reasonable repair, and she helped to clean dusty tack now and again. Stepping back into the stall, she stuck her hand in the automatic waterer to make sure it worked. Cold fresh liquid filled the silver bowl obligingly.

In the distance, the rumble of an old diesel engine could be heard making its way along the rutted dirt road. Wiping her hand on her jeans, Val strode to the end of the barn aisle and watched the beat-up white Chevy pick-up cruise slowly past the ranch house.

It pulled a matching two-horse trailer behind it as it followed the path through the trees and came to a stop just before the entrance of the barn. While waiting, Val had leaned back against the outer wall. Pushing off of it now, the wind-shield caught the beams from the mid-morning sun, and she lifted her hand to stave off the glare.

"Long journey?" She called to the driver.

The door swung open and she stopped to gape at the man that got out.

"You could say that." Jason stood before her.

Damn him, Val cursed Ignacio in her mind. Rotating away from Jason, she covered her face with both hands. Blood rushed to her head, pounding steadily in her ears. This was the last thing she had ever expected. She had no plan to deal with it.

"Is that the way you greet a stranger?" He asked.

"You're no stranger," she countered, turning back to face him.

"Aren't I?"

"No," she whispered it.

They stared at one another. He stood poised in the open space of the driver door, one hand propped on the roofline of the truck. It was the same handsome Jason. But he could use a shave, and new lines had formed at the corners of his eyes. There was a ragged, hungry look about him.

Without the expensive suits, he could have been just another cowboy hunting for work. His thick jacket hung open, rough jeans covered worn boots. She didn't know he owned such clothes.

"Well, I don't think I even know your name." He broke the silence, stepping back to slam the door shut.

Glancing away she battled herself. He was never supposed to have found her, but now that he had, what did it matter if she gave him her name?

"Can't even tell me that much?" His voice sounded tired. Leaning forward he braced his forearms across the warm hood of the truck.

"Kelly," she answered. "Kelly Martin."

"It's nice to meet you Miss Martin. It is still Miss isn't it?" Shoving off of the hood, he rounded the edge of the truck. Crossing to her, he stuck out his hand to shake.

"It's Miss." She let his hand hang in the open air between them, not daring to reach out and touch.

"Is he here? Can I meet him?" Jason's voice was strained.

"I don't think that's a good idea." Val wrung her hands nervously, biting at her lip.

The conversation dropped out. They were left staring at one another again. Bud stamped his impatience inside the metal trailer, blowing out a breath through round nostrils. A crisp breeze picked up, ruffling the leaves in the great trees that surrounded them.

Reaching out tentatively, Jason grasped the ends of her hair that had caught on the wind. He carefully rubbed the brown locks between his fingertips, like he had always done, before gently tugging on the ends.

Val had so many things that she wanted to say to him. All the feelings from before had come flooding back. Her lips parted, but only slightly. She was sucking in more oxygen in a desperate attempt to stay focused. Every instinct she had screamed at her to stop this progression now, but a desire that had long ago been put out was rekindling with a familiar force.

His blue eyes darted across her face. He searched her for a signal to stop. Unable to give him one, she shut her eyes as he leaned in, gathering her consumingly in his arms, kissing her thoroughly on the mouth. Warmth spread, curling tightly inside her belly. She let a low moan form in her throat.

Walking her backwards, he pressed her further into the barn, then up against the nearest wall. His hand pushed up the bottom of her jacket to travel underneath her shirt, stroking along her smooth skin.

The former slow deep kisses gave way to rushed glances as his lips moved down the side of her neck. Arching her back in response, she pressed her hips forward, eliciting an answering groan of desire from him.

"Val... I love you... I love you," he whispered.

Her eyes shot open at that.

"Stop." Growing rigid, she pushed him firmly away. "Jason, we can't do this."

"Damn it." The word was thrown from his mouth in frustration, but he stepped back, running shaky fingers through his tousled hair.

"I shouldn't have let you kiss me." Her breath was short, her heart racing.

"You can't have any kind of real love for that man after kissing me like that. What are you doing, Val? Don't you feel it, too? Am I crazy?" Pausing in his pacing, Jason's eyes pleaded with her.

"Hello!" Camila's voice called from down the aisle. "Kelly?"

"In here!" Val responded, adrenaline shot through her system painfully.

"Oh, there you are. I'm sorry, but I really need to get back to the office." Walking into the barn Camila glanced from Jason to Val.

"Of course. I must have lost track of the time, I'm sorry," Val responded.

"Well, you haven't even unloaded your horse yet," Camila commented happily. "Let's have a look at him."

Val followed obediently down the length of the truck. Camila opened the trailer doors, patting the golden rump soothingly as she stepped in. Bud looked no worse for the wear after the long trip, and backed easily out when asked.

"He's a pretty thing," Camila exclaimed. "I can't see why you didn't send for him sooner."

"I know it," Val replied, taking the thick blue lead rope in her hand.

Walking past Jason on the way to Bud's new stall, she avoided his eyes. Even so, she felt his gaze follow her. Bud sniffed once at his water, then eagerly turned to the fresh supply of hay. Val watched him chomp for a beat before returning to Camila who stood talking with Jason.

"Well, I've got to get back to the house." Camila rubbed her hands together to warm them. "You okay here?"

"Yes." Val assured her with a nod.

"Nice to meet you, uh… what was your name?"

"Jason," he answered. "Nice to meet you too, Ma'am."

Knowing that Jace had been left to nap by himself in her house, Val felt the urge to rush home to him. He was still so little, and almost able to climb out of the crib by himself. Needing to get back, she would have to cut things short with Jason.

"Look," Val began. "I've got to get back."

"Let me meet him." His eyes pleaded with her. "I promise I won't do anything stupid. I just have to see for myself. Please."

"No." Val was firm. "I'm sorry, I need you to let me go."

"I did what you asked me to before. I let you walk out. And sure, I tried to erase you. First it was other women, then it was faster horses, more expensive toys, wild parties and booze. Always lots of booze.

But I can't drink you away, even though I've tried. It's not over for me. I'm drowning Val. Every single day, I'm drowning. Maybe if I could just see for myself, what he's like…"

"I said no, Jason." Val's heart heaved for him, but her instinct to protect her son overpowered it. "I'm not your slave anymore."

The look of pain that flashed in Jason's eyes was too much. Shoving by him, Val rushed out of the barn and into the daylight.

She hadn't wanted to hurt him like this, but there just wasn't any other way to make him stop. Blood pounded in her ears. She didn't look back, but quickened her pace along the dirt path that led to her front porch. Taking the steps two at a time she flung open the door and slammed it closed behind her.

Leaning back against it, her breath came in great gasps. She scrunched up her face to fight back the bursting hot tears. It may be that she would have to leave this home, too. These past months she had worried about Cambric catching up to her, but in reality, it was Jason who had haunted her steps. Would she ever find peace?

"Mum, mum, mum!" The little voice carried through the thin walls of the old house.

Pushing away from the door, she tossed off her jacket, flinging it carelessly on the floor. Kicking off her boots, she took the few steps down the hall and turned right to enter their shared bedroom. Her little man, still lying on his back, gripped his feet in both hands and cackled to himself. He must have just woken up, probably the sound of her slamming the door.

"Nice nap little Bubba?" She smiled into his sparkly blue eyes, so much like his father's.

His coos of delight quickly turned to wailing demands for food. Heading to the kitchen, she strapped him into his high chair as the cries grew ever louder. After nap hunger pains were the worst, apparently.

Sticking her head in the refrigerator she plucked out some leftover green beans and pieces of roast chicken. He wouldn't stop wailing until he had his feast, she knew. Sitting in the chair across from him she doled out the bounty, cutting it all into manageable pieces.

Once the first bean had passed his lips the screaming

stopped, and she blew out a breath. Shaking her head at him, she wondered where he got the powerful lungs.

"This is him, isn't it?" Jason's hushed voice filled the small space.

Val practically levitated with shock.

Shooting up to stand, her chair tipped over backwards, knocking unnoticed to the kitchen floor. She hadn't heard him come in. But it was impossible to hear anything over the sound of Jace crying. There wasn't even a lock on the old front door, now that she thought of it. No need for locks way out here.

"You just let yourself in?" She demanded, incredulous.

"I knocked." He raised his hands in defense, but couldn't stop staring at the baby. "I heard crying and…"

"Damn it, you need to leave," Val protested weakly.

"How old is he?"

"He's just over a year." Val watched him try to do the math in his head. "He's yours, Jason."

"This is the reason you left me." Barely audible now, he spoke almost to himself. "There was never any other man."

"No." Biting her lip to keep it from trembling, she admitted the truth. "There was no other man."

Knowledge washed over him like a shock wave. He covered his face with his hands, tilting his head back towards the ceiling. When he straightened, he exhaled a ragged breath. He took the few short steps towards his son.

Crouching down to eye level, they considered one another. Jace continued to shovel bits of green beans into his mouth.

"Hey, Buddy." Jason's voice wavered, but he managed a small smile. "What's your name?"

"Jace," Val answered.

"You named him for me." He stretched out his fingers to trace along the chubby arms.

"They warned me not to, but he looks just like you," Val explained, forgetting herself as she discussed her baby.

"They." Jason's voice grew steady once more. Angry eyes looked up at her. "How long did you know? Why didn't you tell me?"

"I'm not going to argue with you, Jason. I didn't invite you in here. Maybe it's time for you to go."

"You didn't invite me!" Outraged, he worked to keep his voice level. "My God Val, I have a son that you've kept from me, and now you just want me to what…leave?!"

Unable to meet his fierce eyes with her own, she walked past him to the small sink and braced herself on the counter. Spreading her sweaty palms along the cool surface, she tried to keep her emotions in check. She didn't want him to see how unsure she was about her original decision.

All those endless nights she had spent rocking her crying baby, questioning why she hadn't ever just told Jason the truth. There were so many moments when she had wanted to take it all back. But when the day would dawn, and Jace breathed free air, she knew the sacrifice had been worth it.

"I just want to talk," Jason managed to say calmly, walking up behind her. "Please, Val."

"Okay." She turned to face him, back propped against the white washed pine cabinets.

"When did you first find out you were pregnant?"

"I didn't have a test. I didn't know for sure, but it was a few weeks before New York."

"And you couldn't trust me."

"If The Agency ever found out about him-"

"Didn't you know that I'd protect you? Protect *him*? With my life, Val."

"He would never have been born a free person!" She shouted at him. "We would always have been running, looking over our shoulders."

"And that's not what you've been doing?" He countered. "Running and looking over your shoulder?"

"No. But I guess I should've been."

"Why?"

"How long could you really have lived in hiding? Away from your family. Away from your work. How long would it have been before you convinced me to take Jace home with you? You don't think that The Agency would have figured out he was their captive? It would only be a matter of time before they would come for him."

Lifting her face in defiance, she held his gaze with her own. Tears brimmed her eyes, but she refused to turn away. Softening then, Jason cupped her chin in his hand, ran his thumb along her lips.

"Maybe you're right. Maybe that's the way it would have played out before, but not now. How long could I live in hiding? With you? With my son? Forever, Val. I've spent over a year without you. It's like dying in a prison that I can't escape from. There's nothing left for me out there. Please. Let me stay."

Her hesitation shone clearly in her eyes. Jason seemed to catch onto it, holding tight to the glimmer of hope. Encircling her with his arms he drew her in closer, pressing his advantage. Whispering to her, his forehead rested against hers. Closing her eyes, she let his words wash over her.

"Cambric has been disbanded, Sharon is in prison, and no one can figure out what to do with the thousands of captives they already have. If you won't let me stay with you, then run away with me. Let's get out of the country, start fresh. Just tell me that you love me. I gave you your freedom, but you took mine with you when you left. Set me free, Val."

"Okay." She breathed out the words. "Let's go. Let's be free, Jason. Together."

A word from the author:

Does Val live happily ever after with Jason?
Check out Book Two in The Captive Series and find out:
THE CAPTIVE MISSING

Join my ARC Team!
Click on the link: ARC TEAM - LK MAGILL

Want to know when the next book is ready?
Join my mailing list here…
LK MAGILL NEWSLETTER

Reviews, pretty please…
Each and **every positive review makes a huge difference.** Be it Amazon, Kobo, iBooks, Barnes and Noble; no matter the retailer, I read and appreciate them all.
Thank you and I hope to see you in the future.

Websites:
www.lkmagill.com

Like me on Facebook:
https://fb.me/LKMagill1
Follow me on Instagram:
https://www.instagram.com/lk.magill.author
Check out my Amazon page:
http://amazon.com/author/lkmagill